Lies at Six

Lies at Six

Sarah Scott (signature)

Sarah Scott

A Jolie Marston Mystery

KRILL
KP
PRESS

www.krillpress.com

Lies at Six

© 2012 by Sarah Scott

Lies at Six
is a work of fiction. The characters, incidents, and dialogues are products of the author's imagination and are not to be construed as real. Any resemblance to actual events or persons, living or dead, is entirely coincidental.

Published by Krill Press LLC. All rights reserved.

ISBN 978-0-9846524-3-3

Printed in the United States of America

*For my mother, Lola Calhoun Scott, who has taught
and guided many in her 95 years. Always, her
greatest teaching has been compassion.*

Truth is never pure, and rarely simple.

Oscar Wilde, *The Importance of Being Earnest*

Prologue

Ellis Standifer poured three fingers of Jack Daniel's into a cut-glass tumbler—a finger more than usual—and leaned back. The former mayor of Memphis rested his head against a sofa of dove gray leather only a shade darker than his thinning hair. He took a long sip. The whiskey warmed his throat and softened the February evening's chill.

Outside, the wind moaned as it wrapped around the corners of his building. The noise nagged him. He walked across the slate floor, slid open walnut doors covering the television, and clicked on the set.

When we return—the battle of the pooches. One neighbor owns a Rottweiler, the other a poodle. But guess who's suing who?

"Whom," he muttered. "Who's suing whom." He turned off the news and wandered into the kitchen.

The recessed spots overhead cast a shadowless light on the room's granite countertops and Mary's copper pots. Since his wife's death, only the cleaning woman touched the pots. He opened the refrigerator door. Nothing on its shelves interested him.

A few more sips of Jack Daniel's and the curious anxiety that had plagued him since morning began to ebb. Before long, he quit wondering if he might be ignoring something. He decided it must be only the aftermath of a forgotten dream.

Ellis gazed west at trees whose upper trunks rocked in the unremitting wind. Whitecaps tossed across the muddy depths of the river. Past the Mississippi, he saw the low stretch of Arkansas. Far beyond both, sunset lingered in a thin red streak.

Despite the wintry onslaught, this remained for Ellis the best time of day, this twilight span when downtown paused. He loved the momentary hush after the business types had hurried off to their families and before the musicians pulled out their battered instruments. The time between horns.

Memphians still frowned on honking unless drivers feared a crash, so horn blasts were scarcer than in other cities as large. Yet this quiet place had spawned a world-famous brand of raucous music. Ellis loved the irony. Some of the residents bragged that Memphis had more churches than gas stations. But no choir had sung loud enough to drown out Beale Street. Thank God for that.

He loved every low-down nuance of his adopted city's music, but tonight he wanted a different sound to mask the wind. He put on the Beethoven piece he loved best, the fourth *Sonata Number in E Flat*.

As he listened, he let another sip trickle down his throat. The pianist played with impressive technical precision, but Ellis thought his handling of the plaintive largo fell just short of giving the critical spaces between the notes their due. In that particular movement, the silences carried almost as much weight as the notes. He thought his own mother, still abundantly talented at 90, interpreted the movement in a more heartfelt way. But Ellis had no qualm about how the music he now heard helped to mute the wind's shrieking. He turned up the volume.

Below the floor-to-ceiling glass of his living room, a towboat was nudging a caravan of barges up the river's wily curves. The sky had darkened. The band of red streaking low across it had faded to the color of old blood.

Eyes closed, he relaxed his shoulders and concentrated on the music.

And so Ellis Standifer spent this particular evening—except for the extra finger of whiskey—as he had spent many evenings of his sixty-five years. Familiar comforts reclaimed him. The dragon that had huffed over his shoulder throughout the day now slumbered. Thoughts of making amends, of righting long-ago wrongs, never crossed his mind.

One

One more dead body and Jolie thought she'd scream. She'd bolt into the busy Memphis street, pound her fists on the hoods of halted cars, thump her palms against their windshields. "Forget about it," she'd yell at the gape-mouthed drivers. "Just keep going!"

Instead, Joanna Leland Marston (Jolie, please) checked the placement of her hand-held microphone—six inches below the chin, angled just so—and waited in the February cold for her cues. With the other hand, she fluffed dark copper hair away from her shoulders and face. What was it about a lens that widened bodies yet flattened hair?

To occupy the brief time until her live broadcast, she focused on the noises around her, broke them down as if they were separate tracks of audio: On top, the shrill sirens. Just below that, the barking orders of police and medics. The next layer down, the puzzled mumbling of onlookers. Below it all, the mundane sounds of shoe soles on pavement, of pens scratching paper, of breathing. And in the cloister of these noises, the silence, the absurd quiet of the corpse.

"One minute to Jolie." The noon producer barked in Jolie's earpiece. "You got that, Jolie?"

"Yes, I've got it, Sam." Even for a news producer, Sam was anxious and obsessive. She could picture him now in the control booth, checking his fingertips for a bit of nail left to nibble. "Listen, Sam," she said, "tell Trent not to bother with questions. There's nothing to talk about."

Jolie looked at the white-sheeted lump on the sidewalk. When the cops had lifted the cover for her to get a glimpse, she'd seen decades of hard drinking in the red-veined face and swollen nose. Who the poor man was and what he was doing on this street with his greasy black hair and filthy clothes, she didn't know. But her gut told her he wasn't news. She turned up the collar of her coat and shivered in wait for the next cue.

"Thirty seconds," Sam said breathlessly.

Through the earpiece, Jolie heard the male anchor introduce her report. She fixed pale green eyes on the camera and arranged her features to obtain the right measure of alert grimness, to sharpen the frustrating sweetness of her face. She lifted her head and lengthened her spine in an effort to appear taller than five feet four inches. The upward aim of Marcus's camera would bolster the illusion.

The anchor neared the end of the intro. Sam called out, "You're hot. You're in the two-shot."

"Thank you, Trent," Jolie said in response to the anchor's lead-in. She spoke in a voice that gave scant hint of her Southern roots, a surprisingly deep and strong voice for such a compact woman. Always it held a tinge of hoarseness men found sexy. The news consultants told her WTNW's viewers loved it, that it quickened interest in her stories, lent a sense of urgency to them. Jolie too liked the slight rawness and figured it gave her one more reason not to quit smoking.

"We're live from E. H. Crump Boulevard south of downtown Memphis where a body was found today. Police at this point have few details. What WTNW News has learned so far is that the body was discovered about 10:30 this morning. The identity of the victim, a white man who appears to have been in his forties, is unknown at this time, as is the cause of his death. We'll have a full report with all the latest findings on our early evening news. Jolie Marston, live for WTNW News."

In her earpiece, she heard Trent ask, "What are police saying about the possibility of foul play?"

Jolie checked a grimace. Had Sam even bothered to tell

5

him there was no need for followup questions? Not that it would've mattered. Jolie knew Trent wanted to show how engaged, how concerned he was. It might help him bump up to the evening news. "Nothing yet on that, Trent. As I said, the police don't have much information at this time."

"Okay, thanks Jolie. Keep us posted."

"Will do."

Jolie continued to fix on the lens until the producer's voice said, "You're clear."

She handed Marcus the mic and rolled her eyes. His usually placid, deep brown face broke into a conspiratorial grin. "Another one down."

She lit a cigarette and blew the smoke high in the frigid air. "Yep. Another pointless, inane, idiotic broadcast on its way to Mars."

The officers stood in a clump a few feet away from the body. She walked up to them and flipped open her narrow reporter's notebook. "Hi, gang. Anything more yet?"

The chief of the homicide division, Jim Plonski, glanced over at her, looking like he envied the corpse its rest. She'd seen the calendar in his office where he methodically marked off each day until retirement. His jowly face looked older, but she knew he had another couple of years before he'd hit sixty and could quit crossing off days.

"While you were doing your celebrity turn," Plonski said, "we took a closer look, along with the guy from the coroner's office."

"Anything at all to indicate murder?"

The answer came from Annette Middleton, the newest officer. "Sure. It's likely the same murderer that gets most of them. Mister Mad Dog 20/20. Step right up if you want a whiff."

"Thanks anyway." Jolie smiled back at the thirtyish, black

woman who'd joined the homicide division a few months back. She would give a franker and certainly wittier soundbite than Plonski, but Jolie knew some questions had to be deferred to the cop in command. And in Memphis, that wasn't likely to be a black woman. In PR maybe, but not in homicide. She turned back to the fatigued face of Annette's boss. "Expect you'll have anything official by this afternoon?"

"Check back around three," Plonski said. "You should get something preliminary from the coroner by then. As in acute alcohol poisoning. Sorry to disappoint you."

"You're disappointing my news director who's had to go two weeks without a grisly murder, but you're not disappointing me. I don't think there's a story here."

Plonski shrugged and walked away. Jolie saw Annette scribbling notes about the scene and sidled closer to her. "How's the crime-fighting life?"

Annette zipped her leather police jacket tighter. "Cold is how it is. I feel about as warm as that body over there." She rubbed the soft, blue fabric of Jolie's coat sleeve between her fingers. "You staying all cozy in your cashmere?"

"I'm managing. Yes, ma'am." Jolie nodded toward the huddle of other officers. "These fellows treating you all right?"

"Not bad. Some members of the master race outside homicide…" she gave a tight-lipped smile, "…that's another story. But this bunch is okay."

"Glad to hear it. Why don't you join Marcus and me for a bite?"

"Thanks, but I've got a couple of reports due in an hour. Next to a heater vent, I'm happy to say. Soon, okay?"

"We'll do it," Jolie said and waved goodbye. She liked Annette, she told herself, really she did. It wasn't merely a matter of cultivating her friendship as a potential source.

***

She and Marcus hadn't bothered to talk about where to go for lunch. Delo's Eats was where Marcus headed every day unless the assignment included free food. His squat five-five frame held a lot of Delo's slow-cooked barbecue. But as a Muslim, he shunned pork in favor of beef. To Jolie and almost everybody else in Memphis, God had used only pork on that particular creation day. To order beef bordered on sin.

She could smell the succulent meat from a block away. They swung open the door, a metal-framed plate of cracked glass covered by security bars, and out spilled fragrant steam. Inside, a late lunch crowd jammed the small room's six Formica tables. Jolie and Marcus found two stools together at the high counter.

Jolie took her seat, and then rocked back and forth. Marcus watched her and did the same. Their standing competition was to see whose stool was the most unstable. If they sat at a table, the game shifted to the tilt of the chair legs.

"Okay," she said, "you win. The Coke's on me."

***

At three, Jolie rang up the coroner. Yes, he told her, everything at this stage pointed to alcohol poisoning and only that. No suspicious injuries, nothing to make him think it was anything more.

She called Geena, the five o'clock producer. "Same story, Geena. No story. Just another boozer who's gone to that great happy hour in the sky."

"Shit. You sure?" Her sharp voice held all the disappointment of a good lead lost.

"Absolutely. There never was a story here."

8

"Maybe there were some injuries you could describe."

"There was nothing like that."

"Well, we teased it at noon with your story. We have to do something. And Brad says we need to play up the possible homicide angle, even if only to dismiss it. Got any soundbites?"

"From one of his fellow winos, maybe?"

"You know that's not what I mean."

"I guess I could get somebody from homicide."

"Yeah. Do that. Ask about any sign of foul play."

"I told you. There isn't any."

"So let whoever say that. I need about a minute and a half on this."

Jolie looked over at Marcus. "Slow news day?" she asked Geena. Marcus chuckled.

"C'mon, Jolie," Geena said. "Just get the bite, okay? Or get a couple."

"Anything to uphold the reputation of our newscasts."

"Give it a rest, why don't you?"

Jolie shut off the phone and turned to Marcus. "Is it just me, or do you also think we're making something out of nothing here?"

"I don't worry much about trying to justify what we cover," he told her. "I decided a while back to just shoot and go on. I try to concentrate on getting the best shot I can, no matter if it's the governor or a dumpster."

"One reason you're so damn good."

A smile tugged at his mouth. "I don't know about that. But I do know it makes things a lot easier that way. Especially with this regime."

"You mean since Brad came."

"Since Brad."

"You're lucky," she said. "You get to concentrate on pictures and sound. I have to deal with the content or lack of it.

I have to turn it into something sensational, something guaranteed to make our loyal viewers put down their forks and say, 'Damn, Earl, c'mere and look at this. What's the world a-comin' to?'" Jolie pointed her finger at Marcus. "See, I have important work to do. I have to keep this town more scared than it needs to be."

"That's the job, isn't it?"

"Don't I know that. But it's worse now, and I'm worse at handling it."

"I've got to say, you don't smile nearly as much as you used to."

She looked out the window at the passing businesses. In ten years of covering news in Memphis, she'd been in many of these places. Talked with the managers of auto parts stores and dress shops. Questioned cafe owners about one thing or another. She'd loved reporting, loved pursuing the tantalizing threads, weaving them into a story she could tell. She loved the entrée it gave her into the life of the city.

He made a slow turn of the steering wheel to round a corner. "You need to figure out some way of letting off steam if it's getting to you that much."

"Like what? Throwing darts at Brad during our morning meetings?" She watched Marcus ease up on the gas to let a car cut in front of him. "Nothing seems to unnerve you. You don't even curse. Hell, being a toilet mouth is practically a job requirement in news. You better be careful that you don't get fired."

"I just try to let most stuff roll over me."

"Is that part of being a Koran-toting Muslim?"

A smile spread across his wide, calm face. Muslim or not, he reminded Jolie of a black Buddha.

"Probably has more to do with my daddy dying of a heart attack when he was fifty-five. I figure I don't want a little thing like some fool driver—or some fool news director—to do me in. So I don't push my luck."

"Yeah, well, I've been pushing mine enough lately for both of us."

"Brad's not the sort you want to get riled. You might want to think about going along with him until he feels a little more secure."

"That's good advice, Marcus." She leaned back and stared out the window. "Too bad I'll probably ignore it."

Two

Jolie threw open the newsroom's back door and hurried in her headfirst manner to the cubicle of space she claimed in the open room. In the style of newsrooms everywhere, it was designed for breaking news to be shouted and easily heard. A ring of small editing booths ran along three walls, forming a perimeter around the rows of cubicles where the reporters worked. At the far end of the room was Brad's office, the only room besides the video editors' with a door to shut off the frenzy of ringing phones, clattering keyboards and yelling voices.

Jolie's desk lay waiting for one of the rare spurts when she tossed out all the clutter and restored order. Stacks of published reports, news releases, printouts, and newspaper clippings fought for space on the desktop with a Slinky, three half-used reporter's notebooks with pens rammed through their spiral tops, a Powerful Elvis Prayer Candle, a mug bearing the BBC logo, a computer and monitor, a phone and scraps of paper with scrawled names and numbers. Pinned to one of the fabric partitions was an autograph she'd facetiously requested from a mammoth-egoed anchor just before he left for a bigger market and to whom it never occurred she was joking. Another cubicle wall displayed a creased and ancient photo of blueswoman Bessie Smith. Higher still, looking down on everything, hung a quote in calligraphy from Thoreau:

It is surprising what a tissue of trifles and crudities make the daily news.

The line used to be funnier.

She threw her shoulder bag on the lowest stack of newspapers and with notes and video in hand, headed for one of the editing booths.

"Hey, Rando," she said to the bespectacled video editor whom no one called Randall except his mother. She flung the items on the counter in his cramped room. As Rando looked over Jolie's notes, she read again the hand-lettered message he'd put up a few weeks after Brad's arrival: *Death be not proud. (Why should he be any different from the rest of us here?)* They were reduced to this, she thought: Ineffectual snideness. Laments on a wall. Sarcasm as the defense of the defeated.

Rando tossed the notes he'd read alongside his editing gear and pushed his glasses up. "Should be a breeze to put together."

"Good. Consider it my minute-and-a-half contribution to the ills of the world." As she walked away, she yelled, "And I expect you to make something of immortal value out of it, okay?"

***

From his office, Brad Delano, WTNW's news director, watched Jolie saunter out of Rando's booth. "Has she always been this uppity?" he asked Geena. "Or is she worse since I came?"

"I think it's a territorial thing for her with you."

Brad's thick, dark eyebrows drew together. "I thought only guys got into pissing matches."

"Maybe mostly. I don't know." Brad saw Geena check her watch. He liked that about her. Producers ought to keep track of every second.

"You told me," Geena said, "you never met the news director before you."

"No, he was fired before I had the pleasure."

"Well, he *adored* Jolie. She was teacher's pet. He let her

13

choose a lot of her own stories. Certainly more than any other reporter."

"And look where it got him," Brad said. "The ratings were either flat or falling a lot of the time he was in charge of the newsroom. Can't she figure it out? She's bright enough."

"I guess she's just not real comfortable with the way you do some things." Geena held up her hands. "That's not a problem for me, you understand."

Brad didn't care if it was or not. He wanted it clear that it was time this shop woke up and realized there were turf wars to be fought out there every day. He'd built his reputation on shaking up newsrooms, and this one needed electric shock if it were ever to climb back to number one. Did they really think anybody wanted to see two-parters on the loss of topsoil or a weeklong series—they had let her have a whole goddamn week—on Memphis's elderly? *Hullo*. 18-49 demographic anybody? Old folks ain't in it.

***

When she wasn't out doing a live feed, Jolie usually stayed around the station to watch the early news. This evening she poured a fresh cup of coffee into her mug and went to the station's over-heated smoking room. Damn do-gooders. A non-smoking newsroom would've been a sacrilege in years past. A proposed law threatened to make even this hideout illegal soon.

The smokers' cubbyhole was tucked into an out-of-the-way corner on the first floor. Inside, a brown vinyl couch slumped next to a cast-off recliner. Plastic ashtrays and a few magazines lay in a jumble on a laminated wood table. Jolie had visited smoking pits at prisons that looked nicer. Obviously none of the higher-ups at the station smoked on the job.

From a wall mount, a television monitor fed WTNW's

broadcast twenty-four hours a day. The volume was cranked to
offset the noisy ventilation system.

She lit a cigarette, kicked off her shoes and propped her
feet on the table just as the opening theme music began. At least
they weren't making a lead out of her non-story, but she
suspected they would tease hell out of it before they did get to
it.

Good evening. Elaine, a bright-eyed brunette who had, as
Brad described them when he hired her, "these great pouty lips"
spoke first. *Another stolen car in southeast Memphis. Could
there be a theft ring at work?*

Now it was Devin's turn. He too was a Brad hire. Brad
called him sincere, but Jolie found him pompous and
condescending. *And another body found in Memphis under
mysterious circumstances. Was it murder?*

Jolie threw down the magazine. "Fuck no, it wasn't!"

For the first time since she'd begun working in news, she
found herself unable to watch her own work. She ran back
through the newsroom, stopping only long enough to pick up
her bag and coat, and made a straight shot for the door. She
heard her voice from one of the monitors in the room. The
sound of it sickened her.

You're not to blame, she told herself as she tromped down
the back stairs to the parking lot. You can do decent work. You
have done decent work.

But she wondered if she would ever do it again.

Five years back, she thought she'd seen the worst of it. But
in retrospect, that news director was nothing but a puny
apprentice to Brad Delano. In between the bastards, though,
she'd had a great boss. Last Jolie heard, he was down in
Mississippi, finally hired by a station in Hattiesburg. Was that
even in the top one hundred and fifty markets?

Jolie walked to her car, a vivid blue Toyota sports

convertible, and slammed the door. What she needed was a little time with Jerry Lee.

As she headed west, toward downtown, she popped in a CD and punched up "Great Balls of Fire." Turning the volume up as loud as she could stand, she maneuvered the small car through the darkening streets of the city she knew so well.

Memphis's abundance of deciduous trees loomed in raw outline, their bald limbs spiking upward. Beneath them, spacious parks and lawns lay dead and pale brown. Jolie could see no promise of the lush beauty that would soften the city come spring, nor any hint of the clinging humidity that lurked soon after.

As the Killer plunked and wailed, Jolie chugged west through the long succession of stoplights on Union Avenue. Near the river, the land lost all sense of rise. From anywhere in Memphis, it was hard to believe in mountains.

Despite the flatness, she'd come to love this riverside city. Its sass and sadness pulled as strong and deep as Big Muddy. Pour in a heaping dose of Delta eccentricity, a perpetually hip funkiness and the music. God, the music. It had come wailing up from the low groan of cotton fields and mated with the high purity of Smoky mountain strains. Out of that miscegenation had jumped rock 'n' roll.

Jerry Lee now screamed "Whole Lotta Shakin' Goin' On." Memphis music refused to play white, no matter what color hands were plucking the strings or pounding the keys. Leave white to Nashville.

She jerked the small car into the first available parking space downtown and walked three blocks to Automatic Slim's. Along the way, music spilled from other restaurants and bars. Blues with a pleading sax, bass-heavy rock 'n' roll and a commendable knockoff of the Johnny Burnett Trio's "Rockabilly Boogie." Music was this city's drug. Jolie wished more of the comfy whites who'd fled to the suburbs were junkies.

***

In Automatic Slim's, an after-work crowd jammed the lower level. Several customers lining the long bar called back and forth to each other. Laughter spilled from one corner of the room where a group in their twenties partied. Jolie heard one of them yell, "How could he do that to my copy?" From the looks of their trendy clothes, Jolie figured advertising and PR types.

She scooted through the crowd, aiming for the stairs. As she did, short squared fingers reached out to grab her arm. A thick reddish mustache came in close.

"Is this where all the sexy TV people hang out?" John Beck, a reporter for the city's only remaining major newspaper, the *The Commercial Appeal*, kept his grip on her biceps as he spoke.

Jolie leaned even closer and whispered. "John, I'm confused here. Should I be flattered or insulted knowing the bottom-feeders you take us TV people to be?"

He reared back in mock surprise. "Oh, no, I think you're all glamorous and enormously well-informed."

"Gotta go, John."

His grip loosened and became a hand moving up her spine. "Okay, so only one of you is. It's a compliment, okay?"

"I'm so grateful."

"Let me buy you a brew."

Jolie enjoyed the usual flirtatious sparring with John Beck, and she respected his investigative work, considered it by far the best at the paper. Nonetheless, his offer would have to wait. "Thanks, but I'm due upstairs."

He looked beyond the second-floor railing to a small group of people standing around chatting. "I'll join you."

What John Beck lacked in subtlety, he made up for in gall. "Sorry," she told him, "but I'm meeting someone already. Besides, it's sort of a private get-together."

"Sort of?"

"I was trying to be diplomatic. It's private."

He craned his neck. "Who's giving it?"

"Ellis Standifer."

He lowered his head and looked at her. "And aren't you cozy with the powers that be?"

"Was. Power that was, John. He's no longer the mayor, remember? He is still, however, a good friend."

"I didn't realize you two were so chummy. Is he the someone you're meeting up there?"

"No. Ellis is giving the party for his own sixty-fifth birthday. The someone is the man I've asked to join me."

"How did you get on the invitation list and I didn't?"

"Ellis and I are from the same small town in east Tennessee…Singleton."

"I would've figured Standifer for a country club party instead of this place."

"I chalk it up to his sense of adventure."

"I never noticed that about him. You must know him pretty well."

"I do."

Jolie's friendship with Ellis had begun soon after she'd moved to town ten years ago and he had been on the verge of winning his first term. Since the first time she'd interviewed him, he'd been mentor and wise friend. Her parental stand-in, he once told her, not that she needed parenting. He felt he owed it to her mom and dad, people he'd grown up with in Singleton. "Of course," he'd said with a wink, "if you weren't such a bright, interesting young woman, I might feel no obligation at all."

18

She admired Ellis's sense of fairness and honesty, and the more she'd watched Memphis politics, the rarer she'd found it. Even on a personal level, he'd never been anything less than gentlemanly, and he'd never expected any news favors from their friendship while he was mayor.

Maybe it was because of their shared hometown roots, but she'd felt from the start he was a kindred spirit. Any time an interview with him had been on her schedule, she'd looked forward to it. They sometimes met now for drinks or dinner or a weekend walk along the riverbank. They'd swap local gossip and trade views on their small hometown and the very different place they lived now. Each enjoyed the other's take on things in general, and Ellis felt freer to give his opinions now that he no longer held office. During his tenure as mayor, Jolie had been careful never to let their personal ties override what her work had demanded from him, and she knew he respected her for that. She would certainly never describe him to anyone in the newsroom as a trusted uncle, but that was how she saw him. She could use his perspective on her work frustrations now.

Jolie watched John's eyes scan her face, and she knew his thoughts. "No, I never compromised my ethics. I never cut him any slack."

"Lucky for you he did a decent job running this town."

His tone bordered on peevish, but she knew it had more to do with his not being included upstairs than anything about her professionalism. As she began walking away, she turned back. "Sometime, despite your lofty attitude, I just might hold you to that offer of a beer."

"I wish you would," he said in a tone that startled her by its sincerity.

She began pushing through the crowd again at Automatic Slim's. Actually, if it weren't Ellis's birthday, she would have begged off tonight, called her boyfriend Nick and told him she needed to cancel. The workday had left her in a foul mood, and she longed to be alone with a hot bath and—who would it be— more Jerry Lee? Billie Holiday? Some Aretha therapy? She longed to fill the tub to its limit, lie back, close her eyes and forget this day had happened. Aretha.

Wasn't this exactly the way she'd felt yesterday and the day before?

She began the climb to the restaurant's second floor but paused a moment to work up an opening smile before the last few steps. A dozen mostly familiar people chattered in front of her, among them the conductor of the Memphis Symphony Orchestra, a bank president and his wife, the publisher of the local business journal and a children's book author known for her lurid wit. Nick hadn't yet arrived. Ellis stood with two men who struck her, from their dark coloring and expensive suits, as South or Central American businessmen.

Ellis caught her eye, rose, and waved her over to join them. "Jolie," he called out in his refined drawl, "it's been too long since I've seen you." They exchanged hugs, and her body drank up the warmth of his. Maybe she could just stand here and lean against him all night. Independence be damned. Tonight she wanted a prop.

Standifer introduced his two companions, visitors from Mexico. "Jolie and I," he told them, "are from the same little town." He turned the gleam of his gray-blue eyes on her and smiled wider. "We're overdue for a good long chat," he said. "How have you been?"

She tossed her head back and forth in a non-committal way. "Managing. And you?"

"Too busy. I should run the city again."

Jolie wished, not for the first time, Ellis was still at the helm. But he'd decided it was time to do something else. Study Russian. Travel. With his intelligence, money and still-handsome looks—high cheekbones and a slim nose, a dimpled chin that deepened his face's appeal, kept it from being haughty—he seemed to have everything, short of a woman, a man could want. And who knew about a woman? Their friendship, for all its intimacy, didn't tread there. Jolie decided just then that during their next visit, it would. She would have to figure out a way to couch her curiosity so it didn't come across as bluntly as usual.

"I wish you'd trained your successor a little better," she told him. "Farrell never invites me up to his office for a drink."

He feigned dismay. "I left specific instructions!"

Howard Farrell lacked more than Ellis's elegant charm. If Howard hadn't been riding on his dad's coattails, he'd never have landed the job as mayor. His father, Daddy Joe Farrell, was one of the most influential blacks in town, respected by citizens of every color. He'd built up his taxi business into a large enterprise and donated both time and money to the community. A beloved and admired man. Daddy Joe's son was another matter.

"I haven't seen you since the Curtis Awards," Jolie said. She'd covered the story recently—after arguing with Brad that it was worth doing—when Ellis had received the prestigious award for community service. His aged mother had flown into town for the event.

Ellis began explaining to her what had brought his guests to town. Something about cotton, about studying the market here. What she found more interesting than his explanation was his face, now that she had a moment to scrutinize it. His gently-bred features should look relaxed, especially on this evening. Instead they looked drawn, weary, as if he hadn't had a good night's sleep in a week. What, she wondered, would disturb the sleep of a man like Ellis Standifer? Now wasn't the time to question him. Nick had arrived.

Jolie walked up to him as he made his way across the small upper floor. They swapped a quick kiss just as Ellis asked everyone to be seated.

A waiter with a shaved head and two earrings perched high on the rim of one ear sauntered over to deliver menus. "Are we imbibing tonight?" He spoke in a cheery singsong. "Mr. Standifer has ordered an opening round of champagne."

"Fine," she said. The waiter whisked two full flutes from the tray and set them on the table. Jolie slung her black leather pouch over the back of the chair.

Nick nodded. "Champagne works." His weary tone of voice suggested he came only because she had asked him. She guessed he'd rather be curled up with a basketball game.

They sat at one end of a long table. On a nearby wall hung six 8 x 10 black-and-whites of a young, lusty Elvis. Everyone around the table was engaged in conversation. Jolie gave Nick a tight smile. "Have I told you lately that I hate Brad?"

"Not since this morning."

"Well, I still do. More than ever now." She picked up the menu.

"Is that going to be our topic of conversation tonight? Again? I thought we were here to celebrate with Ellis."

Jolie slammed the menu shut.

Nick reached across and took her hand. "Look, I know you don't like the way things are going, but Brad will be gone someday. Whoever replaces him will have to be better."

"No, they won't."

Several places down, Ellis stood and raised his flute in a toast. "Thank you for being my guests tonight. Let it be known that your presence here requires another year of being nice to me."

Another toast followed the laughter, this one from the conductor. "First let me say, we're honored to be your guests,

Ellis. And we're your dear, dear friends any time you pick up the tab."

Jolie's smile turned wry as she again faced Nick. "So, work sucks for both of us."

The waiter trotted up and took their orders. When he'd left, she studied the fatigue in Nick's near-black eyes. "What's up, lover man?"

He rapped his fingers on the table. "A bigger caseload."

"Not again." Only a year ago, the lawyers on the chief prosecutor's staff had been hit with more cases to add to their already overburdened stack. "Why in hell don't they hire more attorneys?" she said. "I know the city budget looks a little bleak now, but surely they could justify one or two more."

With a flourish, the waiter served Cabernet Sauvignon to Jolie and Nick from bottles on the table. He returned a few minutes later, swooping a bowl of Caribbean black beans in front of her. "For you. By the way, this dish is incredible. The fresh orange is what does it." He slid a plate of mesquite grilled swordfish toward Nick. "And the fish is fresh, really fresh."

"So glad to have your commentary," Nick told him.

The waiter turned on his heel and took off.

Jolie frowned at Nick. "No need to be sarcastic with the guy."

"Well, I don't want a conversational waiter."

"Fine. But I want a hassle-free evening. I really need one. As you said, we're here for a party, and as long as we're here, we might as well be pleasant. For Ellis's sake, if for no other reason."

"Sorry. I'm just fed up."

She could tell he needed to vent. "Then let's talk about it." Her own venting could wait.

His eyes searched the lineup of Elvis images on the opposite wall. "Easton's trying to look good, and for him that means not asking for more funding, no matter how much it's needed. He wants to hold onto this job a long time, and he doesn't give a rip what the rest of us have to do to keep him there."

"Does it help you to know half the council hates him? I overheard one member telling a couple of others that Easton was a—how did she put it?—an ignoramus and the biggest reason she liked lawyer jokes. Nobody stood his defense."

Nick nodded. "Enough of me," he said. "Your turn."

She slid her glass back and forth on the table's polished blonde wood. "I thought you didn't want to hear it. Again."

"Turn about's fair play. So what happened today?"

She told him about the body and the way Brad had wanted the story covered. "What worries me is this: We're heading into the big February sweeps, so for the next few weeks ratings will rule. And you wouldn't believe the mouth-frothing stories he's assigning."

"Nothing new in that, though, is there?"

"But I'm telling you it gets worse and worse. You know, I think Brad would say his granny screwed a rooster for a couple of Nielsen points."

Nick laughed.

"So," she said, "you think I should just put up with it?"

"I didn't say that. I do think you shouldn't be surprised."

Jolie took her spoon and drew figure eights in the mound of beans. Before coming to this city, she'd moved up exactly as she'd planned after journalism school at Michigan State, purposely choosing a very un-Southern J-School. She'd landed her first job at a small station in Battle Creek. Two years there, two more in Albuquerque, then Memphis and WTNW. She'd figured on two or three years here before hitting a top-ten market followed by a move to network. But she was still in Memphis after a decade, and none of the offers that had come her way had included enough reasons to leave or they'd had warning flags that steered her away. Certainly none had been willing to grant the freedom she'd had with her last boss.

"Come on, Joles, eat. You said you wanted to enjoy a nice dinner."

"I did. I still do." She watched him slice off a piece of fish, this man who at 32 was four years her junior. She looked at the dark eyes and brown hair that already had begun to reveal more of his broad forehead.

They'd been lovers two-and-a-half years, outdistancing even her marriage by a few months. No, she would not start thinking about that, not start wondering yet again what might have gone differently. She would keep her mind here with this man, this decent man who loved her, who wasn't—unlike 90 percent of the men she'd known—scared of her intensity.

She put down her spoon and touched his arm. "So, what do I do? I can't just stomp in and quit. What I have in savings wouldn't go far. Should I start flooding downsized newsrooms around the country with resumes on the remote chance I might finally be able to land a better gig?"

"How about something with one of the other stations around here? I'd hate to see you leave town."

They both knew this was as close to commitment as they were likely to come. Nick had divorced not long before he met Jolie. While he'd made clear she was the most interesting woman he'd ever known, he'd also indicated he wasn't ready to share living quarters again. Nor was she. Not long ago, she'd decided their hearts were too covered over with scar tissue for the full-fledged trust needed over the long haul. But for now, it was mostly satisfying for them both.

"Stay here? I know too much about the other newsrooms," she said, "and I don't like what I know. Oh, hell, this is no way to have a nice evening. So how's your fish?"

25

"Not bad."

A tap on her arm came from the banker in the next seat. Jolie turned her attention to the thin-lipped man, trying to look interested in his question about an Egyptian artifacts exhibit in town.

As soon after the dessert as politeness would allow, she and Nick excused themselves. She gave Ellis a goodbye hug.

He grasped her hand. "We'll get together for a nice long visit soon, okay?"

"Soon," she said, "I promise." She looked forward to talking with him without the company of a dozen others. But the way she felt right now, she didn't want any more of anyone, not even if Elvis himself should come calling. Well, maybe if he still looked like he did in those photos.

She headed for the door, Nick closely behind her. Out on the street, they stood for a moment, both knowing neither felt inclined to invite the other home. They bent toward each other to kiss goodnight.

"Hey, Jolie!"

She bucked from a sharp slap on her back and heard a robust, faintly familiar voice. She looked up to see a former sports anchor who'd been with another station in town. His blond hair was cropped more closely than during his time in Memphis, but the self-satisfied look on his face had not changed. She tried to muster a smile. "Hi, Lance. You're in Houston now, right?"

"Yeah. Been at the NBC affiliate there a year and a half. Just back in town for a friend's wedding. Hey, what's going on over there in your newsroom?"

Jolie glanced at Nick. "What do you mean?"

"I've caught a couple of newscasts and seen a ton of promos." Lance grinned. "You guys are really going after the blood, guts, gore, and tears, aren't you? Quite an image change.

Everybody used to call you the white-glove newsroom." He gave a sharp laugh. "Now I hear through my old buds that WTNW stands for Where Trash News Wins."

"What a diplomat you've become down there in big-time Houston, Lancie boy."

"Well, it's true. You can't deny it."

"What the hell makes you—?" She might agree with him, but damn if she would give his smug ego the comfort of knowing it.

"Easy, Joles," Nick said in a low voice.

Jolie cut her eyes at him.

Lance slapped her on the back again. "That's okay, Jolie. We're all ratings whores." With a cackle, he walked off.

"Jolie, don't—" Nick began.

She waved him off with both hands, turned, and made a dash for her car.

***

Ellis deposited his Mexican guests at their downtown hotel and turned the Mercedes toward his condo a short distance away. In the light traffic of ten o'clock, it caught his attention that a white Ford fifty feet or so back made all the same turns. Was it the same white sedan that had pulled out behind him as he left the restaurant?

He slowed for the turn into the basement garage of his building. The Ford paused a moment, then drove on.

Surely, Ellis reasoned, it was nothing but coincidence. So what if a car came the same direction? He'd been on major streets. Still, as he got out of his vehicle, he shot a furtive look around the half-empty garage. He walked at a clip to the elevator. Maybe he should have made a couple of unnecessary turns, an illogical maneuver or two, just to see.

***

That night Ellis dreamed a furious hailstorm assaulted a small plane as he rode in it. Massive ice pellets forced the aircraft into a deadly nosedive. Hail pounded the falling metal with a horrific drumming.

When he awoke in a cold sweat, the only sound he heard was the thudding of his heart.

Three

"Morning, troops. Let's review our battle plan."

The reporters and videographers exchanged glances. Brad Delano had used the same corny words at every morning briefing since his arrival. Jolie's efforts to get the staff to appear in military garb so far had failed, but she hadn't abandoned the fantasy. She looked over at Marcus. He would look fine in a camouflage cap. He caught her glance and winked.

She turned to scan the assignment board. The third line carried the story slug Satanic Teens. And her name beside it. Crap. She swallowed the contents of her BBC mug and walked over to the coffeepot just as Brad's hard-edged voice started up again.

He pointed to the third story with his knuckle. "Jolie, you'll be on this one with Marcus as shooter. I've got the promotions folks teasing it, and I want a lead out of it."

Jolie breathed deeply to offset the nicotine urge making a slow burn up her lungs. "And the story would be . . . ?"

His back was to the group, and he didn't turn around, but she could see his shoulders square. "High school up in Covington. Bunch of teens there doing some weird stuff. We're going for the satanic angle."

"On what grounds?"

Brad swung around to face her. "Enough. Murray's got background and some sources." He glanced over at Murray who flashed a thumbs up.

Brad had sent for Murray as assignment editor soon after becoming news director. They had wreaked havoc together in a succession of markets. Jolie called him Murray the Marvelous, because it was a marvel how he could come up with fluff for news day after day.

What Murray had, it turned out, were the names of five juniors at a high school in Covington, a small town forty miles north of Memphis. He had underlined the only full name. Now he drew another line under it. "This Sean guy is the one I talked to."

Jolie stared at Murray's pasty, round face. "How'd you connect with him?"

"Called me. Said he'd been part of this cult and they were getting into black magic, satanic rituals, that kind of thing. Said something about a cat."

"So *he* called *us*?"

"He's staying home from school today for us," Murray said. "And I made him promise not to call another station. Told the little bugger I'd kill the story if I got wind of anyone else on it."

The craving for a cigarette now flared into her throat. "What kind of evidence has he got?"

"He says he has plenty, but he didn't want to be specific on the phone."

"That's just dandy. And what exactly is this about a cat?"

"I don't know, something about a dead black cat. Brad was talking to me at the time, and I didn't get it all." He looked at her. "That's your job anyway."

At the moment, the marvel was that she didn't spit on him. "So what else? There has got to be more. Tell me there's more, Murray."

"I'm sure there is. Put your vaunted investigative skills to use and find it."

"Did it ever occur to you or Brad that this kid could be lying or just putting us on as some kind of a joke?"

Murray scratched the flaccid skin under his chin. "They're all minors," he said, "so we can't give names, but you know that. Here's his address, and here's the name of a diner where the kids hang out after school, right across from campus. See what you can get there after you interview him. We'll send the satellite truck up there. You'll cut in the truck and be live at five and six. That's about it."

Jolie slammed down her palms on Murray's desk. "That's it? I'm supposed to make a lead story out of some pimply kid's promise of a wicked tale?"

"Run along now, Jolie."

"Don't you—" But she stopped herself, deciding to vent where it mattered.

Brad was now in his office, his eyes fixed on a TV monitor. She stomped in and swung the door shut. "Tell me this is a joke."

Without looking up, Brad sighed. His gaze didn't waver from the full-lipped blonde on his television screen. "What's stuck in your high-and-mighty craw this time?"

Jolie plopped into a chair facing him. "Fourteen years I've been reporting, so I'm not naive. I know we're not doing the live-action version of the *The New York Times*. But this is a new low for this station and for me."

He paused the audition video and finally looked at her.

"Never," she said, *"never* have I had to fabricate a story—a lead story, mind you—out of such damn drivel. All we have is innuendo whispered by some *kid*, for chrissakes! And we're already promoting it! You've already decided it's the lead at five. What the hell happens if I get there and it turns out he's jiving us?"

Brad got up from his chair. "That's not how it will turn out."

"You can't mean you want me to make up a story for you?"

He slammed his fist on the desk. "Of course I don't. But if you're worth a damn, you won't have to. The story is there.

31

Find it! Then make the most of what you find."

"Get someone else." Her hands thumped a steady beat on the armchair. "Let me do a story on that group of Laotian immigrants I've been telling you about. Their landlord's ripping them off. The city's doing nothing to help. It's a helluva story. Send Pat on this teen thing." Pat, the one they called the Crier behind his back, the one who covered child killings and lottery winners with the same degree of trumped-up empathy. "Pat would be perfect for it."

Brad glowered at her, his dark bushy brows almost joining. "I'm sending you. And you're getting a lead story." He went over to his door and opened it. "If you don't think it's worthy of your superlative talents, too damn bad. Blow it off and I'll demote you to nothing but weekend work."

"You're threatening me!"

Brad sat back down and took the blonde's resume video off pause. He watched the animated face on the screen. "You just haven't figured it out yet, have you, Jolie? Your lollipop supply has been cut off."

How she wanted to pummel him. Instead, she stiffened her abbreviated frame and marched from his office.

***

Ellis Standifer stood before the span of glass along his living room's front wall. This morning the mud-laden Mississippi's waters looked almost blue in the clear February sun. He squinted at the bright view with eyes that ached from exhaustion.

For hours after the nightmare had interrupted his sleep, he kept seeing the plane in its headlong dive, kept hearing the hailstorm pelt it.

Around dawn, he had fallen asleep again and only

awakened an hour ago, at ten. He felt as if he hadn't slept at all.

***

At eleven that morning, Marcus pulled the news cruiser, a black Chevy SUV with WTNW painted in bright colors on the side, to the curb. They were in a Covington subdivision after a 45-minute drive from Memphis.

Jolie studied the house, a typical suburban snout-nosed home in a neighborhood full of typical suburban snout-nosed homes with few trees, all of them spindly.

From inside Sean's house, a curtain twitched. Jolie stubbed out a cigarette and grabbed her purse. Patience, she told herself. Patience. Wasn't that the message? This morning before work, she had impulsively pulled open a dresser drawer and drawn out a burgundy velvet pouch tucked away there. She'd reached in the bag and pulled out an ivory-colored stone with the etched markings of the Warrior Rune. An upward-pointed arrow counseling patience.

Patience, my ass. Neither Vikings nor New Agers had to deal with Brad Delano.

A lanky teen with shoulder-length blond hair opened the door before she had a chance to knock. He stood back, hands shoved in the pockets of jeans that rode low on the narrow bones of his exposed hips.

She stuck out her hand. "Jolie Marston."

"Hey, could y'all like park somewhere else?" He rotated his head a half circle to swing his hair to one side. "Maybe down the street?"

"Sure, man," Marcus said.

As he headed down the steps to move the vehicle, Jolie tried again. "Hi. You're Sean?"

He nodded, and she extended her hand a second time. He

clasped it without interest, fingers hanging limp as he glanced toward the floor.

"How're you doing?" she asked.

One lank blond lock already had fallen back over his face, so he flipped it again. "Okay," he muttered.

"Anyone else here?"

"Nah."

"Is there some place we could sit and talk?"

"Uh, sure." He walked up a short flight of stairs and turned to the right. In the living room, an oversized sofa in beige tweed took up most of the space and faced a wall-mounted television.

Jolie studied the hunched-over youth on the sofa, his eyes on the street to make sure Marcus parked out of sight. He looked like thousands of other high school juniors in America must look. Vacant. It pleased her to notice this specimen was popping his knuckles. A sign of life. God, she dreaded the time when her niece and nephew, now an adorable five and two, hit puberty.

She sat beside him on the couch, eased off her coat, and dug her notebook from her purse. "So, Sean, let's talk about this cult. When did you first get concerned?"

***

Ellis got off his treadmill, wiped the sweat from his forehead, and took a swig of water. As he did, he looked at the street below. The white Ford that had been there thirty minutes ago hadn't moved.

Just as he decided to go downstairs and get close enough to the car to see who might be in it, the vehicle slowly pulled away from the curb. He was too far up to get a good look at the license plate.

***

"When you called us," Jolie said, "you said something about a cat. A dead black cat. What's that all about? Did you and your friends kill the cat for some reason?"

The kid looked across the room at Marcus. Since Marcus had returned from parking the news cruiser, Sean had glanced up only at him, never at her. She bet he was great on a date.

"We, uh, we just found the cat."

"Found it how?" Jolie asked. *Found as in stole?*

"It had been, like, smashed by a car. So Jason—I mean, one of the guys—got the idea of doing a sacrifice."

"Are you sure it had been hit by a car?"

"Yeah, it was, like, already dead."

"What did you do?"

"We built us a fire and, like, cut the cat into pieces and burned it. One of the guys made up this chant to Satan and we all did it while the cat burned." He giggled nervously.

"What else did you do?"

"Nothing I guess."

"Really. Tell me, Sean, do you think Laotian and other immigrants generally get a fair shake when they come here?"

"Huh?"

"Nothing. How about guns? Explosives? You guys mess around with any of that?"

He jerked his head back. "You mean like those Columbine dudes and their copycats? Like that? No way. That stuff's sick."

Jolie reached over and put her hand on Sean's narrow biceps. "Sean, why are we here? Why did you call us? You've got to tell me everything if I'm going to make a story out of this. And believe me, I've got to make a story out of this."

"I don't know much else. Mostly we just, like, get together and listen to music, but sometimes now, especially since the cat thing, Jason wants us to chant. And we light a bunch of candles, and we put on these robes." He snickered. "Jason dyed a bunch of sheets black in his mom's washing machine. We drape them around us while we're chanting." He scratched the sofa's rough tweed. "Just stuff like that."

"So why did you call the newsroom, Sean?"

"I dunno. Just to do it, I guess."

"Can you get Jason for me? I really need to talk to him."

"Nah, he's like at school and doesn't know I called you. He'd be pissed. He's like real secretive, y'know?"

"You're sure he won't talk to me? Off-camera?"

"No way. Not Sean."

Her grip on Sean's arm tightened. "Are you telling me absolutely everything? And I'm not talking about whether or not you guys get stoned when you chant. I don't give a shit about that. I want to know what else you and your friends have been up to that you think might be Satanic."

He shrugged. "That's pretty much it."

***

"Marcus, could you toss me the keys?"

Jolie raced down the stairs without waiting for him. The news cruiser sat a block away. She unlocked it, climbed in and slammed the door. Then she opened her sweetly shaped mouth and screamed until her lungs emptied of air.

***

At 4:30, Ellis gave up on trying to snatch an afternoon nap and cued his language lesson. The Russian voice began its repetitive commands. Ellis stared at the slate squares on the floor, trying to concentrate his attention on the rough syllables.

36

At first, he didn't hear the knock. The Russian words obscured the faint sound. When the second knock came, louder, he stopped the instruction and walked toward the door.

No one had buzzed him from the entrance, so his visitor must be a neighbor, someone who lived in the building. Ellis toyed with the idea of not answering, but the lesson, for what little it was worth today, already was interrupted. With luck, whoever stood on the other side of the door wouldn't stay long. He had no energy for company.

A third knock. Insistent.

Ellis opened the door. He only half-noticed the face before he saw the rifle pointed at his chest. He heard the blast before he felt it, and he struggled to translate the sound into Russian. All effort ended as the bullet pierced his heart. He never heard the sound of his body hitting the floor.

***

At three minutes to five, Jolie stood with Ridgedale High School in the background. One of WTNW's bulky satellite trucks, looking as if it were hauling an extraterrestrial search party, idled alongside the black SUV. She had buttoned her coat against the February chill. A twist of coral and blue silk paisley lay underneath, enough of the scarf showing to set off her face and hair. The microphone level had been set. Nothing needed now but to figure out what the hell she would say.

"Do you really think," she'd asked Marcus that afternoon, "Brad would keep me from ever doing a lead story again if I don't do this one?"

"He's not one to mess with," Marcus had said.

So she had dug around for something that would make a story. She'd talked with the high school principal ("Jason's a bully, but the others are just tag-alongs. No serious trouble with any of them.") and had checked with the owner of the hangout across the street ("They sit in that corner over there, all to themselves. Don't say much. Not real popular."). She'd stopped in the local music shop, even in a place that sold candles.

Mid-afternoon, Marcus suggested they drive around and get some file shots of Covington. "As long as we're up here."

"Are you just trying to keep me occupied so I'll stop bitching?"

He offered his Buddha smile. "Who, me?"

Now he stood behind his camera, too focused on his shot to offer comfort or distraction.

"One to Jolie," Geena said through the earpiece.

Jolie shivered and looked up at the sky. The blue had darkened to a twilight gray, and the day's chill had deepened. Above the glare of streetlights and news lights, she could make out a half moon, cold, distant, and uninterested in the knot in her stomach.

In her earpiece, she heard the newscast's theme.

"30 seconds," Geena said.

Jolie heard Devin on the set begin the voiceover introduction.

"You're hot," Geena said as the intro wrapped up. "You're in the two-shot." The anchor introduced her.

"That's right, Devin," Jolie began. "Behind me is Ridgedale High School in Covington. WTNW news has learned that…" She glanced at her notes. *C'mon, get on with it.* "We've learned that a group of students here at Ridgedale High School—" *You already gave the name, idiot.* She took a deep breath and felt it tremble through her stiff body. Her grip on the hand-held mic tightened. She had no idea what to say next. No idea whatsoever. This had never happened to her. Her mind froze.

"We've learned—we've learned—zip." *What had she*

just said? Another breath shuddered through her. The camera was on her, live. She had to talk. She could think of absolutely nothing to say but the truth.

"We've promoted this story. We've encouraged you to watch—"

She could overhear Geena in the control booth. "Did she say *zip*? Anybody hear Jolie say zip?" Then in a mutter, "I can't have heard that right."

Jolie ploughed on. "—to learn details of this satanic cult. And here are those details—"

In her earpiece, she heard Geena whisper *thank God* and begin talking with the sports anchor who wanted extra time for a Titans linebacker trade.

Jolie was only faintly aware of this background conversation. It seemed to be taking place in another universe. In her own, the words began tumbling out unchecked, unstoppable.

"What we have, and I mean all we have, is an over-hyped tale that amounts to nothing. But it's a lead story when it's a big ratings period, isn't it? Because news at WTNW—and, let's face it, at just about any station these days, but especially and disappointingly at WTNW, a newsroom that once was worthy of at least some respect—"

She overheard the director say, "Geena, you need to listen to this."

"—amounts to little more than consultant-run sleaze-mongering."

Into her mind came the image of a violin recital when she was eight. After mangling a series of notes, she had lost her way and had begun bowing wildly, the strings squealing as she'd played on with no idea of how to find her way back to the tune or how to end and flee the stage.

Then, as now, she had been unable to halt. She had no idea

39

what she was going to say next, only that she was going to keep talking as long as they'd let her. All the furor and frustration that had built up since Brad's arrival came gushing out.

Then something happened. Suddenly, she wanted each and every person watching her on TV at that moment to pay attention and *hear* her; although she still didn't know what words would come unbidden next. She knew only that they wouldn't be a mockery of everything she believed in.

Her voice rose a pitch. "You're coming to us every day to give you the news, to tell you what supposedly is worth knowing about that day. Well, forget it. We make a point now of *not* doing that. It's getting worse by the day, and I don't know where it's going to end. We slobber over celebrities, twist facts to make stories juicier, and keep cutting out more and more of what does actually matter, because we're terrified of boring you or, God forbid, asking you to think. So what can you do about it?" She paused, and abruptly felt herself running out of steam. "Hell, I don't know." She threw up a hand. "Rent that great classic *Network* and watch it. E-mail—"

Suddenly Brad's voice bellowed in her ear. "Get that bitch off the air! Cut to the set, then to commercial. Now, goddammit, now! What the hell are you waiting for? Why did you let her keep ranting like this, you dumbfucks?"

Devin's voice, with a discernable quaver, came on. "We'll be right back after this." The next sound was a McDonald's jingle trumpeting burgers.

Jolie kept staring at the lens. Marcus stepped away from the camera.

"What's wrong?" Jolie screamed at him. "Don't they want my live report on the sinister, dastardly satanic cult operating right here in little ol' Covington, Tennessee?"

Marcus walked up and with utmost care took the mic from her hands.

"Where's my goddamn purse?" She walked to the SUV, threw open the door and reached into her mammoth bag. The jitter in her hand made it hard to locate the cigarette pack, hard to shake one from the lineup. The first one broke off just below the filter, and she threw it on the ground. "Dammit! Dammit all!" The next one she managed to get out in one piece but burned her fingers on the match.

Jolie sucked the smoke into her lungs and sat with the door open, cold air rushing in. The familiarity of the cigarette gave her comfort when all else abruptly had turned alien. She watched the satellite crew hastily reel in cables and drive off. She heard Marcus put away the gear as if it were blown glass. A few minutes later, she felt his weight sink the vehicle as he took his seat behind the wheel. She finished that cigarette and lit another off the end of it.

Maybe nothing had happened. Maybe they were still waiting to go live. The good folk of the mid-South, eating their carry-out fried chicken as they sat before their TV's, hadn't really seen her standing right there on the vacant sidewalk, positioned just so, with the high school behind her.

But it had happened. The words had rushed out of her. Perhaps the first unguarded, unscrutinized words she had ever spoken on camera.

Marcus cleared his throat. "Ready to head back?"

His tone was even gentler than usual. Jolie suspected he was worried about what she might do next; concerned she might turn that fury on him if he said the wrong words, or said anything at all in the wrong way. However, the rage that had taken over her, that had pushed the torrent out, had now vanished, leaving her empty, spent and stunned.

She smelled woodsmoke. In a house nearby, someone had built a fire, someone was preparing for an ordinary evening. "Not just yet, okay?" Jolie heard the worn-out tone of her voice.

She knew Marcus would hear it too and know he was safe. "Give me a minute."

She grabbed matches and the pack of cigarettes, slid out of the news cruiser and walked over to the site of her standup. Without thinking, she began pacing the sidewalk, back and forth, back and forth as if she could somehow walk over the words until she'd obliterated them.

After a few minutes, she stopped. Marcus sat behind the wheel, phone to his ear, no doubt talking to the newsroom. The fading light silhouetted his head. The wind had picked up. She pulled her coat tighter. One more smoke. A few more minutes while she tried to keep consequences at bay, snarling to themselves in a low ditch at the edge of her mind.

Ten minutes later, she climbed into the SUV, saying nothing.

"Guess we better be heading back," Marcus said after a while. He waited for her to disagree, but when she merely closed the door, he turned the key.

In the houses they passed, TV screens glowed in the darkness. Jolie watched for the bluish rectangles and the people around them. Even after all these years, it struck her as odd that many of these total strangers knew her face and name, that they sat in their familiar living rooms and watched her every weeknight. Every weeknight here for ten years. Had they seen her blowup? Were they talking about it right now?

***

When Glenda Skinner heard the shot from down the hall, her plump tabby bolted off her lap and the leather-bound copy of *Middlemarch* fell to the floor. She sat immobile. Only her ears felt alive, keenly alert for another blast.

After a few minutes' silence, Glenda slowly rose from the

reading chair in her library and tiptoed to the front door of her condo. She put ear to wood. Not a sound. She started to reach for the knob, but drew back. Do not go out there. Call the police and let them handle it.

The cat's claws had punctured the skin when he'd jumped off her lap. She should attend to that, should clean the small, stinging wounds with hydrogen peroxide. But first she really ought to call the police.

***

Jolie couldn't fault her coworkers. If she were in their place, she would be hanging around to see what happened next.

As she walked to her desk, no one turned to greet her. They all became busy with papers and computers, even though she knew many of them had wrapped up their work for the day. Only Rando looked her in the eye. He gave her a sneaky thumbs-up. She knew damn well several others in the newsroom felt the same way but didn't have the guts to show it.

She dumped her things on the cluttered desk, braced herself, and walked toward Brad's office. The clock above his door read 6:30. In a few small sweeps of the minute hand, it likely would be over.

Why hadn't she chosen another way? Tried PBS's newsroom one more time? Tried anything instead of torching her future with a flame thrower?

Brad's desk faced his office door, and there he sat, glaring. The colonel with a case of flagrant insubordination. Jolie forced her eyes to meet and hold his.

He motioned brusquely for her to shut the door. He gave no indication she was to sit. Usually she did so unbidden, but she sized up such a move this time as an opening round mistake.

She concentrated on breathing. In, out. Deeper. In, out. Don't think about a cigarette. Don't look away. In—

Brad interrupted the third intake. "That," he said, his voice hard, "was the most asinine thing I've ever seen. It also was the most self-serving, self-righteous and self-destructive."

"Look, Brad, I'm—"

He held up his hand. "I don't want to hear it. Maybe the GM will. He's waiting for us."

Top Dog Trousdale. A name she had given the general manager, one that had caught on in the newsroom. Oil paintings of his beloved bird dogs lined his office walls. Jolie realized Top Dog would blame Brad as well as herself. It meant his news director couldn't control his pack.

Brad brushed past her out the door and turned rigidly to make sure she followed. Jolie had no doubt everyone was watching. She threw back her shoulders.

On Trousdale's credenza sat his lead crystal decanter, something Jolie had seen emerge only for celebrations until now. A half-full highball glass rested near his elbow. "Sit down, please," he said after Brad shut the door. Trousdale's south Georgia accent carried a cold edge. She knew he had added the "please" only because he fancied himself the epitome of the well-mannered Southern gentleman, but his etiquette would not extend to offering his aged bourbon.

Jolie glanced at Brad's face and saw it pale. She walked in front of him across a thick rug and sat in the red silk chair beside his, both of them facing Trousdale.

Following the intimidation pattern of top dogs everywhere, the GM made them wait. He leaned back, and then leaned forward on his elbows, locking his hands. He looked back and forth at both of them. Finally, he spoke to Jolie.

"If it were any other reporter, you wouldn't be here in my office. You'd be picking up the contents of your desk from a paper sack out by the trash. But you've been with this station a long time. In the past, you have been known to do good work. Won some awards for us. It is only for that reason that you are sitting in front of me at this moment."

"Sir—" she knew he liked to be addressed that way "—if I could, I'd like to explain."

She saw Brad squirm, shift his weight in the high-backed chair. "Jim—"

Trousdale ignored him. "I am deeply disappointed in you, Jolie. It is beyond my grasp how you could be so disloyal to this station, how you could blaspheme all of us who work so hard."

"I agree that I should have voiced my concerns another way. I hold to what I said, but I should not have used my standup to say it. I'm willing to apologize on air for that."

Brad jumped up from his chair. "You can't let her do that! You can't let her go back on the air."

"Of course I won't." Top Dog motioned for Brad to sit. "It's unconscionable Jolie would even suggest it." His deep drawl lowered to a growl. "I'll tell you exactly what I told the *The Commercial Appeal's* TV columnist. I told him, 'Ms. Marston's comments were an insult to our viewers and staff. She is no longer a part of our news operation.'"

So this was what "you're fired" sounded like. Of course, Top Dog, with his commissioned paintings, his expensive bourbon and his hand-loomed Persian underfoot wouldn't say, "You're fired." Much too crude. That was more Brad's style, and she knew Brad regretted not being the one to say it.

"Sir, as long as you're firing me, may I say something?"

"Is it anything you haven't already told everyone within a hundred-mile radius of this office?"

Jolie kicked a heel against the rug. "Do you know what someone told me the other night? That WTNW now stands for Where Trash News Wins." She heard the tremor in her voice and spoke louder to push through it. "Do you care that we're a joke? You must. You're the same GM who was here when we did decent work, when we covered local news with about as much depth as it ever gets." She looked over at Brad. "Since Brad's arrival, our integrity has plummeted. We pander. And if you ask me, we outright deceive. Today I was told…ordered…to concoct a lead story out of some kid's flimsy fantasy of evil. When I questioned the assignment, Brad threatened me with the weekend shift…no more weekday reports. Do you know this kind of intimidation is happening in your newsroom?"

Trousdale took a slow sip of his bourbon and rocked the ice in his glass. "We are within three ratings points of being number two for our five-to-seven news block. Within five points of being number one. As you know, we used to be number one, were for years. But we've been mired in the number three position for longer than I care to remember. Thanks to Brad and the techniques you demean, we are now nipping at the heels of our competition. We've gained seven ratings points since he came. Seven. I hired him as news director to do what he's done at other third-place newsrooms in the country, and as long as he's doing it, I have no complaints."

"So," she said, "the ratings justify the trash and to hell with our reputation, is that it?"

Trousdale stood and walked over to one of the paintings, a glossy-coated setter with his foreleg up to point. He looked at the picture a moment, and then turned to Jolie. "It's fine for you to pontificate and shake your finger, but where exactly do you think the money comes from that lets you go out and do your job? Do you know what a seven-point climb means in increased ad revenues? It takes good ratings to pay for the nice salary and benefits and steady raises you've had since you joined us."

"I know it does, but—"

"If ratings and ad revenues didn't matter, we'd just turn this place into a documentary shop."

"No doubt she'd love that," Brad said.

Jolie leaned forward. "That's not what—"

"And we'd go broke," Top Dog said, "which means I'd be out of a job. Why do you think we abandoned documentaries ourselves? Because we do our market research. God in heaven, we spend a fortune on market research. Not to mention the consultants. And you may be certain we are following the results and advice we pay dearly to get."

"As we should, sir," Brad said.

Slimy weasel.

Top Dog sat back down. "I think we're through here."

Brad started to speak, but Top Dog shot him a silencing look, rose, and stood at his desk.

***

Halfway down the hall, she spoke, not turning back to look at Brad. "I'll clear out my desk later tonight after everyone's gone to Huey's to yammer about me over beers. I don't need an audience."

"Make sure you're out before morning. Leave your keys on your desk."

If I don't leave them up your rear.

"Oh, and Jolie—" He stopped to be sure he had her attention. "I've been thinking about something." He paused again.

She turned to face him. "Don't string it out, Brad."

"I've been thinking what fun newsrooms all over the country will have with an aircheck of your implosion. You know, some way or other, your standup is bound to make the rounds."

47

She blanched. "You wouldn't."

"Oh, I'd go further, but our gentlemanly GM wouldn't like that. I'll just have to settle for seeing you become the industry's laughing stock."

She knew he was right. Hadn't she often laughed at videos that stations sent around of absurd or stupid things that had happened on-camera?

"If anyone calls me for a reference," he said, "I'll tell them about Jolie Marston's Last Stand. At your age, that's probably what we can call it, isn't it?"

"You do anything illegal, you bastard, and I'll sue."

"I won't have to do anything illegal. Hell, some viewer at home is probably posting it to YouTube right now. You've screwed yourself royally."

"All the screwing I see around here is done by you. And we're probably talking literal screwing after you get your newsroom filled with grateful little bimbos from fourth-rate markets. But they'll all have great lips, won't they, Brad?"

"They'll be young too." He walked past her into the newsroom.

She made herself follow.

But the staff wasn't standing around waiting to size up the depth of her demise. Something was happening. She knew it the second she walked into the room. There was the heightened pitch of voices, the palpable frenzy crisscrossing the rows of desks.

Pris, the ten o'clock producer, grabbed Brad's arm with red lacquered nails. "Ellis Standifer's dead. They're saying foul play."

Jolie felt the blood drain from her face.

"Who's on it?" Brad shouted.

"Mark and Brenda are on their way," Pris said. She tucked a lock of short, henna-colored hair behind one ear. "Somebody found him at his condo."

Brad looked around. "Geena! Where's Geena?"

Somebody yelled, "She ran downstairs to find a director."

"Are we on the air with this?"

"Not yet," Pris said. "But—"

"Why the hell not?" Brad shoved her toward her computer. "Write something up. I want us on the air pronto. You've got one minute to get copy ready." He threw a glance toward the 5:00 anchor. "Devin, get on the set. Tease that we'll be covering the story the rest of the evening. And listen up, all of you. I want something on the air every ten minutes, even if it's only a crawl that says what we've already said." He pointed to a nearby reporter. "You, go work up a bio. Get Rando to pull archive clips for you."

Pris's nails began tapping out copy on her keyboard. Brad watched her a moment, then swung around to Jolie, his face smug. "The highly esteemed former mayor murdered. Probably the biggest story this year. You would've been covering this." His voice grew callous. "Guess I'll just have to put a pro on it instead."

Jolie's lower lip trembled. She clamped her teeth over it. How could Ellis be murdered? How could this whole impossible day be happening?

She went over to Pris. "Okay if I read over your shoulder?"

Brad pushed her away. "Get your ass the hell out of my newsroom."

She whirled to face him. "Are you happy now that you've got yourself a juicy murder?"

He smirked. "Couldn't happen at a better time."

"God, Brad, your belly must stay raw from all the slithering."

"Out!" He pointed to the back door.

"No, thanks," she managed to say. "I'll go out the front."

Four

So this is what it felt like to be on the outside. Jolie had been in the thick of whatever was happening for so long, she had forgotten it could be any other way. This, she saw, would be the worst part: being excluded, standing outside the clique of information.

She ground out her cigarette on the station pavement and drove the low-slung convertible out of the parking lot.

At her fifth-floor downtown apartment, she called Nick. "Bad news. Real bad news."

"Joles, are you hurt?"

"If you mean am I injured, no. Not physically. What I am is…fired."

"You're what?"

"Canned." Her voice shook. "Axed. Kicked out. But there's more."

"Want me to come over?"

"Now. Hurry."

"Anything I can bring you?"

"If you've got any heroin tucked away, any opium, any horse tranquilizers, bring them on. But don't let me near the hemlock."

"I'll be right there. Just give me time to grab some clothes for tomorrow."

After Jolie hung up, she sat unmoving, staring at nothing in particular. It all was too much to be real, much less something she could absorb. Ellis's murder (how awful that phrase sounded), her firing (how improbable that one, despite her shared enmity with Brad). No, not possible. Neither of these horrible events was even remotely possible. To think she'd never again get to talk to Ellis, that he'd never get to do any of the things he was planning for the rest of what had seemed a charmed life, to think his mother would have to grapple with his absence and the way he'd died. Too much. Too much. Too much.

She found herself chanting these words aloud. Her voice grew louder until she was nearly screaming, and she didn't care who in her apartment building heard her. She walked over to the dresser and watched her reflection in the mirror as she yelled, "Too much! Too much!"

Glancing down, she spotted the ivory rectangle left on the dresser this morning. The Warrior Rune advising patience. What did any of it, especially Ellis's death, have to do with patience? She raised her middle finger toward the rune.

***

When Nick entered Jolie's apartment, she was sitting in the dark, feet up on the sofa, hands wrapped around her knees, her head tucked in, spent. He turned on a table lamp and brushed the length of her reddish-brown hair. "Hey, Joles," he whispered.

She threw up a hand in a limp wave. Next to her on the coffee table lay a drained tumbler and overfilled ashtray.

"Tell me how to help."

"Just be here," she mumbled into her knees.

They sat silently for several minutes, his hand stroking her hair. Finally, she looked up at him with red-rimmed eyes. She decided to focus for now only on her firing. Loathsome as it was, it was easier to speak about than Ellis. She could not deny her firing. But Ellis's death she could put off making entirely real for a little while longer. Telling Nick would take that away.

"I had a major, major screw up. Beyond major."

"What happened?" he said softly.

"I lost it, plain and simple. I fucking lost it. And we were live."

"No."

"Oh, yes. I can't believe I did it either. I mean, everything I said was right, was the truth and needed to be said. But what a stupid, self-destructive way to do it."

She told him the details of the baseless assignment, her on-air blowup, the meeting with Trousdale and Brad's glee in banishing her from the newsroom. As she spoke, she watched his face shift from bewilderment to shock.

He leaned back and blew out a breath. "Oh, man." Then he leaned over and gave her a hug far longer than ever before. She collapsed into it.

Eventually she pulled back and looked at him. "What am I going to do now, Nick?"

He reached for her hand. "Nothing for a bit. Nothing needs to get decided for a while. I strongly suggest you give yourself time to think about what you want to have happen next. It might have nothing to do with news."

She held out her empty glass. "I know what I want right now."

"Okay, but how about some food? I can make you a sandwich."

"I'm not hungry."

"Just something to nibble on. You need at least a little food." He returned in a moment with a refilled glass and a bowl of chips.

She poked her finger in the tumbler and twirled the ice as Nick stood over her.

"Sit down," she told him quietly. "That's not all that happened on this godawful day."

"What do you mean?"

Why put it off? He'd know by morning anyway. Hell, it probably was on national news already. Still, she who rarely was at a loss for words, couldn't figure out a way to start.

Jolie dropped her head and covered her eyes. "What I have to tell you next is even worse than my little drama, bad as it is."

She looked up at him. His look of alarm told her she'd better get it out quickly. "Ellis Standifer was murdered."

Nick's mouth dropped open. "Ellis murdered? Why would anyone murder him of all people?"

"I don't know, Nick. I don't know."

He held her close again. "Oh, Joles. That's terrible. I know he meant a lot to you. I'm so sorry."

In a moment he asked, "When did this happen? I haven't heard anything."

"Word got to us…to them, the newsroom…right as I was being booted out the door."

"Damn."

"Yeah."

"But why, for Chrissakes? Was it just some random killing?"

She felt the anger toward Brad, toward herself rise again. "That's what I'd be finding out, if I still had a job." She laughed in a bitter, sharp burst. "My dear friend Ellis Standifer has been murdered, and I can't cover it. I'm out of the loop. I'm so far out of the loop I might as well be on a dinghy in the middle of the ocean."

The phone jangled, and Nick answered, and then put his hand over the receiver. "Do you want to talk to Colin Fisher with the *The Commercial Appeal*?"

Jolie waved away the call. But as Nick made excuses for her, she walked over to signal she would take it in a minute. Nick stalled as she circled the room to collect her thoughts.

She was still pacing when she took the phone. "Hi, Colin.

Here's your quote: In hindsight, yes, I would've handled things differently, and I apologize if I offended any viewers. But I don't apologize for my opinion. I know a lot of viewers agree with me. They must."

"Certainly *I* do," he said in his clipped voice.

"Great. Then back me."

"I'm not here to go on a crusade, Jolie. What you did tonight was make news, not report it. And I'm reporting that you made it."

"As if anybody's going to care, with Standifer murdered."

"Ellis Standifer? Are you kidding? How? A robbery?"

"I don't know. You mean you haven't heard he was killed?"

Colin's voice grew defensive. "I just got back from dining with friends. Besides, it wouldn't be my story. You're my story."

"But of course."

"What's your next move? Are you going to try to stay in town?"

"Colin," she said wearily, "I don't know my next move. I have no idea. Probably take a bath. Right after I clear out a decade's worth of work at dear ol' WTNW."

***

Soon after the call, Nick drove her to the station and stood nearby as she emptied her desk. In the top drawer lay a video with *Blaze of Glory* written on its spine and a note: *I thought you might want this someday. You're very talented, and it's been great working with you. I'll miss you, but there's bound to be something better out there for you. Let's stay in touch. Marcus.*

When she and Nick were back in her apartment, they

watched the video. When the abrupt cut to the anchor desk came on, he put his arm around her and squeezed hard.

"Here's what I want to know," she said, her face turned away from him,"Is something like this going to happen again?"

"No," he whispered. "No."

She pulled away from his embrace and faced him. "I mean it. Maybe the next time I have to deal with some inept clerk in the checkout line? Some bratty kid in the seat behind me on the plane who won't stop whining? Am I just going to lose it again and keep on losing it?"

"You won't, Joles. Trust me, you won't."

They said nothing more for several minutes. Finally, he kissed her cheek and got up off the sofa. "I hate having to say this, but I need to be in court by eight. Won't you please come to bed too? See if you can get some sleep?"

She shook her head and reached for another cigarette. "I want to see the news."

"You sure?"

"I'm sure."

Ellis Standifer's murder, of course, led on all three stations. He had been killed at his downtown condo a few blocks from where Jolie lived. The footage of the crime's aftermath made even Jolie, hardened to murder scenes, wince. Splashes of Ellis's blood covered the floor, walls and furniture. The cameras lingered on the gruesome stains.

She wanted that blood back in him, coursing through his living, breathing body. The longing to see him again was acute.

Plonski, at a news conference, described the weapon as a Winchester Model 70 30-06, a common type of rifle but unusual in the commission of an urban crime. The shot entered Standifer's heart, exited his back, and lodged in the living room wall, only blocks from where Jolie now sat. Plonski looked even more bushed than usual. No, he said, there were no suspects; there was no known motive, that was all he could tell them.

Standing beside Plonski was the beefy deputy mayor, Ed Dempsey, who used to head the vice squad. Jolie thought of him as Mayor Farrell's token white goon.

As the newscasts ended, she said a quiet "Hallelujah." On none of the competing stations was she the kicker, the flip bit of information that closes each newscast.

Jolie stuffed a wad of chips in her mouth, picked up the remote control and began running through the channels. Pink-haired evangelist Jan Crouch, who made Tammy Faye Baker look subtle and bald, glittered in all her gaudiness on the Trinity Broadcasting Network. She introduced a smiling male singer about twenty and touched him often with diamond-laden fingers.

Jolie studied TBN's fancy shots from crane-mounted cameras, the huge jewelry of everyone who appeared, and the immense stage with its overdone sets. No manger scene on this network. Understandable that they had to keep begging. High tacky doesn't come cheap.

When the young man began singing in a syrupy twang, Jolie turned off the set and ran a bath, hoping a dreamless sleep soon would follow.

***

By the time she dragged her hangover from bed the next morning, Nick had been at work two hours.

The newspaper lay on the kitchen table where he had left it. She had to turn it over to see the headline on Ellis, and she was sure Nick planned it that way when he refolded it for her to read. She would grapple with the story on the murder and all its sidebars a little later. Braced now with aspirin and a mug of stout coffee, she flipped to the television page. *Marston canned after on-air outburst.* Jolie sucked in her breath and began reading. At least Colin quoted her correctly. And skipped the bath part. He concluded with: *Ms. Marston tells me she has no idea what she will do next.*

After a second cup of coffee, she turned back to the front page. A quick scan of the first paragraphs in the lead story showed little in the way of hard news that hadn't been on TV the night before. The skimpy details were fleshed out with quotes from "stunned" people in high places including the governor. There were sidebars detailing Ellis' background, his achievements, and what he'd done since leaving office. An inside page covered in photos highlighted his years as mayor.

Jolie tossed aside the paper. She would keep an eye on its online version for anything newer.

She walked into her sparse living room and looked at the box plopped on the floor last night. How could fourteen years' work in three newsrooms fit into one container not much bigger than a suitcase? She lifted from it a familiar square of paper:

It is surprising what a tissue of trifles and crudities make the daily news.

Except on this morning, the news was not trifling. The death of a friend, the death of her career. Slaughtered. A florid word, but it would do.

Jolie crumpled the Thoreau quote and threw it at a row of awards lining one wall.

Colin's final line in his column had spoken truth and terror. She had no idea what she would do next. She kicked the newsroom box toward the wall.

***

Violet Standifer lifted her 90-year-old fingers from the

57

keyboard and closed the lid. She put a hand on her chest, trying to ease the labored thumping under her bony ribs. From a silver frame on top of the piano, Ellis smiled at her in a photograph taken when he was an invincible seventeen.

She laid her head on the lid's cool wood. Could a heart rip apart from grief? Could her own heart tear open and spill out onto the keys, leaving her emptied, unable to feel, drained of all life? What a gift that would be.

With only a vague awareness of what she was doing, she reopened the lid and began playing the largo to Beethoven's *Sonata Number Four in E-Flat* again. This time she held the pauses until a listener might wonder if another note would ever come. Only then, in that half-instant when the question might arise, did she sound it.

Five

The second day after her firing, Jolie awoke with her usual morning hunger pangs and took them as a sign to get busy. Yesterday she had told herself she could have one day to do nothing except stare at the pink-haired lady on TV, but that was it.

After checking the newspaper and finding little more than a rehash of Ellis's murder, she scooted a straight-backed chair close to the kitchen table. At the top of a yellow sheet, she wrote *Options* and underlined the word. She sat staring at it, pen poised.

She poured coffee. Maybe she should've taken one of the offers that had come her way, not held out for a dream job. Instead, she'd become stuck in the Mississippi mud, hadn't she? Just as she had seen other people do. It was a comfortable ooze, the way it quelled any dramatic action, any decisive move. No need to rush and you couldn't if you wanted to. Just slow down and sway to the city's funky, mud-laden beat. The living was easy.

Easy, of course, if you were white and weren't poor. Or hadn't just jabbered your way out of a job.

To the task. Rent was due in two weeks.

For damn sure, she could kiss off a future in TV news. She chewed on the end of the pen. So, what did people do when they left news? She made a list of former colleagues and looked up their work numbers.

Roger Wilhelm had worked his way up to head of internal PR for Federal Express. He now flew all over the globe from the company's Memphis headquarters. Jolie considered it a good omen that he was in town when she called.

"Here?" Roger said after she told him she needed work. "The hard-nosed Jolie Marston working as a PR hack?"

"Yeah, well."

"I can't see it. Much as I liked working around you in the newsroom, it's just a very different atmosphere here."

"So maybe's that's exactly what I need, Roger."

"Even if I thought you'd like it here—and not for a minute do I think you would—I couldn't hire you."

"Why not?"

"You know why, Jolie."

She wanted, perversely, to hear how he would phrase it. Besides, until then, she had not thought of her future as being shot anywhere outside of news. "Tell me. Why?"

"Because the very skills you need for this job are the same ones you failed to demonstrate. I saw your standup, and I'm not in the least surprised you're looking for a job."

This was a different man. Roger had been a tepid reporter. She imagined him now, ensconced behind the authority of a vast slab of mahogany and several underlings.

"The corporate leash," he went on, "is even shorter than the one in news. It wouldn't work, Jolie."

Jolie's eyes traced the walls and ceiling, measuring her situation. "Here's what I need to know then. Is that going to be the case with any PR position in town?" She heard a squeak and imagined Wilhelm leaning forward from a high-backed leather chair, planting his elbows on the silken wood.

"You're asking me to be straight," he said, "so I will be. I think your chances are nil. Anyone in the PR business in Memphis who didn't see that newscast will know what happened soon enough. Image is everything in this line of work. Image and being able to say diplomatically whatever you're told to say." She heard the chair squeak again. "I wish I could help you," he said, "but…" She imagined Roger leaning back, dismissing her.

Jolie punched in Greta's number. Greta had opened her own video production company after leaving news.

"It's bleak," she told Jolie. "The market's glutted. Every Tom, Dick, and Harriet think they can start up a video company. We're all scrounging. And the way the technology keeps heading, all of us pros might be irrelevant soon."

Two strikes. Jolie forced herself to make a third call.

The school superintendent, Evan Smith, could play spin-doctor with the best of them in public, but in private conversations he was known not to mince words. In the past, Jolie had admired that. Maybe there would be something in their public information department.

"Can't even think about it," Smith said.

"Why not?"

"I don't need a loose cannon on this staff."

"I'm not a loose cannon!"

Smith snorted. "It's out of the question."

Was this his revenge for her story last month on his staff's expense reports?

Roger Wilhelm and Evan Smith were right. She wasn't cut out for such work. She would hate it. It gave her satisfaction to decide she would refuse to do it.

***

Jolie changed into snug jeans, a sweater and wool jacket, gear for a blustery walk along the Mississippi. She habitually exited her apartment with the expectation of being recognized. That hadn't ended, not yet. Just as she was about to go out the door, she returned for a gold and green chamois scarf that set off her eyes. Fired she might be, but she damned sure did not want people saying she looked awful.

Two blocks from her fifth-floor apartment overlooking the river lay a familiar stretch of riverbank called Tom Lee Park. The park's length had become a favorite walk when she needed to think through anything or just wanted fresh air. Today, under a brisk wind, she gazed at the roiling brown current and the flat Arkansas farmland beyond it. The park's name honored the heroic actions of *a very worthy Negro*, as the marker said. Tom Lee, with his boat Zev, saved 32 lives when a steamer sank in 1925. Lee's marker, a stout obelisk, stood only blocks from where another black man, this one named King, had stood on a balcony in 1968. Between the two sites lay Beale Street, where blues strutted nightly to ghostly notes from the rowdy backrooms of W. C. Handy's day.

Jolie often felt that, as a white person, she ought to have a pass to be in parts of Memphis. Unfortunately, Beale Street was no longer one of those areas. It had been glossed up to draw white tourists with money, to make them feel safe and comfortable strolling the clubs late at night. She felt Beale Street should have remained the opposite of such predictable ways, but any chance of that was hauled away with urban "renewal" in the 60s.

The open park where she now walked lay exposed, bereft even of the cottonwoods that once had lined its bank, a clearing considered idiotic by all but the city officials who ordered it. The expanse no longer offered any shelter from a wind gaining strength by the minute under darkening skies. Jolie wrapped her scarf tightly around her neck and tucked her head. Occasionally she braved a glance at the river and noticed whitecaps skimming its wide, murky surface. The cold gusts urged her back to shelter, but she shoved her hands deep into the jacket pockets and propelled herself to the end of the park and back.

Her mind kept straying to why on earth anyone would want to kill Ellis, but each time her thoughts wandered that way, she corralled them to the task at hand.

By the time she re-entered her apartment, only one disturbing thought held. She might have to leave Memphis. Leave Nick, leave news, leave a town that had embraced her, a town she had come to hold dear.

After taking off her jacket and scarf, and rubbing her cold cheeks, she turned on the television. WTNW had Devin on the set with a *Breaking News* banner across the lower third of the screen.

"...nothing taken from the condo and no sign of forced entry. So, to repeat, Memphis Police now say burglary definitely was not a motive in the murder of Ellis Standifer. We'll of course continue keep you posted with the most up-to-the—"

"Shut up, Devin." She hit the power button.

If not a burglary, what could have been the reason? Out of habit, she began making a mental list of all the people to call, all the ways she might dig up more information. Not until she reached for a notepad did she catch herself.

***

"Leaving town's the only option that makes any sense," she told Nick soon after he arrived that evening. They sat in her living room, speakers nearby playing an Al Green-Lyle Lovett cut from *Rhythm, Country & Blues*, a beloved CD from 1994.

"But to go where?" Nick asked.

"I haven't figured that part out yet."

"Grad school?"

"To study what? With what? I have got maybe two thousand in savings. This isn't the time to take out a loan, if I could get one. And I refuse to borrow from my parents. I'm a self-sufficient woman, or ought to be."

63

"How about looking for something with a newspaper?"

"They turn up their noses at TV people."

"Yeah, but you've made it clear you're not a TV type."

"I'm not a newspaper type either. Anything larger than some low-paying weekly wants reporters with newspaper experience and plenty of it. So many newspapers have downsized or just flat-out folded the last few decades—Memphis's *Press-Scimitar* being a case in point going back to '83—that experienced reporters go begging." She sighed. "Let's face it, my job prospects suck."

"Glad to see you're not cynical."

She pushed her feet against the coffee table. "You don't spend fourteen years in news without becoming cynical. It's a trait that's cultivated and applauded. Belief in anything gets hard to come by."

By morning, Jolie had narrowed her one humiliating choice. She explained it as Nick shaved at the long mirror above her bathroom vanity.

"At least in Singleton, I could live cheaply. Give myself a sabbatical until I figure out just what it is I want to do with the rest of my life."

He threw her a sideways glance. "How long do you think that would take?"

"God, not long, I hope."

He rinsed his razor and began shaving the other side of his face. She used to stand mesmerized as her father daubed foam on his cheeks and chin, and then slid the razor along to reveal pink skin beneath. After he would leave for work, she would climb up on the step stool, rub the soft, damp bristles of his sterling-handled brush over her face. It had been a grave disappointment at age five to learn she would never grow a beard.

She watched Nick make a careful sweep from ear to chin.

"So, what do you think about my moving back?"

He spoke to her image in the mirror. "You want the truth?"

"Of course I do."

He rested his razor against the sink. "I think you're making a mistake."

"What the hell else can I afford to do? Singleton's cheaper than Memphis."

She watched him pick up the razor again and begin on a new streak of skin. "Want to come to Singleton to work?" She knew neither of them took her question seriously, but she threw it out anyway.

"Not enough Jews in that town for me. What are there, two?"

"Four, but the Gupton's son is away at NYU."

"Never to return would be my guess. No, Singleton would not be a good fit for me with a last name like Ellsberg. I like big cities, remember? It's hard to grow up in Atlanta and not feel stifled in some place small."

She moved to stand beside him, talking to him in the mirror. "I'm going to miss our routine."

He looked at her. "Routine?"

"You know. The way we spend some nights and just about all our weekends together. Hear music, go to movies, art galleries, restaurants, that kind of stuff."

It was in a Midtown gallery that they had met. Nick had come up as she'd stood by a fifties-era photograph of the Mississippi Delta. "I've been watching you," he'd said, "and I'm not sure which you're observing more—the photos or the crowd. Seems to me you're at two exhibitions."

She had made sure not to let an opening line like that go to waste. Their conversation had lasted six hours.

Jolie sat on the edge of the tub. "You really think I'm making a bad choice to go back there?"

"You asked." He continued to shave.

"You know, Nick, I'm telling you about my limited options, and it occurs to me there's something you're not mentioning. If you think my leaving town is such a bad idea, why aren't you offering to put me up for a while?"

"That's not fair."

"What's not? Why isn't that a viable option?"

"Jolie, that's why we've worked as a couple. Neither of us pushed the other. You know damn well it wasn't that long ago I divorced. I'm not ready."

"Bull. You'd be ready if you wanted to be."

He whirled around, shaking the razor at her. "You're one to talk. You have kept yourself closed off to me. I don't know who has your heart—maybe your ex, maybe nobody—but I know for damn sure I don't. So don't start in on me about not making any leaps of faith with you."

He stuck the razor under the faucet and tossed it on the bathroom shelf. "Go to Singleton." He reached for a towel and buried his face in it as he dried off. When he spoke again, his voice was kinder. "Maybe it is the best place for you. Maybe it would do you good to have your parents close by."

"Why? Did God switch mothers on me?"

Six

On an annoyingly bright day in late February, Jolie and a loaded U-Haul pulled her little blue Toyota eastward. She watched the terrain's gradual ascent, first to the rounded hills of middle Tennessee, then to the higher, ancient limestone of the east. Each portion—middle, east and west—lay neatly separated from the others by the Tennessee River as it looped through the state.

Jolie's only stop except for gas and food had been at Shiloh, near the first crossing of the Tennessee. An ironic, supernatural peace pervaded the grassy acres, scene of one of the bloodiest battles of the Civil War. For years, it had been a favorite stop of hers.

She knew debate lingered about what had, or might have, happened here. It was 1862, early in the war. Confederate General Albert Sidney Johnston, the highest-ranking general on either side of the conflict, had triumphed the first day at Shiloh, driving Grant and Sherman, the giant figures of the Union, back to the river. But Johnston was killed late in the day, and Northern troops got reinforcements during the night. Southerners still argued the point: The South might well have won the war if not for Shiloh, if not for losing Johnston and failing to capture Grant and Sherman. Because a Northern loss would have meant the abominable continuation of slavery, Jolie wasn't sorry about the outcome.

She wandered through the long rows of grave markers. In only two days, 23,746 men from both sides were killed, wounded, or captured. It was said peach tree petals, dislodged by gunfire, fell like snow. The wounded were gathered at a pond on the north end of the orchard. Their blood turned the water red.

It was hard to think of either side claiming victory. The dead had been flung into trench graves, seven hundred to a hole. Federal dollars later put the Yankees in individual graves; the Confederate bodies remained tossed together. She walked by the sunken earth where they still lay.

Back on the highway, Shiloh's curious serenity stayed with her until she finally crossed the Tennessee river again at Chattanooga, marking her return to the state's eastern third.

***

Jolie wanted to slink back into Singleton unnoticed and remain unseen until she could leave again. But she knew the small town she'd deserted in sassier years wouldn't ignore her. The church she had endured, the high school where she'd felt stifled, even the stoplights where she'd exchanged flirtations on a long red waited to ridicule her. To tell her she had not become what she had vowed to become when she'd left. As she passed the city limits sign, she realized this was her first trip back without an exit date.

She urged the U-Haul up the long grade outside town. In the distance, a bluish haze hovered above the upthrusts that formed the foothills of the Smokies. A lot of people, she reminded herself, enjoyed living here. They liked having the bustle of Chattanooga and Knoxville only an hour or so away. But they liked better Singleton's quiet predictability. She knew it was just this contentment that drove away some people and seduced others. As a teenager, she had claimed the town got its name "because there's not a single thing to do here." Like every teen before her who had uttered the phrase, she was sure she'd coined it.

At the first traffic light, a once-familiar face craned its

wrinkled neck and scrutinized hers. Jolie turned away without smiling. Screw Bessie Rumfield and her perpetual frown.

Jolie trundled through town well below the speed limit. Past the older homes near the courthouse square, past the smaller homes on the lower part of Lander's Hill, to the larger homes and the last street before the topmost one. She pulled into a drive leading to a white, two-story Dutch colonial with wide, navy shutters—the Ozzie and Harriet house. As she turned off the engine, she paused to gather the remnants of her pride.

"Joanna, honey!"

Jolie knew her mother would sound just that sugary on her deathbed. She approached with outstretched arms, fingers flitting. Jolie shut her eyes for a moment before climbing out to receive the hug. Despite the display, she knew their unvoiced thoughts were the same: How long?

***

Charlotte Marston loved her daughter, to be sure, and she felt Jolie returned her love, but she knew they remained, at bottom, unfathomable to each other. Charlotte never understood her daughter's adamant spirit that would have its way and to hell with the consequences.

Charlotte fit Singleton's society like a cashmere-lined kid glove. Marriage to a top officer of the largest of the town's banks automatically assured her place unless she trespassed socially against her peers. And Charlotte was not about to trespass. Her recipe for social security came down to this: take care to always look good, even at home; exhibit beneficence appropriate to her position, a task made easy by the charity work of her social clubs and church; be an attentive wife and mother; call sick friends, write prompt thank-you notes and entertain expertly; at all times in public be pleasant. Yes, there were jealousies, occasional unkindnesses to endure, and disappointment to wrestle when it became clear her husband never would rise above senior vice president, but in time she became adroit at deflecting any threat to her harmony. She had watched her own mother, until the day she died, maneuver society's waters wavelessly as a judge's wife. Why hadn't she been able to pass those virtues on to Joanna?

She could understand why her experience-hungry daughter had not wanted to remain in Singleton. There was little to keep a bright, ambitious girl who longed to be worldly. But she could not comprehend Joanna's lack of interest in marrying again. (She had even become willing to overlook her boyfriend's Jewishness.) Why didn't her daughter long for children? And why on earth did she want to work so hard?

Now, though, had come this bewildering arrival in a rented moving truck. Charlotte's sweetheart-shaped lips like her daughter's, dressed with the light touch of pink used at home, pressed together as she encircled her returning child.

***

After clearing the dinner table that night, Jolie followed her father into the den. Walking behind him, she once again wished for his height and not her mother's diminutive stature. Stuart Marston's hairline had receded since her visit a few months back, and the deep red strands looked thinner, or maybe she was only now noticing. She watched him settle into his green leather easy chair and prop his feet on a matching ottoman. She dropped into a nearby chair. It was, she noticed, newly upholstered. Fawns ambled across a leafy brocade. Had her mother ever gone so much as a month without redecorating something?

Stuart kicked off his shoes. "So how's my girl?"

She scrunched down in the chair. "Utterly lousy. But you figured that much."

"Jeff called me at work today. Said to tell you he'd get in to see you when he could. Things are busy right now. A couple of short deadlines he's dealing with."

"Jeff? Don't you mean Jefferson?" Jolie's only sibling, five years her junior, had decided last year that Jefferson sounded more appropriate for an upscale architect in Chattanooga, so he'd taken the full name that used to be a source of humiliation.

Her dad chuckled. "We never should have named him that. Can't believe I let your mother talk me into that."

Jolie leaned forward. "So, have you got any ideas about why Ellis was murdered? Mom just blames it on the big, evil city."

"Darling, I don't have the slightest idea."

"Surely you must have heard some rumors through the years."

"None. You have to remember, he moved to the other end of the state a long time ago. You'd be the one to pick up rumors."

"And they're damnably non-existent," she said. "I never heard a thing." She watched Stuart fill and light his pipe, stand up and begin pacing. She guessed the next topic.

He walked through a few more puffs. "From what little I know so far," he said at last, "it sounds like you definitely won't be returning to the station."

"Not that one." She stretched out her legs and clasped her hands across her lap. "Not any one."

"I knew from our phone calls your were getting more and more frustrated, but how—?"

"How did I end up here?"

She told him the story, watched his jaw tighten its lock on

the pipe stem.

"I understand your frustrations with the news," he said. "Any thinking person shares them. And your new boss sounds like an idiot." He puffed and considered his next words.

"But…" she prompted.

He sighed and put down his pipe. "I'm sorry you burned your bridges."

***

The next morning, Jolie filled a copper pitcher with dried flowers. Her mother had said "just any old way," but she knew better. No matter how much she fiddled, the eucalyptus and wheat fronds looked lopsided. Why did being at her parents' house make her feel six years old again?

The phone rang. She wiped her hands and picked it up.

"How are you doing, Joles?"

Nick's voice sounded much too far away. "Oh, I'm managing," she said. Since their argument that morning as she had watched him shave, each had been polite if a bit skittish toward the other.

"You sure?"

"Well, at the moment I'm throwing the first pity party of my life, but I'm sure I'll get bored and throw out the guests before long. How are things with you?"

"Fine. Busy. Same ol' same ol'."

As he described his frustrations at work, Jolie listened with only half a mind.

Back last summer, on the second anniversary of their meeting, they had driven her convertible under a full moon to a juke joint in the tiny Mississippi River delta town of Iuka, Mississippi. On the way home, they'd stopped by a field to make love on a blanket laid between rows of tufted cotton. The evening perfectly fit her idea of romance, but she was relieved when he hadn't suggested a deeper commitment.

He had been on target to accuse her of holding back. Since her divorce at twenty-three, she had kept her heart to herself, extending it for a few brief illusions, only to yank it farther back in. As much as she cared about Nick, she had held herself at one remove from him, just as she had from every man since Rich Peretti. It was safer this way. As a result, until Nick her relationships had sported the shelf life of quarks.

She realized he'd stopped talking. "Well," she said, "I sure hope things improve at work."

"So do I."

"What's happening with Standifer's murder?"

"Not a whole lot, although that's not keeping it from continuing to be the lead story day after day."

"Must not be anything else going on. Bet the producers are praying for a tornado. So there's nothing new at all?"

"I guess there is a little news. You remember it was a rifle that killed him."

"Right."

"No casing was found, but the rifling on the bullet might be a help."

"Right," Jolie said. "The marks left on a bullet from whizzing through the barrel can be as unique as fingerprints."

"So," Nick said, "the police are hoping that indentation or scratch or whatever it was will help track down the weapon. And they said only one of the neighbors was home and noticed anything. She heard a loud shot about the time they figure he was killed…around 4:30 that afternoon…but she didn't see anyone suspicious."

"So who alerted the cops?"

"She did," he said. "But she didn't see anyone."

"What was her name?"

"Skinner, I think it was. Gloria, Glenda. I'm not sure. Not a familiar name to me. So how was the drive over?"

"Okay. Keep me posted on Standifer."

"I will. Give your parents my best."

"Let me know anything you hear about him. Immediately."

"Joles, do you really…?"

"Humor me, okay?"

***

Jolie thought the diminutive two-story cottage looked as if it belonged in England. All it needed were lace curtains and a thatched roof. It stood at the end of a gravel drive, shielded from a paved road beyond by tall oaks and pines. The nearest neighbor could be seen only through a gap visible along the brick path leading from the back door. The isolation suited her just fine.

A light gray wood stain covered the planks of the cottage's well-maintained exterior. Behind a rounded, cherry red front door lay pine walls and floors, and a stone fireplace.

The owner had been eager to get the place rented, particularly to "someone from a nice family." She had patted down the lapels of her lace-trimmed blouse. "Since you're Charlotte's daughter, I could let you have it for…how does four hundred fifty a month sound? I feel I can't charge as much as I could if it were closer in, but it is newly painted."

Jolie hoped her face hadn't shown her astonishment. Four hundred fifty for a fairy-tale two-story twenty minutes from town?

But she hadn't bargained for the quiet. Now, three weeks after her move to the woods, she played music almost nonstop during her waking hours, raiding the considerable CD collection she had built up over the years. She had so many that she'd never bothered downloading much online. She even had a turntable and a decent collection of vinyl LP's.

Jolie missed the deadening comfort of a newsroom's clatter. "Disquieting" she called the silence, loving the pun. At least she hadn't lost her irony along with her job.

Her furniture created its own kind of noise. The lemon, lime and black prints, the sleek leather and tubular chrome furniture that had looked terrific in the high-ceilinged, open rooms of her downtown apartment now merely looked silly.

When she heard the CD player click to a stop, she hunted through the rows of music for an old Leonard Cohen that had been running through her mind. Soon his subterranean voice began eking out "Like a Bird on the Wire," singing about the crazed attempt to live freely.

She gazed out the window toward the woods. A few feet away, a squirrel raced down the thick trunk of an oak.

Singing about the attempt to figure out how much we can ask from life.

She tapped lightly on the window, hoping to get the squirrel's attention, but it turned and ran.

Jolie looked around for the burgundy velvet bag and spotted it where she'd flung it on a corner table in the living room. She tugged open its string, reached inside and pulled out a tile. The etching on the Rune resembled a person with outstretched arms. She flipped through the small cloth-bound book until she came across the reading for *Algiz*, the Protection Rune. *Control of the emotions is at issue here.* "A little late for that," she muttered. *New opportunities and challenges…along with them will come trespasses and unwanted influences.* Oh, goody.

As she stuffed the stone back into its bag, the phone rang. She turned down Cohen's croaking and answered.

The call was from her mother, inviting her to dinner the

next night. Martin Everett would be there.

For the first time since her return, Jolie found herself looking forward to something.

Seven

Martin Everett liked being Singleton's bon vivant. He relished being told he was the town's most interesting inhabitant and, at fifty-five, one of its handsomest. Along with his spunky mother Agnes, he also was one of its wealthiest.

Despite never having exercised his mind in a profession, Martin loved to learn, particularly about his passions: food, wine, books, and Avantis. He revered those forward-thrusting, wedge-shaped cars first made in 1963 that still looked futuristic. A few years ago, he had begun writing a column for the quarterly *Avanti* magazine, and his lively comments always garnered the most reader response of any pages in the publication.

And as much as Martin loved to learn, he loved to talk. He could be a spellbinding raconteur with his emphatic drawl, even if that drawl did take its time to wend its way to the end of a sentence. The wit his listeners got along the way made it worth the wait.

Martin lived amiably with eighty-three-year-old Agnes in their history-filled home. Agnes liked to think of herself as a *grande dame* in the mold of Alice Roosevelt Longworth. She would steer a guest toward the closest sofa, quoting her heroine: "If you don't have anything good to say about anybody, come sit by me." As a result, Agnes and Martin always knew the best gossip.

On this particular evening, Martin was dining with Charlotte and Stuart Marston and their daughter Jolie. Martin always looked forward to talks with Stuart about their abiding fascination with Thomas Jefferson. Although he knew Jolie less well, her determined spirit attracted him and, like most of

Singleton's residents, he found her television work to be glamorous.

To ward off the chill of the mid-March night, Martin wore over his starched white shirt a plaid vest whose vivid red brought out the blackness of his hair with its slow intrusion of white. The vest also set off his hard-won figure. Most of his life, he'd fought off the results of his epicurean pleasures with a three-mile-a-day run. A troublesome knee at fifty halted his running and prompted a switch to the YMCA pool. Agnes wouldn't hear of installing a pool in the extensive yard. Martin teased her that he would put one in the minute she died, just have the grave diggers come on over to the house after the funeral to save time.

Only his desire to keep his youthful looks drove him to exercise, and he had never set out to run or swim without wishing he were doing something else. He resented the effort it now took to maintain his reputation as a man who enjoyed life to its fullest without remorse or reckoning. But maintain it he would. He'd sooner shoot himself than be defeated by a *crème brûlée*.

He arrived at the Marston's door with two bottles of Premier Cru Chablis from his basement wine cellar. "I pulled these out in honor of Jolie's return," he told his hosts. Martin knew one of the attractions of his company at dinner was an excellent bottle or two of wine. His donations were particularly welcome in a town where anything bought locally other than beer had to come from the price-gouging bootlegger whose specialty was sickly sweet cherry vodka.

Jolie came up from behind her mother. "Hey, Martin."

Martin greeted her with an enthusiastic hug. "It's great to see you, Jolie! Welcome back." Although he was itching to confirm rumors, he knew information would have to be extracted carefully, tactfully. He and Agnes already had decided she wouldn't be back here unless something had gone wrong in Memphis.

During an opening round of artichoke soup—he knew Charlotte worked and worried over her menus when he was a guest—Martin glanced at his hands, saw the grime of engine oil on them from one of his Avanti cars, and shoved them under the table. Before the next course, he excused himself. On his return, as he cut into his steak Bearnaise, he felt Jolie's curious eyes on him. But her question was about something else.

"So, Martin," she asked, "what are you hearing about Ellis Standifer's murder?"

"Joanna," Charlotte said. "Please."

Martin waved off her concern. "I'm intrigued by the subject, ghoulish as that sounds." He shifted his glance from Charlotte to Jolie. "He was well thought of in Memphis, wasn't he?"

"He certainly was," Jolie said. "Especially for a politician. And he'd been a damned good friend and mentor to me."

"I'm sure you will miss him. I don't know how his dear mother will continue on."

"Oh, my, isn't that so?" said Charlotte.

Martin nodded to her and turned back to Jolie. "It seems totally improbable. Why do you think it happened?"

"Beats me. Somebody comes into his condo and blows him away with a rifle. Curious, because in Memphis you'd expect a handgun. Apparently it wasn't a forced entry."

"Nothing was taken, right?"

"So they say. Do you suppose his mother knows something?"

Martin saw Charlotte blanch. "Jolie, you wouldn't!" She gave him a practiced smile. "How's your mother? Agnes is such a remarkable woman."

"As plucky as ever. Probably cheating at bridge as we

speak."

The murder wasn't mentioned at the table again. Martin was not surprised when Jolie followed him outside at the end of the evening.

"You never answered me earlier," she said, the husky urgency in her voice stronger than usual. "What are you hearing? And for that matter, why do you think he was killed?"

"Two theories," he said without hesitation. "Ellis enjoyed gambling from time to time. Let's just be blunt and say often. I suspect he could have found himself way over his head in one of the high stakes games he favored. Can't you just see him in a tux, nonchalantly tossing a few thousand on a poker table?"

"Absolutely, although murder doesn't jibe with the scene. And he had plenty of money or so it always seemed."

"Maybe he got in with a dangerous crowd."

"But if his murder was payback for a debt," Jolie said, "why wasn't anything stolen?"

"Because it was a matter of evening a score."

"So what's theory number two?"

He tugged on the ends of his vest. "The more plausible one, I think. I happen to know he'd been having an affair with a woman in Nashville."

"Who?"

"Her name's Mary Ellen Hargrove. Captivating woman and a talented one too. A portrait artist. She's Louis Spencer's cousin."

"Who's that?"

"Your parents know him. He's one of the Chattanooga Spencers up on Signal Mountain, but Mary Ellen lives in Nashville, in Belle Meade."

"All this tells me," Jolie said, "is that these people have money, but I expected that. And I'm not surprised he was seeing someone. His wife's dead."

Martin's brown eyes twinkled. "Mary Ellen's husband isn't."

Eight

The downpour would have to stop sometime. The cluster of gray clouds that perched between Singleton and the ever-shining sun eventually would scoot on.

The unrelenting rain began in late March, shortly after the last of Jolie's unpacking. She'd been able to break the lease on her Memphis apartment. The landlord told her she completely agreed with everything Jolie had said in her on-air rant. Talking with her, Jolie realized she had become a champion to some people. The knowledge gave her at least a little comfort.

She looked out the rain-specked window of her cottage. Impromptu ponds dotted the gravel drive.

Putting order to her belongings had given her time to ruminate, and by the time the last DVD was shelved, the last book stacked in the built-in pine bookcases, Jolie had reached a conclusion. Time to start drumming up work. The thought filled her alternately with excitement and nausea.

Within two days of her decision, she had purchased a video camera, an editing system, and a few lights. Her parents had urged her to let them provide the money for the equipment. She'd agreed only after drawing up a written agreement for repayment.

Within a week's time, she had set up a simple website, had placed an ad online and in the local newspaper and had ordered business cards and brochures. Marston Productions. She thought the name sounded businesslike, a far cry from *Weddings by Betti*, the only other video operation in town. She hated to think she might have to shoot weddings, catering to the whims of nervous brides and interfering parents, but shoot them she would to keep from going any deeper into her modest savings.

The promotional literature now sat in a dozen of Singleton's stores, although delivering it hadn't been easy. The shopkeepers, familiar from childhood, took the cards and brochures only in exchange for answers.

"What are you doing back in town?"

"Oh, I just needed a little break from city life. I'm in reassessment mode." She offered no further information, but she knew what they were thinking: *I'll bet she did get fired, just like I heard.*

Jolie felt she had let them down. Before, the questions had been, "When are we going to see you up there with Anderson Cooper?" and "What's it like to be a TV star?" She had achieved about as much fame as anybody who'd left Singleton, with the exception of Ellis Standifer. She was their glamour girl. And she had come back to walk dull among them. Their disappointment was palpable.

As Jolie made her deliveries, she took a close look at the town she thought she'd escaped. At its center stood a staunch red brick courthouse with white columns that, to her, summed up what much of Singleton wanted to be: dignified at all costs. The courthouse struck her as a fortress against the rabble looming at the town's perimeter. It shouted: *We have order here*. Minutes away from its Georgian symmetry, rednecks might sit on sagging porches and toss chicken bones to their dogs. A few miles beyond, gamecocks might fight to the death with metal claws. But here, here where law reigns, we are respected and respectful.

Maybe so. But Jolie usually described her hometown to people as the place where the fire station had burned and the sheriff's department had got busted for bootlegging.

Sitting on its prosperous haunches overlooking the courthouse was another red brick structure, one much larger than the courthouse. The First Baptist church declared, *By God, we have religion here.* Holy rollers please worship elsewhere. Yet Jolie always would remember it as the church that once threw out a tavern owner because using liquor in any way was against the covenant. The vote was taken by deacons who kept their booze well hidden and drank privately, with dignity.

***

The knock on her red door could barely be heard above the drill of the rain. Jolie opened it to see Martin in a gray Burberry raincoat that set off his curly, gray-flecked black hair.

He gave a slight bow from underneath his wood-handled umbrella. "A continual dropping in a very rainy day and a contentious woman are alike."

"Sexist."

"So saith Proverbs."

"King James was a sexist too."

"Will you forgive me in exchange for offering up Ellis Standifer's paramour a week from tomorrow?" His dark eyes sparkled.

"You mean meet her?"

"In the adulterous flesh."

"I want to meet her husband. I want to see if he smells like a murderer."

"That can be arranged."

"Sign me up." She pointed to his umbrella. "Put that thing down and come on in. Even misogynists don't stand in the rain at my house."

"I am sorry about that one. It was the only thing that came to mind."

"You're forgiven if you grovel the rest of the time you're here."

He snapped his fingers. "Tough luck for me, but I have to run. I just came by to tell you Louis Spencer—the cousin, remember?—invited me to a fiftieth birthday party for his wife, and I'm to take a guest if I like."

Jolie's arm shot up.

After Martin left, Jolie sat on the pine-planked stairs leading to her bedroom. Ellis's murder and Memphis itself felt impossibly far away. Why did she even care anymore about finding his killer? The effort seemed pointless. Was she looking for some twisted version of redemption that had little to do with Ellis and a lot to do with herself?

***

Violet Standifer fingered the ad she had clipped from the Singleton newspaper. A year or so ago she'd seen a magazine article about old people who put their life stories on video. It had been in the back of her mind since then, but she hadn't given it much thought until the local newspaper ad for Marston Productions appeared. Now she thought of it often, a welcome relief from the piercing sorrow over losing Ellis.

But who would care about what she had to say? Only one person might, and that possibility was remote.

She lay the ad aside and pursed her narrow lips. Perhaps it was better to take some things to the grave.

***

The brochures had been on display a week, the sunshine only two days, when the first call came in. "Jolie, honey, this is Martha Croswell. Your momma told me you have your own little TV company now, and I saw one of your brochures at Togs for Tots. Well, here's why I'm calling: My son's turning

85

four Thursday but we're not having his birthday party until Saturday. That's April fifteenth. And it would just be wonderful to have you come film it all."

"The fifteenth? Sure."

"That is, if your price is, well, you know…"

"I'm sure we can work something out, Ms. Croswell."

And work it out they did, although Jolie hoped never to shoot anything else with as little pay or as much clamor. Twenty-two sugar-loaded preschoolers, who wanted to stand right in front of the lens and grin, too close for focus and too far away to accidentally step on their toes. By the time she'd gone through a two-hour party with four fights, three crying jags and one scraped and bleeding elbow, she was looking fondly on the idea of a tubal ligation. When she returned home, instead of walking immediately to the CD player, she poured a hot bath and reveled in the silence of her tree-enclosed home.

As she lay there, she thought about meeting the husband of Ellis's lover in a couple of days. Would she meet a murderer? Why was she letting the lover herself off the hook so easily? Was there some reason she might have been driven to hoist a rifle and blow away Ellis's life? Jolie looked forward to being able to size up both of them.

* * *

Louis Spencer's home, a neo-Gothic stone structure, spread its two-story expanse atop one of Chattanooga's moneyed hills. Pink and white dogwoods dotted the rolling lawn.

A butler admitted them through the arched oak door. "Hired just for the evening," Martin whispered to Jolie after they had passed him.

She surveyed the murmuring clusters inside. Soft Southern laughter spilled from tan, blonde matrons who looked as if they spent their days on tennis courts and massage tables. Men in linen jackets and two-hundred dollar leather belts slapped each other on the back and grinned. Everyone seemed to be resting easy on their stocks and bonds.

Jolie leaned over and whispered to Martin. "I don't have to tell you how ecstatic Mom is that I'm at a party given by one of the Signal Mountain Spencers. She's so glad to see me…how did she put it…spending time with the right sorts of people."

Martin cut his eyes at her. "Little does she know."

A short man with red hair, a ruddy face just starting to droop, and gray-green eyes with a few late nights still left to go waved and walked over at a clip. "Martin, my friend!"

The two men exchanged a hug, and Martin introduced Jolie to Louis Spencer.

"I know your parents, of course," Louis said. "Please give them my regards." He turned back to Martin with an up-and-down look. "It's time you and I made another New Orleans jaunt. You're looking too slim."

After Louis left, Jolie returned her attention to the crowd. "So which one is she?"

Martin searched for a moment. "See the woman by the mantel? That's our Mary Ellen Hargrove." Martin resumed his search. "And the man across the room, the one in the aqua sweater, is her husband Dick."

Jolie spotted a man with a thatch of gray hair. He was talking with three other men. One was demonstrating a putt. "I see him," Jolie said.

Martin took her elbow. As they walked toward Mary Ellen, she noticed them and offered a dazzling smile. "Martin, come join us."

During introductions, Jolie sized up Ellis's lover: a striking woman with a curvy, energetic build, straight black hair cut stylishly short and penetrating gray eyes. Fitting eyes for a portrait artist.

If Mary Ellen mourned her lover, she exhibited no sign of it. She smiled and teased her two male companions. Her lilting voice often broke into laughter.

After a few minutes chatting about New York—Jolie was the only one who had not been recently—she and Martin left the trio. They walked across the room toward Dick Hargrove.

"She's quite a flirt, isn't she?" Jolie said.

"That she is. And an effective one. As I've told you, I find her enchanting."

Jolie lowered her voice. "Was there talk of leaving her husband for Ellis?"

"Louis said there wasn't as far as he knew." He steered Jolie toward the husband.

"Hey, Marty!" Dick Hargrove greeted him with a vigorous handshake and a slap on the upper arm.

When Martin introduced her, Jolie extended her hand, bracing for the shake. Instead, Dick held her hands in both of his. "So nice to meet you," he said.

Like his wife, he appeared to be in his late forties or early fifties. Despite a yellowish tint to the skin that suggested years at a pack a day, he had health club shoulders and a quick step. Jolie smiled back, but was that a hint of malice in his dark blue eyes? Enough to commit murder?

"Jolie just moved from Memphis back to east Tennessee," Martin said.

"Are you from this part of the state originally?" Dick asked her.

"Yes. Do you live in Chattanooga?" From the corner of her eye, she noticed Martin giving her a curious look, but she ignored it. She knew full well from Martin's earlier comments the Hargroves lived in Nashville, but she had in mind a path for this conversation.

"No," Dick said, "I live in Nashville."

"I just got tired of all the crime in Memphis," she told him. "You're better off where you are in Nashville, I think. It never has seemed as rough to me."

"Nashville does like to think of itself as more refined." Dick laughed. "Despite that country music element."

"I worked in news," Jolie said, "and it seemed like every day in Memphis another violent crime occurred. One of the worst recently was when Ellis Standifer was murdered."

Hargrove's face lost its blood and turned more yellow. He sucked in a deep breath and said, "Yes, I heard about that. Terrible."

"Did you know him?" Jolie said. "I only ask because it seems likely. He knew so many people."

Dick clasped his hands behind his back. Jolie wondered if he were trying to hide a tremble.

"We'd met," Dick said. "But I didn't know him well." He reached over and gave Martin another pat on the upper arm, one less hearty than the first. "I see my wife signaling me. Better not keep her waiting." As he walked away, he called out, "Nice to meet you."

Jolie and Martin watched him. Instead of joining his wife at the mantel, he hurried to the bar. They saw him take a long slug from a highball glass the bartender handed him.

"Curious how he interprets that signal from his wife, isn't it?" Jolie said. "But he was quick with the lie, I'll give him that."

"I can't believe you mentioned Ellis's name to him."

Jolie gave Martin a look of wide-eyed innocence. "Why, Mr. Everett, I certainly wouldn't know anything untoward about his wife, now would I?"

"You scoundrel. But he did look uncomfortable, didn't he?"

"Very."

"I never cared much for him," Martin said.

"Why's that?"

"One, there's something cold about him, despite all that glad-handing. Two, Louis says he has a furious temper. And three, my name's not Marty."

Jolie moved in closer and wrapped an arm around one of his. "So, Marty, tell me what Louis says about Dick Hargrove's temper."

Nine

Jolie's next work-related call a few days later came as a jolt.

"Hello," said an elderly woman. Her educated drawl sounded more deeply Southern than east Tennessee's nasal pitch. "This is Violet Standifer. I saw your advertisement recently. You are Stuart and Charlotte's daughter, I believe?"

"Yes ma'am." How long had it been since she had said "ma'am" to anyone?

"Am I right," Violet said, "that you used to live in Memphis?"

"Yes, ma'am. I'm very sorry about your son. I'm not sure if you're aware of it, but Ellis was one of my favorite people, a very dear friend. I thought the world of him."

"I knew he was very fond of you."

"The last time I interviewed him was the night he received the Curtis award. I noticed you were with him, but I didn't have a chance to say much more than hello. I was on deadline." Jolie couldn't let the opportunity pass. "They still haven't arrested anyone?"

"If so, they haven't told me."

"This must be very difficult for you."

"Yes, well. Perhaps they'll come up with something… The reason I called you is about your little film business. Do you come to people's homes to film them?"

"Sure, I do my work in homes. Anywhere I need to."

"I see. When do you think you might be free to come to my home?"

"Actually, I could come tomorrow."

"Well, why not?" She sounded resigned. "Why not."

***

Violet Standifer's home harkened back to the days when the well-to-do often lived close to the center of town. Despite rubbing noses with a nearby cafe and offices, the two-story, ivy-covered brick retained its dignity.

Jolie walked up the shrubbery-lined path to the front door and swung the brass knocker monogrammed with a swirling S. Its tap sounded too weak to rouse anyone. She lifted her fist to knock when the door opened.

Violet's white hair was pulled back in a loose bun. "Hello, Jolie. Thank you for coming."

Jolie took the extended hand and was startled by its coolness and frailty. She feared she would crush the thin bones if she squeezed, so she responded with the only tepid handshake she'd ever given. "Nice to see you again." She looked at the gray-blue eyes and high cheekbones, features she had seen often enough behind the mayor's desk at city hall. The slim nose they shared, combined with those cheekbones and small, intelligent eyes, gave both a patrician air. The one feature they didn't share was Ellis's dimpled chin.

"Shall we go into the parlor?"

Violet led Jolie through opened double doors into a high-ceilinged room that exactly fit Jolie's image of what a parlor should be. High-backed Victorian furniture on tall legs, a crocheted antimacassar across the back of a green horsehair sofa, lamps with fringed lampshades atop claw-footed tables. Violet's floral print dress suited the scene. Her own khaki pants and denim jacket felt coarse.

"Would you like to sit down?" Violet indicated the sofa and seated herself in one of the rose-and-green patterned chairs facing it.

Jolie sat on the stiff sofa. "I'm very sorry about Ellis's

death. I will really miss him. But it can't compare to your loss."

Violet looked at Jolie, then away.

"Besides being a good friend, your son gave me good advice, kept me from flying off the handle more than I did, made connections for me when I was new in town and in so many ways made things easier for me."

"This is nice to hear, isn't it? It's just the kind of thing I can see Ellis doing."

"I was dying to go to California once to cover a quake because Memphis sits on a fault line. I knew the general manager at my station would be a tough sell, but I also knew Ellis thought we needed greater public awareness of Memphis's potential for an earthquake. He and I talked, he called up the GM, and my videographer and I were on a plane that night."

Violet released a small laugh. "Oh, my." She looked more closely at Jolie. "I remember most of my pupils, even now, and I don't believe you were one."

"A lot of my friends took piano from you, but I never did. My parents stuck me with violin instead." Jolie winced at her choice of words, but it betrayed the level of enthusiasm she and most of her friends had shared for their music lessons, no matter what the instrument.

"Do you ever play now?"

"I haven't touched the violin since I quit taking lessons in third grade." She tried to sound less hostile. "I do wish sometimes I could play something. I really love music."

"What kind?"

"Just about everything. Blues, rock, jazz, classical, even a little country." Jolie nodded toward a gleaming grand piano in a corner of the room. "Do you still play the piano?"

"Every day. I still can reach an octave."

The pride in the woman's voice was clear, and Jolie considered it must be no mean feat to stretch eight notes with those delicate hands. "That's wonderful." She straightened and waited. Surely, she had not been summoned to discuss music.

Violet rose, walked over to a table, and picked up a small, bisque figurine of a shepherd boy. She seemed not to be aware she was holding it. "When I called to discuss your coming by, I had in mind your recording something for me. The idea," she said in her cultured drawl, "was for me to talk as you filmed me." She shook her head. "It seems a little foolish now, though, doesn't it?"

Jolie saw income slipping away. "I'm sure it's not. Besides, everybody feels a little awkward talking to a camera at first. I know I did." She gave a confident smile. "I'll make it comfortable for you. I'll be here right at the camera, so you can talk to me, really, instead of a lens. Honest, it'll be easy."

Honest, it could be like pulling teeth. Sometimes people froze when the camera began recording. And you could never tell in advance which ones would be the ice cubes. But she would figure out a way to make it work. She would figure out something.

Violet sat down again and unconsciously rubbed the figurine. "I would like to have it recorded. Writing is not the same thing, is it?"

"No, that's true." How tentatively Ellis's mother spoke, always asking. The ratio of interrogatives to declaratives was a hefty one.

"I think it's a wise thing you're doing," Jolie said, although she still wasn't sure what she was there to do.

"Do you?"

"Oh, definitely. It's good to make a record of anything that matters, and the kind of keepsake that has your face and voice is something to treasure."

"I'm not sure who will treasure it now."

"That's not always for us to say. What matters now is that

you get it down, get it recorded for posterity." Whatever that meant. Jolie's words sounded shallow even to her own ears.

"I suppose you're right," Violet said, "although some things I feel I need to talk about trouble me still, after all these years."

Jolie wondered what those things could be. Whatever they were, she decided she'd better fetch her equipment now before this opportunity passed and Violet decided it might be too difficult to talk. "I'll run out to the car and get my gear. Won't be but a minute."

***

Jolie set up a tripod and mounted her small video camera on it. She set her focus, and then zoomed back to a medium shot. It felt odd to do something she had rarely done since her broadcast classes at Michigan State. Fortunately, she'd practiced enough since she'd bought the camera recently that she didn't have to look for the right buttons every time.

"Great. Now if you'll talk a little, I can set my audio level. Tell me your name, why don't you, and where you were born."

"My name is Violet Gilman Standifer. I was born 90 years ago in Birmingham, Alabama."

So that was the origin of the rich accent. "Got it. Stand by."

She saw the woman's straight back stiffen. Don't say *stand by*. She's not an anchor. She leaned away from the viewfinder for a moment to smile at Violet. "Okay, I think I'm all set up. Just relax, take a deep breath or two, and start talking whenever you like. We've got all the time we need." She again fixed her eye to the viewfinder. Through it, she could see the slight mouth relax and the shoulders loosen a fraction. "Remember, just talk to me. It might seem like I'm not looking at you, but I am. I see you right here through the camera."

The frail hand pulled back a wisp of fine white hair that had slipped from its bun. "Oh, dear. I'm not sure where to begin now."

"Let's start at the beginning. You could talk about your childhood a little. Tell me about your family."

"I suppose I could do that, couldn't I? Although the story I want to tell happened when I was a young woman. Well, I'll get to that soon enough." She gave a sigh that sounded like the exhalation of an age-old breath. "I had a sister, Rachel, who was three years younger than I. She's dead now. Everybody's dead now, aren't they? My mother's name was Leonora. Leonora Evans. And my father was Joshua Standifer. Their families were both from Birmingham, and they were sweethearts from grade school." She smiled at the memory.

Jolie congratulated herself at the change to a gentler tactic. But when nothing more followed this, Jolie again leaned away from the camera to communicate eye-to-eye. "You're doing great. Just tell me whatever comes to mind."

"Well, I always loved music, didn't I? When I was seventeen, my father and mother sent me to the Lippincott Conservatory of Music in Montgomery. I had wanted to go to the Institute of Musical Art…they call it Juilliard now…but they wouldn't hear of my going that far away. Certainly not to New York City."

This time the long pause required another prompt. "Tell me about the Lippincott Conservatory. Did you like it? Did you have boyfriends?"

Violet looked down. "Could we stop for a moment, do you think?"

"Sure."

She pressed her lips together. "This is more difficult than I expected, isn't it?"

"You're doing fine. Really. Is this something you want to

pass on to relatives?"

"Ellis and his wife had no children."

"His wife…I can't remember her name…died during his first term, as I remember."

"That's right. Mary had cancer."

Jolie noticed a coldness creep into the refined accent. "That must have been especially hard for him if they didn't have kids. Losing his wife like that."

Violet looked aside. "I'm sure it must have been hard on him, yes. He was such a tender-hearted man." Her gaze returned to the camera. The blue eyes so like her son's filled with tears. "He was…" She pulled a small, white linen handkerchief from her dress pocket. "I'm sorry."

"No need to apologize, Ms. Standifer. I know it's hard for you. You and your son were very close, weren't you?"

Violet dabbed her eyes. "I didn't see him as much while Mary was alive. She always had something planned that kept them from getting over here, and she seemed so busy when I visited there. I didn't like to impose. Ellis was always good to call, though. It's just that he and I became much closer again after her death."

She tucked her handkerchief in a dress pocket and clasped her hands in her lap. "For some reason, Mary didn't care for me. Perhaps Ellis told her I preferred he marry someone else, a lovely girl he was fond of when Mary entered the picture. But it certainly wasn't my place to tell him to do anything. No, I'd seen how awful that sort of coercion could turn out. Mary did not like me. Of course, I wouldn't wish such a cruel death as she had on anyone, would I?"

Jolie seized the opening, chiding herself as she did. "Your son died a cruel death too." She watched Violet flinch. "I can't stop thinking about it," Jolie said. "Do you have any idea why it happened?"

With only the slightest movement, Violet shook her head.

"Did he ever mention someone having a grudge against him? Mention any trouble he was having?"

"I've wondered and wondered about it," Violet said. "I can see no reason at all."

"I hope you understand, I just had to ask." Jolie waited a minute before speaking. "Are you ready to start back up? We can pause for a bit if you want."

"I suppose I'm ready." Violet repositioned herself and faced the camera.

Ten

Violet's Story

"I suppose it was Ellis's death that prompted me to call you. That, and Beethoven. Although this all feels very strange now, and I'm not sure I did the right thing."

Violet considered her situation. It would be rude to stop now, after asking for this very thing to happen. The Marston girl deserved better than that. She took a deep breath and held herself more erectly.

"The other day I had Ellis on my mind and was feeling very sad, so I sat down to play the sonata he always begged to hear me play when he came home. It has helped me at other times in my life when I've been grieving, and I thought it might help me then.

"In the midst of the piece, just as the barest of notes sounds—it's a forlorn section—it came to me clearly what I needed to do. I needed to speak. My life has been a long silence, it sometimes seems to me. With no sounds to complete it. I suddenly became very weary of the silence." She looked down at her hands, turning them over before looking up again at the camera.

"As I mentioned, there were a few young men who were keen on me. I thought I was in love with a couple of them, didn't I? But…when I met Grant, I understood that I had not been. In love with them.

"Grant Milburn. How odd it is to say his name aloud after all these years. After carrying it silently in my heart.

"You must think me awful. He was not my husband. Please don't misunderstand, I did love my husband, and we had an agreeable marriage.

"Odd, how I don't feel disloyal talking to you about this. Perhaps it is because everyone who could be hurt by what I have to say is gone.

"The truth is, I loved…still love…Grant Milburn. More than I've ever loved anyone except my son, but that's a different sort of love. I've often wondered if we had spent our lives together in the sort of day-in, day-out way of couples, would the romance have faded? But I suppose the point is, it never did. And the way it ended…my heart still aches from that.

"Oh, he was handsome! Tall and broad-shouldered. Thick black hair. A full mouth, just like Clark Gable's, and that same devilishness about him too. Grant's eyes were the same blue as cornflowers, exactly that bright blue. When I looked at those eyes, I never wanted to look away. "

Violet smiled to herself at the memory.

"We met at Ruth Anne Kenworthy's. She was a friend of mine at the music conservatory in Montgomery. Her family lived on a big plantation in Mississippi, just north of Oxford. The summer after my second year, during our break, Ruth Anne invited, oh, I guess nearly a dozen young people to a weeklong house party at the plantation. Twining Roses, that was the name of her home. A huge thing it was. A curving staircase in front and balconies on the second and third stories. And there must have been ten servants! Someone always standing around to wait on us or scurrying off to get whatever we needed. But what I remember most was the scent of the place. Ruth Anne's father grew hundreds of roses in a garden by the house. Especially in early evening, just as the fireflies were starting up, the smell was pure heaven."

Violet leaned forward, warming to her tale.

"I wasn't able to get there as early as the other guests. Mother had been quite ill with influenza and only the day before had begun to recover. I was afraid of flu back then, weren't we? We had heard so many horror stories about the Spanish flu. It had been terrible in 1918. Any mention of flu caused worry. I was so afraid I wouldn't be able to attend at all, as selfish as that sounds."

"My friends were gathered behind the house when I arrived. Someone was playing banjo, an instrument we weren't allowed to play at Lippincott. I stood on the veranda for a moment watching everyone, and that is when I first saw Grant. He was leaning back against a tree, one knee up against it, his arms crossed over his chest, listening to a boy from our class. But he was looking around, not paying much attention. And he looked at me. When he did, I saw his eyebrows raise just the least bit. I thought my heart would pound through my dress! He just stared at me. Stared and stared, propped up there against that big tree. I'd never seen a fellow be that bold. I stared back as long as I dared, then lowered my eyes. All these long years, I've never forgotten that look he gave me."

***

Violet's gaze locked into the window opposite her, but she did not see beyond it. Nor was she wholly aware of the young woman with a camera. Not for years had she spoken freely, not for decades, she supposed, and now she was revealing herself to a near stranger. Still, what did it matter? What did anything matter anymore? Ellis's murder eradicated what scrap of sense was left in the world. But she would not talk about that today. She would never talk about the depth of her grief. It was a story running beneath words, far below them where there is nothing but pain. No, she would never honor that horror by telling it.

She had expected the story spilling from her today would ease her heart a bit. Perhaps that was why she was doing this.

Looking for some little release from an old pain, she no longer had room to carry. If so, her battered, weary heart was disappointed.

The young woman cleared her throat. If it was a signal to resume, Violet chose to ignore it. Now that she had brought Grant back, she wanted to be alone with him for a moment. Without looking at the woman, Violet lifted a finger delicately to indicate her wish for a delay. But it was too late. The moment was lost. The only person with her now was Charlotte and Stuart Marston's daughter. Perhaps if she began talking again? She returned her gaze to the lens.

***

"Ruth Anne and I were visiting with…wasn't it Stan Mabry? Oh, yes, I remember now. Stan had been a bit sweet on me, so he kissed me hello on the cheek and held my hand a moment. It was then Grant walked up. Poor Stan hadn't a chance after that, although I never was keen on him to begin with. A momma's boy, that's what we girls thought. Too good to be exciting.

"I remember Grant's words exactly: 'Well, Ruth Anne,' he said, but looking straight at me, 'your little party just got a lot prettier.' Then he broke into a big smile and introduced himself. When I extended my hand, he kissed it and winked at me. Oh, he was a brash one!

"That night we were having a concert by some of the students. I hoped, of course, that he'd come sit by me, but Lizabeth Tilson…not a shy bone in that girl's body, she was what we called fast…ran up to him as he walked into the music parlor. She just trotted right up and put her arm through his! Just before they sat down together…what choice did he have after that…he looked around the room. I glanced away just as

102

he saw me, so he wouldn't think I'd been staring at him. He told me later he was searching for me. I knew he was, didn't I?"

Violet paused a long moment to linger with the memory.

"The next day the boys all left early for a fox hunt while we girls stayed to make decorations for our dance that night. Twining Roses had an enormous ballroom. The whole week I was at the plantation I felt as if I were in a dream and never more than at the dance. I remember there were these long murals on the walls of the ballroom. Ruth Anne told us they'd been hand painted by a man from New Orleans. And the floor was parquet wood from Brazil. Shiniest thing I ever saw. I guess one reason that time is so beautiful in my memory is because of the tragic thing that happened soon after." Violet took a deep breath. "But I'm getting ahead of my story."

"In fact, Twining Roses was the grandest place I'd ever seen. My family was very comfortable financially, but Ruth Anne's family was...or at least it seemed to us...rich beyond measure. All those servants! I remember she told us that Yankee officers had stayed in their home while they were traveling through Mississippi. Her great-grandfather was away in the war, and her great-grandmother was there all alone with her babies. Well, not alone with all those Negroes everywhere, I guess, and no telling how many they had then, but...

"They, the officers that is, let her great-grandmother stay on there in the house while they were there. They used it for a headquarters for a while. Ruth Anne even showed us where some of the Yankee soldiers had carved their names and their hometowns on the back of a door, the one in the foyer just under the stairs. The story is that the Yankee general was so furious at those soldiers for defacing that beautiful home that he had the men horsewhipped and made them eat nothing but grass for three days. 'If you're no better than brute animals,' he told them, 'then that's how you shall be treated.' I don't remember

103

the general's name, or if she even told me. I've wondered if it might have been Ulysses S. Grant. But I don't know if he even came down that way. It certainly couldn't have been that beast Sherman, now could it?"

She rearranged herself in the chair before continuing. Her posture remained erect.

"But I'm getting away from my story. I can't seem to keep my thoughts in a straight line lately.

"Well, as I said, the big dance was to be that night, so we girls set about decorating the room, hanging ribbons and bows everywhere. The places we couldn't reach, we just called to a servant to help us. One was never far away from you, no matter where you were in that house. All of us were to perform at some point in the evening, all, that is, except Grant and a couple of others who also weren't from Lippincott Conservatory. Then, when we weren't playing, we'd dance to whoever was. All I could think of was what it would be like to dance with Grant, to be that close to him, to those eyes. I knew I would die if he didn't ask me. But I thought I might die if he did!

"I knew I looked pretty that night in my dress. It was light blue, my best color, and it showed off my waist, which was a few inches smaller then, and smallest of all the girls except Lucy Rule's and she was just a stick.

"He noticed me right off, too, and I could tell he liked what he saw, even from across the ballroom. We didn't have dance cards, so it was all left to chance. When the first piece began, "Tea for Two," who ran up to him but Lizabeth? And he was already walking my way! But she just pulled herself right up in front of him and stood there with that silly smile of hers. He had to ask her after that. But the next dance, Grant came up and said I looked 'especially lovely' and would I care to dance? After that, we danced every dance together, except when I played. And he sat those out, just watching me. I saw Lizabeth with her bottom lip stuck out. She always thought she looked cute when she was in one of her petulant moods."

Violet laughed to herself.

"The last song of the evening was "Alice Blue Gown," and he held me closer and hummed the melody in my ear. Waltzing with him to that song, in my blue gown, I felt the whole world was pulling us together, bringing us to each other."

Violet sighed, looked away from the camera, and closed her eyes.

It appeared she needed a break, and Jolie wanted to check her footage.

It was a few minutes before Violet opened her eyes. She seemed startled to find Jolie there. "Oh my, I've kept you waiting. And before that, I was just going on and on, wasn't I?"

"That's exactly what you're supposed to do. You're doing great, Ms. Standifer."

"Do you mind if I go upstairs a moment?"

"Of course not."

When Violet returned and sat across from the camera again, she was wearing a necklace. A large round gem of at least two carats gleamed in the center. Eight similar but smaller stones, four on each side, lay along a gold filigree chain.

Jolie's mouth dropped. "Wow. That's gorgeous."

Violet smiled and patted the stones.

"What kind of stones are those?"

"Alexandrites. Not a very common stone. From Russia generally."

"There's a reddish-blue hue to them. They look like reddish-blue diamonds."

"Only sometimes. Let me show you." She walked toward the window and beckoned Jolie to follow. When the stones caught the April sunlight, they glowed a pale violet-blue.

Jolie laughed. "Like a mood ring, but better."

"Pardon?"

"Oh, nothing."

"I've noticed that when I am under those ugly things..." she drew a long cylinder with her hands "...those, oh those ..."

"You mean fluorescents?"

"Yes. Under those lights the stones have a greenish cast."

"That's a stunner of a necklace you're wearing, whatever light it might be in." She fiddled with the camera a moment. "Ready to keep going?"

Violet settled in her chair and folded her arms across her lap. "Yes, I think so."

She straightened, but said nothing.

"You were at the dance."

"Oh, yes."

***

"After that, the rest of the week we were inseparable, or as inseparable as young people under supervision were allowed to be at that time. My girlfriends teased me for ignoring them, but I didn't care. They played mahjong and made music for hours with the boys, but I wanted to be alone with Grant. I didn't know how I was going to stand going back to Montgomery and Lippincott and not be able to look up and see those cornflower eyes.

"We wrote each other every day for a month after Ruth Anne's. I kept pestering my father and mother to let him visit. Finally, they relented. I think they saw how much I was in love with him and wanted to see for themselves if he were a gentleman or not. So mother sent an invitation to Grant's family.

"He came in September, just before I was to return to the conservatory. He looked handsomer than ever. We went to see a

Buster Keaton movie and held hands all the way through it."

Violet halted and pressed her lips together before saying more.

"The four days he visited were even more wonderful than before, until that awful thing the day he left. The last night he gave me this necklace and asked me to marry him. I couldn't say yes fast enough, even though I knew he should've asked my father first. But, as I told you, he was brash. And not as respectful of his elders as I'd been brought up to be. But what did I care about that? I was weak-kneed with love for him." Violet pressed her lips together.

"The next morning, after breakfast, Grant and I told my parents. My mother just looked worried, but my father was livid with rage. You see, Grant had told them he was a Catholic. My parents hadn't known that or he'd never have been invited to visit.

"My father said he would never allow his daughter to marry a man who worshiped the Pope. He said, 'What about children? How would you rear your children?'

"'They would be brought up in the Church,'" Grant said.

"'I take it you mean the Catholic church?'" my father roared.

"'Yes, sir.'" Grant said.

"'Impossible!'" my father said, and he stormed out of the room.

"I had known my father would hate the idea of my marrying a Catholic boy, so I hadn't said anything. And you know how naive young people can be. I was just certain that because of how much I loved Grant, Daddy would come around and let me marry him. It was unthinkable that he wouldn't. I don't know, I might have eloped if he'd refused. Yes, I might even have done that."

Violet's fingers unconsciously played with the necklace.

She paused as a shudder coursed through her.

"Grant was furious when he heard what Daddy had said.

"Grant's train wasn't until that afternoon, and he and my father had planned to go fishing that morning, before the argument I mean. You would think he would have canceled it, but not my father. Mother told me later she figured he held to the trip because it would give him a chance to be alone with Grant and make certain he never came near me again. My father always had to be absolutely certain he had his way. That's why it was absurd for me to ever think I could've won him over."

"So only an hour after this argument, my father and Grant set off with fishing equipment for a lake about 30 miles away. Grant, even as bold as he was, must have dreaded the thought of it, knowing how angry we'd made my Daddy. I'm sure he wished the boat trip had been called off. But as I said, that wasn't my father's way. That would have looked like he'd let this young man get his goat, and he couldn't do that.

"The weather already was turning foul. Even when I first woke up, I remember seeing dark clouds, because I thought they were so out of place when I was so happy, about to marry Grant, or so I thought until after breakfast when we told Daddy. By the time he and Grant set off, it was already sprinkling. Mother said, 'Do you think you should go in this weather? There might be lightning,' but my father was determined.

"After they left, Mother and I sat in the parlor and did embroidery. I still have the piece I was working on, a pillowcase edge of a kitten in a basket. I never finished it."

Violet clutched her hands together and waited a few moments before continuing.

"Mother and I hardly said a word. Both of us kept looking out the windows. The rain had become a downpour, and there was thunder and lightning, still distant but moving our way. The worst of the storm, though, was the wind. It was blowing so fiercely! Mother and I both were thinking that Daddy's boat wasn't that big and could overturn easily.

"We must have sat there listening to the storm and the winds whip around for three or four hours. Then all of a sudden, there was this pounding. We thought at first it was thunder, but then we realized it was somebody at the door. We both ran to it, didn't wait for Jenny to answer it. She was old and slow and we were frantic with worry.

"It was Grant pounding on the door, pounding with both fists. I opened it and he just stood there, the most awful look on his face. He pointed to the porch floor a few feet away. There was a big lump, water puddling around it. 'What?' I asked him. 'What it is, my darling?' I looked back and forth from him to the lump, but it didn't make any sense. My mother rushed past me, threw herself on the lump, and began shrieking and crying. That's when I realized what I'd been looking at was my father's body.

"Grant later told us the boat overturned in one of the gusts of wind. They had been way out in the middle of the lake, trying to get back in, but the wind was against them, blowing them back two feet for every one they gained. He said he kept telling my father to go to the other side of the lake where they could take cover, but Daddy refused. When the boat turned over, my father and Grant both spilled into the water. Daddy couldn't swim. Grant tried to get to Daddy and get him to the boat, but Daddy kept fighting him. And the boat kept getting farther away. Grant was afraid he would drown as well. I guess by the time Grant finally got hold of him, he was already…gone. I hate to think of it to this day, to think of Daddy dying angry at me. And poor Grant. How awful it was for him to watch him die, to be unable to save him."

She closed her eyes a long minute.

"I don't want to speak of the funeral and my mother's grief.

It was all so sad. I'm not sure I ever heard her laugh after Daddy died, even though she lived another twenty years.

"Grant and I continued to write each other, but the gayness was gone out of our romance. It was unthinkable for me to marry soon after my father's death. I told Grant we must wait at least a year, even though he hoped it wouldn't be that long. But it would have been disrespectful to my father to have married right away. I kept telling Grant that.

"He tried to talk me into it, especially the times he came to visit me at the conservatory. He was insistent, but I couldn't say yes. I blamed myself for my father's death and for making my mother so sad. Something had changed for me after that awful storm. I still hate wind. Whenever it picks up, I put on Rachmaninoff and play it loud enough that I can't hear the wind roar.

"I decided it was best to break things off. I offered to return the necklace, but he told me to keep it as a 'remembrance.' That's the word he used.

"He wrote to me a few times more, but I answered with just very short notes or not at all, because Mother said I shouldn't give him false hope. I guess it was best for me too, to pull back. After a couple of years, his letters stopped.

"Soon after they did, I learned from Ruth Anne he was engaged to a girl, a Catholic. Then I heard they had married. A few years later, Ruth Anne wrote me they'd moved from Mississippi to La Grange, a tiny little town in west Tennessee, and he was running a department store in a bigger town nearby, managing it for somebody. He had a son. Not long after that, I became engaged to Ellis's father."

Violet turned her attention from the camera for a few moments, then looked back at the lens. Her voice was distant.

"How I wish that storm had never happened. But my father wouldn't have relented. If I had eloped, he probably would've disowned me. He did not like to be crossed, and I'd never gone against him on anything before, not anything that mattered. Or on much at all really. I don't think he would've put up with it. So there was no way for things to have worked out, was there?" She looked down again at her clenched hands.

"Now that I'm saying all this, I realize there isn't anything more about my life I want to tell. I don't need to say any more, except to say I loved my dear, dear Ellis, and I miss him so."

She looked down at the necklace. "I haven't had my remembrance on for years. Perhaps I'll wear it every day from now on."

Eleven

The next time Jolie knocked on Violet Standifer's door, she had already made up her mind what she would do. She wanted more from this visit than just a music track for Violet's video. She wanted to find out anything at all the old woman might know about her son's death.

Despite early May's sunshine and 80 degrees, Violet greeted her in a long-sleeved, lace-collared dress. Her face was wan, unbrightened by the sparkling necklace around her narrow neck.

Jolie unloaded her equipment and set a microphone on top of the grand piano. While she adjusted the audio level, Violet ran scales. For the track, Jolie had requested the Beethoven largo Ellis loved. She would use it at the open and close and perhaps at periods in between.

When Jolie signaled she was ready, Violet leaned back from the keyboard and took a deep breath, her eyes closed. She took a second breath. As she exhaled, she lifted arched fingers, held them a moment several inches above the keys, then brought them down on the first slow, somber chords.

Jolie sat transfixed. The notes and the full pauses between phrases ached with halted longing. As the music progressed into more forceful measures, still there was restraint, a passion made graceful for being held in check. As it returned to the spare notes and silences of the opening theme's sorrow, Jolie's eyes glistened with tears.

Violet again rested her hands in the air and then reached for her handkerchief.

Jolie sat in wonder, wonder at Violet's soulful playing, at the ability of notes to soften and open the heart.

She quietly turned off the camera and walked around to the piano bench. Although she wanted to hug the frail figure, she was afraid Violet might read her action as an unwarranted intimacy. She looked at the desolate slope to the curved back and lightly put her hands on the bony shoulders. She brought her face close. "Thank you, Ms. Standifer."

Violet reached back with knobbed fingers, cold despite the recent exercise, and patted Jolie's hand. "Thank you for asking me to play." She stood and closed the keyboard. "Would you like another cup of tea?"

It would mean two more cups than Jolie had drunk in a year, and the hot liquid wasn't welcome on a day like this. "Yes. I'd love one."

By the time Violet returned, Jolie had put away her gear. The two women sat on either end of the horsehair sofa.

"Ms. Standifer, forgive me if I'm intruding, but do you think the police are any closer to finding out who killed Ellis?"

"I like to think so. But...oh, I would hate for things to get ugly."

"What do you mean?"

"A couple of days ago I had a call from the police. Apparently there had been some unpleasantness."

"What sort of unpleasantness?"

The refined Alabama accent muted. "They wouldn't really say. But it sounded terrible. Ellis was an honorable man, and I would hate to see his name besmirched."

"Are you saying they let you know they had some new information about him but wouldn't tell you what it was?"

Violet nodded.

"Those jerks. If you don't have a right to know, who does?"

"It happened when I'd called the number they'd given me, hoping for some word. It's been nearly three months now since… I asked if anything had turned up. The man I spoke to was reluctant to say anything at first, but I kept asking, 'Haven't you learned anything?' I suppose I made him feel he had to say something."

"Was the man's name Plonski?"

"Yes, that's it. He had called me to ask some questions soon after Ellis died. He had left his number. Plonski. It sounds Polish, doesn't it?"

"Yes, ma'am. I've interviewed him dozens of times."

"I see."

"We haven't really gone into why I left news, and this isn't perhaps the best time to do that, but if I were in Memphis, Ms. Standifer, still at my old job, I'd be covering Ellis's death. And it's bugging the hell out of me—excuse my language—that I'm not."

Violet grabbed Jolie's hands between her own. She took in a long breath and drew herself up. "You're such a smart young woman."

Jolie saw a question in the woman's face. "What, Ms. Standifer?"

"The police are taking so long, and getting any information out of them is such a chore. I suppose I don't have a lot of faith in them, do I? I'm so afraid they'll just forget about him. You know people there. Will you promise to see what you can find out about who killed my dear boy and why?"

"Remember," Jolie said, "this is a high profile murder. They need to solve it if for no other reason than public perception."

"I shouldn't have imposed on you."

"No, no. That's not what I meant. And to tell you the truth, knowing how overworked homicide is, I don't have much faith either."

She squeezed Jolie's hands tighter. "I'm so discouraged."

114

Jolie released her hands, rose, and kissed the cool, doughy cheek goodbye. "I promise I'll do whatever I can."

She had no idea what that might be, but she'd figure out something.

Violet put her hand to her forehead and closed her eyes momentarily.

Jolie studied the pallid woman. "Are you okay?"

"I'm so sorry," Violet said. "I wasn't feeling well before, and I guess that piece just took everything out of me. I'd better go lie down. I have been rather faint lately. Will you come back soon?"

"I promise," Jolie said and meant it. She hated to think of Violet living as a recluse. "And maybe you'll play for me again. If you feel up to it, that is."

"I'd love to. Nobody hears me but myself now that I've stopped giving lessons and having recitals. I used to play for Ellis when he came to see me. Chopin was one of his favorites. Such a torrid choice for him I always thought, but then, maybe not…"

Twelve

The quick-talking blonde turned from her male co-anchor and gave the camera a wide-eyed look. *Up next: Is there an arsonist on the loose here in Chattanooga? Plus, an arrest could come soon in the death of former Memphis mayor Ellis Standifer. And, we'll meet a man who prefers to see the world from stilts.* She beamed toward the lens. *Right after this on tonight's news at six.*

Jolie's attention quickened. While she had read the Memphis newspaper's website daily looking for anything on Ellis, she hadn't watched local news in a week, a fact that amazed her. During her tenure in news, she'd seized any chance to catch another station's newscast, to critique their reporters and anchors. She wondered if this small rebellion signaled a lasting change.

Big John's Warehouse, a burly man yelled in an east Tennessee twang. *Y'all come on down for Big John's biggest-ever clearance. It's our Beat the Heat Marathon Sale.* Behind him a grinning woman in a bikini sat on a massive block of ice. *Now through Thursday*, he hollered. *Remember, Big John's expecting you!* On his last word, the woman kicked up a leg and aimed a red-nailed finger at the camera, snapping her gum all the while.

The rapid-fire blonde reappeared to introduce the story of a possible arsonist. Jolie took a long drag on her cigarette and thought about the anchor's dirty little secret. The truth was, she and many others in the newsroom hoped mightily it was an arsonist, a deceptive and determined one who would set many more fires, bigger fires, highly visual fires, before his detection and arrest. Fires looked great on TV. If fatalities should occur, the more hardened staffers might go so far as to refer to them, after a few beers and only among co-workers, as crispy critters, a term that now made Jolie blanch. The reporters, videographers, and producers would consider themselves decent folks at heart, and probably they were. Certainly, they didn't wish anyone dead or injured. The jokes helped, that's all. They helped to keep a necessary distance.

After a dull voice-over about a 7-11 robbery, the male anchor took over. *In Memphis*—Jolie raised the volume—*police now think they might be closer to an arrest in the troublesome murder case of former mayor Ellis Standifer.* Behind and to the left of the anchor, a photo of Standifer's elegant features appeared. *Standifer's body was found in February in his downtown Memphis condo, a rifle shot to his chest. No sign of forced entry or of anything taken. This morning at a news conference, police revealed that important clues have been found in Standifer's dwelling, clues that could lead to the killer. Police refuse to say more at this time. It remains to be seen—* Jolie winced at the inane, ubiquitous sign-off—*what the next steps will be. In other news—*

Damn! Jolie hit the power on the remote control, and the screen blacked. The story told her only that the pressure was on homicide to come up with something, anything, and they had found a clue that might be useful, might even be decisive, but might just as easily mean nothing. So they were touting their progress—if there'd really been any—but keeping their asses covered. She would've held their feet to the fire if she'd been on the story.

Jolie pressed the speed dial on her portable phone for Nick's number. He answered on the third ring, out of breath.

It had been four days since they had talked. They were phoning less frequently now, and a hint of strain had crept into their conversations. She knew they both sensed it.

"I need some information."

"What do you mean?"

"Not about you. About Ellis Standifer. Both Plonski and the news say something's turned up, but I can't get anything more than—"

"Why on earth are you talking to Plonski?"

She bristled. "I'm not. Ellis's mother spoke to him. They found something…an unpleasantness was how Ms. Standifer put it…in his condo. But, get this, they wouldn't tell her what. I need to know."

"Jolie."

"Don't give me that 'Jolie' shit. I didn't leave my curiosity at the WTNW door. I want to know what's going on."

"Don't you think you're a little hung up on this?"

"I am not! This is not just some guy I never met who suddenly got murdered. You know damn well Ellis's death is personal for me. Besides, I'd do anything to help his mother, and she's really worried."

"Since when did you become such a softie?"

"Since headlines started being about real people."

Nick sighed. "I'll ask around. Again."

"Thanks. A lot. So how are you?"

"Fine. But I need to go."

"Sure. Fine."

"Look, I'll call you tomorrow night and let you know what I've been able to dig up, okay?"

"Call early. I'll be waiting."

***

Jolie woke up as hungry as always and munched on the remains of a packet of graham crackers on her bedside table. Sunlight seeped into the room, and the clock read 6:35. She had decided last night it couldn't hurt to pursue another avenue of information besides Nick. But Annette Middleton, Jolie's favorite on the homicide squad, wouldn't be in for a while because of the hour's time difference.

When the papergirl tossed the Chattanooga newspaper on her doorstep, Jolie hurried to pick it up, but she found only three column inches that revealed little more than the empty TV report from the evening before. By the time she'd eaten a bagel, taken a walk and completed as much of the crossword puzzle as she had the patience for, it was eight in Memphis.

Annette picked up after the first transfer. "I've missed seeing you around, girl. No one to smart-mouth with me anymore."

"Same here, believe me. Listen, I need to check with you on something about Standifer's murder."

"What do you mean?"

Had a slight chill come into Annette's voice? "His mother's a friend of mine," Jolie explained, "He was a friend of mine too. And I…well, I just need to find out what I can."

"I'm not sure there's much I can tell you."

This was going to take all the charm, chutzpah and persistence she could muster.

***

Nick called soon after seven that evening. "I didn't get much. I did find out it was a photo they found in his condo, but I couldn't get anything more. Don't have any idea what the shot was. Sorry."

"The photo was of a local prostitute."

"No kidding? How'd you know that?"

Jolie ignored his question. "The woman's name is Monique. They found the photo secreted away in a locked chest

119

hidden behind a shelf of books. Something they had missed on two earlier searches. The photo had been torn apart, then taped back together, as if Ellis had thrown it away but thought better of it."

"Why did you need me to dig for you? You know way more than I do."

"It took a lot of wheedling."

"I never would've figured him for the type to pay for it," Nick said, "but you never know. Did you get any info about what the photo was like?"

"She was wearing a corset, leaning back on a bed. She's a black woman with long curls, very heavy makeup. Lots of turquoise eye shadow."

"Whoa."

"I know. And get this: The photo was signed, 'Cuddles.' No name, just 'Cuddles.' Sounds like they knew each other pretty well."

Jolie thought she had known Ellis. Now she wondered how much he'd hidden from her and everyone else. She knew he hadn't been perfect, but somehow she couldn't help feeling disappointed.

"So they think this hooker might have done it?" Nick asked.

"They called her in for questioning but didn't arrest her. The cops are checking out her alibi, expecting it won't hold. Blackmail, they're figuring. Ellis was probably paying her to keep quiet about the sex. She demanded more money. He balked. The guys in homicide were relieved finally to have a suspect, and the chief prosecutor, your very own boss, was of course thrilled it might be a prostitute."

"Sure, an easy guilty verdict. So," he said, "how did you manage to unearth all that?"

"Oh, I just did."

They chatted a while about his work. Before they hung up, he said, "You're sure sounding more like a Southern girl. You know that?"

"Don't give me that shit."

"That she-e-et?"

"Up yours, Ellsberg. That's not what I said." But in fact, she had noticed the laziness creeping into her speech, had heard the elongation of vowels. She saw no reason to fight it. Unlike in the past, it wasn't likely now to keep her from getting a job, not in Singleton.

Thirteen

Martin's languid drawl was even slower than usual. "I have some sad news, Jolie. Violet Standifer died. They found her in her bed this morning."

"No," Jolie gasped.

"Apparently she died in the night. The cleaning woman…who comes once a week, so thank God this was her day…found her. Yesterday's mail had been collected, so she was alive then. Looks like the heart condition she had was to blame."

"And there's no chance of anything else? I only ask because of—"

"No. The doctor thinks her heart just gave out."

"She wasn't well the last time I saw her a few days ago. She mentioned feeling faint lately." Jolie wondered if she'd been the last person to see Violet alive.

She had only begun to lay in the music on the video. The charged notes moved her each time she played the piece, even through the editing speaker. Was that the last time Violet had played at her beloved piano?

She wondered about the effect of the "unpleasantness" on Violet. "Martin, they found out something about Ellis. It's not very pretty." She gave him the details of what she had learned from Annette a few days ago, not long after her last visit with Violet. "His mother knew only something troubling had been found, she didn't know what, but you know she worried about it."

"Of course she did. Do they think there's a connection between this photo and Ellis's murder?"

"They're hoping."

"Do they know about Mary Ellen and her hot-tempered husband?"

"They found out about her from Ellis's phone records, e-mails and letters lying around, but they'd much rather bring in a black hooker than a rich white man."

"With his rich white lawyer. Wonder if they know about Ellis's penchant for gambling?"

"Yeah," Jolie said. "They know about that too." She chose not to mention how. It had helped smooth things with Annette to offer something in trade. Jolie was surprised they hadn't already stumbled across the fact.

After the call, Jolie watched the video of Violet yet again. She had been alive, talking. Now she was gone. Just like her son.

Until Ellis's murder, Jolie had been spared death at close range. She had seen plenty of it in news, but that was always at one remove. Now two people had passed on to whatever "on" was.

Although Jolie had enjoyed time with Violet, her death was almost a comfort. She knew the woman enough to know she'd lost her reason to keep going. Death likely came as a friend.

***

On a temperate day in mid-May, Jolie sat in the Singleton office of White and Winstead, Attorneys at Law. She listened to Jerry White clear his throat several times as he shuffled papers. Occasionally he looked up to smile. A letter the day before had informed her she was to inherit personal effects from Violet Standifer's estate. She assumed it had to do with the video and what she was to do with it.

White, Violet's executor, gave his throat final clearance, leaned back, and smiled more warmly. Jerry had moved to town only five years ago, so Jolie didn't know him, but she sensed the respectful manner he used to greet her was due mostly to her family's standing in the community. It wasn't the first time strangers had been especially courteous after learning her mother was Charlotte ("so gracious," "such a lovely woman") and her father was Stuart ("do anything for him"). Jolie had become accustomed to gaining favor on the strength of her news celebrity. It was odd to be favored not because of who she was but because of who her parents were. She realized now it was a privilege she had enjoyed unaware throughout childhood.

"Violet thought quite a lot of you," Jerry White said.

"How do you know?"

He winked behind his wire-rim glasses. "What I mean is, she's been mighty generous to you in her will."

Jolie leaned forward and squinted at White's round, boyish face.

"I gather you didn't know she left you her alexandrite necklace."

"Is this a joke?"

Jerry's smile widened, making his face above a red bow tie look almost cherubic. "Not at all."

"But it must be worth a fortune! Why on earth would she leave it to me? I only recently got to know her."

"It was only recently…very recently…the will was revised. She called her lawyer three days ago and said she wanted to make a change. It's not the first time I've seen that happen soon before a person dies. They get everything squared away in this world, and they're ready to move on to the next."

Jolie leaned forward, her pale green eyes wide. "Three days ago? You mean last Friday?"

"That's right."

The day after Violet had played for her. She tried to incorporate the information. "Do you know how many times

I've seen her? I mean, not counting growing up? Not that I saw her much then. I wasn't even a pupil of hers. I've seen her a total of two times. Two times since I moved back here."

Jerry slapped his palms on his wide oak desk. "You left quite an impression."

"I was doing a video of her, that's all. She wanted to…but I don't need to go into that. I really liked her, sure, but…" Jolie heard the tremble in her voice. "I don't even know what she wanted to do with the damn thing after I finished it. Did she tell me what to do with this video?"

"There is something in her will about it." He ran his finger down the typed page. "Here it is. You are to keep it and any materials related to it. I need one copy to deliver to someone, but I'll get to that in a minute."

"That's it?"

"That's all. Just keep it and give me a copy. And take the necklace."

"But I hardly knew her."

"It is kind of sad, isn't it? She was a reclusive soul. Ellis meant the world to her, but he was a widower and had no children."

Jolie erupted in a nervous giggle. "She couldn't stand his late wife." Jerry laughed with her, and she felt the tension ease.

"So maybe," he said, "that's why nothing goes to his wife's family. Violet Standifer could be a feisty little thing, couldn't she?"

"She could?"

"Once she had another lawyer file suit against the city because the garbage man kept throwing her can around, you know, back when everybody had those metal cans. This guy just banged the hell out of one can after another. She would buy a new one. He'd bang it up even worse than the old one. She'd leave notes for him not to do that. He paid no mind. Finally, she

125

up and filed suit for destroying her property."

"What happened?" This was a side to the tentative woman Jolie hadn't seen. But her playing made it obvious she had passion.

"Never went to court, of course," Jerry said. "The mayor called her after he got word of the suit, promised her garbage can would get better treatment in the future."

"Did it work?"

"Bet your swee… It certainly did." Jerry colored slightly. "I understand the guy took very good care of her trash after that."

"Go, Violet! So what about the rest of her estate?"

"The house is to be sold and everything in it. That and most of her savings and stocks go to the Lippincott Conservatory of Music in Montgomery."

"That makes sense since she went there. So why not have the necklace, or whatever price it could bring, go to the school too?"

Jerry shrugged and broke into yet another smile. "She liked you. Her lawyer asked why she was making the change, because the bequest surprised him too. She said she felt a great affection for you and that you had seen the necklace and loved it, that you were *enchanted* by it was how she put it. And she told him you knew her story. You'd listened to her story."

"She paid me to."

"What did she mean, you knew her story?"

"She told me about her life, things that happened a long time ago. For what it's worth, my fondness for her had nothing to do with the fact that she was paying me." She watched Jerry close the file folder. "You said 'most of.'"

"Huh?"

"You said she left 'most of' her savings and stocks to Lippincott. What about the rest? Where does it go?"

"Actually all the stocks go to Lippincott. It's just a part of her savings that she left to someone else."

"Who?"

Jerry glanced out his window toward the courthouse in the square. "I'm not sure. She left twenty thousand dollars to a Rebecca Folsom of Memphis. I have no idea who she is. Her lawyer meant to ask Violet for her address. In fact, he was going to have his secretary do that on the day she died."

"Have you tried tracking her down?"

"Yes indeedy." Jerry slid the folder in a drawer. "There's no listing in Memphis information for a Rebecca Folsom, not even an unlisted phone. She may have moved to Timbuktu for all we know. The next step is to put a notice in the Tennessee Bar News saying it is presumed she lives in Memphis and asking if anyone knows how we might reach her. If that doesn't turn up anything after a while, it'll be time to pay someone to look for her."

"So what about the second copy of the video? Who gets that?"

"She does."

Fourteen

Jolie discovered one benefit to her return to Singleton: She could ignore much of what she disliked about it. Instead of being forced to sit in a high school classroom pervaded by anti-intellectualism, as an adult she could seek out the minority of adults who loved books and ideas. In place of the what-will-people-think muzzle that silenced non-conformity and had chafed her teenage spirit, she could do pretty much as she damn well pleased and be with others who did the same as long as she didn't parade it around the town square.

It was only natural she liked to be around Martin and his mother.

Now the two of them bent near as Jolie held the alexandrite necklace under a Tiffany lamp in the Everett library. Beyond the room's windows and the long terrace it overlooked, dogwoods mixed with pines on the estate's back acreage. The late-day sun highlighted the varying shades of green. The scene matched the beauty of any piece of jewelry.

"I remember this," Agnes said to her son as she touched the stones. "She wore it for Ellis's wedding in Memphis. We took the train."

"I don't remember the wedding or the necklace," Martin said, "but as long as I live I'll remember the train ride and that huge man who sat near us and snored like an asthmatic hog with apnea."

Agnes straightened to her erect stance. "Now, Jolie, you mustn't hide this away. Wear it every time you come to see us."

"Maybe I will. If you ever want to borrow it, please do."

"The only time I'm likely to dress up again is for my funeral. And I'm afraid I couldn't return it to you for some time in that case. If you're very good, never."

Martin excused himself to finish cooking dinner. Agnes and Jolie sat in the cozy room whose gray-green hues and walnut bookcases seemed like an extension of what lay out the window. Jolie took a sip of the sherry Martin aptly described as "dry as the desert after global warming."

"It always seemed odd," Agnes, said, "that someone as quiet and remote as Violet could spawn an outgoing son who went into politics. Of course, there was that passionate way she played the piano. I've sat through more than one wretched student recital…forgive me, Jolie, if they included you…just to hear her play at the end."

"She's a lot more interesting than I would've guessed," Jolie said.

Agnes chuckled. "So are most people."

When they joined Martin in the kitchen, he was adding a grating of nutmeg to the bread pudding mixture. "Has the mysterious Rebecca…what was it? Fulmer? Fuller…turned up yet?"

"Folsom," Jolie said. "And the answer is nope, nada, nuh-uh."

Martin shook the nutmeg remnants off the grater and tossed it in the sink. "Not even a hint of who or where she might be?"

"As her executor, Jerry thinks he might have to hire a detective. Or one of those nanoheads who can find out anything about anybody on the web. For what it's worth, I looked for her in cyberspace but she didn't turn up. At any rate, nothing's going to happen soon. Jerry and his wife and kids went to Vermont for two weeks."

"What if she turns up in the meantime?"

"His secretary promised to give me a call as soon as she notifies him." She tapped her fingers on the delicate sherry glass. "I think I know the connection. I think the woman's a relative of an old love." She told Martin and Agnes about Violet's love for Grant and her father's death.

"Well, well," Martin said, "that certainly whets my curiosity." He put bread pudding in the oven. "That can cook while we eat our stir-fry. Let's skip the dining room since it's just the three of us."

Jolie helped him carry steaming bowls of rice and sweet-and-sour beef and vegetables to a round oak table in an area off the kitchen. From here, she could look through a bay window to a tiered rock garden some seventy feet long on the left side of the lawn. Masses of purple and yellow irises flowered between huge rounds of limestone. Through open windows, Jolie could hear frogs croak in the small pond at the garden's edge. Lily pads floated on the water.

"Are you the gardener in the family, Agnes?"

Martin answered before his mother. "Of course. Fortunately Ralph, who does all the work, never breathes a word in refute. It's one of mother's favorite things about him."

Agnes smiled and gave a light shrug.

"Mother's way of gardening is to wander around and point out to Ralph what needs to be done. She's fond of saying, 'You have to stand back from the dirt to see the design.' You always have been a great one for seeing design, haven't you, Mother? I call it gardening by remote control."

Jolie smiled at them both and felt her shoulders softening. These two made Singleton a much more entertaining place to live.

An hour after eating their fill of bread pudding, they sat once again in the library. Agnes looked at her watch. "Goodness. I see it's past my bedtime. Y'all will excuse me won't you? I'm awfully tired for some reason."

"Tired, my ass," Martin whispered after she left the room. "She's got an Ellery Queen she can't wait to get to. She's

130

probably read it six times already."

Jolie laughed. "I envy your relationship with Agnes."

"I take that to mean you and Charlotte aren't shopping for matching mother-daughter outfits?"

"Hardly." Jolie made a sweeping gesture that took in the floor-to-ceiling shelves jammed with books. "Nice collection to choose from."

"You must be looking at the lower shelves. The sleaze is up on the top shelf for when I get weary of good writing. You're welcome to borrow either."

"I'll probably ask for the trash first. It could be the only sex life I have."

Martin smiled at her. "There are good reasons to go out of town." He sipped the espresso he had drawn for them both. "I have a suggestion. Something that might keep us from waiting however long it might take for Jerry White and company to find our elusive Rebecca."

"Go on."

"Why don't we put an ad in the Memphis papers, in the personals?"

"Old-fashioned, but appealing. We could hit some online sites too plus theirs. Where's a piece of paper? Let's figure out what we should say."

Martin pulled a pad and pen from a desk drawer and handed them to her.

"I'll e-mail it in the morning," Jolie said. "The print ad won't be cheap."

"That's all right. Have them bill me." When Jolie shook her head, he held up his hand. "I insist on it. Should we run it for, say, a week, and renew if nothing turns up?"

"Sounds good."

After fifteen minutes, they had worked out the wording:

Parties trying to locate Rebecca Folsom of Memphis. Monetary gain due her. Must be able to prove identity. Call 423-745-6822.

The number was Jolie's cell which, to save money, was her only phone. She thumped her pencil on the table and frowned. "I don't know about that 'monetary gain due her.' Sounds like something out of Dickens."

"Precisely why I love it. The whole thing is like something out of Dickens. A reclusive old woman dies without heirs, leaving thousands to mystery woman with no known connection to her. It's wonderful." He broke into a grin. "I knew you'd bring some excitement to our little hamlet when you returned. I don't want you to ever leave."

"Not until the first chance I get."

"No. Don't tell me that."

"Okay. I'm going to stay forever because I can make such an incredible amount of money here taking video of birthday parties for bratty three-year-olds. Plus, I have the assurance that I'm not missing out on anything, because I live in the cultural nexus of the universe. Gosh, I missed Yo-Yo Ma playing cello with the symphony tonight, didn't I? And the opening of the Monet retrospective." She threw up her hands. "Oh, what to do, what to do? So much going on in Singleton every minute."

She picked up the sheet on which they had jotted down the copy. "We need to change this 'Parties trying to locate' to 'Urgent need to locate.' Now, I know that's a little less nineteenth century, but it adds a good edge."

"Whatever you like."

She heard the distance in his voice and looked up. "Uh oh. I pissed you off, didn't I, talking about Singleton that way?"

"You're entitled to your opinion."

"Oh, c'mon. Nobody says that unless they disagree with you and are being civil between clenched teeth."

Martin shrugged.

Jolie reached over and laid a hand on his shoulder. "Apologies, okay? I forgot the rule. Criticism within the tribe is permissible. Criticism from without is not. It was my choice to become a quasi-outsider. Okay, a near-total outsider. But maybe now I need back in just a little."

As she tried to get to sleep later that night, she felt lonely in a way that made her ache. She wished there were some man in town who could hold her interest besides Martin.

Perhaps she should forget mental compatibility, start seeing someone who lives in his body all day and is at ease with its hungers, at ease with lollygagging in the physical, in no hurry to button his shirt. Maybe that was what she needed to do: Hang out at the local tavern, find some hunk, and follow Jackson Browne's advice to don sunglasses and have at it 'til dawn.

***

The ad would be in the next day's paper in print and online plus on a couple of other Memphis websites. She had no idea if Rebecca Folsom could lead her to Ellis's murderer, but it was an avenue worth exploring, and whatever the outcome, she wanted to know who this woman was. The police were pursuing the prostitute and Mary Ellen Hargrove's husband as suspects— or at least she hoped they were. And there was the weakness for gambling that might have led to Ellis's death. Lots of possibilities. Not enough substance to any of them so far.

The lead that intrigued her was Monique. Lying down on a regular basis with a prostitute you called "Cuddles" could lead to intimacy with all kinds of trouble.

Jolie rang Annette's office in homicide. Instead of information, all she got was a voice message announcing Annette was out of the office for two days.

So most of the day Jolie puttered around barefoot, doing

133

small chores. The windows of her cottage opened to viburnum-scented air. On a swing through the living room, she moved a matched pair of forged iron candlesticks from a corner to the stone mantel. She stood back to assess the effect. Too tall?

She moved the candlesticks to the other side of the mantel and eyed them again. Yes, that was better. They were balanced by the floor lamp a few feet away on the opposite side of the fireplace.

Fortunately, no one had pointed out how like her mother she was in this habit of rearranging things. Her illusion that they had nothing in common remained firm.

As far as snagging video work went, Jolie was still contacting local businesses. She had targeted those with little web presence that likely had the bucks for upgrades. She'd explained to the owners that video would give them an edge with search engines. She had showed them examples of well-done but inexpensive online videos. She had tried not to show how new this knowledge was to her.

Jolie had spent long hours at the computer to educate herself. So far, a couple of probable jobs dangled but with no definite dates.

She loathed marketing herself and found it to be the most despicable part of self-employment. So much time and effort had to be spent just trying to get the work that it could take more energy than the work itself. The hustling required an uneasy self-promotion.

She moved into the kitchen, sat on the linoleum, and ripped open a cardboard box that had sat in a corner since her move. In it lay the items that had decorated her cubicle in the newsroom. She pulled out the Slinky, tossed it from hand to hand, and peered into the box. A couple of reporter's notebooks, the Bessie Smith photo. And all that stuff underneath.

She tossed in the Slinky and toted the box to the back of the downstairs closet.

Fifteen

As soon as Nick picked up the phone, Jolie asked, "So have they cracked this Monique's alibi?"

"You should know. You're the one with the contacts. Care to say 'hello' first?"

"Sorry. How are you?"

"I'm ok. What I heard is, this Monique claims she was home with the flu, but of course, nobody buys that. It's just a matter of proving her wrong."

"Any more photos, anything else turn up?" Jolie asked.

"Nothing I've been able to find out about."

"Do you know for sure if they're questioning the Hargrove man from Nashville? The husband of the woman who was having an affair with Ellis?"

"You'd think so."

"Any talk about getting in trouble over a gambling debt?"

"Nothing."

"Damn." Jolie fired up a cigarette.

"We had a hell of a thunderstorm this afternoon," Nick said, "and for a while…"

"So I wonder if they've really narrowed it down to this hooker or if they're just going for what's easy."

"I don't know," Nick said tiredly.

"Keep me posted, okay?"

"I need to go now."

Jolie glanced at the clock. Twenty to seven. "A date?" she asked, keeping her voice casual.

"Not really. Just catching a movie with a friend."

"Someone I know?"

"Probably not."

136

"Try me."

"I don't think…"

"Go on. Who is it?"

Nick sighed. "Marci Schmidt. From the office."

"Don't think I know her."

"So I better go."

"Sure." She forced her voice to sound light.

Jolie hung up, fell into the sofa and propped her feet on the coffee table. He had a right to see other women. If the situation were reversed, she wouldn't want him telling her to avoid other men. Was she feeling a twinge of longing or merely territorialism? Did she want to be with him or want only to stave off yet another alteration in her life?

***

The afternoon sky hinted at a late May storm, but the darkness could as easily pass over. Just in case, she popped a baseball cap on her dark red hair before setting out on a walk. Lately, she'd begun exploring the land around her house whenever her lurking restlessness came too strongly to the surface.

In Memphis, she'd enjoyed strolls by the river, but these walks, into territory familiar only at a distance, became an exploration as much as a form of exercise. But exercise they were. Four pounds had attached themselves to her since she had moved to the slower pace of Singleton and given up working out twice a week at a health club.

Temperatures in the low eighties made the treks pleasant, but soon she would do them in early morning or near sunset to avoid the sweltering humidity.

Someone, perhaps her landlady, had planted peonies along the gravel drive leading to her house, and the plants now drooped from heavy pink and white blooms. Jolie picked up her pace as she entered the narrow two-lane blacktop that led eventually to town. A neighbor's dog, a bristly, black critter with a large white V on its chest, sidled up, its tail wagging. Without slowing, she reached down to pet it. The dog licked her hand and matched his gait to hers.

Considering the standstill in other parts of her life, the brisk movement of her legs felt defiantly good. No calls had come in for video work since her project with Violet. Attempts to locate the mysterious beneficiary had so far proved fruitless. The ad would expire in two days, and Jolie hadn't yet convinced herself it warranted another run. So far, the only response had been a teenager who'd hung up the minute Jolie told her to mail proof of identification and a woman named Rebecca Follins who'd tried to persuade Jolie it was she and not a Rebecca Folsom they wanted.

As Jolie turned off to follow a one-lane road, she and the dog parted ways. The patch of darkness overhead had moved on. Her cell phone clock showed she had been walking forty-five minutes. In another five, she'd turn around and head back. Soon, she promised herself, she would work up to a 2 hour round trip.

As she pulled out the key to open her front door, her cell began ringing. "Hello?" she said breathlessly.

"Who is this?" a woman asked, her tone curt and coarsely nasal.

"This is Jolie Marston. And who is this?"

"Where am I calling?"

"I'm in Singleton. In east Tennessee. And you are…?"

"Why is it you want to find Rebecca Folsom?"

"Are you Rebecca Folsom?" It was hard to believe this rough woman could have any connection to Violet Standifer.

"Maybe I know her. What's this about money?"

"She is due some money."

"How much?"

"I'd rather not say."

"I mean, is it just some measly fifty dollars or something some dude wants to lay on her out of the goodness of his heart?"

"No. It's more than that. Much more. It was left to her in a will."

"Whose will?"

"A woman here in Singleton." The woman's secretive demeanor made Jolie less forthcoming than she might have been.

"I need to know how much."

"Why?"

"'Cause if it ain't worth her time, I'm not bugging her, you understand? Besides, how do I know you're not just trying to set her up? Take advantage of her?"

"No one's trying to take advantage of her."

"Then tell. How much?"

"Twenty thousand, that's how much."

The woman at the other end didn't speak for a minute. When she did, her tone had shifted from hostile to curious. "So what are you, some lawyer or something?"

"No, a friend of the woman who left her the money. A lawyer is trying to find Rebecca too, but lawyers' methods can take a long time, and I want to see that she has the money as soon as possible. It belongs to her."

"Why should you care?"

"There's no need to go into that."

"So what do you know about her?" the woman asked in a hard twang.

"Nothing. Otherwise I wouldn't be running an ad, would I? I know only her name and that she was left the money. I don't even know why she was. I'd like to meet her, find out who she is, what her connection to…this woman is. I was very fond of the woman."

"So why can't you tell me her name?"

"Because I don't know that you're not setting *me* up."

Instead of a reply, Jolie heard nothing, the connection broken. But her still-intact news instincts told her this woman was not a fraud. She either was Rebecca Folsom or knew how to get in touch with her. And would.

***

"What's you're guess, Matty?"

Matty pressed her weight into the iron as she smoothed out a stubborn wrinkle on one of Stuart's shirts. She and Jolie were in the large kitchen of the Marston's hillside home.

"What I think," Matty said, "is that this is a girl Mrs. Standifer had by that fellow she was so in love with, the one you told me about that wasn't her husband. I think she's been hiding all these years that she had a daughter, and the guilt got to her, so she left her the money."

"You and mother need to cut back on *The Young and the Restless*. She had the same idea."

"Yes indeed, that's what we both figure. And we think it was pretty stingy of her not to leave that poor girl more money after she set her out for adoption and when she left so much to that music school."

"You could be right. But it might be something much less exciting. Some second cousin or something."

"Mark my words. It's more than that."

"Maybe so. After that phone call, I'm more likely to join you and mother and give it the soap opera version."

"You just wait. What's Mr. Everett say?"

140

"Martin thinks Rebecca's probably the daughter of an old friend of Violet's, and that Violet really loved Rebecca as a child, the daughter she never had and all that, but they'd lost touch. He admits it's just a wild guess."

Matty shook her finger at Jolie. "More than that. Mark my words."

Jolie nibbled a pretzel from a pile she had dumped into a bowl on the counter. "Your son and his family doing okay out there in Tacoma?"

"Just doing fine."

Matty had been coming to work for the Marstons since Jolie was in second grade. She came two days a week and often when they entertained. Years ago, she had given up her starched white uniforms for street clothes.

In childhood, Jolie had loved the black woman's diminutive size, so close to her own. Jolie now towered four inches above Matty's sixty-inch frame.

Growing up, Jolie had appreciated that Matty wholly accepted her just as she was. She didn't feel she had to live up to anything, as she felt with her father, or that she should be someone else, someone nicer, as she did with her mother.

Occasionally one of Charlotte's friends tried to lure Matty from the Marston household. Matty merely hinted at this to Charlotte when such occasions arose, and the next paycheck, still meager by city standards, contained a little more money.

Matty's relationship with the Marstons was as complicated as are many between white Southern families and the black women who have worked long years for them.

In times past, Matty sometimes got a little too happy on Saturday night and Stuart had gone down to bail her out of the drunk tank, a fact Jolie only learned from him since her return. When she asked him why he did it, he'd shrugged. "Matty wasn't disturbing anyone. Probably never would've been in jail

141

if she'd been white." Now in her mid-fifties and beginning to gray, Jolie doubted Matty needed bailing out much anymore.

In the hand-me-down manner of many such employers, Matty drove their old cars. Stuart traded in his vehicles, but Charlotte's cars, usually safely respectable Buicks, were passed on to Matty, and Matty drove them until the next one came along four or five years later.

What Matty offered the Marstons was secure order. A sparkling home, shirts ironed just the way Stuart liked, watchful care of their children when young and a mutual trust that had come only through the proving ground of years. Jolie hoped her parents realized how much they depended on her.

"Oh, I almost forgot." Matty walked across the kitchen to retrieve a large brown envelope. "This came for you in today's mail."

Jolie took the thick packet. The return address was *The Commercial Appeal* newspaper with the name *C. Fisher* handwritten just below. Why would Colin send her something? She ripped open the envelope with her finger.

Inside she found a stack of papers with a note on top: *Thought you'd want to see what some of your supporters have sent me. Best, Colin.* The sheets underneath included a few letters—one written by hand on decorative personal stationery—and several printouts of e-mails. She began with the handwritten letter.

I think it is shameful that Jolie Martin was let go. She is the best reporter in town, bar none. If you talk to her, tell her I am behind her 100% and think WTNW should hire her back.

Sincerely,

Judy Roswell

She held the letter with shaking hands. Judy Roswell, whoever you are, may life be good to you. Jolie read the others, all of them more or less along the same lines. Most even got her name right.

"Thanks, Colin," she said in a whisper. She looked up for Matty, but the tiny woman had left the room.

***

It had been too easy, Jolie thought, and far less satisfying than her fantasies about a pair of broad shoulders would have led her to expect. She sat now on her back porch in the sunshine, sipping iced tea and thinking about the past night. No one had been hurt, they'd taken precautions, and her vanity had been given the stroking it went after.

This morning she felt as if someone had scooped out the ventricles of her heart.

Country music had been blaring predictably from the jukebox when she'd entered Singleton's only halfway decent tavern. She hadn't sat alone at its nicked and sticky bar for more than ten minutes before he'd come in. He'd taken a seat an empty stool away, studied her as he sat down and, after a few sips, struck up a conversation.

"You're Jolie Marston, right? Remember me?"

She scanned the narrow face with its small, pleasant features and blue eyes whose droop gave them a tired sincerity. His skin had seen a lot of sunshine, but no gray showed in the light brown hair, so she guessed him to be about her age. "Singleton High?"

His straight-across mouth widened into a grin. "That's one way you might know me."

"Okay, I'm stumped. What's the other one?"

"I used to mow the grass some at your folks' house. They

143

still live up on the hill in that white house with all the boxwoods? It'd take me forever to trim around those things."

"Yes. But, I'm sorry, your name…?"

"Billy Welton." He toyed with the label on his beer bottle. "We weren't actually in high school at the same time," he said. He peeled away an even, quarter-inch strip from the top of the label and tossed it on the counter. "I was a few years behind you. I'm a year younger than your brother Jeff." He offered a sheepish look. "I guess I woulda been just another kid to you."

Jolie laughed and shook his hand. The song ended, and the sound of pool cues hitting balls, of balls rolling across felt into pockets, of curses and shouts could be heard from somewhere around the corner. The music shifted to a fast, foot-stomping number. The game noise once again became background.

Billy cupped his beer in one hand and slid it toward her, then scooted to the barstool between them. "You back in town visiting?"

"Yeah, I'm just back here for a while." She decided to ward off any more questions with a few of her own. "So what are you up to?"

"I work for my brother's construction company, mostly building houses. You remember Luther? He was a year older than you."

"Sorry, I…"

"I was in Memphis once. Saw you on TV there."

"Really. So, do you like building houses?"

"It's all right. Slow now. Mostly remodels these days, nothing big."

Jolie surveyed the work-hardened shoulders under the taut cotton of his clean t-shirt. "What do you like about it? What don't you like? Tell me."

Billy smiled at this unaccustomed attention. "Gosh, I don't know. I like being outside. I couldn't handle no desk job.

Course, soon it'll get hotter 'n' hell. But, I figure, it still beats wearing a tie." He grinned at her.

Jolie watched his tanned, sinewy arms as he tore another neat strip from the label.

"What I really like," he said, "is finishing up a job, getting everything just right. There's a real good feeling all us guys on the crew have then. My brother hires good workers. Now you'll have to excuse me if it sounds like bragging, and it very well may, but it's true. Take Jimmy. He does the best trim work of anybody, anywhere. Bar none. Once I asked him what…"

Jolie let her eyes wander from his earnest face to his well-formed chest.

During the second round of beers ("…but them sheetrockers. I got nothing good to say about…") Jolie reached out and put a hand on his forearm. When this stopped his monologue, as she knew it would, she gave him an up-and-down look. "So, Billy Welton, would you like to come back to my place?" She watched his face turn from incredulity to delight.

"Why, sure." He looked down at his bottle, giving it a pleased-with-himself smile. "Hell yes."

He began kissing her as soon as they were inside her front door. Yes, she told herself, this is good, this is healthy, this is necessary. This needs another beer.

"One moment," she said and headed for the kitchen. She returned with two bottles of microbrew. As Billy began drinking his, she unbuttoned his shirt and pulled its tail from his jeans.

He sat his beer on the floor and lifted her black cotton tank top over her head. He stood back a moment, said "Oh, my, ain't this sweet?" then reached to unfasten her lacy black bra.

During their lovemaking, he kept trying to slow her down. "Easy, easy," he cooed. "No need to rush this thing." But Jolie was in no mood to linger and coaxed him to a climax soon after her own. The moment he pulled away from her, she grabbed a cigarette and tossed her head back against the pillow. "That sure felt good."

"Hey," he said after a minute, putting an arm around her and pulling her close. "If you want to hear a good story, then I ought to tell you about this run-in my buddy Jimmy had with a sheetrocker this one time."

Jolie watched the cigarette's fire and occasionally muttered, "Really?" or "Hmm."

After finishing the cigarette, Jolie kissed the still-talking man beside her. "Good night, Billy. You've worn me out. I need to sleep now."

The next morning, as day broke through the bedroom windows, he kissed her and moved a hand to her breast. She rose from the bed and put on her robe.

"Jeez, I've got a busy day ahead," she lied.

He pushed himself up and narrowed his eyes. "So you're saying 'wham bam, thank you, sir,' and I should get my ass out of here. Is that it?"

"No, not at all." She heard the hollowness in her voice and made herself look him in the eye. "It's just that I've got a lot to do."

"Sure. Sure you do." He sat up and began putting on his t-shirt.

She hated to see the gorgeous shoulders go, but it was time for the rest of him to leave.

He stepped into his jeans, adjusted their fit, and zipped them. "You want to do something sometime?"

She shrugged. "I don't know. My life's pretty hectic."

"Yeah," he said, his voice suddenly harsh, "visiting takes up a lot of energy."

She hadn't bargained for sarcasm. 'Look, I'm in a

relationship with a guy in Memphis. Sort of. Maybe we've already split, and I just haven't understood that yet. But at any rate, I don't have any business getting involved with someone else right now."

"Goddamn, I only asked if you wanna do something sometime. I didn't ask you to marry me. Cripes, you women."

"Sorry." She rubbed her forehead with her fingers. "This is getting too edgy here. Last night was…we both enjoyed last night. Can't we just leave it at that?"

He gave her a tight, insincere smile and saluted. "Whatever you say, ma'am. You're in control."

She had watched his back as he'd turned and walked heavy-footed from the bedroom. A few angry steps later, she'd heard the front door slam, a sound that had jarred loose unexpected tears.

***

The voice on the phone this time sounded distinctly different, refined and well modulated. "I understand you're trying to locate a Rebecca Folsom."

"Yes, that's right. Are you Rebecca?"

"Could you please tell me why you want to find her?"

"Did someone tell you to call me?" Jolie asked.

"Yes."

"Was it a woman who called here a couple of days ago?"

"Yes, but I'd like to have the information myself."

Jolie's nose for news told her she was talking to Rebecca, but she'd play along.

"Okay. A Rebecca Folsom of Memphis has been left twenty thousand dollars in the will of a woman who died in Singleton. That's where you're calling. Singleton's a small town in east Tennessee, but maybe you know it."

"I've heard of it. Who is the woman who died?"

"Who do you think it might be?"

"A Ms. Standifer would be my guess."

Jolie's pulse quickened. "That's exactly right. Are you related?"

"How will the money be transferred?"

"Probably a wire transfer to your account. But that's to be worked out with the lawyer who's handling her estate."

"Could I have his name and number please?"

Jolie wasn't about to let her catch slip away. "Not until I meet you." She hadn't planned to go to Memphis until that moment. Now it was unthinkable not to talk face-to-face with this woman and find out more. "I have a video to give you." She'd given a copy to Jerry White as he'd requested, but why couldn't she make another copy and hand it over herself?

"I don't see why that's necessary. You could mail it to my post office box."

"It's necessary because I'm the one who put the ad in the paper, not the lawyer. Because of me, you'll be getting your money sooner. Besides, I was a friend of Ms. Standifer's. She was a dear old lady. I'd like to meet someone who meant as much to her as you obviously did. She made a video just before she died and wanted you to have a copy."

"Why hasn't the lawyer contacted me?"

"It's not for lack of trying. You're a tough woman to track down. I'll make it easy for you, though. I'll make the drive over. We can meet for coffee or lunch someplace. Then I'll give you the lawyer's name and number."

"Singleton can't have that many lawyers. I could just get their names and call them."

"She's not local." A bitter taste arose in her mouth. The lie was indecent, the kind of deception she detested when practiced by news people, but here she was, panting for her story and lying to get it. She promised to explain to Rebecca when she met her.

"How soon could you be here?"

"Soon. Probably in a day or so. Give me your number and I'll call you when I've got things squared away." She hoped Nick would welcome putting her up.

"I'll call you back tomorrow morning around ten."

Why was this woman so secretive? "One more thing," Jolie told her. "You'll have to bring ID to show me. Driver's license and a credit card or something else."

"I assumed that."

"And you'll need to tell me why Violet Standifer left you this money. You have to tell me about your connection to her. Then I'll give you the lawyer's name and number."

After the call ended, Jolie checked her phone and made note of the number.

***

Jolie knew it would be difficult to convince Martin he shouldn't join her for the meeting. "This woman's aloof," she explained. "No, more than just aloof. Downright tight-fisted with information. It's going to be a struggle to get her to open up to me. If I bring in some strange guy, I know, I just know, I'll get nothing out of her."

They were sitting in the porch swing on Martin's back terrace, sipping lemonade late that afternoon. He brought the slow rocking to a halt and gave Jolie an imploring look. "Couldn't you tell her, oh, maybe that I'm your husband? Just make it matter of fact. Don't make a big deal out of it. She'll forget I'm even there."

Jolie gave Martin a wry smile.

"After all," he said, "the ad was my idea."

149

"Yes, I agree. You're paying for it, and I appreciate that, but I'm the one she talked to." She put her hand on his shoulder. "Sorry, pal, but I'm absolutely certain from our conversation that I'm likely not to find out a thing if you're along. It's nothing personal."

"You promise to call me as soon as her reticent rear is out of sight?"

"Count on it."

***

Jolie's excitement awakened her at three a.m. After that, until she gave up around dawn, sleep came only in spurts. Last night Nick had said, in a voice she judged neither eager nor displeased, "Sure, you can stay."

The phone didn't ring until ten-fifteen.

"This is Rebecca Folsom."

"I can be in Memphis tonight," Jolie said. "I'm leaving in about an hour. I'll call you when I get in town if you'll give me your number."

"I want to make the arrangements now," the woman said. "Meet me at 1:30 tomorrow at the Hilton Memphis. The hotel is out east."

Jolie remembered the place, a tall cylinder of glass near the interstate. "Fine. I'll buy you lunch."

"If you like."

So what was her prying going to cost her? Never mind, that's why God invented plastic. "How will I recognize you?"

"I'll be wearing a yellow sheath. And I'm tall."

Sheath. The word struck Jolie as odd. She must be connected in some way to the clothing industry. Anyone else would have said dress.

"When you look for me, look for this head full of auburn

hair," Jolie told her, "and a woman who's not nearly as tall as she wants to be." Jolie got the sense this woman didn't watch a lot of local news which could be an advantage in not scaring her off.

***

Other drives from Singleton to Memphis over the years had been a return to her life there, to a higher pitch of activity. This time, as she began the long, downhill roll west to the far side of Tennessee's stretch, she felt as if she were coming from no place in particular and going nowhere definite.

Even Nick's hug at his front door didn't feel like a return to something familiar. It was as energetic as before, and his kiss had its old intent, but on seeing him again, she found it odd they'd been lovers more than two years.

Later, as she lay against his bare shoulder, Jolie decided it was his smell she'd missed as much as anything. She rubbed her nose against his skin and inhaled deeply. The scent was intensely male, one of soil and toil. As if, in the naked labor of sex, a deeply buried and age-old essence rose up, laced with the salt of his sweat. An ancient smell that prep school, college and a law degree could not wholly bury nor disguise. She extended her tongue and licked a swath along his shoulder, then filled her nostrils again.

One plunge into that unknowable world where mental superiority held no power always had been enough for them. After that, they had been content to return to the familiar. But this time she felt a need to make love again, to store up a dose of maleness.

She licked him, the warmth between her legs rising, no longer pent up. He stroked her spine in response. She knew the stroke, that contented pat that knows the world is back in its place, the mind has regained control, the urge is satisfied.

She kissed his chest, saying between kisses, "It's been a long time."

"Um," he said before sitting up, running a hand over the crown of his head.

She closed her eyes, imagined a bare chest, and muscled arms swinging a hammer.

Nick turned to her and chuckled. "You wouldn't believe what Squeegee did Friday." Squeegee was the nickname Jolie had given one of other lawyers in Nick's office. The only time she had met him, he'd been cleaning his car windshield with a long-handled sponge, a ritual, Nick informed her, that took place every day before he left work.

Jolie propped up a pillow and lay against it. "So what did Squeegee do?" But she found she didn't care, that she had little interest in Nick's world now.

"You know how he is," Nick began. "Has to have everything just so. This client…"

Jolie sat up straight as a bolt of certainty shot through her.

"What is it?" he asked.

"Nothing. I'm listening." Although it wasn't nothing. It was about their relationship and had come with abrupt clarity: their time together had passed. They didn't have enough to keep them holding on to each other in some nebulous future, four hundred miles apart. What was the point in continuing when it became more strained, more distant every time they talked?

Her eyes searched his face as she groped for words. He might be hurt for a while, but this would not be a heartbreak he would carry around the rest of his life, she was sure of it. Besides, he already seemed to be seeing someone else, however casual that might be. Time to break it off. Now.

"I have to get away from us." She spoke to the surprised look on his face. "I'm not talking about right this minute. No, I am. But every minute from now on too. I live way at the other end of the state now, Nick. I'm not with you anymore physically. I can't linger emotionally."

He faced the wall. "So that's it?" he said with a prosecutor's edge to his voice. "Tell me, did you make up your mind before or after we made love?"

She ignored his question and reached out to touch his shoulder. "Neither one of us deserves this half-assed tether between us."

He turned in bed to face her. "So that's your official declaration?"

"Oh, Nick. I know we care about each other. I wish it could be different, with me still working here at a job I enjoyed, and you actually enjoying your work situation, and we could be together."

"That's the basis of happiness together for us, isn't it, Joles? First comes work, and then comes us."

She reached over to stroke his forehead. "Maybe. Maybe we just didn't have it for the long haul, for the come-what-may."

He rolled back over. "See you around, Jolie. Been nice."

"Nick, I..." She wished their feelings toward each other were stronger than any circumstances, but to pretend that was pointless. She rose from the bed and collected her clothes, feeling her now-small life was even emptier.

***

Rebecca Folsom accented her five feet eleven inches with a sure stride and a tilt of the chin just a notch higher than nature intended. She pranced into the hotel lobby in a snug-fitting, canary yellow dress of nubby silk that hit her long, shapely legs mid-thigh. Over her shoulder hung a lime green leather bag. Her smooth black hair was swept into a tight chignon at the nape of her slender neck. Arched eyebrows rose above a perfectly formed nose and high cheekbones. She liked turning heads.

With her coffee-with-cream coloring and golden-hued eyes, Rebecca knew she was what in centuries past in the South had been called a "high yellow." Now the term she heard time and again was "exotic." She'd developed what had become an automatic reply: a smile that lifted one corner of her mouth, a smile designed to be enigmatic.

At the entrance to the hotel's restaurant, she noticed a 30-something woman with a small build and sweet face topped by a head of freedom-loving hair. She looked faintly familiar as she scanned the room. Rebecca walked up, out of her line of sight. "You're Jolie Marston?" The name also had a familiar ring.

Jolie wheeled around. Rebecca saw her pupils widen as they gave her a quick scan. No matter the age, sex or preference in partners, Rebecca knew she could rely on that effect when meeting someone new.

"Are you Rebecca Folsom?"

Rebecca extended long fingers. "Nice to meet you."

Jolie gave her hand a vigorous shake. "Same here."

After they were seated, Jolie leaned forward and clasped her hands. "You're a model, right?"

"I do some modeling now and then."

"I knew it! But do you get enough work in a town this size? I mean, Memphis is no Mecca of fashion. I'd expect somebody like you, the way you look, to have high-tailed it to New York long ago."

"I have my reasons for staying here." Rebecca suspected Jolie already had reached the common conclusion of strangers, deciding there was a generous older man lurking somewhere, probably with a wedding ring on. As was her habit, she offered nothing to confirm or contradict the assumption.

"I'm really glad you decided to meet with me," Jolie said, leaning forward even more.

Rebecca had a mental image of Jolie rubbing her hands together in glee.

Suddenly, Rebecca drew back. She was an infrequent news watcher, but wasn't Jolie Marston a reporter for one of the TV stations? If so, Rebecca wanted this conversation to be over fast. But why had the call come from the other end of the state?

"Do you live in Singleton?" Rebecca asked, keeping her tone detached.

"I do now. I lived in Memphis until about three-and-a-half months ago."

"But you're in Singleton now." She waited for the explanation.

"Yeah. I…I'm, uh, taking some time off."

"You're a reporter on TV." Rebecca decided to state it as a matter of fact.

"I was. I'm not now."

After they were seated, Jolie said, "Singleton's my hometown, and I might as well tell you I'm back there because I got fired. I've got nothing to do with the news now."

Rebecca felt easier but far from trusting this stranger. She watched Jolie's eyes narrow and saw the distrust was mutual.

Jolie asked, "Now, how did you say you knew Violet Standifer?"

"I didn't." Rebecca picked up the menu and put it down moments later. "The artichoke salad," she told the female server who appeared. "And a glass of Chardonnay."

"Caesar salad, I guess," Jolie said, "and just water."

"So," Jolie said when the server had left, "is that how you stay so slender, by ordering salads? Of course if I did the same I might not always have to fight the five or so pounds that want to attach themselves to me in the worst way. And the way I'm built, every one of those pounds shows. That's not true for you is it, as tall as you are?"

Rebecca suspected the chumminess was just a way to get her to open up. "It's not much of a problem. But I don't eat a lot."

"Damn," Jolie said. "It's unjust."

Rebecca smiled faintly. "Then again, I suppose you've never minded being white." She watched the fair complexion redden.

"Sorry," Jolie said. "Even as light-skinned as you are, I guess it's not always easy, is it?"

Rebecca's face remained placid.

After a few more awkward minutes of contrived chit chat, the server placed the salads and drinks on the table.

"To be on the safe side," Jolie said, "I really do need to see some ID from you. I mentioned a credit card and driver's license. Do you have those handy?"

Rebecca languidly produced the documents.

Jolie studied the pieces of plastic and laid them on the table. "On the phone, I told you I'd need to know why Violet left you the money."

Rebecca retrieved her identification with a long ruby fingernail and slipped the cards back in her purse. "Twenty thousand, wasn't it?"

"That's right. So why did you mean so much to her?"

"Actually, it surprised me. I didn't really know Violet Standifer."

"Then why? How did you meet her?"

"Once when she was visiting in Memphis I met her. It was when I was a teenager."

"You stayed in touch after that?"

"No."

"Wait a minute. Are you telling me she met you once, years ago, and as a result left you twenty K?"

Rebecca offered her mysterious smile, hoping it would halt further questions.

"This doesn't make sense," Jolie said. "What did you do to impress her so much?"

Rebecca shrugged. "Think of it as a guilty conscience award." She looked hard at Jolie. "You know how those white liberals can be."

That had shut her up. Before Jolie could muster up another question, Rebecca said, "I'll need to get in touch with the lawyer. Do you have her card?"

"Not exactly," Jolie said. She shoved back her plate. "Look, I lied." She rushed on. "I don't like it but I lied. My curiosity got the best of me. I had to find out who you are. So I said it was a woman lawyer, out-of-town, but it's not. It's Jerry White. I don't have his card, but he's in Singleton. Hold on." She pulled a pen and reporter's notebook from her purse, opened the notebook, and began scribbling. "I don't know the number off the top of my head, but here's the firm's name, White and Winstead." She stopped with the pen in midair. "How about if you just give me your number? I promise I'll have him get in touch with you."

"I can get the number."

"Save yourself the trouble, why don't you?" Jolie said.

Rebecca said nothing.

Jolie ripped the top of the paper from its spiral binding. "Okay. Here."

Rebecca grasped the paper between two lacquered nails. "Thank you. You said something on the phone about a video."

Jolie reached into her purse and handed over a DVD of Violet's story. "I'm not sure what this will mean to you. Do you know a Grant Milburn?"

157

She took the video. "I've never heard of him." She tucked her napkin beside the plate of half-eaten salad. "I need to be going."

"Already? But…"

"I need to be somewhere." Rebecca slid out of the booth and walked away, calling out over her shoulder, "Thank you for lunch."

***

Jolie wiped her brow and propped her tennis racket up against the bench. Martin had just beaten her 6-2 and 6-1 before she begged off a third set. He looked as if he hadn't broken a sweat.

Jolie took a hearty swig of water, and then lit a cigarette as they sat on the bench. "I know I keep repeating myself, Martin, but she was gorgeous, exotic. The way a bird of paradise flower would look if it became human. You should've seen her."

He rolled his eyes toward her.

"Oh, sorry. I forgot I banished you." Jolie blew out a puff of smoke. "The one thing I couldn't figure is any connection to Grant Milburn or to Ellis's murder, but who knows? I raced out in time to see her leaving the parking lot. Get this: She drives a pale yellow Jaguar sedan. The license plate reads YOUWISH. I definitely suspect a sugar daddy somewhere."

Martin grinned at her. "You sexist. Maybe she gets a discount on the clothes she models. Maybe she got a good deal on the car secondhand."

"Could be, I admit. Or she might really be able to make a fabulous living modeling in Memphis, but I doubt it."

"I doubt it too." He stood to stretch out.

Jolie tapped her racket against the side of her leg. "Damn her, she had breasts too. With that thin body! Of course, the

158

boobs could be fake."

"I gather you didn't think about introducing her to Nick while you were there?"

Jolie batted the racket harder against her calf.

Martin gave her a close look. "Do I detect some trouble in the trans-state romance?"

"It no longer exists."

"I'm sorry."

"Don't be. I'm the one who called it off." She watched a man on the next court deliver a pounding serve. "Now that's a pair of shoulders, so broad they're almost flat on top."

"It's a relief to know the fair sex never judges men primarily on their physical characteristics. It's such a tacky thing men do, don't you think?"

She kept her face a blank. "It certainly is."

***

Jolie held a small, round mirror to the light flooding her bathroom window. The sun's rays revealed several wayward eyebrow hairs. She picked up the tweezers and yanked. "Do that too much and they'll quit growing." Her mother's admonition from long ago rang in her ears. What did it matter now anyway? With a rebellious intent, she resumed her tweezing. Just as she was poised to tackle the last stray, a thought struck that caused her to toss the tweezers in the sink. She ran downstairs and ripped open the cardboard box that held her newsroom paraphernalia.

Her hunch was right.

But by two the next morning, she'd decided it might not be. To end the confusion, she rose, cued Violet's video, and fast-forwarded to what she wanted to see. As she watched, a look of relief spread over her face.

Sixteen

"Hi, Annette, it's Jolie. I hate to bug you again, but I need to get a little more info."

"Look, Jolie…"

"Please." She knew she was pushing the homicide rookie to the limits of their loose friendship. "It's just that this is important, and it won't take you long. I promise."

"It won't take me long to say no, either."

"Doesn't take any longer to say yes."

"What is it?" Annette said in singsong, but her tone sounded warmer.

"I need to track somebody. The license plate reads YOUWISH."

"That's appropriate. It takes longer to say than no, but I like the sound of it."

"Ah, c'mon, Annette." Rebecca had called Jerry White, but she hadn't left her number, acting just as cagey as she had with Jolie. Annette was her only hope.

"I'll see. Call me back around 4:30."

***

To keep from spending the day fretting, Jolie sent out more brochures and called more businesses to hustle video work. By the time she called Annette back, she had a training video for the local hospital lined up. At least one job lay in her future.

Annette dispensed the information hurriedly. Jolie spewed her thanks. As soon as she hung up, she placed another call.

"How did you get in touch with me?" Rebecca's carefully articulated voice held a hard edge.

"That's not important. I need to see you."

"Why? You met me. That's what you wanted."

Jolie searched for something persuasive that wouldn't be another lie. She found nothing but desperation. "I really need to see you. I'll explain then."

"But why?"

"Please. It won't take long. We'll meet wherever you say. Please."

To her surprise, Rebecca agreed.

***

Martin poured glasses of Châteauneuf-du-Pape for Jolie, himself, and a half-glass for Agnes in the Everett's formal dining room.

"I want to eat in here," Agnes said, "now that those heavy old draperies are down and the summer curtains are up."

Jolie looked around at the softly hued room. On the walls, ladies and their suitors danced in a pink, green, and cream landscape. Crisp white Battenburg lace hung on either side of the antique windowpanes. Sunlight streamed through them on this clear evening.

Martin walked over to a massive sideboard topped by silver serving pieces and heavy crystal decanters. He lifted the stopper from one of the decanters. "If you drink a drop from one of these, you're likely to sue us for lead poisoning, if you've brain enough left to do it." He swirled the brown liquid inside. "Agnes, why in the world do we keep brandy in these things? A slug of it would be akin to gnawing a wall's worth of lead paint."

"Yes, but they don't look right empty."

"No brandy for me tonight," Jolie said. "Thanks all the same."

The aromas of olive oil and garlic filled the room as Martin opened a swinging door to the kitchen. He returned with huge bowls. "Just something I whipped up from my little Betty Crocker cookbook," he told Jolie.

"Oh, goody. Jell-O for dessert?"

"With miniature marshmallows." Martin heaped a rich tomato sauce with zucchini, garlic, sun-dried tomatoes and olives over rigatoni. He sprinkled feta cheese on top and passed around a loaf of homemade olive sourdough.

"This is so yummy," Jolie said after a few bites. "I've hit my limit on microwaved frozen dinners. Lately I just eat bagels. I know it's breakfast if the bagel has margarine on it instead of cheese spread."

After dinner, Agnes excused herself. "An old S. S. Van Dine is waiting for me. The Greene Murder Case." She laid a hand on Jolie's shoulder. "I'm sure you've never heard of it, dear heart. It was big back in the twenties."

"And it still holds up?" Jolie asked.

"Actually it does. Some of the phrasing is quaint, but then so is some of mine nowadays."

Agnes left for the gray-green comfort of the library, and Jolie and Martin took their wine into a pine and brick-walled sitting room.

Jolie sat on a love seat by a woodstove that waited for cooler nights. She slipped off her sandals and put her bare feet up on the blue plaid cushions. "I'm headed to Memphis again tomorrow. I'm meeting with Rebecca the day after."

"This is a surprise. Why?"

"I just need to talk to her once more, that's all. There's something I've got to check out."

"Fourteen hours round trip is a long way to check something out."

"I'll have to figure out somewhere to stay overnight now

that I've torn Nick's welcome mat in shreds."

Martin moved to the edge of his tall rocker. "Let me go with you this time. I want to see this creature. You don't have to introduce me. I'll just be some anonymous onlooker." He began rocking again and gave her a sideways glance. "I'll put us up in a suite at the Peabody for the night."

"We might be able to work something out, Mr. Everett."

***

They had made the trip quickly in one of Martin's Avantis and sat now in the sumptuous and vast lobby of the Peabody hotel in Memphis's downtown. The lobby's centerpiece was a circular fountain with lollygagging ducks. Far above them hovered a skylight that emanated, through hand-painted cherubs, a gentle, approving light.

"You belong here, Martin," Jolie said as she looked around at the familiar scene.

"I used to come with Mother as a child. We stayed here a few times before it got rundown and was just a history-filled dump. I'm glad it's again 'the South's grand hotel.'"

"So is everyone who remembers when it wasn't," Jolie said.

She noticed people gathering between the fountain and the elevator, forming lines on either side of a red carpet rolled out by bellhops. From her years in Memphis, she knew the ritual well. As the opening notes of John Philip Sousa's "Stars and Stripes Forever" began, the ducks started waddling out of the fountain and onto the carpet. Onlookers applauded as the mallards filed into the elevator on the way to their rooftop quarters. When the doors closed, the bellhops began rolling up the carpet. In the morning the now-legendary march would reverse itself.

Jolie and Martin figured only mint juleps could suit the occasion. When the drinks arrived, she took a sip. "Do you realize this is the first one this Southern girl has ever had?"

He gave her a look of disbelief. "I'll have to fix you one of mine. I use a family recipe credited to General Howell from Revolutionary War days."

"But of course."

"A double handful of fresh mint, a pint of water, a cup of sugar, and the juice of six limes. Boil that for ten minutes and run the liquid through a sieve. Toss out whatever doesn't go through and mix the rest half-and-half with good bourbon. Serve in sterling julep cups."

"A whole cup of sugar?"

"I've never had a complaint. After a couple of rounds, everyone's comparing me favorably to the good general."

Jolie craned her neck toward the bar. "I didn't see anything boiling on a stove over there." She nodded toward a north-facing door. "My old apartment's just a short walk from here. Feels like a thousand miles away." She studied the tourists and locals relaxing on well-cushioned sofas and chairs, in the room where the Mississippi Delta was said to begin. "I don't know," she said. "I just don't want to be around people much anymore. You're one of the exceptions. Mostly I'd rather avoid folks. I don't want the second question."

"The second question?"

"Yeah, the one that comes after, 'Dear Jolie, it's been so long, how in the world are you?' The second question always is, 'And what are you up to now?' At least half the time I know they know the answer. They just want to hear my version of it."

"Get creative with your answers."

"How so?"

"Just smile sweetly and say, 'I'm a gypsy harlot now.'"

Jolie laughed. "But the caravans are *such* a lumpy place to

164

do business."

"That's the spirit. Or tell them you test illegal drugs for a living. Since they're just looking for gossip anyway, you might as well give them something juicy."

"God, I'd love to have the nerve to do that."

"So there are some things even you don't have enough chutzpah for?" He smiled at her. "Speaking of your moxie, what time did you say we're meeting Rebecca tomorrow?"

"Eleven. The Hilton Memphis is on our way out of town, so we can just head on out from there."

"Are you still not going to tell me why you want to see her? I was hoping the bourbon would loosen your tongue."

She shook her head. "It's just a hunch at this point." She wasn't about to confess that the Runes had counseled silence.

When they had finished their drinks, they went up to their suite, two plush bedrooms on either side of a spacious living room. They dressed for dinner and returned downstairs to Chez Phillipe. The elegant dining venue in a private cove off the lobby might well be the only French restaurant without duck on the menu.

Jolie wore her necklace and slowed before every mirror. As long as she had to show her face in the Peabody again, she might as well do it with style. She silently thanked Martin for her attitude.

***

Jolie paced near the door as Rebecca entered the modern lobby of the Hilton Memphis the next morning. The hotel "out east" was a 180-degree difference from the historic Peabody downtown. Martin stood a few feet away pretending to read a newspaper.

As Rebecca strode through the entryway, Martin lowered

his paper to gape, a gesture that went unnoticed because everyone else turned to watch too. As soon as Rebecca walked past, Martin slid Jolie's small video camera from a tan leather briefcase.

Jolie wanted the meeting on video, if there were any way for Martin to sneak and get it. She knew it wasn't probable he'd get close enough to record their conversation, but it was worth a try. Martin had been a quick study on the gear's basics.

Rebecca wore a vest of supple ivory-toned leather over a short, bronze-colored skirt. This time her smooth black hair turned under just at shoulder level. Jolie wondered if the woman had any female friends. They would have to get used to being ignored.

"Can I buy you a cup of coffee?" Jolie asked.

"I could use an iced latte." Rebecca turned and walked into the restaurant, leaving Jolie to follow.

As Rebecca headed for a table, Jolie said, "Let's sit in one of the booths. They're a lot more comfortable." She walked in front of Rebecca and toward a booth with no customers nearby.

Martin wielded the video camera as if he cared only about the contemporary furnishings and general crowd. When he safely could, he zoomed in on Rebecca. A few minutes after the women sat down, he slid into an empty booth next to them, his back to the tall woman.

Even before a waiter could hurry over to take their orders, Rebecca spoke. "Why is it you have to see me?"

"First I want to ask you something. What did you think of the video I gave you?"

"It was a sad story, but I couldn't see what it had to do with me. Why did Ms. Standifer want me to know about all that?"

"I think I know."

"Well?"

Jolie wasn't sure how she wanted to confront Rebecca.

166

"Let's order first, okay?"

After the waiter came and went, Jolie said, "I asked you here because I think I know who you are." Jolie saw a flash—of fear?—shoot through Rebecca's eyes, but otherwise her face betrayed nothing.

"What's that supposed to mean?" Rebecca spoke in an uninterested voice that sounded forced.

"Just that," Jolie said pleasantly. She waited for Rebecca to say something more. They sat in silence.

The waiter put their iced lattes on the table. When he left, Jolie stared at Rebecca's topaz eyes. "You're Ellis's daughter, aren't you?"

Rebecca's hand, as she lifted her glass, shook so that it nearly spilled the creamy liquid.

Her hunch had hit its target. She knew Martin sat dumbfounded. She watched his back lean closer, knowing he strained to hear what might come next.

Finally Rebecca spoke. "What makes you think that?"

"It just struck me the other day," Jolie said. "I was thinking about eyebrows, dumb as that sounds. I was plucking mine and wondering why I bothered anymore. I happened to recall yours. Your eyebrows and all your other perfect features. Then it hit me. I went to a box of things I used to have at my desk in the newsroom. Underneath the pile was a photo of Ellis with me, back when he was mayor. Same high cheekbones and tall like you too. But it was the identical arched brows that did it. That, plus Violet's generosity to you. Did you know she knew?"

Rebecca stared at the table and shook her head. "No. That was her first grandmotherly act toward me." She looked up at Jolie, her features tight. "Nice, but a little late for intimacy, wasn't it?"

"I hope you saw more of Ellis," Jolie said softly.

"At first."

Something told her Rebecca would say more if she waited.

"He used to come by all the time," Rebecca said after a long pause, "back when I was little. He used to bring me the prettiest dresses. I guess everybody in the neighborhood knew where they came from, but they were kind enough not to say anything, at least not to me. When I turned six, he stopped coming."

"Did you know why?"

"He came by the night of my birthday and brought me a frilly pink dress. It made me think of cotton candy. Then he and Mother went off to talk. Of course, I eavesdropped. I was fascinated by him." She paused and tapped bronze colored nails against the side of her iced latte. "I heard him tell my mother I was getting old enough to put two-and-two together, so coming by was a risk he couldn't take anymore. I asked Mother the next day what that meant, and she told me. Not surprisingly, that happened to be the time he began running for office."

"That must have been when he ran for city councilman, several years before he became mayor."

"I guess he figured I'd start blabbing that the nice Mister Ellis who came around was the same Mister Ellis on TV and in the papers. Wouldn't do for an up-and-coming married politician to have a child by his black girlfriend, now would it? Certainly not in Memphis."

"So you didn't see him after that?"

"Oh, he'd drop by every two or three years and bring a load of presents, but he always seemed in a hurry to get away. I will say one thing for him, though. He was good about sending Momma checks regularly. They used to come every month on the first, like clockwork, until she died."

"Was your mother married?"

"Not at that time. Her husband had been killed in a car wreck." Rebecca took a long drink and shook the ice in her glass. "So now your curiosity should be satisfied. And I'd appreciate it if you'd do me a favor in return and light a fire under that lawyer to get my twenty thousand to me."

"I'll certainly try. But if you'll excuse my bluntness, you don't exactly look like you have to shop at Goodwill."

"So I like nice clothes. Nice clothes cost money."

"I'll see what I can do."

"Of course you will," she said in a doubtful voice.

"Jeez, that must have been hard for you as a kid."

Rebecca looked away.

"Had you been close to him before you turned six?"

"His visits were the highlight of my childhood. He'd tell me about interesting places. And he didn't just bring clothes. He also brought books. A lot of times, he read to me. I'd get up on his lap. That's how I got my nickname, Cu—"

"You're Cuddles!" Jolie whacked her forehead with the back of her hand. "You're Cuddles!"

"How did you know?"

"The photo the cops found in Ellis's condo after he died," Jolie said. It was of a black woman and signed 'Cuddles.' But wait." She studied the face before her. "What I heard was that the photo was of a sleazy woman, heavily made up, thick black curls."

Rebecca met her gaze head-on.

Jolie studied the features, the hair, and the expertly applied makeup. "I don't get it."

"You've never heard of wigs? Makeup?"

"But why? Why would you send him a photo of you that way?"

"I sent it when he was elected mayor the second time." Her voice was hard. "To show him what the child he was ashamed of could be."

"No wonder it had been ripped."

169

"Ripped?"

"Yeah, but then taped back together, as if he meant to throw it away but had second thoughts." Jolie saw Rebecca wince, but she had to know more. "That photo. Police said it was of a woman called Monique, a known prostitute."

"That's such a crude term. Please."

"What then? Call girl?"

"That's a little better at least."

"And I thought you were a model."

"That sounds better still, doesn't it?" She gave her half-smile. "I also tell them I'm from the Virgin Islands."

"Aren't you just Little Miss Irony? When did you start…in this line of work?"

"At nineteen, when I was a sophomore in college. I dropped out soon after that. College seemed like child's play."

"Did your mother know?"

Rebecca gave her a scathing look. "Of course not."

"And did Ellis know when he saw that photo?"

"I'm sure he did, and I made a point of getting word to him, just in case there was any doubt."

Suddenly the defiant tilt of the chin fell. "Why," Rebecca said in a weary tone, "couldn't you have stayed out of my life? I have the police trying to pin his murder on me, treating me like some two-bit streetwalker. And now you have to drag up stuff that's none of your damn business."

"I didn't mean to hurt you. Really I didn't."

Rebecca took a deep breath and collected herself. "What gets me is, even after he'd stopped coming to see us, I was proud of him. He was my secret. He made me special. Better. Smarter. When he was elected mayor, I wanted so much to tell someone, but I couldn't. Momma made me promise to never, ever say a word to anyone. She said he would stop loving me if I did."

Rebecca lifted her chin again. "I thought if I were good enough and smart enough, he'd claim me someday. He would stop being ashamed of me. So I got all A's, and I was always teacher's pet, and I made myself as pretty as I could, and I started college, but none of it ever mattered. I'm sure he never gave me a thought except every two or three years when his guilt would get the best of him and he'd sneak by."

"He cared enough to send money regularly. He cared enough to tell his mother."

Rebecca's gold-hued eyes showed a spark of interest. "He did tell her, didn't he?"

"Yes, and you know that can't have been easy."

"Maybe she just heard about it some way and confronted him."

"I doubt it," Jolie said gently. "I heard all kinds of gossip during my years in news, and I never heard even a whisper of anything like this. His mother, living at the other end of the state, what would she hear? Besides, in a small town like Singleton, if gossip like that got out, I would know about it. I have a friend who knows everything about everybody in that town. And I know he never heard anything like that."

From the next booth, Jolie heard an abrupt cough. "So," she said to Rebecca, "that story about his mother meeting you once."

"I never met her. I made that up." Detachment once again laced Rebecca's words. "I better go now."

"Look, can I ask you just one more thing?"

Rebecca didn't answer but she didn't make any move to leave.

"Do you have any idea who killed your father?"

The eyes grew wary. "No."

Jolie emptied her coffee, figuring the meeting was over. But as she pulled out her purse to pay the check, Rebecca said,

"Did you know my father well?"

"Yes I did, or thought I did. I liked him a lot. You know, Rebecca, Ellis couldn't have held office in Memphis if the truth had gotten out, so while his behavior toward you was shameful, at least it's understandable. I hope he at least remembered you in his will."

"I've asked around. He left everything to his wife's nieces and nephews. Seems he didn't want to be embarrassed by me, even after his death."

"I'm sorry, Rebecca. That sucks."

"Yes, it does, doesn't it?"

"Violet must have known about his will. I wonder if that's one reason she left you the money. By the way, I think the reason she wanted you to have the video was to give you some sense of who your grandmother was." Jolie put down a tip. "Can I ask you something else?"

"Is there the remotest likelihood you'd listen to me if I said no?"

Jolie laughed and Rebecca broke a smile. "Tell me," Jolie said, "what's it like being physically perfect?" It wasn't at all the question she'd planned to ask, but she was encouraged by a hint of friendliness between them, and she hoped the question might lift Rebecca's spirits.

"I beg your pardon?" Rebecca said, but her voice indicated her amusement.

"I'd love to know what it feels like, just for a day, to look like you. Hell, just for a minute."

"You're hardly an unattractive woman."

"Yeah, but flat-out gorgeous I ain't."

Rebecca giggled, a curiously girlish sound coming from such a creature. "Except for the times when some creep is hitting on me, it beats being ugly." She shrugged. "So, I got lucky that way. But not so lucky in other ways."

172

"Okay, now here's that final question."

"I thought you just asked it."

"Nah, that didn't count." Jolie grinned as Rebecca shook her head. "What I really want to ask is impertinent as hell, and rude and—"

"I don't know why I'm in the business I'm in."

"Do you enjoy it?"

"You are impertinent, aren't you?"

"Well?"

"The money's great. Every time I think of getting out, maybe going back to college, I think about living on, say, thirty-five thousand a year with two weeks of vacation. I think how long I'd have to work my way up in some boring corporation just to make what I'm making now."

"But someone like you, I mean, you could get a man with bucks—" Jolie snapped her fingers "—like that."

"I've had helpful men friends from time to time. But they'll bail on you in a wink, always when you need them the most. I learned that at an early age, didn't I?"

"I'm sure you did."

"I like being able to earn good money on my own. And I've developed a pretty good clientele." She smiled again. "You'd be surprised at some of the people I know."

"No doubt. I like your frankness," Jolie said, "and your pride."

"Thank you. I'll call when I need a character reference. Now is the inquisition over?"

"See, you're smart too. Your daddy was smart."

Rebecca drew up taller. "My mother was smart."

"Are you…are you on your own? I mean, do you have a pimp?"

"I work with someone, a manager."

"Does he have other girls?"

"You must have been great in news. Yes, he has other girls and a few boys."

"So, what's his name?"

Rebecca let go a haughty laugh. "Not a chance." She slid her purse over her shoulder. "And now I'm leaving." She walked away under the gaze of every other patron in the cafe. Martin shot video of her exit.

After Rebecca was out of sight, Martin extended his hand across the back of the booth. "Brilliant, Ms. Marston. But twice I nearly spewed my cappuccino across the table. The first time was when you said she was Ellis's daughter. I'd barely absorbed that information before you came out with your 'Cuddles' deduction. So the photo tipped you off?"

"It did. But after I'd made the connection, I remembered Violet saying something about Ellis not having any kids. So I thought I'd gotten it all wrong. I looked at the video again. That's when I saw that what she'd said was 'Ellis and his wife had no children.' I'd just made the assumption that he had no children, period. She was being discreet, very discreet, while still being truthful. She wasn't going to deny her only grandchild."

"You seem to assume Rebecca didn't kill her father," Martin said.

"I don't think she did."

"What rules her out?"

"She has an alibi, for one thing," Jolie said.

"Which you said the police think they can crack."

"Yes, but so far they haven't or they would've arrested her. But mostly it's my instincts." She turned to Martin and smiled. "She doesn't smell fishy. I've learned to trust my nose."

"No, she smells like two-hundred-dollar-an-ounce perfume. Usually the higher-priced brands don't use fish oil." He leaned toward her, excited. "Let's say you're right—"

"Let's do."

"Then who did kill him?" He looked her up and down. "How do I know you didn't do it? Your avid inquiries may be merely a ruse to cast suspicions elsewhere."

"Oh, right. It's something I used to do regularly whenever we had a slow news day. My news director was *so* appreciative." She hoisted her shoulder bag. "C'mon. There's something else I want to check out. Okay if we drive back downtown before we leave the big city?"

"Anywhere's fine. I'm just your mascot."

"And you're doing a helluva job, Toto."

Seventeen

Martin found a parking spot two blocks from the tall building downtown near the Mississippi river where Ellis had lived. He and Jolie walked into the arched, marble-floored entry.

Jolie was unprepared for the sadness that met her. Several times over the years, she had been in this lobby on her way to see Ellis for a chat or to attend one of his parties.

She had to remind herself that today she was here to find out about the building's security system. She knew that to get through the second glass door and to the floors above, they would need a security card unless someone buzzed them in.

"Let's try this," Jolie said. She wrote down the number from a small brass sign near the second door and made a call from her phone.

The building manager promised to be right down.

***

The robust woman gave them a brisk smile. "I have a contract with the developer to show any of the condominium units not yet sold." The woman scrutinized Jolie. "Do the two of you live in town? You do look a little familiar."

Before Jolie could answer, Martin spoke in his soft drawl. "I lured her away to come live with me down at the family place near Hattiesburg. But she's talked me into having a place to stay when we come back here for visits." He smiled indulgently at Jolie. "She does love to come up here and spend money. I've never seen a woman who could throw money away like she does."

Jolie returned his smile and reached an arm around Martin's waist. She gave a sharp pinch.

"Ow!"

The agent's eyes darted uncertainly from Martin to Jolie. "Shall we look at one of the units?"

Jolie watched the woman slide a card with a magnetic strip into a slot by the second door. With a smooth movement, it swung open to admit them.

"What sort of accommodations are you looking for?" the agent asked. As she spoke, she fussed with dark blonde curls.

"Something with two bedrooms," Martin said. "And something with room to entertain, don't you think, honey?" He turned to Jolie and smiled.

Jolie smiled sweetly. "Whatever you say."

"I have something on the fourth floor that sounds perfect for you two." The agent steered Jolie and Martin to a walnut-lined elevator that took them to the unit.

In a moment, Martin called out from the master bedroom, "Come see these closets, sugar babe." Jolie walked across the wide hallway's terrazzo floor to the master suite. She joined Martin at a walk-in cedar closet as large as her cottage's bedroom.

The agent came up behind them. "What do you think?"

Martin turned to Jolie, his face innocent. "Do you think it's big enough?"

Jolie forced a worried look. "I suppose it would do. It would only need to hold the clothes I'd bring up from Hattiesburg." She turned to the agent. "What about security?"

"Our card system is extremely reliable, and the building has backup power in case of an outage."

"That's good," Jolie said. "Do you have security cameras?"

A look of concern flashed across the woman's face before she resumed her businesslike manner. "No, the owners have chosen not to have them."

"Why is that?" Jolie said. "Especially after…that awful murder, I mean."

"Yes, that was so unfortunate. Oddly enough, when the issue was brought up at a tenants' meeting, Mr. Standifer was the chief opponent."

"Really. Why?" Jolie asked.

The woman began leading them down the hall toward the elevator. "I recall Mr. Standifer making the argument that people thought crime downtown occurred much more frequently than it actually does. And of course, the crime rate here is relatively low. Nothing for you to be worried about at all." She studied Jolie's features again. "Now why is it you look so familiar?"

Martin gave Jolie a quick hug. "Oh, people are always telling my little darlin' she looks like someone they've seen before."

Jolie cut her eyes at Martin. "Back to the matter of security. Is there ever a guard on duty?"

"No. That too was discussed, but the residents didn't think the cost justified having one." She glanced down quickly. "There's some discussion about that again now. And installing cameras as well."

When they exited the elevator downstairs, Jolie noticed a woman in her sixties pulling her security card out of her purse. While she was inserting it into the slot, a handsome, college-age man walked up and greeted her. Jolie watched through the glass security door as he mouthed the words "I forgot my card" and gave a helpless shrug. The woman smiled as he held the door for her to enter and followed behind.

"Should we do that?" The agent looked at Jolie.

"I'm sorry. What did you say?"

Martin put a hand on her arm. "She's talking about the

sauna and exercise room. Do you think we have time to see them, honey?"

"Oh. No, not today." Jolie smiled at them both. "Perhaps soon though."

***

"Did you see that?" Jolie asked Martin as they walked to his car.

"The woman letting a younger version of Brad Pitt in?"

"Yeah."

"Maybe she knew him."

"Maybe, but I got the feeling she'd never seen him before."

"I would've let him in," Martin said.

"I'll bet you would have. But what that tells me is that all Ellis's killer had to do was to look friendly or at least non-threatening."

"Hard to do when you're toting a rifle."

"Yeah, but he could've had it in a box or something. In fact, if his arms were full carrying a big package that would give someone all the more reason to open the door for him."

"Or her," Martin said. "Don't leap to gender-based conclusions, sugar babe."

"Or her. But don't ever call me that again."

"I promise, honey."

A brassy blonde approached as Martin unlocked the Avanti. Behind her followed a man whose wide stomach formed a shelf for his tie. The woman grabbed Jolie's arm. "Aren't you Jolie Marston?"

"Yes."

"My husband Bill here and I used to watch you all the time, didn't we, Bill?" She turned to him and nodded, but his face remained immobile. She returned her attention to Jolie. "We were just saying the other night we haven't seen you on the TV in a while."

"No, I don't work there anymore."

"Really? What station you with now?"

"Not any. I'm not in news anymore."

"Oh." The woman and her husband walked off without another word.

"I bet you used to get attention from strangers a lot," Martin said sympathetically.

"Yeah, but who needs it?"

Martin unlocked Jolie's door, opened it, and began walking to his side of the car.

"Let's not leave yet," Jolie blurted.

"What?"

"The woman who heard the shot…the only one who heard anything…might be home. I want to talk to her." Jolie slammed her door and began walking back to the building.

Martin sighed, locked the doors again, and followed.

***

"The woman who called the police…her last name was Skinner," Jolie told Martin. She scanned the polished brass nameplates inside the condominium building's outer door. After a moment, she pointed to a name and unit number. "Bingo." She pressed the button beside the listing.

"Yes?" a tinny woman's voice said.

"Hello. I'm Jolie Marston, and I'm from Singleton, Tennessee, Ellis Standifer's hometown. I was a good friend of his mother's. I hate to bother you Ms. Skinner—" Jolie heard a faint chuckle from Martin "—but I wondered if I might come upstairs to speak with you a moment. I promise not to keep you long."

"Well," the woman answered uncertainly, "I suppose you could." She paused. "Could you show me some identification? Because, you know..."

"Absolutely. And if it's any reassurance, I was a reporter at WTNW for years. But I'm not here to do a story, Ms. Skinner. You've been hounded enough that way, no doubt. I'm only here to talk with you a moment."

"I thought your name was familiar."

"I do have a friend with me, a man who knew both Ms. Standifer and Ellis. May he come too? If not, we'll understand."

"Yes, I suppose so."

"Thank you," Jolie said. "We won't even need to come in."

***

Glenda Skinner's bookish, middle-aged face looked pleasant when she answered the knock, but she did not invite her guests inside after looking at Jolie's driver's license. She did not open the door beyond a few inches. Martin kept looking around, hoping the building manager didn't show up.

To lay the groundwork, Jolie spent several minutes describing to Ms. Skinner her close connections to Ellis and his mother. After the woman seemed comfortable, Jolie asked in a voice of concern, "You were the only one to hear the shot, weren't you?"

Glenda Skinner nodded and adjusted her owlish glasses. "It was just two doors down, so I couldn't help but hear it."

"Why do you suppose no one else did?" Jolie looked up and down the wide corridor. "There must be six or seven other units on this floor."

"Everyone works. Except for Mr. Tuell. He lives between Ellis and me, or where Ellis used to live I should say, but he's off on a five-month trip to China." She nodded toward the left side of the hall. "Eleanor Wiggins usually is home during the day, but she was visiting her daughter in Boise. Everyone else, as I said, is off at work during the day. I don't work."

"And that was about what time?"

"4:30," Ms. Skinner said. She glanced inside.

Jolie figured she longed to return to the solitude of a book. "We won't keep you much longer."

Martin gave the woman a warm smile. "You're so kind to talk with us."

"When you heard the shot," Jolie said, "did you open the door to see what happened?"

The woman gave a tight shake of her head. "I've gone over and over this in my mind. If I had opened it, I might have seen who it was. But I just couldn't." She gave her guests an imploring look. "For all I knew it was some mass murderer who would kill me too, don't you see? For weeks afterward I was terrified."

"We understand," Martin said.

"When did you open the door?" Jolie asked.

"Not until I heard the police sirens. I was the one to call the police. I called right after I heard the shot."

"It's good that you did," Martin told her.

"And there was just the one shot?" Jolie asked.

"Yes, just the one."

Jolie looked at the thick carpet beneath her feet. "I don't suppose you heard footsteps or anything else?"

"Not a single thing. I do wish they'd find whoever did it. I'd feel so much easier."

Jolie nodded. "So would I."

***

Martin shifted the '63 Avanti into a higher gear as it

finished climbing the steep mountain west of Chattanooga. This was his favorite part of the drive, the climb, and the descent that followed. Now on the mountain's slender perch, they passed the hamlet of Monteagle and the entrance to The University of the South, a remote private school which he and everyone else called Sewanee.

Beside him, Jolie had opened the car's vanity case, a tiny compartment tucked into the glove box, and was studying her eyebrows in its mirror.

Martin glanced over at her. "There's something we need to keep in mind."

"What's that?"

"I'll admit what Rebecca had to say about her childhood and her relationship with Ellis was touching, but maybe we shouldn't be so quick to believe her."

She flipped down the small mirror and closed the case and glove box. "Not believe her? I told you, I don't think she was lying."

"Just keep in mind that any call girl worth her high heels has to be an actor. Think of all the roles she must have to play with various johns."

"But she seemed really sincere."

"No argument there," Martin said. "I'm just saying, her seeming sincerity proves nothing."

"But what would she be lying about? Not being a prostitute surely."

"No. But we have no proof he was dear Uncle Ellie or whatever she might have called him. She could just be some hooker who serviced him once a week. Some hooker who may or may not have blackmailed and then murdered him. That picture proves nothing."

"So you think the whole story about Cuddles is made up?"

"It could be. Instead of Cuddles being her childhood

nickname, that might be the way she signs the photos she gives to all her regulars. Her version of a business card. A friendly reminder to keep calling, johnny boy."

"I'm not buying that one. What about the money Violet left her, the video she wanted her to have?"

"So that's a little harder to explain. Still."

"You know, Martin, I'm the one who's trained to be cynical, not you."

He shifted to a lower gear as the car began rumbling over the miles of curves that spiraled down the mountain. "I'm just saying, keep in mind that "Sunday School teacher" isn't on her resume."

Eighteen

For the next few days, Jolie kept mostly to herself, except for the training video she finished and delivered. It had been an easy gig, and the hospital's staff director loved her work and said he would hire her again. She was at her computer preparing the invoice when the phone rang.

"You Jolie Marston?" Jolie recognized the nasal voice, the same female twang that earlier had led her to Rebecca.

"Yes," Jolie said, and then added in what she hoped was a knowing way, "but I forgot your name."

"Yeah, right. I'm calling 'cause she's been beat up. She's in the hospital."

"Oh, dear God."

Jolie was able to extract few details beyond the name of the hospital. As soon as the woman hung up, she called Martin.

"So I'm going back to see her," Jolie told him.

"It could be dangerous for you. I'm serious."

"Never mind that. I want to know if the person who mauled her is the same one who killed her father."

"That's a question for the police, don't you think?"

"Since when did you become so cautious?"

"I've always been cautious," he said. "I just don't want anyone to think I am. But this is a different kind of recklessness you're talking about, Jolie."

"The woman's been assaulted!"

"That's horrible, detestable, and I hope they put the bastard in stocks and flog him on the half hour. But this kind of risk goes with the job, doesn't it? Anyone who sells sex for a living knows violence can always be just under the bed. It probably was some overzealous client with no connection to Ellis's

185

murder."

"I can't believe you're saying this! If nothing else, where's your curiosity?"

"Intact and as keen as ever, but I don't want you getting in over your head."

"I don't need to be protected. I'm not some babe in the woods."

Martin sighed. "So when are you leaving?"

"In a few hours."

"We'll get there faster in one of my cars."

***

What Jolie hated most about hospitals was the smell. A determined, invasive odor that threatened to wipe out anything living. Utterly sterile. Utterly manufactured. Not a place for both the first whiff of life and the last. Not a place for the striding beauty of Rebecca Folsom.

Martin stood behind Jolie as she tapped lightly on Rebecca's door and took a few hesitant steps inside. Rebecca's private room looked as antiseptically tidy as hundreds of other rooms in the complex must appear.

She halted in the dim light. She did not want to see what she was about to see. Yet the pragmatic side of her was prepared for anything. In one hand was her video camera. If Rebecca wanted evidence about what had happened to her, whether she wanted to use it legally or not, Jolie wanted to make sure she had it.

Jolie tiptoed to the edge of a partially-drawn curtain. She saw long legs under a white blanket. "Rebecca?" she called softly, but there was no answer. She took a few more steps, then halted, too dizzy to go farther.

God in heaven, why couldn't they have left her face alone?

Her lovely, perfect, other-worldly face? Jolie grabbed the thick cloth of the curtain by the bed to steady herself. Behind her, she heard Martin's sharp intake of breath.

The sensuous mouth had been pummeled to twice its normal size and was the same bluish color as her swollen cheek. A thick pouch of skin turned one of the tiger-like eyes into a slit. Above it, near the hairline, a knot rose, wide as an angry fist. On an exposed part of an upper arm, Jolie saw a band of four blue-black stripes, the gruesome imprint of a hand.

Rebecca's head lolled over toward her visitors, first seeing Jolie, then Martin behind her.

"I'll wait outside," Martin whispered to Jolie.

Jolie put the camera aside and walked toward the bed. "Hello, Rebecca," she said gently.

There was no response beyond a blank, defeated stare.

"It was your friend who told me what happened," Jolie said. "The one who first put us in touch with each other. I'm so sorry. I'll do anything I can to help."

Rebecca rotated her head a few inches, turning toward half-opened blinds.

Jolie walked around to face her. "I hope they have you completely zonked on good drugs. You deserve good drugs for this. Are you hurting? If you are, I'll get a nurse."

Rebecca's thickened lips parted, and she drew in a labored breath. "Dho whay," she mumbled.

It took Jolie a moment. "Okay, I'll go. I guess I shouldn't have come. I'll go." But she found herself unable to leave. "Look, you've got to tell me who did this to you. Was it a client?" Her voice grew insistent. "Was it somebody just off the street you've never seen before? Or was it maybe the same person who killed your father? Please, tell me. Nobody should be allowed to get away with this. We can't let them get away with doing this to you, understand? We can't."

Rebecca lifted a slack arm from the sheets and gave a weary wave. "Dho whay," she repeated in painful syllables.

Jolie sat on the corner of the bed, careful not to disturb the battered body. "I'll go away just as soon as you tell me who did this." She picked up her camera. "We need to get this on video. We need evidence for the police, the court. I know this may seem rude as hell to you, but I'm trying to help you. The truly rude jackass in all this is the one who put you here."

A listless hand covered the discolored face.

"C'mon," Jolie said. "Please. We need this." She held up the camera and began recording.

Rebecca's hand moved from her face and swatted toward the camera with a vehemence that surprised Jolie.

"Okay," Jolie said, lowering the gear to her lap. "You win. I don't like it. I don't agree. But okay. On one condition: You tell me who did this."

Almost imperceptibly, the gaze hardened. "My fa di dis."

Jolie worked to decipher the words. "Your what? Your father?"

Rebecca made no motion to disagree.

"Your father is dead! What are you talking about?"

Rebecca pointed to the camera, then to a chair.

Jolie sighed. "All right, dammit." She put it on the chair. "Now talk."

"He star id," she said groggily.

"Yeah, right. How can you blame this on a dead man? Somebody walking around now, with breath in his damnable lungs, that's who did this."

Rebecca shrugged and looked away.

Jolie leaned forward. "You know how dogged I can be when I want to know something. Why not go ahead and tell me now what bastard beat you to a pulp?"

"Sqoo id." Rebecca pressed together her fluid-filled

188

eyelids, a gesture that looked painful.

"Screw it? No. Do you know the man? Or woman? Was it a client?"

A slight motion of the head back and forth made Jolie feel triumphant. She would get her answer.

"Was it that guy you call your manager?"

Silence, and no movement.

"It was, wasn't it? Why?"

Rebecca pointed her finger at Jolie.

Jolie's hands flew to her chest. "Me? Why me?"

"Somn saw ud togeder."

"That creep would beat you up just for talking to me? Why do you let a man control your life like that?" She looked at the bruised and dejected face. "I'm sorry. It's obvious why."

"He dodn wan me dalkin to reporer."

"I'm not a reporter. Tell him I'm not a reporter. I was fired! I shoot kiddie birthdays now!"

The slightest trace of a smile formed on the puffy lips.

"What do you mean your father started it?"

"He wan bus ja rom."

"Ja Rom? Jerome! Your manager's name is Jerome, right?" Jolie figured the pain medication had broken down some of Rebecca's armor or she never would have revealed this much.

"He ca be ully."

"Ugly indeed. Are you saying your father found out what you did and wanted to bust your pi—your manager for it? Ellis found out from that photo you sent him, didn't he?"

"He ha ja rom. Tho I do somein else if he us ou bunus."

The translation took Jolie a moment, especially "ou bunus." Out of business? "So that was his way of making an honest woman of you, huh, to put your employer out of business? What do you think of that idea?"

Rebecca's thin shoulders drew into a shrug. A wince

189

followed.

"Is anything broken?"

"Jus sore."

"No kidding. Tell me, did you get the money Violet left you? I checked with Jerry White soon after I saw you, just as I promised you I would, and he said you should get it soon."

"Came las wee."

A worried look crossed Jolie's features. "He didn't take it did he?"

Rebecca gave her head a minute shake.

"Good. At least you'll have that." She ran her hands over her face. "Listen, I'm really, really sorry if I got you in trouble. I mean really sorry. If this is the result, I won't try to contact you again. I'll stay out of your life, I promise."

As Jolie started from the room, Rebecca said, "You purer tha me now."

Jolie stopped and turned. "Purer?" When she figured out the word, she laughed. "Prettier! I'm prettier than you now, am I? So I am." She walked back over and clasped Rebecca's blanketed ankle, squeezing the slender knob of flesh over bone. Thoroughbreds, she thought, must have such ankles. "That won't last long, but in the meantime, don't get near any mirrors, all right?"

The ankle pulled loose and the foot gave Jolie's thigh a push. Jolie saw again the glimmer of a misshapen smile.

***

When Jolie re-entered the hospital corridor, she found Martin propped against the wall outside the room. She signaled for him to wait a minute, and then went to the nurses' station. After a couple of minutes, she came up alongside Martin, leaned back against the solid concrete, and hugged her sides.

"What a pity," he said.

Jolie said nothing.

"Did she give you any indication who did it?"

"Her pimp."

"You must mean her *manager*."

"Yeah, I forgot," Jolie said. "And he'll get away with it. She won't press charges. One of the nurses told me that when the police came by, she blew them off."

"Did she say why he assaulted her?"

"She said it started with her father. That he wanted to bust the guy. Ellis's way of trying to make her change careers." Jolie's head dropped and she kicked a heel hard against the concrete wall. "She told me our meeting together also caused it."

Martin put a hand on her shoulder.

She looked at him, her chin trembling.

His grasp became firmer as he steered her away from the wall. "Let's get you outside where you can suck on a cigarette."

After they had walked several blocks in the sunshine, she stopped. "I'll keep my promise to stay away from her, but I'll be damned if I'm going to back off on anything else."

"And what if her pimp is Ellis's killer? What if you're his next target?"

"The timing doesn't fit. Ellis didn't get killed while he was trying to bust this guy. He was killed only a few months ago, long after he was out of office."

"I could see this fellow waiting," Martin said, "biding his time."

Jolie stopped walking. "Maybe. With Farrell in now as mayor, this Jerome guy's got free rein to run his operation and a better chance at getting away with..." She tugged on Martin's sleeve. "Let's get back to our hotel. Now." She began walking briskly.

He caught up with her. "What's the rush?"

Nineteen

Jerome Daunton was a slicked-back man. He liked his world the way he liked his longish, black hair: nothing sticking out. His meticulous control made Anthem Answering Service both the best-run message center in town and the best-operated prostitution ring.

Jerome Daunton did not like voice mail, or voice messaging as those sticky-voiced ads called it. It took constant attention to dissuade his business clients from switching. He would contrive stories, wholly believable because of their basis in common frustration, of customers who'd switched and begged to come back after angry callers yelled at them about getting lost in voice-mail hell.

So far, only a handful had abandoned his friendly-voiced employees, thanks to his persuasions and hefty discounts. He needed his customers, if only to keep the IRS off his back.

To the clients of Anthem Answering Service, Daunton appeared to be a respectable businessman in his late forties. He might not have their Rotarian look. He might toss out words in an unsettling staccato. He might be tieless and wear his hair longer, but he ran a good operation.

A few customers also used Jerome's other business. It amused Daunton that they knew nothing of the connection between the two. The secret also held within the answering service, with the exception of three good-looking women who worked part-time in both businesses and could keep their mouths shut unless paid to do otherwise. Not that there was much threat now.

Jerome attributed the answering service's smooth running to his managerial flair and the devotion of Dorothy, a

193

grandmotherly type. She'd been with him for almost the entire thirteen years Anthem had been in operation. Jerome knew Dorothy was aware of the second business, but she'd never said a word about it. He figured that as long as Dorothy never had to deal with it, it did not really exist for her. No one but Jerome recorded the few written transactions of the shadow enterprise, and those notes stayed hidden in a safe at his sprawling estate on the outskirts of east Memphis.

Anthem's name was Jerome's tribute to Ayn Rand. He admired the strong individualism in her novels. He considered his every action based on self-interest. And he thought anyone who wasn't a loner was stupid. Stupid and weak.

He had thought of going with Fountainhead as the name for the business. He smirked at the allusion. But he'd decided in favor of Anthem because he liked the anonymity of the book's hero and the subservience of his beautiful, blonde lover. A particularly sweet touch considering the novel had been written by a woman.

In his sparsely furnished office at Anthem, Daunton reached for the dark gray jacket draped over the back of his chair. He had a headache, it was nearly 5:30, and he wanted the forty-minute drive home to be over. From the corner of his eye, he saw Howard Farrell walking past his office window, headed for the front door. Daunton threw down the jacket and yelled for Dorothy. She appeared immediately.

"Anybody else here?" he asked.

"No, sir, everyone but me left at five." She glanced at the clock. "I was waiting around in case you might need me for something."

"Head home."

The front door opened. Dorothy gave her boss a questioning look. "You want—"

"Head home."

The current mayor of Memphis tapped on Daunton's open door but didn't wait for permission to enter. He strode across the office, smile on his face, arm extended. "Jerome. How's tricks?"

Jerome hated the question, the same stupid question Farrell asked every time he saw him. Did the man really think it was clever? Jerome looked at the mayor, imagined him with his tongue cut out of his yapping mouth. The picture amused him, but he didn't let himself smile. Instead, he shook Farrell's hand and motioned for him to sit, but Howard already had lowered himself into one of the black leather chairs facing the desk.

"Dempsey's joining us," Farrell said. "I told him to give us a few minutes first."

Jerome's headache sharpened. The last thing he needed was a blast of Ed Dempsey's bravado.

"What's up?" But he already knew why Howard needed to talk to him alone. Farrell considered his persuasive skills nigh onto irresistible in a one-on-one.

"I know re-election is a long time away," Farrell began.

Did anyone or anything hold an iota of surprise anymore?

"As you know, early money matters. Your support's always meant a lot to me, Jerome." Here Farrell paused to widen his what-a-good-boy-am-I smile. "I'm hoping I can count on you."

Jerome refused to smile back. "I don't think I've let you down yet."

Farrell's smile relaxed a bit. It left his eyes entirely. "No, and Howard Farrell hasn't let you down either, has he?"

Spoiled SOB. In exchange for laissez faire, Farrell hit him up for campaign funds at least every six months. He suspected the money ended up in Barbados, Howard's preferred getaway the last couple of years, and never saw the greedy hands of a campaign manager.

"Of course you haven't," Daunton said. "How about

195

bourbon? That's your favorite, isn't it?"

Farrell leaned back. "Bourbon would be real nice right now. Sure."

Jerome walked over to a credenza and pulled out a bottle and highball glass. "As I remember, you take it straight."

"Good memory. That's just exactly how I like it."

Daunton poured a glass and set it on a small table beside the chair.

Farrell looked up at him. "You're not going to join me?"

Daunton rubbed the space between his eyes. "No." He sat down again. "You'll have your cash in three weeks." Let him wait a little.

"Fine, Jerome. That's just fine. Give Ed a call when you're ready. I'll send him around to pick it up."

"Anything happening I should know about?" Daunton asked.

Farrell swirled the golden liquid and thought for a moment. "Can't say there is."

Daunton heard Dempsey's loud exhale beyond the door before he saw him. The man had a perpetual case of the put-upons. Daunton watched the deputy mayor enter the brightly lit office.

Dempsey let out another sigh as he dumped his bulk into the chair next to Farrell's. He didn't speak to either man and looked down at Farrell's glass.

"Want a bourbon?" Daunton asked.

From his thick neck, Dempsey nodded.

Daunton served him, sat, and waited. He knew they wanted a favor beyond the so-called campaign funds. Only the specifics were in question.

Farrell watched his aide gulp down half the glass, then spoke to him. "Ed, why don't you tell Jerome why we wanted to pay him a visit."

Dempsey rolled his tongue around the inside of his mouth, poked it into the crevice above his front teeth. "We figure it's time for a little party."

Daunton thought it was time these two had a few *birthday* parties. Had they for a moment considered themselves past the age of sixteen? He had no doubt what was coming next. And it pissed him off.

"We figure," Ed said, "you might be able to help us out. Get us some girls."

"How many?"

Ed looked over at his boss. "Let's see, four guys. What? Six girls, seven?"

Farrell gave Daunton a boys-forever-will-be-boys smile.

"What else?" Jerome said.

Dempsey shrugged. "Oh, you know. A little something to get us in the mood."

Cripes. Couldn't they get their own damn drugs? But he knew the answer to that. Hadn't he supplied Dempsey...and by extension, his boss...often enough since the election? "When?"

"Two weeks from now," Ed said. "That Saturday. Send the girls to my house around eight. And don't let them come empty handed."

They wouldn't. They'd be carrying top-grade cocaine, a little meth, a handful of poppers and half a case of Mumm's blanc-de-noir, Howard's champagne of choice. And it wouldn't cost them a cent.

He missed the old days. A lot of discretion, a little pressure to influential customers when need be, that's all it had taken. He'd been left alone to do things the way he wanted, without interference except for the time Ellis Standifer went after him. That didn't last long, because Daunton ran a business that important men in Memphis wanted and wanted to keep private.

The shakedowns for favors to the current mayor had started

when Ed Dempsey became the head of vice. Now that the bombastic fool had moved up to become the mayor's number two man, it was worse. Dempsey thought he owned the girls. He never paid, never wanted a hassle if things got a little rough. At least Farrell didn't leave any marks. For Howard, the girls were a way to show off his importance, not his depravity.

Ed drained his glass and held it out. Daunton refilled it, but not before topping off Howard's.

Jerome pointedly looked at his watch. Quarter to six. These guys looked in no hurry to leave. At least the bourbon would run out after another round.

Farrell looked at Dempsey. "Got a joke for our host?"

Ed stretched his legs. "Yeah, I got one."

Didn't he always? Daunton had come to the conclusion that much of Dempsey's success in life lay in dirty jokes. Would he have become head of the vice squad if he couldn't remember a punch line? Daunton doubted it. He imagined a thick rope around the steroid-swollen neck. He imagined Dempsey choking on his opening line.

"There was this girl name of Wanda, okay? And this Wanda, she…"

The image took too much work to pursue. Daunton leaned his throbbing head against the back of the chair and feigned interest.

***

Jolie learned only the sketchiest outlines of Anthem after phoning Annette. Neither Jerome Daunton's name nor his back-door operation was news to the department. Annette promised to call back as soon as she could do some checking.

Jolie had spent the next several hours in the Peabody's suite by the phone. Martin had tried to talk her into going down to one of the dining rooms for supper, but in the end, they had ordered room service. She nibbled two bites of a roast beef sandwich before setting it aside for another cigarette.

Annette's call had not come until morning. She'd found out Ellis Standifer had indeed shown interest in busting Jerome, but nothing had ever come of it. During Standifer's tenure as mayor, a couple of Daunton's girls—no, not Monique—were arrested. Arrests of street hookers were common, but not of Daunton's girls. Someone in vice told Annette the women had been questioned at length, but it never went much further; at least her source didn't think so. Maybe, Annette suggested, Standifer hadn't tried all that hard because Daunton's carriage trade no doubt included friends.

That made sense to Jolie. Those friends would be most unhappy if their shenanigans got curtailed. Campaign support could dry up. Relationships of long standing could turn icy. Ellis liked being elected when he chose to run, and he liked being liked.

Annette had one more piece of information: After Standifer left office and Farrell took over, no more arrests took place.

Because Jolie no longer had the media pull to cajole information from sources, she'd had to play tit for tat by telling Annette about her discovery that Monique was Ellis's daughter as well as Cuddles. Or so—Jolie felt compelled to add—so Rebecca said. On the whole, Jolie thought Annette got the better end of the deal, and she hoped the policewoman would remember that the next time.

***

"Don't the Farrells own a cab company?" Martin asked.

"Second biggest one in town," Jolie told him.

They sat in the Peabody's bustling pastry shop eating

almond croissants for breakfast. Around them stirred a noisy crowd, a mixture of shorts-clad tourists and business people in suits juggling attachés and steaming lattes.

"How convenient," Martin said. "When Farrell's out-of-town customers ask where to find a little action, the drivers can lead them to Daunton. Farrell probably gets a nice cut."

"I wonder if Daddy Joe knows?"

"Farrell's dad? Maybe not," Martin said. "Or maybe he just figures a gentleman has a right to a little fun. But you're the one who knows them, not me."

"I know Daddy Joe's well-respected and does a lot of volunteer work. Neither can be said for his son."

"Then how did he get elected?"

"I figure people were voting for Daddy Joe when they elected sonny boy. Certainly, Daddy Joe has the clout. And he got the black preachers to help him get out the vote. I remember, too, that Howard picked up a fair number of white votes, because the lineup of white candidates was weak."

"Why didn't Ellis run again?"

"He'd made it clear two terms were it for him. That left a vacuum for Farrell. But as far as I can tell, Farrell's filled it with little more than hot air." She signaled the waiter for a refill. "Memphis politics, I'm afraid, is still recovering from Crump even though his reign was mostly way back in the '30's and '40's."

Martin chuckled. "The loved and loathed Boss Crump."

"This city stayed under the thumb of Crump's machine politics for decades. He did make some big improvements to this town, but he was corrupt to the core. His legacy, as I see it, is that he gave vice a sturdy foothold and self-governance an amputation. But I don't know if we can blame Howard Farrell entirely on Edward Hull Crump."

"How popular is Farrell?"

"Several blacks I know are embarrassed by him and his divisive tactics, but a sizeable chunk of the black population likes his methods. They want somebody in power who they feel is on their side and giving hell to the rich white boys. Understandable, given the history of this city." She ate the last of her croissant and wiped her fingers. "You have to remember, Daddy Joe pulls in a lot of votes for his offspring. People know he gives a lot to the community. Some of us just wish Howard hadn't been one of his gifts."

***

They set out for the long drive to east Tennessee after breakfast, riding in silence. Martin still worried about Jolie's interest in a vengeful man who thought nothing of landing a woman in a hospital. He was relieved to hear she had promised Rebecca never to contact her again, but he had his doubts she would keep her word.

While Martin was no stranger to the *demimonde* himself, he preferred risk-taking to be amiable, secret, and without the possibility of riling anyone dangerous. He knew such finely gauged restraint must be foreign to the woman beside him.

She sat, scrunched down in the leather seat, her arms crossed, her light green eyes staring straight ahead.

He glanced over at her. "Your choice," he said. "Do you want to take the interstate back or go the scenic way? Which would you like better?"

"Don't care," she muttered.

He thought the back roads might provide more stimulation, more chance of diversion. "We could start out on 57," he said, "and go through Germantown, Collierville, and head north to pick up 64 a little later. That would take us through La Grange. I haven't been there in ages. If we see a nice bed and breakfast, we could take time to look around and leave tomorrow morning."

He wasn't sure she'd even listened to him. It was a full minute before she responded.

She scooted up in the seat and fixed her eyes on Martin. "You said 'La Grange,' didn't you?"

"I did. One of my favorite small towns." He leaned the Avanti into a curve. "All the charms of the antebellum South, but without the slaves."

"Do you know who lives in La Grange?"

"Besides ghosts in hoop skirts and Rebel uniforms?"

She thumped him lightly on the shoulder. "Grant. Oh, what was his last name?" She beat her palms on the dashboard. The rhythm increased and then halted. "Milburn! That's it. Grant Milburn. Let's go pay a call on the dashing, or I'd guess, formerly dashing Grant Milburn."

"Who in the world are you talking about?"

"Violet Standifer's old flame. The one she talked about on the video. She said he lives in La Grange."

"Lived, more likely. Violet was 90 when she died. What are the chances this guy's still guzzling Ensure, especially if he was older?"

"I got the feeling they were about the same age. Maybe he is dead, but let's definitely find out."

Delighted to see her spunk return, Martin agreed. "But" he asked, "what will you tell him? Will you tell him what Violet said about him?"

Jolie's drumming resumed, this time on her thighs. "I don't know. I'll figure that out if we find him."

"Someplace other than in close proximity to a headstone?"

"Yeah. Of course, with my curse of late, if he is alive, and I do talk to him about Violet, it will probably cause him to have a fatal heart attack."

"At least he'll leave this world knowing he was loved."

"Maybe he'd even let me get him on video. Make it a companion piece to Violet's." When Martin passed the city limit sign for La Grange, he downshifted to the ordained speed of 30, then he slowed to 20, 15.

Even fifteen almost seemed like speeding in La Grange. Along either side of the road, well-tended homes staunchly unchanged from the 1830's stood guard over the tiny community's devotion to its past. Martin and Jolie agreed it was the perfect place for Violet's long-lost love.

Twenty

Russell Wiggam carried Jolie's overnight satchel and Martin's tan leather suitcase up a winding staircase. "Just follow me," he called out behind him. "The servants seem to be on strike again."

Jolie and Martin swapped smiles, glad they'd found Russell and his wit. They had spotted the bed-and-breakfast lodging on a side street just off La Grange's four-store downtown. A discreet marker in the same careful calligraphy used on the waist-high street signs indicated they had arrived at Havenwood. They opened a picket gate and walked up a brick path between wide boxwoods. The house's colors echoed those of most other homes they saw here: white clapboard with dark green shutters. Martin clanged the brass knocker.

Jolie decided the word for Havenwood's proprietor—except for his eyes—was jaunty. Although Russell looked as if he had less red hair than in years past, his was a lively face under thin horn-rimmed glasses. But there was a worn look to his eyes that suggested an old and weary man. His voice alternated between a crawl and a strut. At the moment, it was on full-charm crawl.

"It took several bouquets of flowers and contraband cigars to the historical committee just to get the approval for one upstairs bath. The committee probably would demand grandmother's Limoges china in exchange for another one." He gestured toward a door at the end of the hallway. "The hard-won bath is there. And I can promise the hot water won't run out even if you fill that big old clawfooted tub to the limit."

He swung open a bedroom door. "This is your room," he told Jolie.

Across polished wood floors stood a four-poster bed with a ruffled canopy of the same lilac and white floral print as the bed skirt, pillows and tie-back curtains. The bed faced a rosewood armoire as high as most ceilings, although not within two feet of scraping distance here.

"Dang!" Jolie said. "I forgot my lace frock and satin slippers."

"Well, ma'am," Russell said, "after a night in this bed, you'll awaken with your hair in ringlets and a cameo 'round your neck."

In Martin's room, the two men began comparing the ages of their houses. Jolie backed out of the door with a wave. "I'll see y'all in a bit. I think Prissy's trying on my whalebone corset again. I'd better see to that."

In her flower-flecked room, she kicked off her shoes and flopped on the bed. Two ceiling fans cooled the air. Above the soft whirr, laughter faded down the hallway and stairs.

***

When Jolie came down a half hour later, she found the men in the living room, still talking. She noticed a nervous liveliness in Martin, as if he were on the verge of something fun.

She pulled out her cell phone. "Hey, Russell, any chance you know Grant Milburn?"

"Of course. Not especially well, but I know him. This is La Grange."

Her hopes rose. "So he's still alive?"

"Some folks say you couldn't accuse anybody in this museum of a town of being alive, but he passes. Do you need his number? It should be listed."

The entire listing of M's took up only one column in the thin phone book. About midway down, there it was. Grant

Milburn. It startled Jolie to see a name from Violet's memory blatantly printed just below Milbanks Auto Repair.

"Yes," a frayed female voice said when she called.

"May I speak to Grant Milburn please?"

A weary sigh. "Who is it calling?"

"Jolie Marston. But he doesn't know me. I'm friends…or was…with someone he knew." She didn't think she ought to mention Violet's name to someone who might be Milburn's wife.

At the other end, the receiver clanked on a table. Jolie heard muffled voices followed by a shuffling sound. She could hear the receiver being lifted, but it was a few seconds before anyone spoke. Finally a gruff man's voice said "Julie who?"

"Jolie. Jolie Marston. Look, I was friends with someone you used to be close to. Violet Standifer. I'd like to stop in to visit for a few minutes. I just happen to be in town, and…I know you meant a lot to Violet, I mean she talked about you before she…" Jolie realized the man would have no reason to know about Violet's heart failure. "I'm sorry, but Violet died the first part of May." She paused for reaction but heard none and went on. "She and I got to be close. Because you meant so much to her, I'd like to meet you."

The only thing that met her was silence. After half a minute, she spoke again. "Mr. Milburn? You still there?"

In answer, he cleared his throat roughly.

"Okay if I come by?"

"Violet's dead?" asked the graveled voice.

"Yes. I'm sorry. She was a wonderful lady, wasn't she?"

"What of?"

"She'd been having heart trouble for some time. But apparently it was an easy death."

"Easy? Easy for you to *say* maybe. Probably the only thing easy about it, young lady."

"According to her physician—"

"What does he know?"

"Well, she did have a lot to cope with. I'm not sure if you knew that her son Ellis, who used to be mayor of Memphis, was killed."

"Read about it."

"So may I come over?"

"Why do you need to come here?"

Good question, Jolie thought. Because I'm determined to do something, although I'm not sure what, to help a dead woman, her dead son and his battered daughter, and any little thread I spot looks like hope? At this point, she had no idea. "It would mean a lot to me. Please."

"When?"

"What about right now?"

"Not now."

"When then? I am only in La Grange for the night. Could we meet in the morning before I leave?"

"Come around nine tomorrow morning if you have to."

"Great." This was not the time to mention a camera.

***

Jolie and Martin spent the rest of the day exploring La Grange with Russell. He fed their appetite for the town's history, telling them how *La Belle Village* already was a well-upholstered town when Memphis was an upstart ruffian. "The Civil War was hard on this town, a terrible thing. We hadn't recovered from that when yellow fever hit west Tennessee, including us, in 1878." Russell stood erect, hands behind his back, as he recounted the story. Several homes were torched to ward off the disease.

The trio walked a few blocks to the stately Immanuel

Episcopal Church. Because it was locked, they jumped up to peer into the high windows that ran along the red brick exterior on either side.

"Pews from this place became coffin planks in the war," Russell said as he continued his tale. As if pestilence and war weren't enough, a succession of tornadoes leveled many of the old structures. But there was still another blow to come. The townsfolk didn't want the changes the railroad would bring. "They didn't like change then, don't like it now. So they opted not to have it go through. So we kind of froze in time."

"Now it doesn't seem like such a bad bargain," Martin said.

As twilight seeped into the village, fireflies started to flicker in low, upward flight on the broad lawns. Cicadas began their one-noted chorus.

Russell suggested they amble west. "There's a story I want to tell y'all. Another one."

Jolie touched Russell's arm. "That's one thing I love about the South. In other parts of the country, people exchange information. Down here, they tell stories."

Russell grinned. "And the facts aren't always critical. I well remember my daddy telling me, 'Son, there's no excuse for a dull story.'"

They turned off the main road onto Pine Street and walked several hundred yards until they reached a discreet drive off to the right.

"Here," Russell said. "Come this way." He walked down the private drive, past tall magnolias and massive holly bushes. Through the greenery on the left emerged a two-story home, one of the largest in town. Massive brick fireplaces flanked either end. Above the central entrance, over a narrow porch, rose a balcony.

"Every time I look at this house," Russell said, "I see Yankee soldiers wandering in and out of it. The North occupied

La Grange from 1862 to 1865 when the war ended. This town became that devil Sherman's West Tennessee headquarters." Russell walked to the edge of the lawn and stopped at a crepe myrtle laden with vivid pink blooms. "The house is known as Westover of Woodstock. The story I want to tell y'all is about the young woman who grew up here, Lucy Holcombe Pickens, known at least in this part of the South as 'the Queen of the Confederacy.' I think she could've given Scarlett a few lessons in coquetry."

Jolie sat cross-legged on the edge of the grass. "Tell us," she said. Martin leaned against a thick maple, as Russell remained standing. She could tell he relished an audience.

"She was a red-haired beauty described as spoiled and lazy. Many men courted her, including Francis Pickens, said to be brilliant, handsome and 30 years her senior. The tale is, she wouldn't consent to marry him unless he received the ambassadorship to Great Britain, a job he'd refused. He tried to withdraw his refusal, but someone else had taken the post. He was offered instead the ambassadorship to Russia. Lucy decided that was good enough, so off they went, becoming great friends with Tzar Alexander II and Empress Maria."

Russell strolled back and forth on the brick sidewalk leading to the stately home. "Lucy gave birth to a daughter in the royal winter palace, and the tzar and his empress were the godparents. When the Pickenses returned to this country, he became governor of South Carolina, which, of course, was where the war began at Fort Sumter. Because of Pickens's enormous influence, and no doubt Lucy's own, her lovely countenance was put on Confederate money, on one-dollar notes and hundred dollars notes."

He looked up at the balcony. "I suspect Lucy complained the one dollar bill wasn't much of an honor and wouldn't dear Francis, please, do something more respectful. That's my guess as to how she ended up on the C-note."

Jolie tossed aside the blade of grass she'd been twisting around a finger. "Curious. It was more than a hundred years later before the U.S. got around to putting a woman's face on its currency."

"That's the South for you," Martin said. "Ever in the avant-garde."

"At least," Russell said, "the money with Lucy's face made for pretty wallpaper after the war."

As they strolled back toward Havenwood, Jolie pumped Russell for more information about Milburn. She didn't glean much. He lived with a housekeeper as cranky as he was crusty. Not much was known about a son, beyond the fact that there was one somewhere, or had been. Grant had been a widower fifteen, maybe twenty years.

***

When Jolie came downstairs the next morning, Martin had a spatula in one hand and an omelet pan in the other. Russell was halving oranges and putting them in a juicer.

"Don't worry," Russell told her. "I won't put you to work. Martin insisted."

She took a seat at the counter. "I'll watch. It's not often I get to see two men on kitchen duty."

"I'll drive you over to Milburn's after breakfast," Martin said.

After they had eaten, she said, "I think I'll just walk." She opened the front door and stepped out into the early June morning.

The town still seemed asleep at 9:00. Only one car passed along the street. In the homes, many shades remained drawn. Her determined footsteps clopped on the broken sidewalk.

Occasionally she stopped to shoot video of the quiet houses.

Russell's directions soon led her to a modest one-story built early last century. It had none of the charm of its older neighbors. The lawn was neat but barren of more than a frazzled shrub on either side of the entrance. Jolie climbed the steps, wondering if she were being watched from behind the slight opening in the curtains.

When she pushed a doorbell, a tinny ring sounded from inside. Almost immediately, the front door opened. A tall, rigid woman, her brown hair streaked with gray and pulled into a tight bun, came into view. She said nothing.

"Hi," Jolie said, taking a step forward. "I'm Jolie Marston."

"Come in," the woman said. Jolie recognized the exhausted voice and pegged her for the housekeeper Russell had mentioned. The woman stood aside as Jolie entered.

A smell hit her, musty, as if a window hadn't been opened since the house's construction. Woven into it was the stench of rotten fruit.

The woman gave a faint nod of her head, and Jolie followed her into what appeared to be a living room just off the hallway. Underfoot lay a worn carpet of faded roses that Jolie guessed once looked pink. Sepia-toned photographs, close to the color of the rug, crowded a mantel. Many of them showed a dark-haired young man who appeared as brash as Violet had described. Jolie's heartbeat quickened.

Without offering Jolie a seat, the housekeeper disappeared into the narrow hallway. She reappeared briefly for no apparent reason before walking out again. Jolie guessed they had very few visitors.

She looked at her choice of seats. A dark brown sofa wore a greasy sheen on its tattered brocade. An upholstered chair with wide arms sat nearby, its seat deepened to a crater.

A man shuffled into the room.

"Mr. Milburn? I'm Jolie Marston. Thanks for letting me stop by." The hand that shook hers slid like rough paper across her palm, its sound as strong as its touch.

Milburn settled into the sag of the creaking chair and waved her toward the couch. "Have a seat," he barked.

Jolie perched near him on the edge of the filthy sofa and studied his face. The hair still grew thick, although its sleek blackness had faded white. The full mouth "just like Clark Gable's" now was a clamped and narrow line. The eyes, however, remained the blue of cornflowers. They stared at her now in the harsh glare of a high voltage lamp.

"So, here I am," he said.

"Yes. Thanks." Jolie's camera was out of sight. The subject of shooting video would have to be approached delicately. She wished she had Violet's story to show him.

"As I mentioned on the phone, Violet and I became close. In fact, in her will she left me the necklace, that beautiful necklace you gave her."

Milburn's blue eyes pierced her. "You have it?"

"Yes." She leaned forward with her palms on her knees. "Before she died, Violet told me a heartbreaking story. But it's one you know, isn't it?"

He looked at her as if she'd said something very stupid.

"I'm sorry." She wasn't sure why she was apologizing. "But it's such a spellbinding story."

"What's so damn spellbinding?"

"What isn't? The way you met at this lovely old plantation. The way her father was opposed to the idea of marriage. That awful way he died."

"No need to dig that up."

She decided to try for a zinger. "The way Violet never loved anyone else as much as she loved you. She never loved her husband that way. Did you know that?"

212

The aged face turned away. "She married him, didn't she?"

"Yes, but she felt she'd be disloyal to her father's memory if she married you. She couldn't. At least she thought she couldn't."

He turned toward her. "That's what she told you?"

"Yes."

"What else did she say?"

"Lots. It's all on video. I could have it sent here overnight." She could have Violet's interview Fed Ex'ed, and she expected no argument from Martin if she suggested they stay another night. She pointed to Milburn's DVD player and TV. "Then you can see her for yourself," she told him.

He looked at her. "You're saying you got all this on a film somewhere?"

"Yes. You could watch it. Tomorrow."

"What good would that do?"

"I think she'd love to know you watched it."

When he looked back, the cornflower eyes were hard slits.

Jolie felt she had inexplicably lost her argument and searched for another approach. "If you don't watch this," she told him, "you'll wish you had. You'll always wonder what she said, what she looked like." Jolie leaned forward, her hands on her knees. "If you don't say 'yes,' I'm gone. I'm headed back to east Tennessee where I live. I'm leaving in a few hours. You won't have another chance if you change your mind later. But if you say 'yes' now, I'll stay over, I'll get the video here, and I'll show it to you."

He studied her for several long moments, then raised himself from the chair, took a few steps and stopped. "Get it here then." He left the room.

***

213

Howard Farrell turned to his deputy Ed Dempsey as they sat in his office. "So you like my idea?"

"Sure," Ed said. "What's not to like about it?" Dempsey knew his boss's idea to name a four-story city building after his dad would be loved by some folks, not by others. But what did he care? Even if his brat of a boss might want to change the name of the Hernando de Soto Bridge over the Mississippi, what did he care? Let the city council members who'd have to vote on the idea care. Let them give a shit.

"I love it," Howard said. He jerked his head toward the door, indicating to his deputy that the meeting had ended.

Ed lifted his bulk from the chair and began walking toward the door.

"Oh, one more thing," Farrell said.

Ed stopped but didn't turn around. "Yeah?"

"Stop by the jewelry store on Union. Taylor's. I bought Janet a necklace for our anniversary and want to give it to her tonight."

"Can't you get your driver to do that?" Ed said over his shoulder.

"He's off for the day."

Ed stuck a toothpick in his mouth, clamped his lips around it and walked out. As if, he thought, a jewelry store wouldn't gladly deliver a purchase to the mayor.

In the car, Ed drove with a slowness fed by resentment. Pick up a fucking necklace. Farrell wanted his white boy, his honky sidekick to do the running. Never mind that this white boy had worked long and hard for every dinky promotion that had come along. Worked long and hard for the one lucky break that made him head honcho of vice when the former commander, a guy who'd spent four nights out of seven in a bar laughing at Ed's jokes, resigned and recommended him. Worked long and hard now kissing black ass.

Always somebody's ass to kiss. And the asses just got bigger the higher up you went. When he ran vice, it'd been the know-it-all ass of his chief. These days he put his lips to the backside of a man who'd be a petty thief if he weren't Daddy Joe Farrell's only son.

Always somebody's ass.

Twenty-One

The video arrived at Russell's in La Grange the next morning, thanks to help from Jolie's mom. Fifteen minutes later, Jolie stood out of breath at Grant Milburn's door. The worn-out housekeeper answered, once again without hello.

"I'm back to see Mr. Milburn," Jolie told her.

"Just a minute." She shut the door in Jolie's face.

When it opened again, it was Milburn who stood in front of her. "I've changed my mind. I don't need to watch whatever it is you've got." He began to close the door.

Jolie held her hand against it so it wouldn't close. "You'll regret this," she yelled into the few inches that remained open. "You know you will. This is your only chance."

"Get out of here," he said and pushed against the door. But she shoved back, and it shut no farther. She caught a whiff of the house's mustiness.

He said nothing but stepped aside. She stepped across the threshold, one hand holding her video camera.

He glanced down as they walked into the shabby living room. "What'd you bring that thing for?"

"I just did." She put the camera aside and pulled the DVD from her shoulder bag. "Violet's really wonderful on this." She began playing it on his system before he had a chance to stop her.

He sat, his hands thrust in his pockets, looking away

The video began, and Violet's delicate face appeared. *I had a sister, Rachel, who was three years younger than I...* Jolie saw Milburn's eyes swing to Violet's image. After a few minutes, Jolie sensed the old man had forgotten she was in the room.

Violet's voice continued: *"As I mentioned, there were a few young men who were keen on me. I thought I was in love with a couple of them, didn't I? But...when I met Grant, I understood that I had not been. In love with them."*

Jolie watched Milburn's head jerk back.

"The truth is, I loved...still love...Grant Milburn. More than I've ever loved anyone except my son, but that's a different sort of love. I've often wondered if we had spent our lives together in the sort of day-in, day-out way of couples, would the romance have faded? But I suppose the point is, it never did."

The papery hands were out of his pockets and clutching each other.

When the video reached the closing notes of Beethoven, Jolie ejected it and sat back down, waiting for Milburn to speak.

He unclasped his hands and scooted them over his face. "It's bull."

"It's what?"

"I said it's bull."

"Are you saying Violet was lying? I don't think—"

"You don't know what you're talking about." He popped his knuckles. "That isn't the way it happened at all. And she left out the biggest part, the worst part."

"Then tell me what happened." She got her video camera. "Tell me the way Violet did."

"Why the hell would I want to do that?"

"Because I really need to hear your side of things. And as long as you're setting the record straight, I might as well record it."

"There's nobody for it to matter to."

"You have a son yourself, don't you?"

"Did have. But he wouldn't have cared even when he was alive."

Jolie reached over and touched Milburn's sleeve. "Violet

needed to tell what was in her heart," she said quietly. "Maybe you should do the same."

He pulled his arm away. "Why did she need to tell all that stuff?"

"I'm still not entirely sure myself," Jolie said. "The more I think about it, I think it had a lot to do with her son's murder. I suspect it was a way of telling about her heartache over that without ever actually touching on it. Because that would have been too hard to ever put into words. So she could talk about something else that broke her heart, something that could be expressed, even though she'd held back from expressing it all these years." Jolie leaned back and pulled a pack of cigarettes from her purse. "Mind if I smoke?" A chipped ceramic ashtray indicated he might not, and she took his silence as consent. "You know, it's sort of like when we get wrought up about one thing, but we're actually upset about something else, something deeper that we're not putting our finger on. Maybe she only thought she needed to talk about you."

Milburn gave a slight shake of his head.

"At least that's my theory most of the time," she said as she exhaled. "At other times, I think she just wanted to tell someone about how you were the grand love of her life. To unburden herself after living a lie all these years. Poor woman. She was such a recluse she had nobody but me and my camera to tell her story to."

"Whatever her damn reasons," he said, "she told it wrong."

Jolie wondered what had happened in the course of Grant Milburn's long life to turn him from a self-assured charmer into a rude grump. "Then you need to tell it, don't you think?"

He got up, shoved the hands back into his pockets and paced the room. Jolie watched him, watched his concave chest heave, and waited. If she said anything more right now, she feared he might send her away.

218

In a few minutes, he sat back down. He pointed at the video camera and shoved his hands in his pockets. "Turn that thing on."

Shocked at her luck, she stubbed out her cigarette and hopped up. "It'll only a take a sec to set things up."

In four minutes, she was ready. "Just look at the camera, or if it's easier, you can look at me."

Milburn ran his hands over his lined face once more and stared into the lens.

He got up, took a few steps, and stood with his back to her. "This is a damn fool idea if ever I heard one." He turned around and pointed to the camera. "I think you need to get that thing and go on home, young lady."

Jolie hit the pause button. She decided to meet his gruff and raise him.

"What the hell are you afraid of?" she said, standing to face him.

"Certainly not you."

"Then why in the world won't you let me do this?"

"Because you got no reason to."

"No reason? Don't you want the truth told? If what Violet said is a lie, don't you want to counter that? Don't you want it on record the way it really happened?"

"Why should you or anyone care? It happened a long, long time ago."

"You're chicken! You're afraid to delve back into the past, afraid to face whatever emotions it might bring up in you." She watched the blue eyes tighten, the lips compress. She waited and stared back, her own face tense and unmoving.

He stalked to his chair and pushed himself back into it. "Turn that goddamn thing on."

She sat back down with the video camera and began recording. A small hidden smirk crossed her face as she looked through the viewfinder.

"For one thing, the dress wasn't even blue. That dress she wore to the dance. It was yellow, as certain as I'm sitting here.

"She was pretty. She had that right. Had the prettiest smile I ever saw too. She would tilt her head down, then look up kind of sideways at me and smile. Made me feel she'd never smiled at anybody else like that. I didn't know back in those days what trouble women could be."

He stopped, as if unsure what to say next.

"Tell me about the first time you saw Violet," Jolie said. "Tell me about that. And take all the time you want."

Milburn grunted, leaned his head against the grease-stained chair and shut his eyes. He was silent so long Jolie again thought she might lose this lucky opportunity. In a moment however, he heaved a sigh and began speaking in an adamant voice.

"My family used to have money. Before my time, that's for damn sure. All my life growing up, I was told about how much we *used* to have. But my grandfather liked horses and whiskey too much to hang onto what he'd come by. So all I ever heard was how much we used to have. We *used* to have servants. We *used* to give fancy parties. My grandmother *used* to have all this jewelry.

We sure as hell didn't have it when I was coming up, although we thought we had to act as if we did. Always scrimping at home and pretending to the world like we had everything we could want. Not that anybody was fooled. They all knew we were just scraping by on what little we had left.

Still, in a small place like Oxford, it meant something that your people at least once had money and a high position. And folks thought a lot of my mother, because she was always doing all this charity work. That let her—and us—still be part of the nice families, even though we were the ones needed charity. My pap spent his life working in the local gin mill, some two-bit office job. It sure didn't bring in much, and most of that went to pay off Grandpap's debts. When Grandpap died, he owed nearly everybody in north Mississippi. I got so damn tired of being poor.

"It surprised me Ruth Anne even invited me to that party. 'Course it thrilled my mother no end. All I could figure was, Ruth Anne needed to even things out, have enough boys for the dance and whatnot. And she knew I wouldn't be like a lot of boys and just hang back hugging the wall when it came time to dance. Back then, I wasn't about to miss a chance to hold a girl."

He stopped, and then straightened in his chair. "No need to ramble off into all that other stuff.

"I couldn't remember why Violet came late...don't remember that part about her mother having the flu...I just remember she was the last one to come.

"I wasn't leaning against any tree when she saw me. I was teasing a couple of the girls, Lizabeth, and another one. I felt this tap on my shoulder, and I turned around. Ruth Anne was standing there with this pretty girl, one I hadn't seen before, so of course I'm interested. Introduces her as Violet Gilman. I asked where she was from, things like that. That's when she first gave me one of those up-from-under smiles of hers. I decided right then and there she was the one I was going to spend my time on.

"I'm surprised she didn't tell you about the rose I gave her the last night there, because she told me she slept with it under her pillow every night from then on. At least until her old man... But there's a lot of things she didn't tell you. And one damn big thing, like I said.

"So I went to visit her family. They were well off, that was easy to see. She and I got on that week. She couldn't get enough of me. It was 'Grant, darling' this and 'Grant, darling' that. Course I was keen on her too. Damn right.

"She told right that her father had a hissy fit when we told him we wanted to get married. Gilman yelled to high heaven about my being Catholic. That mattered a lot to her good Methodist family. And my guess is, they might have done some checking with the Kenworthys and found out we didn't have money either. A poor Catholic. No way in hell her pap was going to let her marry that.

"So then we went out fishing…Gilman and I…the next morning, and this storm came up." He turned sideways to face the wall. "You heard the rest from Violet."

***

Jolie paused the camera and said softly, "Could we talk about that morning?"

He wheeled around. "Why in God's name would I want to talk about that?"

"Sorry." She reached around and massaged her neck, stiff from leaning over the camera propped on a table for stability. Bringing in a tripod didn't seem wise. Too much gear might have rattled him enough to refuse to do this. "You said there was one big thing Violet didn't tell. What was that?"

"She wouldn't want it told."

"I got the feeling Violet wanted the truth told, at all costs. She was tired of hiding, tired of lies. I'm sure she'd want you to tell."

"Then why didn't she tell it herself?"

"Well, maybe…maybe she just forgot."

"This she wouldn't forget. Not this."

"There is no one who needs protecting anymore," Jolie said. "No one can be hurt. And there is no one's honor to defend

222

now."

"Honor?" Milburn roared. "What do I care about defending her honor? What do I care about that? Her precious honor. Or her feelings? What did she care about mine? Not a damn bit, not one damn bit. She said to hell with me, that's what she did."

Jolie eased down to the viewfinder and resumed her work. She wasn't sure if Grant even thought about the video camera any longer and whether or not it was recording.

***

"After...after that business with her father...I went to see her at that music school in Montgomery. It must've been three, four months after he died. Stayed in a local boarding house. We'd go walk in the woods just outside town. Had a little place for ourselves up underneath a big cedar. The branches came down so that you couldn't see underneath even if you were standing a few feet away. It was cold as hell, I remember that. Winter. We'd snuggle up together under that tree and talk and whatnot. Well, one day the sun broke out, and it turned warm. We'd felt so trapped from having to sneak around and from freezing out there under that tree. I guess it made her a little wild. She..."

He cleared his throat and looked at the wall. "The upshot was, she got pregnant. First time and pregnant. When she wrote me about it, I borrowed money from every friend I had and came back to Montgomery to see her. Begged her to marry me, even got on my knees to that woman. I mean I begged and begged. She wouldn't even consider it. Said it would dishonor her father. He was dead! What did he care? Wrote me about a month later that she'd gotten rid of it. That's how she phrased it. Gotten rid of it. Like the kid never happened. Some doctor there in Montgomery. Every town of any size had one back in those days. Said she was paying him off by giving his children music lessons. Sounds like a hell of a lot of music lessons to me. What I want to know is, what else was she giving him?"

Grant pushed himself up from the chair and stood. "You wanted the truth? There, you've got it now. Pretty ugly, isn't it?"

Still recording and keeping him in view, Jolie called out, "What happened next?"

"Put that thing away! I'm finished with talking. You can cajole me until you're blue in the face. There's nothing more to tell."

She hit the stop button. "Did you keep seeing each other?"

"Of course not. She didn't want anything to do with me after that. Oh no, she went back to her pretty little parties and fancy music school boys like nothing had ever happened. She quit answering my letters. I went back once to Montgomery. Rode first class in a box car. But she wouldn't even see me. Sent one of her girlfriends to tell me to go away."

He flinched. "I got nothing more to say, so don't even try me."

***

On her slow walk back to Havenwood, Jolie thought about the bitterness Milburn had dragged around since his youth. As for Violet's abortion, could it be that casting aside one child meant she could never cast aside another, even if the other was her son's illegitimate daughter?

Jolie knew Martin had hoped La Grange and Milburn would take her mind off Rebecca. But it hadn't worked. The battered face had drifted through her dreams both nights as she lay in the canopied bed. She wondered what would happen when Rebecca walked out of her safe hospital room.

***

Martin drove past Chattanooga, past Cleveland. As they neared Singleton, Jolie stretched her legs along the length of the floorboard. "I almost wish I hadn't met Milburn. Violet might have loved him until the day she died, but he seems almost to hate her."

"Maybe he's just masking his hurt with anger."

"Thank you, doctor."

"Cut it out. The only emotion society permitted men of his generation was anger. It's not all that different now."

"I guess you're right."

"What do you mean, 'you guess I'm right?'" Seems to me I have an innate claim to more authority on the subject than you."

"Okay, okay."

They rode in silence for a while before Jolie spoke again. "Speaking of emotions, Russell's fun, but there's something sad, kind of lonely about him, don't you think?"

They had just turned onto one of Singleton's outlying roads. "I'd go with lonely, yes," Martin said. "He and his partner started the bed and breakfast. Then his partner died years ago with AIDS. Russell didn't say a lot about Eric's illness, but it was clear it was tough on them both."

As they neared the stoplight at Murphy's hardware store, Jolie said, "You know, Mother says the word is out in our little hometown that you and I are seeing a lot of each other."

"Is it? I'm not surprised."

"I mean, after all, we're taking these out-of-town trips together." Loyalty fought her compulsion for candor, and candor backed down. "And it's just fine with me if they think that." He turned his head and gave her a conspiratorial smile.

225

Twenty-Two

"Matty, do you trust your memories?"

The Marston's housekeeper put down the towel she was folding and stared at Jolie. "Now that's a peculiar kind of question if ever I heard one. And wouldn't you know, you'd be just the child to ask it."

"Matty, I'm 36 now. I'm not a child."

"Whatever you say. *Child*." She grinned to herself as she picked up the towel again.

"Back to my question. Do you?"

"Do I what?"

"You know, trust your memories."

"I guess."

"You ever wonder if other people remember things the same way as you?"

"Nah. They're always getting it wrong."

***

"Hi, Nick."

"Hello, Jolie." His voice was flat.

"I just wondered how you're doing." Her call had more to do with a nagging question, but she felt obligated to ease into it. "What's new with you?"

"Not a lot. Why are you calling?"

So much for laying the groundwork. "There's something I have to ask you. Remember that night you gave me the heart-shaped box?"

"Why are you bringing this up?"

"Because I'm choosing to be irrational at the moment. So,

226

do you remember it?"

"Of course I do."

"Tell me everything you remember about it." When he hesitated, she said, "Look, I'm not after emotional confessions. I just want to know the facts of what you remember."

"What the hell for?"

"It's a project I'm working on. Just for me."

"This is bizarre. You dumped me, remember?"

"Please."

He sighed. "We had dinner at some Asian place out east. Then we went back to your apartment. You opened the box. It was made of some kind of wood. And I'd put this silk scarf inside, because you loved silk scarves."

"What else?"

"That's about it. Besides the lovemaking. But I suppose you want to forget that."

She ignored the jibe. "What was I wearing?"

"You really expect me to remember that?"

"I mean, when we made love. What was I wearing?"

"Nothing. That *is* the usual uniform."

"So that's the way you remember the evening."

"No, I made it all up. Of course, that's the way I remember it."

"For one thing, the box was papier mâché not wood. How could you think it was wood? And we ate ribs at the Rendevous. You're not even in the right part of town." She heard the sharpness in her voice. "And I wasn't bare naked when we made love. I wore the scarf. I thought for sure you'd remember that."

"What does it matter?"

"I just want you to remember it correctly, okay?"

"Who says your memory of that night is more accurate than mine?"

"I have the box!"

"And I suppose you have the tab from the Rendevous and a photo of us making love while you wore the damn scarf?"

Why was she ruining this memory? What did it matter?

Nick said, "This is an inane conversation."

She couldn't argue with him about that.

Twenty-Three

To hell with her promise. Jolie couldn't let what had happened to Ellis's only child go—that was all there was to it.

On this humid June night, she had worried herself awake around three. She lay there now, the sheet clammy underneath her sweaty body. The cottage had only a window air conditioner, and that was in the living room. She didn't feel like getting up to turn on the ceiling fan.

Ellis had been right. Jerome Daunton's prostitution ring must be broken. That was the only way to protect Rebecca and give her a shot at an independent life.

But why should she be the one to try to save her? It kept coming back to an image of a six-year-old in a frilly pink dress, heart newly broken by a father. To an image of a face swollen and bruised in a hospital bed.

Still, Jolie knew these images, poignant though they might be, fell short. Yes, she wanted to see Rebecca free to live her own life, but truth is, Rebecca probably wouldn't spend twenty seconds worrying over Jolie's fate in any situation. She hardly seemed to spend that fretting over her own.

Jolie's reasons were complicated, bound up in her fondness and, yes, love for Ellis Standifer. Although he might have been a lousy father, he had been a great father figure to her. Ellis had befriended her, helped her and never failed to be there when it was sharp-eyed wisdom she'd needed. She wondered now if his affection for her would've gone to Rebecca instead, had circumstances been very different. Whatever the case, wouldn't she be failing him if she didn't now try her damnedest to complete what he'd started?

She rolled over and sat up on her elbow. Wouldn't he tell

her to stay out of this, that it couldn't be done, that she would only put herself in harm's way? Maybe. Nonetheless, he'd be proud of her for trying, in spite of his caution. Or at least that's what she decided to tell herself now.

Maybe Ellis's wasn't the only case of transference. As long as she was wallowing in psychobabble, shouldn't she explore whether her quest was because she could no longer right wrongs—or pretend she did—through her job? What exactly did she need to prove?

She rubbed her face hard against the damp sheet as if to wipe away her doubts. First light began to eke into the room. It wasn't in her to do nothing, that's all, it just wasn't in her. If other, maybe less noble reasons lurked, she didn't want to dwell on them.

She thumped her feet on the floor, went downstairs and began making notes. As she slugged back coffee and smoked, the excitement of pursuing a story coursed through her once more. By seven, her plan was in place.

One step of it remained in question. Should she bother pitching the story to her nemesis at WTNW? Why give Brad Delano anything? Halfway through her third cup, she figured she would never have a better way to one-up her ex-boss.

Of course, she wouldn't get any credit, but she'd have the satisfaction of showing Brad that even out of the newsroom and out of town, she could do the story he wouldn't let her cover.

She'd keep Rebecca out of this. This was a story ready and waiting for anyone who put in the effort, and she could lead them to all the keyholes without leading them to the room that held Rebecca.

When Jolie rang the newsroom, she didn't identify herself to the woman who yelled "News" into the receiver, but she didn't need to. It was the practice of newsrooms never to ask who was calling. She thought it was Geena with a cold who answered, but perhaps it was someone new.

As she waited for Brad to pick up, a tingle ran through her. He wouldn't welcome the sound of her voice, but he'd damn sure welcome her story. And he just might regret firing her, even though he'd never acknowledge it.

"Delano."

"It's Jolie."

Silence at the other end. After a moment, she spoke again. "I'm calling because I have a helluva story for you. Right there in River City."

"Sure you do."

"Do you want to listen to me or not? Because if you don't, I can call one of the other stations. And this is one juicy tale."

"Hold on." She heard him slam his office door, heard the familiar moan of his chair as he sat back down. "I'm listening."

She told him about the prostitution ring fronted by Jerome Daunton's legitimate Anthem Answering Service. She told him about Ellis Standifer's attempts to shut him down and about the current policy of toleration under Howard Farrell. She told him she'd made contact with two of the women working for Jerome, had even had lunch with one of them. Very classy lady. Now a very sore lady lying in a hospital bed. No, she wouldn't give names. But Jerome Daunton definitely should be a suspect in Ellis Standifer's murder.

By the end of the conversation, Brad's tone was almost friendly as he thanked her. "But," he said, "I have to ask why you brought this to me?"

"Because I know a great story. And you know I do. You've gotta give me that."

***

Two days later, Brad called back. "Look, I took the story to

Trousdale since it could take us out on a limb."

"And."

"He doesn't want to do the story."

"That's ridiculous! And Top Dog's reason would be…?"

"He said it wasn't worth the legal bills."

"Bull. Top Dog's probably humping Daunton's women and doesn't want to mess up his good thing. What do you think? Don't you think it's worth pursuing?"

"It doesn't matter what I think. Trousdale made it very clear he wants nothing to do with the story. If it even is a story."

"What do you mean, 'if'? You know it's at least worth checking out. At the very least. C'mon. Challenge him."

"Still the same old Jolie, aren't you? I figured you'd have learned by now."

"Learned what? To be a kiss-ass sycophant? Oh, sorry, I'm being redundant in describing you, aren't I?"

The phone slammed in her ear.

***

By the end of the week, she'd heard much the same from the other stations in Memphis.

On the back porch of her rental cottage, the morning sun already had heated the earth. She threw her feet up on the railing and parked her elbows on the wide-armed chair.

When had the porch gotten so filthy? The floor planks had a thin layer of dirt. Overhead, cobwebs clung to the eaves. She went inside for a broom and came out swinging. As she swept, she thought.

That afternoon she placed small ads for her video business in the newspapers of nearby towns and enlarged the one running in the Singleton paper. All included online ads for the same price. She called video production companies in Chattanooga and Knoxville, each an hour away, and pitched her talents. She put on lipstick and made the rounds of stores in town to see if any needed more brochures. Only the children's clothing store did.

***

The idea struck Jolie the next day as she leaned down to pick up the local newspaper from her front porch. Forget TV. John Beck, the investigative reporter at *The Commercial Appeal*, was dogged, talented and as best she could tell, fearless. She hadn't seen him since running into him downstairs at Automatic Slim's the night of Ellis's birthday party. From that exchange, she guessed he wouldn't mind hearing from her now.

During his tenure at the Memphis newspaper, John had won awards and built a reputation as relentless and exacting. The grudging respect he'd always shown her probably had increased after her explosion and firing.

John Beck also was ambitious, and Jolie needed ambition on this story. Raw ambition that didn't stop too long to assess the risks. He'd come down from the Midwest three years earlier and was in Memphis only until he could land a job someplace larger.

He returned her call that afternoon. "I've missed seeing you around our merry little crime scenes. Missed that Lauren Bacall voice of yours too. Where are you these days anyway?"

"Back in east Tennessee. Singleton."

"Isn't that the little town that brought forth you and Ellis Standifer? Don't tell me you're living there."

"Got my own little production company," she said with what she hoped sounded like pride. "It's going okay."

"Really." He sounded unconvinced. "What's up?"

She repeated the story she'd told all three Memphis TV

newsrooms by now, but on this go-round she caught a decided difference in her listener. She knew from his questions she had him hooked.

"So," John said, "you going to come into town and help me out on this?"

From their half-flirtatious exchanges in the past, she guessed this was a come-on. He was cute in an arrogant sort of way. It would be fun to work with him, even though he might regard her as little more than his gofer because she came from TV, not a newspaper.

If the story got a big spread in the city's most influential newspaper, Farrell's office couldn't ignore it. Daunton surely wouldn't dare to hurt Rebecca after he was exposed. Ellis's mistake, Jolie decided, was in failing to line up the power of the news media before he went after Daunton. He might have been mayor, but he'd been too quiet about his efforts. She would play it smarter.

***

Charlotte wound silver ribbon around white wrapping paper.

Jolie sat beside her mom at her parent's dining room table, watching the expert fingers. "Who's the gift for?"

"Beth Smith's daughter Karen is getting married. She's probably too young for you to know." Charlotte gave one end of the ribbon a twist with the scissors blade and watched with satisfaction as it spun into a tight curl. "I hope wedding presents will come your way one day soon."

"They did once, Mom, remember?"

"They did, didn't they? It's been so long, I almost forgot." She looked up and smiled sweetly, then began twisting the other end of ribbon. "Wonder what Rich is up to these days?"

"I don't know, Mom. Every week when I call my ex I forget to ask," Jolie said with all the sarcasm she could muster. She pushed back her chair. "I need to get over to Martin's."

"I think it's wonderful you and Martin are spending time together. Who knows where it might lead?"

"Who indeed."

***

"Do you want me to come along?" Martin asked when she told him about her plans to return to Memphis.

"Thanks, but I don't know how long I'll be there. Someone is letting me stay at her house."

She had called a Memphis friend, a guitar shop owner with a roomy old house. Jolie was relieved, first when Betsy Radcliff turned her down her offer of money and second when she told Jolie she'd be on vacation and could have the place to herself.

Twenty-Four

"You want to knock off for the night?" John Beck said in his Illinois-born nasality. He reached over and rubbed Jolie's tight shoulders. "Let's grab a couple of beers and shoot some pool."

She leaned back and pointed to the knot along her right shoulder blade. His short, squared fingers dug at it, kneaded its unyielding tension.

The two of them had been staring at computer screens from the *The Commercial Appeal's* in-house research library for five hours. They began their search by looking through files on Jerome Daunton and Anthem Answering Service. They found a blurb about Anthem moving into a new, larger building and another about Anthem winning a small business award. Not a smidgen of scandal anywhere. The stories on prostitution arrests proved equally unfruitful. In desperation, they began pulling up the paper's stories mentioning Ellis Standifer, and there were hundreds.

Yesterday they had stopped by the Tennessee State Patrol's local office to look at prostitution arrest records. Nothing listed for a Rebecca Folsom or a Monique, either as a single name or with any last name.

John planned to go by Anthem tomorrow to sign up for their answering service using a pseudonym. He would let it be known in a subtle but sure way he would like to meet women, being new in town.

"Aren't you worried you might be recognized?" Jolie asked.

He gave her a yeah-right look. "Newspaper faces aren't known all over town. We aren't *celebrities*. Besides, I'm

shaving off my mustache. And morning is haircut time."
"So despite your snide remark, you are concerned."

***

A half hour later, they entered a Midtown pub known for its microbrews on draft and antique billiard tables. After ordering pints of pale ale, they staked out a game table in a back corner.

Jolie racked the balls. John grabbed his stick and broke, landing the 6-ball in the far right pocket. As Jolie leaned over to line up her shot, aiming for the 3-ball to the center left pocket, he sidled up beside her.

She raised back. "Hey, no fair distracting the competition."

He moved away, hands held high. "I'll keep a fer piece away from ye now on, ma'am."

"No need to be *that* rash."

After she pocketed a crucial shot during the second game, John whispered into her thick hair. "I might have known you'd know how to knock balls around."

"You bet your ass I do."

Working alongside John got her adrenalin going, as did the playful tension when they weren't working. He was at least as good as his reputation. She liked to watch him work, watch him think though possibilities and ways to dig up more information. It was humbling being nothing more than his helpmate, but she reasoned it was a temporary situation for a good cause.

John had arranged for her to get a researcher's salary for a couple of weeks. Beyond that, he couldn't promise anything. She knew he wouldn't use her much beyond that anyway. This was his story now. She might have brought it to him, she might have helped him, but it would be his name on the byline. No way he'd share the glory of what could go into competition for a Pulitzer, what might land him that NY or LA job.

After two more games of pool, he walked to the jukebox and popped in several coins. "Lost in the Ozone Again," a decades-old song by Commander Cody and the Lost Planet Airmen, began to blare. Good, he was cool about music. He reached for her hand and pulled her onto the ten square feet of parquet allotted for a dance floor.

John danced with an energetic grace that astonished her. "Hey," she said over the music, "I thought all the good dancers were in TV news. You know, where all the exhibitionists hang out."

They danced a sexed-up jitterbug, touching often. When the next song, Otis Redding's "Try a Little Tenderness" began, he moved close and ran his hand slowly up and down her spine. She leaned her face into the crook of his neck, and her lips felt his skin, damp and salty from dancing. While his scent didn't have Nick's unexpected earthiness, it was undeniably male. She smiled into the moist skin. What a sucker she was for a man's smell.

Even so, she didn't know that she particularly liked John Beck. After working beside him for three days, she had discovered he was even more arrogant than she'd assumed. Every other sentence began with "I," and rarely did he show concern for her. But there was the adrenalin.

She studied him as they spun around. His brown hair grew thinly from his broad forehead in a nondescript way. His mustache had a lively reddish cast. (She'd be sorry to see that go.) He had a newspaperman's physique, not bad but one that had seen too much of a desk and not enough of a weight room. She suspected he prided himself on that. Let the TV *celebrities* be hardbodies. Most of all, he had a presence that said, I'm someone to be reckoned with.

When Robbie Robertson's "Crazy River" came on next, they improvised a snaky crawl to the steeped-in-the-bayou sounds. He stood close behind her, his hands around her hips.

Jolie knew John wasn't surprised when she went home with him that night.

When they arrived at his place, he put on David Sanborn and turned out the lights. The jazzman's alto sax wailed as they danced, laughing as they groped to find each other until their eyes adjusted to the dark. They swayed and touched, twirled and wound around each other. She licked the cool sweat from between his breastbone. He leaned back and put his hands behind his head, reveling in her attentions.

Before the third cut of Sanborn, they were dancing naked.

***

Jolie's stomach growled when she awakened to a bed John already had left. The comforting aroma of coffee filled the air. She slid from the covers, washed her face, and rubbed toothpaste around her mouth with her forefinger. When she leaned over and spat out the sweetish green remnants of paste, she found herself only inches from a layer of grime scaling the sink.

The only washcloth she could find for a shower lay in a corner by the toilet, hardened and reeking of mildew. She would do without. As she opened the shower curtain, she encountered a ring of slime around the tub and a tangle of hair in the drain. She yanked the curtain closed.

In the kitchen, a harsh string of overhead fluorescents cast a rude clarity on the morning. John faced away, digging in a chaotic utensil drawer. Metal clanged on metal. She looked around at the precarious stacks of dirty dishes in the sink, the empty cans and bottles on the counter.

"Jesus, John, why don't you hire a housecleaner?" she said. "I know you make enough."

"Good morning to you, too. Are you always this pleasant before breakfast?"

"Sorry." She extended her hands in a gesture of apology. "I know. I don't live here. It's not my apartment."

"I guess it's just not something I notice," he said with a touch of defensive pride. He nodded toward the coffeemaker. "Want a cup?"

"Sure." She poured coffee into a chipped mug and walked up to him. "I want to see this face." He'd shaved off the mustache. "You really look different. It always dumbfounds me how little it takes to change a man's looks."

"Wait until I get my hair cut. And add these." From his shirt pocket, he removed a pair of black, squarish glasses and put them on."

Jolie smiled at him. "You say your last job was being a Buddy Holly impersonator?" She spotted a Snickers bar lying on the counter, unwrapped it, and began munching.

"I've been thinking about this story all morning," John said.

"And?"

"I need this girl Monique. Rebecca. Whatever you want to call her, the story's got to have her."

"You won't get her," she said around a lump of chocolate. "She won't talk."

"You're sure she's out of the hospital?" John asked. "I could get to her there."

"I'm sure. She left." Jolie had called the hospital a couple of times. The first time a nurse on the floor said she was improving—that had been two days after Jolie's visit—and the second time, a day later, a different nurse said she'd checked out that morning.

"Then how do I get in touch with her?"

"We've been over this before, John. You don't. She told

240

me to stay away. I promised her I would."

John stared at her. "I didn't promise."

"I can't, John."

"Why can't you?"

"I don't want to see her hurt again. If Daunton thinks she's still talking to me, God knows what he'll do to her. I'm the reason she ended up in the hospital, remember?"

"So? You stay out of it. Just give me the number or address or whatever you have, and I'll handle this on my own. Daunton will never know, so she'll be fine. I won't even mention your name to her."

"As if she couldn't figure that one out. She's smart, my friend. Way too smart for what she's doing with her life." She tore off another bite of Snickers.

"What's so wrong with what she's doing? I never understood why the world's oldest profession has to get such a bad rap."

"It's the system that sucks," Jolie said. "Johns get off, pimps get rich, and women like Rebecca get pummeled."

"But you told me she likes her work."

"At least that's what she tells herself. I'm not convinced." She refilled her mug. "If she were working entirely for herself, I wouldn't care. She'd be running her own show—a pretty distasteful one considering you can't be too choosy—but at least she'd be hanging onto all the bucks her back earns her."

"Then, dammit, help me do something about it."

"I'm trying," she said. "It bugs hell out of me that her pimp could very well be guilty of murdering Standifer. You should go after that instead of trying to cajole me into handing you Rebecca." She stuffed the last of the candy bar into her mouth.

"You know as well as I do that the cops don't have solid leads on anybody. And they can't arrest Jerome Daunton just because it would be convenient if he'd done it. Besides, you told me it could be a jealous husband or Standifer's gambling that did him in." He walked over and looked in her eyes. He lifted a hand to stroke the curve of her cheek with his forefinger. "Help me out here, please. We both want the same thing, Jolie. This is a dynamite story, and you know it or you wouldn't have sought me out in the first place. I'm damn glad you did, but don't abandon me now. I need your cooperation all the way if I'm ever to expose Daunton, and I need Rebecca's story. We're hitting dead ends, and you know it."

She looked away.

He gently turned her face back to his. "Help me expose Daunton to help Rebecca. Get him in jail and get her out from under his thumb. We'd be doing it for her sake."

"That's what I've tried to tell myself. I'm not always convinced." She studied John's eager face. "You can do this story without her if we just keep digging, do more research. You don't have to have her to tell it."

He crossed his arms over his chest but remained standing close. "C'mon now. Think. What research? Are we going to go out on the street and start interviewing men until we get one who'll lead us to Daunton?"

"You're smart," she said. "You'll figure out something. Signing up at Anthem will help."

John settled into his stance. "Let's say you're doing this story all by yourself, and you can get an interview with a hooker who is the former mayor's illegitimate daughter and who now works for a supposedly upstanding businessman who—surprise, surprise—turns out to be the city's major pimp. You can't get an interview with the former mayor, he's been murdered. The pimp isn't about to talk, and the johns aren't too verbose either. What would you do?"

She waved him away. "I don't want to see her hurt."

"Then help me nail Daunton." He unfolded his arms, put

them on her shoulders and begin kneading.

Jolie saw through his manipulations. She'd be doing exactly the same thing in his place.

He kissed her lips lightly. "Please," he said as she leaned back. "It comes down to you. You know we've got a dynamite story. If."

She pushed him away. "Persuasion's not going to do it, John." She gingerly added her cup to the pile in the sink, retrieved her purse from a living room chair, and slung it over her shoulder. "I'm heading out for a while. Half an hour, an hour. I don't know."

"I'm leaving for my haircut," he said, "but I'll be back here soon, around ten. If you come back before then, use this." He flipped her a spare key.

***

Once in the street, she breathed deeply and took in her surroundings. John lived in a tree-shaded part of Midtown known as Cooper-Young. Here, ample two-story homes mixed with modest bungalows and trendy restaurants. John lived on the second story of one of the more spacious houses.

Half a block away, a lawnmower rumbled. The sharp scent of cut grass filled her nostrils as she walked along a sidewalk humped by tree roots.

Ten minutes later, she'd left Cooper-Young and stood at the entrance to Overton Park, a massive stretch of woods and fields. She made sure to stay within sight of a group of guys playing soccer. The justified buzz described Overton Park as a place for men to pick up men, but she also knew of a few murders and rapes in this seemingly bucolic park.

Vast cumulus clouds floated beneath a vivid blue backdrop. Although the solstice wouldn't officially arrive for another week, the heat and humidity declared summer long ago here. She already was growing warm in last night's jeans. But she opted not to leave the open sunshine for the shade of the woods. In the open, there should be no threat of harm for a woman alone. She felt a sudden appreciation for the woods around her rental house where she felt safe roaming. Jolie walked in a wide circle around the soccer players, and then paced back and forth before plopping on the grass. She ran her hand across the soft top of a dandelion bloom.

It wasn't as if Rebecca wanted her help. What right did Jolie have to break her promise and interfere again? And if for any reason Daunton should find out, what then?

No, she couldn't risk it. She couldn't risk putting Rebecca in danger again.

A fly landed on her sweaty arm, and she swatted it away.

Still, if a humdinger of an exposé could lead to Jerome Daunton's downfall, the risk would be worth it. And there might never be as good a chance to dethrone him as she had now with John Beck.

If they brought Daunton's operation into the public eye, the men who could afford his high-class roster would no longer dare to associate with him for fear of their own exposure. He'd have to lie low or leave town. That could give Rebecca her opportunity to break free. What she did with that freedom wasn't Jolie's business.

The soccer players whooped as one side kicked the ball past a startled goalie.

The conclusion was as distasteful as it was obvious. John needed to talk to Rebecca. She had blithely assumed it wouldn't come to this, ignored the likelihood that it would. But she now saw no other way to pull the story together.

He wouldn't have to use Rebecca's name. He might not even need to say she was Ellis Standifer's illegitimate child, although Jolie knew it would be a fight to keep John or his editors from using such a juicy description. He wouldn't have to have her photograph, but he needed her quotes. Maybe there was no way to talk Rebecca into giving them. Still, Jolie had to try.

A few freckles had popped out on her pale skin by the time she rose and began the walk back to John's.

***

"Okay, I've thought about it," Jolie announced when John answered her knock. His close-trimmed cut, coupled with the erasure of the mustache, made him seem like someone other than the man she'd made love with last night. She walked to a sofa piled with newspapers and cleared space to sit. "One condition."

"Which is."

"*I'll* call her. I'll be the one to see if I can set something up."

"Fine," he said carefully. "But I thought you wanted to stay out of it."

She kicked her heels against the carpet. "That's chicken. That's deceiving her."

He looked at her and nodded slowly. "If you'd call her for me, that would be great."

She pulled out her cell phone. "Let's get this over with."

"Hello," said a sleepy voice.

"Hi, Rebecca, this is...please don't hang up on me, please don't...this is Jolie."

"I told you..."

There was no distortion in her speech now. Jolie liked to imagine the bruises had vanished without a trace. "I know you did. I know. And I don't ever want to see you hurt again. But

245

this is really important. I need to see you. Or, at least, I need to have you see someone. This could mean your freedom, Rebecca, especially with the boost from the money Violet left you."

"Why do you have it in your head that it's your job to rescue me?"

"Because you're not crazy enough to want to work for Jerome any more."

"So, what, you're going to be my new manager?" Her tone was icy.

"I just want you to talk to someone. That's all. Anywhere you like."

"I told you. Leave me alone."

Jolie put down the dead phone. "I've got her address," she said to John. "Maybe if I talk to her in person and if she sees you, maybe then."

***

After John left to sign up for Anthem's message service, Jolie washed dishes and cleared the counters. While she was philosophically opposed to cleaning up after men, she needed something to occupy her time. Besides, his mess drove her crazy.

"So," he said when he returned, "that's what color the counter is. Thanks."

"I had to do something with myself. How did it go with Daunton?"

"It didn't. A receptionist, a fetching blonde one, I might add, told me he's out of town. But I made an appointment to meet with him day after tomorrow." He opened the refrigerator and grabbed two cans of cola. He tossed one to her. "Let's go find your friend."

Twenty-Five

Jolie and John said little to each other on the drive to Rebecca's house in John's 1959 Ford Fairlane. Last night she had thought the car was cool. Today it just seemed like an act. She looked at John, intent on driving. She'd always thought he was cute, so what happened? But the whole world seemed disgusting this morning.

"Look, it's great that you're doing this," he said without taking his eyes from the road.

"And it's just dandy that you think so."

"No need to be nasty. I just want to say I appreciate your doing this."

"Rebecca's not likely to share your appreciation."

They were headed toward one of the newer and decidedly suburban parts of town. 1321 Lilac Lane, an address that had come from Annette.

John twisted the wide steering wheel hard to the right and pulled into a subdivision. On either corner stood a wood plank wall with wrought-iron lettering: Woods Meadows.

Jolie pointed toward the sign. "Where is the roomful of idiots who think up these names?"

Lilac Lane lay two streets down from the entrance and showed no trace either of woods or meadows. Instead, it displayed close-cut lawns and twiggy trees, neutral house colors and double garages that faced the street like angular snouts.

"By the way, how did you get her number and address?" John asked. "She give it to you?"

"Hardly. I noticed her vanity plate and used my connections to ferret out the rest."

He looked at her and nodded. "Good work."

"Oh, thank you, great newspaperman."

"Cut it out. So what did the plate say?"

"'You wish.'"

"C'mon, tell me."

"I just did. The plate says 'you wish.'"

He threw back his head and laughed. "I'm definitely looking forward to meeting this woman."

1321, when they came upon it, blended with its neighbors. A red brick facade halfway up, beige siding above that, cream shutters freshly painted. No vehicles to be seen.

"She drives a yellow Jag," Jolie said. "I'd keep mine in the garage too." She rubbed clammy palms against her jeans. "Park a couple of houses down, okay?"

John stood behind Jolie as she rang the doorbell. It gave a pleasant tinkle, as if nothing sinister ever could intrude. When they heard the high click of a woman's footsteps, they turned to each other, and John gave a broad smile. Jolie thought she could make out an eye coming up to the peephole, then moving away. *Please let us in.*

The varnished oak door opened slowly at first, then widened quickly as a woman with skin the color of Ivory soap and a head of mouse-brown curls beamed at them. "Aren't you Jolie Marston?"

Jolie stared at the woman. "You—yes, that's who I am. And you're…?"

"Well," she said in a sugary voice, "I'm Patsy Morris, don't you remember?"

At that moment, a cheerful, towheaded girl raced up, grabbed her mother's hand, and fixed her eyes on Jolie. The woman leaned down to her daughter. "It's Jolie Marston, Missy. You remember Jolie from the TV station?"

"I'm sorry," Jolie said, "but…"

"Oh, I don't know why I should expect you to remember

248

me." She giggled. "You must meet so many people. You did a story on my husband's ball team when they gave all those teddy bears to St. Jude's. Now you remember?"

"Yes, I remember now." Brad had sent her on the story because she was stalled on an investigative report until one of her contacts got back in town. Some slow-pitch men's softball league had donated a hundred teddy bears to the famous children's research hospital in town. She'd picked up a couple of soundbites and thrown the story together with little thought, her interest on hold for the pending story. Funny, she couldn't recall the bigger story.

The woman's girlish face looked slightly worried. "So what is it that brings you here now, honey?"

John spoke up. "Sorry, but we knocked on the wrong door. We must have a bad address."

"Oh, well, maybe I can help. What address is it y'all are looking for? This is 1321." She pointed to four-inch-high brass numbers near the door.

"Yes, we know," John said. "We must be on the wrong street."

"What street y'all looking for, honey?"

When John didn't answer, the woman turned to Jolie. "Y'all out on a story? I thought you'd left the station."

"Sorry about the wrong address," Jolie said. "Do you mind telling me how long you've lived here?"

"Oh, not long. We just moved in here two months ago."

"Really? Who'd you buy it from?"

"Fellow name of Gus something. Poor boy. He'd no more than moved in here than he got transferred out to Kansas and had to sell. Wouldn't that be just awful?"

"Did you ever meet a tall, nice-looking woman who lived here?"

"I never heard of anybody living here but that Gus fellow,

and I don't know who had it before him. Never even met Gus. He'd already packed up and left when we first looked at the place."

***

Jolie toyed with the paper wrapping on her corned beef sandwich. She and John had squeezed into the confines of a tiny corner deli downtown. "I'm stumped," she told him, "absolutely stumped. Any ideas?"

John chomped into a pastrami on rye before speaking. "I need to finish a piece on redevelopment in south Memphis," he mumbled through his food. "Tell me where you'll be about five, and I'll call you. I can't think about our next move until then."

She gave him the number at her friend's empty house where she was staying.

Because she could think of nothing else to do, she spent the afternoon back with the newspaper's archives, pulling up more online stories about Ellis Standifer. Nothing unfamiliar or remotely helpful came up.

She walked down a long corridor to a back door where the paper's smokers huddled. At the moment, only two male employees stood there, saying nothing after they'd greeted each other. After lighting up, Jolie strolled toward the front of the building and busy Union Avenue. Looking west, she could see downtown's collection of buildings—the banks, the restaurants, the hotels.

The hotels.

***

"Just the parking lots of the hotels," she told John. It was late afternoon, and they had settled into a couple of the battered

250

but comfy chairs at Betsy's, her temporary quarters. Four guitars and an upright bass were propped against a nearby wall. Betsy not only owned a music shop but was an adept musician herself.

Jolie grabbed a pen and paper from her purse. "Hotels and the motels nice enough to be promoted to motor inns. She must meet some of her johns in these places. We'll just have to wait and watch for her car."

They began a list of all the reasonable possibilities. "At least the car will be easy to spot," Jolie said.

"If she hasn't traded."

"So throw me a better idea if you don't like this one."

"I guess it's as good as anything."

"Damn right it is."

***

By eleven that night, they had driven through the parking lot of every hotel on the list. The above-ground lots were easy; those with garages required a tedious drive from floor to exhaust-choked floor. Still, they'd found no pale yellow Jaguar with a YOUWISH plate.

Figuring Rebecca worked late and slept late, they made one more round at the airport locations before calling it a night.

"So," John said as they began the drive back, "would you like to stay at my place again tonight?"

"I guess not." She yawned. "I'm beat. Thanks anyway."

They rode in silence most of the drive. As they neared the empty 1930's two-story that belonged to her friend, she turned to John. "I've got an idea that could work."

"We need one."

"Let's go in separate cars tomorrow. That way we can afford the time to stake these places out, to wait a few hours if

251

need be. That car is bound to show up sooner or later."

"Sounds boring as hell," John said, "but I'm willing to give it a try. For a while at least." He leaned forward as if to kiss her.

She pretended not to notice and hurried off.

***

Late the next morning, Jolie had stationed herself and her small blue convertible on the lot of a three-story chain hotel in east Memphis. John drove to a competitor not far away.

Every hour or so they checked in with each other. At two, he came by with sandwiches which they ate sitting on the curb, talking about strategies they'd come up with to pass the time. Both confessed to reading books held at eye level to notice anyone driving by.

At five p.m. and again at ten, they met for coffee.

"Too dark to read so I go for music," John said.

"Mouth-frothing talk radio for me," Jolie said. "That crap keeps me awake."

At midnight, they met for an ample breakfast at an all-night café close by on Poplar. Three hours later, they agreed by phone to wind things up for the night. Tomorrow they'd stake out two different hotels in the same part of the city. Jolie bid John goodbye and drove to Betsy's house, a welcome refuge while her friend was out of town.

***

By 3:30 the next afternoon, John's Fairlane was a moisture-laden oven. He reached for a handkerchief to wipe his face. He had grown tired of this stakeout, tired of the whole business. If they didn't get something solid by the end of the day, he was ready to talk about giving up, at least for now.

252

Just as he tucked the damp handkerchief back in his hip pocket, he saw it. The pale yellow Jaguar turned into the lot and rumbled slowly toward him. It took a moment before John had a clear view of the license plate. Sure enough. He sat up and craned his neck. Behind the wheel sat a light-skinned black woman wearing sunglasses. John leaned into the closed door of his car to keep from attracting attention as she drove past. He watched her pull into an open space four rows away. As soon as she did, he jumped out of his car and began walking toward the Jag.

The woman emerged and shut the car door. He quickened his pace and called out to her when he was only a few feet away. "Rebecca?"

She halted and looked his way.

In that brief moment, John took her in. Her lovely face, her spectacular long legs on five-inch heels. Rounded breasts beneath a low-cut blouse and a skirt that barely covered taut thighs. A full mouth gleaming with deep ruby lipstick. He realized he'd stopped breathing. He also realized she was waiting for him to speak.

"I'm John Beck," he said and extended his hand.

The hand that met his was limpid, a disappointment. It was as if she weren't really touching him.

"Could we talk a moment?" he said. "In your car maybe? Or mine? Anywhere's fine. Anywhere you like."

"Why not here?"

"Sure. Fine. Sure." He took a breath that shuddered through him and addressed the dark glasses. "I'm a reporter for the *The Commercial Appeal*."

She started to walk away. He stepped in front of her. "Please, just listen to me. I need to talk to you."

"Jolie Marston," she said. "She's the reason you're here, isn't she?"

"Yes, but she's just after what I'm after. This is a huge story, a monster story. We could put Jerome Daunton away for life. You'd be done with him. But it won't happen without you."

She pulled off her sunglasses and aimed golden eyes at him. "Then it won't happen."

"This could make you a free woman, don't you understand? They'll get that sleazebag Daunton on some federal rap and put you in the witness protection program."

"And give me plastic surgery so no one could recognize me. Maybe they could even turn me into a white woman. Wouldn't I be lucky then?"

"Please, listen to me. You could live anywhere you wanted, any way you wanted, and you'd have the money to do it." He wasn't sure if the particulars of his offer were true, but he thought it sounded convincing.

"How can you be this naive and be a reporter?"

He crossed his arms over his chest. "What are you saying?"

She turned to leave. He reached out and wrapped his hand around her upper arm. He tried to think what she meant, but all he could think was that he was touching her, he was touching her wet dream of a body. He loosened his grip but didn't remove his hand.

"You are such a boy." She jerked her arm away. "Leave me alone."

"I'm doing the story anyway. If you work with me, it can mean shutting down Daunton forever. No one will put you in the hospital again."

She opened her red lips wide and laughed at him. "I can't believe how stupid you are."

"Tell me," he urged. "Tell me what I'm stupid about."

"You'll figure it out, choirboy."

"Tell me. Tell me!"

"So you think your big newspaper's going to do an expose on Jerome, do you?"

"Of course they will, if I give them enough to make a story. They'll back me."

She shook her head. "So very naive."

"What? What are you trying to say? Quit taunting me and just tell me, dammit."

"How do you think Jerome got to be so powerful in this town? Not by contributing to United Way."

"Are you saying he has enough pull to stop a story on my paper?"

"*Your* paper." She gave him a disdainful look.

"What are you saying?"

She offered the suggestion of a smile and looked away.

"Talk to me. Please."

She put her sunglasses back on. "One night Jerome was in a very loquacious mood. We were sitting around his place, doing a little nose candy, and he started talking, bragging. Now I don't remember, if he said it was the publisher, editor or some big shot on the board. All I remember is he said he had some mucketymuck at your paper in place. That's the term he uses when he's talking about having somebody where he wants them. They're in place. And he's got somebody at *your* paper in place."

"Maybe it was just the cocaine talking. Maybe he was just trying to impress you."

"I can see you don't know Jerome."

"So what's he got on them?"

"What do you think? You do know what I do for a living, right, choirboy?"

"Of course I do. So you're saying Jerome's clients include—"

"You are so quick. She smirked. I'll bet you went all the

way through college."

He bit his upper lip. "Are you sure about the clients?"

"You might say I have personal knowledge. That's why I know there will never be a big story about Jerome. He's got too many of Memphis's upstanding people *in place*."

John leaned hard against the heated metal of the car behind him. "I suppose he has a lot of people with political power under his thumb too, or at least responsive to pressure?"

"From the mayor's office on down, choirboy. The ones he can't get with sex, he gets other ways. Money. Drugs sometimes. But mostly it's sex. Jerome is very fastidious about his business. He doesn't leave much to chance."

John stood there shaking his head.

"I knew you'd be surprised," she said. "Otherwise, you and Jolie wouldn't have made fools of yourselves trying to talk to me." She swatted, as if dismissing a fly. "Now go away. You've made me late." She spun on her tall heels and walked off in long, rapid strides.

***

Four cars away, a hefty man tilted back his head and dribbled the last of a Pepsi into his open mouth. He crushed the can, threw it on the floorboard, and swung open his car door.

John had jotted down only a few notes when he felt the tap on his shoulder through his car's open window. He looked up at a familiar beefy face under thinning blond hair.

As John saw it, Ed Dempsey was Farrell's flak catcher and flak giver. The deputy mayor protected his boss, did his dirty work, allowing Farrell to convey nothing but slick charm. John detested them both.

He'd spoken to Dempsey more than once. Their last conversation had been an acrimonious exchange over the mayor's push to replace a patch of green downtown with a parking lot.

Dempsey leaned fat, red hands on the sill. "What're you up to, sonny boy?" He spoke in a rough-edged voice.

God, he was tired of being called boy. "Nothing much. How about you, Mister Deputy Mayor?"

"Nothing much. Like you." He reached into his coat pocket and pulled out a toothpick. As he did so, he left his jacket open for a long moment.

John saw the pistol he was intended to see. "So, Dempsey, you going to tell me why you came over to say hello?"

Dempsey rolled the toothpick around his mouth with his tongue. "Now, let me think, why did I come all the way over here? Was it to tell you how much I like your new look, sonny boy?"

"You've been watching those 1940s movies again, haven't you, Dempsey? Take my advice, okay? Stay away from anything earlier than 1950. Doris Day did some nice things. *Pillow Talk*, *That Touch of Mink*. You should check them out."

Dempsey withdrew the toothpick, spat on it, and dropped it into John's lap. It landed in his crotch.

John glared up at him.

As Dempsey stared back, he pulled out another toothpick and planted it in his mouth. "Time to quit being a smart ass, Beck. Not that you know how to be anything else. But it's time to go on to some other story."

"Other than what?"

"Other than you know what."

"I don't know what you're talking about. Give me a clue."

Dempsey looked around before leaning in closer. John could smell onions and beer on his breath. "What's the matter, John boy, can't you get it for free?"

"Are you one of the guys Jerome Daunton has—what was

that term—in place?" John asked.

Without dislodging the toothpick, Dempsey spat again, this time on the Fairlane's door. The hit caused a faint sizzle against the hot metal. "Listen, I got no time to play games with you. You know damn well what I'm talking about. If you want to keep yourself in one piece and keep on turning out the lying crap you've been turning out for years, you'd better stay off this story. Stay away from that bitch Monique. And stay out of business that ain't your business." Dempsey threw the second toothpick on top of the first and walked off.

John watched the deputy mayor get in a white Lincoln and screech away. After his hands steadied, he tossed the toothpicks on the pavement and started the engine. He drove north, toward a county-owned expanse of land, forgetting all about the plan to meet Jolie at four for barbecue.

He parked alongside a lake and opened his car door but didn't get out. Three ducks swam in small circles on the smooth water. Otherwise, the place looked deserted. He switched off his cell phone without checking messages.

He'd had people ask him, beg him even, not to do certain stories, and he'd always ignored their pleas. But he'd never been threatened, and certainly not by someone as nasty and as close to the political center as Dempsey.

***

At 5:00, Jolie grew tired of waiting and took a table at Gridley's. After being handed a menu, she opened up the newspaper she had brought with her. John had the piece on south Memphis redevelopment and another about a risky bond rating for an outlying city. She read both, mostly to study more closely his writing style.

Jolie wondered what she might have covered if she had still

been reporting. Probably an arson fire in north Memphis that merited only four inches of copy on page three in the paper. No doubt, it was the much-hyped lead on WTNW if the crew got good flames.

Rich smells of pork and seasoned sauce wafted through the restaurant. She decided to order rather than hold out any longer for John. In a few minutes, a heaped plate of juicy ribs, cole slaw, and baked beans sat in front of her.

After she'd eaten, she called John again, her third try since she'd arrived at Gridley's. She left another message. Nothing she could do but wait. She purchased iced coffee to go and drove back to settle in for the evening's hotel stakeout.

Twenty-Six

By eight that night, Jolie gave up and left the lot of the Midtown hotel where she'd parked the past few hours. She had tried approximately 30 times to contact John in his car. Calling his home, she got only his voice mail. When she called the newspaper, they told her he hadn't been in since morning.

She drove back to east Memphis, to the hotel lot where she'd heard from him last, but she saw no sign of his Fairlane. She headed back west, to his Midtown apartment. Maybe calls there weren't getting through for some reason. As she drove, she called his number once more. Again the call didn't go through.

His car wasn't in sight when Jolie turned into his backyard drive. When she banged on his door, he didn't answer. Because she still had the key he'd given her, she went inside the dark apartment and walked through its high-ceilinged rooms, turning on lights and calling for him. Before leaving, she scribbled a note for him to call her at Betsy's. She placed it on the lap of a chair and moved the chair a few feet from his front door. Even in his messy apartment, he would see this.

On her way out, she thumped on the downstairs door hoping to ask the woman who lived there if she had seen him. No one answered.

She had grown weary of waiting for a yellow Jaguar to show up. Now she was stuck waiting for John too.

***

At Betsy's, Jolie showered and dried her hair, thankful that with Betsy out of town, she had nothing to explain to anyone.

She checked the phone for messages that might have come while the water and hair dryer were running. She told herself it would be silly to go back to John's. He'd see the note; when he got in, he would call.

From Betsy's bookshelves, she pulled out a biography of Robert Johnson, one of several books on famous guitarists on her shelves. Jolie nestled into a chintz-covered sofa in the living room. Later in the evening, she closed the book and turned on the local news.

One station led with its exclusive on a welfare fraud case, but the other two, including WTNW, led with the arson fire. Both newscasts displayed the requisite flames. A fire wasn't news on TV without flames. On WTNW, a reporter Jolie didn't recognize, a woman in her early twenties with a mound of dark hair, covered the story. Jolie wondered if she were looking at her replacement.

***

When she woke soon after two a.m., the TV still droned on. Even before she had fully regained consciousness, her stomach rumbled for food. She dragged herself up and forced her eyes open. With a start, she realized John still hadn't called.

Maybe this wasn't unusual behavior for him. Still, he'd been careful to call and meet as planned until their four o'clock appointment.

Considering the Fairlane's brakes, a wreck didn't seem unlikely. Should she be calling emergency rooms? The police? Not yet. Later if need be, but not yet.

She microwaved a turkey dinner from the freezer and watched CNN. Half an hour later, she climbed into bed with the hard-luck story of Robert Johnson.

Late the next morning, she emerged from a deep sleep,

groggy and hungry again. She called the paper. No, they hadn't seen John today.

After three pieces of toast, she put on shorts and a tee shirt and walked to the nearest newspaper stand. She wanted the print version to pore over for distraction. If she hadn't heard from John by noon, she'd make those unpleasant calls.

She sat at Betsy's kitchen table, a long expanse of well-nicked pine, and began to scan the paper's story on riverboat gambling. Several times, she caught herself staring at the words, her mind on John. The phone startled her when it finally rang.

"Hey. It's John." His voice was maddeningly casual.

"Where the hell are you?" She tossed aside the paper. "Why haven't you called?"

"I guess I should have."

"Damn right, you should have. So, what happened? Did you find Rebecca and decide to play john, John?"

"I really could do just fine without the sarcasm."

"Where are you?"

"Home."

"You just get there?"

"No. I slept here."

"You slept there! You had to see my note. And why didn't you answer when I called?"

"Sorry. I needed time to think."

Was he talking about their relationship? Did he imagine they were getting involved? "Think about what?"

"This story."

She felt relief, but it didn't last long. "What about this story?"

"I, well, I don't think we have enough here."

"We'll find Rebecca, John. If we keep digging hard enough, we'll track her down."

"I think we should talk."

262

She lit a cigarette and blew out the smoke between nearly clenched teeth. "I don't like the sound of this." When he didn't answer, she said, "You want to meet somewhere or what?"

"The phone's good enough." He paused. "I've met Rebecca." He told Jolie about his encounter with her.

Jolie speculated with John on who those people Jerome Daunton had in place might be. When she thought he had told her everything, she was more confused than ever about why he'd want to drop the story. Then he told her about Dempsey.

"Oh, shit." She rose from the table, gripping the phone. "You're not going to let him scare you off, are you? That only makes the story stronger."

"Is that how you read it?" John said. "I've had a lot of time to think about what that Neanderthal said to me. I spent last night thinking about nothing else. I'm wondering if Dempsey doesn't get a cut of Daunton's earnings. After all, he used to head vice, so he's had plenty of opportunity to get his nose dirty. He sure as hell has some reason he wants me off this story. If he has his hands in Daunton's pie, fine. I'm not willing to get killed or even battered and bruised over it. As I said, I never was against prostitution in the first place."

"Dammit, John!"

"Jolie, it's crazy to pursue this. Why can't you let it go?"

"Because it's something Ellis started that I can finish for him, that he can't finish. I owe him that. And his mother."

"Well, I don't owe Ellis Standifer or his mother a thing. They're dead, Jolie. And aren't you forgetting the reason Ellis can't finish is because somebody murdered him? Very possibly because of what he started?"

"But I'm doing it the right way. They wouldn't dare hurt one of us. I've talked to too many people now—people in news—people in homicide. They wouldn't dare."

"There are terrible fates that fall short of murder, you

know."

"I'm telling you, nobody's going to hurt us. Don't go squeamish on me."

"Get off my back, okay? It wasn't you who was shown a gun and threatened by the mayor's right-hand goon."

"At the least," Jolie said, "you've got to slap charges on Dempsey. You can't let him intimidate you like that. Who's your editor? I'll go talk to him."

"Forget about it, Jolie. Go on back home to your east Tennessee hills and forget about it."

"I said, who's your editor? It's not as if I can't find out quick enough, so just tell me."

"You're wasting your time."

Without waiting for an answer, she grabbed the newspaper again and found the listing she wanted. "Mike Jantsen. He's your immediate boss, right?"

"Look, it's pointless to contact him."

"Why? Is he chicken too?"

"Up yours. Mike's a pro. Of course, as a TV *personality* you might not know about that. But I also can tell you he has two girls in college. He can't afford to get killed or lose his job over any story, and I don't blame him."

***

An hour later, Jolie sat in Mike Jantsen's immaculate office. She hadn't thought there was such a thing as a tidy newspaper editor. Jantsen was making nice so far, inviting her in a gentle voice to take a seat, offering her coffee. On the credenza behind his desk, she noticed photos of his wife and the two college-age daughters John had mentioned.

Mike Jantsen did not strike Jolie as a man who'd risk much of anything for a story. Still, she presented her evidence. He listened with hands folded on his desk, only interrupting once or twice to clarify something.

"That's pretty much it," Jolie said when she'd finished. "But it's plenty for a story, wouldn't you say?"

Mike Jantsen leaned back and rocked his chair several times before answering. "John called me a little while ago," he said quietly, "so a lot of what you told me is a repeat of what he said."

"So what's your verdict?"

He leaned farther back, stretched his arms forward to touch the edge of his desk, and rocked twice more. "I think this Rebecca-Monique character is setting you up." His chair leaned toward the desk, and he grabbed the desk's edge. "I think—"

"But doesn't the fact that John got threatened prove she wasn't?"

He held up his hand. "I heard you out. Now please hear me out. Dempsey didn't hold a gun to John's head. John just happened to see the gun. I spoke with the mayor's office right after John called. Granted, Howard Farrell isn't the most upstanding of men, and his administration isn't filled with saints, but he promised me he'd talk with Dempsey. Said Dempsey's carried a grudge against John ever since John did a series on the vice squad back when Dempsey ran it. Maybe you don't remember, but he headed it for a few years."

"I remember. I reported news for years in this city. Remember?"

"Oh, yes. Excuse me." If there was irony in his tone, it lay well hidden. "The major point is this," he said. "It isn't news that prostitutes operate in this town. Prostitutes operate in every town. It would be news only if they didn't. The gift from Ellis's mother does make Rebecca, Monique, whatever you choose to call her, a little more credible if the story is that she's his daughter. But do we really want to besmirch the name of a well-respected man just to announce he had an illegitimate daughter? He was no longer in public office, and he's dead now. What does it matter? Although it might seem as if all news people are panting to print or air salacious stories, that's not true in every case."

"You don't think his death is tied into this some way?"

The chair started to rock again. "I spoke with homicide about that after I talked with Farrell. Plonski…no doubt you remember him…said they're pursuing every lead as to a possible killer including this supposed daughter of his. He did tell me off the record…and I won't print this until we have more, because I respected Ellis, and I respect the rules of journalism…that there could be a Nashville connection. It seems there was a married woman."

"Mary Ellen Hargrove. But there's more at stake for Daunton and Dempsey."

"That's a matter of opinion. Plonski thinks, and I agree, that this Rebecca woman might very well turn out to be nothing more than an annoying sideliner. The term he used was 'a gnat.'" He leaned forward and stopped rocking. "So you can see, we don't have much. And I'm certainly not going to put John in harm's way."

"I thought you said he wasn't really threatened."

She noticed the smallest tightening of his facial muscles. "I doubt that he was," Jantsen said. "But Dempsey is known for having a short fuse. I don't want to see him throw a punch or two at John. That's what I meant."

"If he has a short fuse, then—"

"John has one too. I wouldn't put it past John to say something that provoked whatever Dempsey might have said to him." He stood up and walked around toward her, his hand outstretched. "Thanks for coming by. It must be frustrating to be out of the news loop after all these years."

"That's not why I'm here."

"Thank you for coming by," he repeated calmly as he opened the office door.

***

Rebecca gripped the end of the narrow rubber hose between her teeth and tightened the circle around her thin biceps. She eased the needle into the pale cocoa of her skin and waited. Waited for the rush of well-being, for the sure and lovely serenity and the oblivion that followed.

The wiry woman who had sold her the packet stood ten feet away in a corner, half hidden in the dim cavern of the vacant building. A fat rat scurried along a side wall. Rebecca eased down on the plunger.

Her eyes flew open as a steel wall slammed into her at a thousand miles a minute. The force yanked her forward, then thrust her back and froze the beating of her heart.

The woman pursed her lips and kept watch. After a couple of minutes, she scuttled over, hiked up her ragged cotton skirt, and leaned down. Beneath the velvety skin on the inside of the wrist, nothing throbbed. No life came from the startled gold eyes. The woman clucked her tongue. Such a pretty one. She walked into the empty hallway and counted again the wad of hundred dollar bills Ed Dempsey had pressed into her palm a few hours ago.

Twenty-Seven

Two thoughts fought for attention. Rebecca was dead, and Jolie herself might be to blame. God, she was tired of people dying. Her hand trembled as she struck a match and held a cigarette to her lips until its tip flamed red.

She had returned only a few hours ago from Memphis, had just finished unpacking, when the call came. At the other end she heard the nasal twang of the woman who had first put her in touch with Rebecca.

"I just hope you're happy," the woman had said.

"Why? What?"

"She's dead. You done got her killed."

Jolie jumped up from the couch. "Who?"

"You know who."

"Not Rebecca?"

"Who the hell you think I'm talking about?"

"No. No! God no!"

"I just hope you're satisfied."

"What are you saying? How was she killed?"

"Everybody's gonna say OD. But she wasn't no OD. She was always careful."

"Are you telling me Rebecca was a junkie?" Jolie couldn't envision a needle in those graceful arms.

"She used, but she was careful. Snorted it lots of the time." The woman paused. "Well, she sure ain't using any more."

"You said she died of an overdose?"

"So they'll say. Made to look like one, you ask me."

"Who do you think killed her?"

"I ain't about to speculate on that even if I might have a good idea."

"Jerome Daunton?"

"I said I ain't saying nothing. Except this. Why did you have to go poking your nose in her life? It wasn't none of your damn business!" Sobs interrupted the rage. "I thought I was helping her out when I called you that first time, thought I was gonna get her some money she wouldn't have to account to no one for. It would've been enough for her to get away somewhere for a while, maybe get away from the heroin too. That's what she'd talked about. Instead, all I did was get her connected up to you and your damn poking around."

"I never meant for anything like this to happen," Jolie said. "Never." She rubbed her forehead hard with the back of her fist. "I wanted to see her free of Jerome too. I wanted her not to have to be beholden to a thug."

"Well, she ain't any more."

"I'm so, so sorry." Jolie slumped against the wall. "When did this happen?"

"Last night sometime, looks like. Didn't nobody find her 'til this morning."

"Do they know who gave her the heroin?"

The woman gave a short, sharp laugh.

"I mean, are they even investigating?"

"Didn't I tell you? They're saying it's just another junkie OD. Got no reason to think anything else, they say."

"What else? What else can you tell me?"

"Ain't no more to tell, now is there?"

"Well, where? Where did they find her?"

"Some building that'd been standing empty for a while. Couple of drunks found her."

"What else?"

"Nothing else. I done told you everything. I just wanted you to see what you and your snooping and prying has led to."

In a few minutes, Jolie was on the phone to Plonski. His

269

worn-out voice seemed to know a call, any call, rarely meant anything he'd want to hear.

She told him what she'd learned about Rebecca's death. "So that's why I don't think it was a typical OD. She was always really careful."

"Jolie, there's no such thing as a careful junkie."

"But this friend of hers said—"

"This friend who's also a hooker?"

"Well, probably, but…" She tried another tactic, feeling ridiculous. "Can't you at least check into it?"

"I already have. I got a call when they figured out who she was. She had plenty of track marks on those pretty arms. And those were her fingerprints on the syringe. Believe me, there wasn't a damn thing to indicate this was anything other than one more junkie overestimating the load. It fits. Vice tells me there's some very potent stuff on the streets right now."

Were those some of Ed Dempsey's former lackeys telling him that? "Did you know Ed Dempsey threatened John Beck, the *The Commercial Appeal* reporter?"

"What do you mean 'threatened'?" His voice showed little interest.

Jolie suspected there wasn't a thing she could say that would extract curiosity from this man. "Dempsey didn't exactly pull a gun on John, but he showed him one. He told John to back off a story the two of us were working on."

"What story?"

"One that would expose what's behind Jerome Daunton's answering service."

"Did Beck file a complaint?"

"No."

"And what evidence do you have about this Daunton thing?"

"Not that much so far, but…" But the story was probably as

270

dead as Rebecca without her to help tell it. She told Plonski what she knew, but he voiced little surprise.

"Daunton probably supports Farrell in a big way at election time," Plonski said. "Dempsey's just watching out for him is my guess."

"But what about Daunton being a pimp?"

"I heard a rumor like that. But that's vice's job to pursue. I got my hands full here without bothering with who's poking who. Memphis isn't exactly the quietest town in Tennessee, you know. Folks do tend to kill each other. And I'm paid to pay attention when they do."

One more call needed to be made. John answered on the third ring.

"I really am sorry," he said when she had told him about Rebecca. "But if she got killed because she knew too much, that just hardens my determination to stay the hell off this story. If she simply died of an overdose—which is exactly what I suspect—then it makes her claims all the more unreliable. Either way, I've got an editor who just dumped two stories on me with absurdly short deadlines."

"Will you at least file a complaint on Dempsey? Tell them he threatened you?"

"Maybe he was just showing off."

"You know better than that!"

"Do I? Give it up, Jolie."

She didn't answer.

"If," John said, "they had come back with a report saying her death looked suspicious, I'd dog this story. But they didn't. For chrissakes, you've got the head of homicide saying nothing like that happened. What more do you need?"

"You're wimping out, John."

"I'd call it exercising judgment."

"I'd call it cowardice."

271

"You know, Jolie, you shouldn't have blown the money your mother gave you for charm school."

"Up your chicken ass."

***

The Commercial Appeal dismissed Rebecca Folsom's death with an ordinary and brief listing in the obituary column. The notice made no mention of the cause of death. Nor did it mention a father.

Twenty-Eight

"Hello." Martin called out from behind the raised hood of one of his Avantis. "Be just a minute."

The sight of Martin's erudite rear in dirty overalls, bent over the engine of a car, lifted Jolie's mood. "I don't believe it," she said. "You're a grease monkey."

He eased back and laid down the wrench. "'Deed I am." He grinned and wiped his hands on a blotchy rag.

"Nice car," she said. "I haven't seen this one."

He gently closed the hood. "I don't take it out as much as I should. This little princess is a twenty-fifth anniversary edition LSC. 1988. Only twenty-five of them made."

"25? Wow. So what are you doing to the little princess?"

"Just tweaking her a bit here and there."

"You like doing that, tweaking a bit here and there?"

"Sure." He opened the driver's door and motioned for her to look in. "See the instrument panel?"

"Yeah?"

"I put all those gauges in. They used to be digital. Didn't work worth a damn. Replaced them with good old reliable analogs, even if that did take away some of the authenticity. Too early in the evolution of digital, I guess. A sign of forward thinking but not an accurate one, and these gauges need to be accurate. So I swapped them out."

Jolie snapped her fingers. "I did the same thing to my Toyota before breakfast. Just after I overhauled the engine."

Martin laughed. "Aren't you the clever girl?" He patted the car's low roof. "The '87's and '88's had TV as an option."

"Not for the driver, I hope."

"Good point. No, strictly for second-row viewing. My

guess is somebody who lived with a backseat driver thought it up."

He wiped his sweaty forehead with a clean linen handkerchief retrieved from a chest pocket of his overalls. Jolie thought, who but Martin?

"Care for a glass of tea?" he said. He stuffed the handkerchief back into the pocket as if every car mechanic kept a linen hanky on hand.

"Thanks. We can talk here if you want to keep working."

Martin looked closely at her. "Anything in particular you want to talk about?"

Jolie waved off his concern. It wasn't a matter she wanted to return to just yet. Being here, around Martin's cheeriness, gave her the first breather she'd had since learning about Rebecca's overdose.

He leaned back and stretched. "I've been working on this carburetor for a couple of hours non-stop. It wouldn't hurt me to take a break."

As they walked through a narrow brick passageway into the kitchen's side door, Jolie smelled the sweetish air. "Fresh corn?"

"I picked it up at the market this morning and made some relish. I'll have to give you some."

"Please." She sat on one of the high stools around the kitchen island and watched Martin pour tall glasses of tea from a chilled silver pitcher. He dropped a sprig of mint into each.

"You're really something, Martin. From corn relish to carburetors."

He winked at her. "Aren't I a catch?" He hopped on a stool across from her.

She looked around the room, reluctant to break the spell of his well-tended world.

"I think you have something to tell me," he said. "Is my

274

guess right?"

She nodded slowly and turned to him. "For a few moments there I could pretend it hadn't happened. Thanks for the reprieve."

He locked eyes with her. "From what?"

"Rebecca died of a heroin overdose."

She saw disbelief move over his face. "She was a junkie?"

Martin listened carefully to all she had to say, his face growing more troubled with each additional bit of news. "That beautiful creature," he said at last. "That poor, luckless, beautiful creature."

Jolie drew circles with the base of her glass. "So, I just have to give the story up, I guess, and try to figure out a way to live with that."

"I know that goes against your nature, Jolie, but it sounds like good advice to me."

"Maybe. Maybe it's not worth pursuing now that Rebecca's gone. But I wish somebody would expose this slimebag Jerome and whatever connection Dempsey has to him."

"Maybe Memphis doesn't have the inclination to uncover that part of itself," Martin said. "Daunton does perform a service many people, and no doubt a number of powerful Memphians, consider useful."

She looked at him, her eyes widening. She slapped her hand on the counter. "You're absolutely right!"

"Usually my being right doesn't bring this much glee to others."

She began thumping a beat on the counter with both hands. "I need to go out of town with this story. *Watchworld* for instance." She leapt from the stool.

He glanced at the clock above the sink. "Are they in New York?"

"Yeah."

275

"Are you determined to call them no matter what? Is there no way I can talk you into letting the whole thing drop?"

"I have to make this one last effort." She took her phone out of her shorts pocket. "This could work."

Jolie knew *Watchworld*'s coverage ran the gamut, and often the stories tended toward slick entertainment. On occasion, however, the national television show did investigative pieces well. She hoped the prostitution and illegitimacy angles would be juicy enticements to pique their interest on a more serious level.

In a few minutes, she had the numbers she needed. "This is Jolie Marston," she told a receptionist for the program. "I've got a hard news story for you, and I need to speak with one of your producers. I'm an investigative reporter for WTNW in Memphis."

Martin came up close to her ear. "Present tense. Past tense," he whispered. "They're all the same, right?"

She smiled and covered the mouthpiece. "I'll be truthful with the producer. But first I need to get to one."

She told her story to an assistant producer and to his boss, a segment producer named Penelope Chisholm who made it clear she was rushed for time. Jolie figured that was her standard pace and refused to leave out anything that struck her as significant. At the end of her spiel, she offered the clincher: "I've got video of her before she died. She was stunning."

"Do me a favor," Penelope said. "E-mail me all this so I'll have it in writing. Be sure you've given me everything. I'll need phone numbers, addresses, all those kinds of things. And send me the video. By the way, this will be an exclusive for *Watchworld*, won't it?"

"Absolutely."

"Otherwise, we're not interested. You understand."

"Sure." She smiled and gave Martin a thumbs up.

***

Jolie sent Penelope the video and e-mailed not only details but the story as she would write it. Penelope replied that the segment was set tentatively to air in mid-August and to tell her immediately if anything new cropped up.

After that, the spurt of activity slowed, and Jolie found it difficult to concentrate on anything. Her next video shoot, a promo for the local historical museum, wouldn't get going for three weeks. The meetings with the museum's enthusiastic executive director so far had proved fruitful, and Jolie was glad to have something to look forward to that didn't hinge on murder.

In the meantime, though, the accusations lurked. Had she brought on Rebecca's murder? Should she never have intruded? The questions scurried endlessly through her thoughts.

***

"Why is it," Martin said from one of the wicker chairs on his terrace, "I feel I'm looking at a woman who's 56, not 36?"

Jolie sat across from him, rocking slowly in the big swing. "Thanks, pal. We vain people eat up compliments." She kicked the swing so it almost collided with the 180-year-old bricks in back.

"Sorry, but it bothers me to see you looking this—"

"Unwell? That's what my mother calls it. My dear sibling Jeffy didn't put it quite so politely when he was in town the other day. Haggard was Brother Jefferson's word."

Martin walked over and put an arm on her shoulder. "Are you getting enough sleep?"

She slumped and gazed at the floor. "Some." The truth was, damned little. Each night her worries had been waking her around three a.m. Last night, tired of lying there fretting, she got up, put on Aretha—the best company she could think of at that hour—and danced in the dark, twirling herself into dizziness. Good ol' Aretha therapy to the rescue once again.

Martin came over and sat beside her on the swing, stopping its motion. "If you think you're responsible for her death, you're not."

Jolie's gaze remained on the floor, but her lips tightened.

"She was a junkie, Jolie. And, as you well know, I never was sure she was telling you the truth in the first place. She also worked in a very dangerous profession. My guess is, the life span of your average prostitute is short."

Jolie pushed back hard, causing one end of the swing to veer wildly against Martin's planted feet. When she saw the unintended effect, she said, "Sorry, I'm acting like a brat."

He got up and began pacing over the sunset-hued squares of the terrace's sandstone floor. Behind him, on the long stretch of lawn, birds flitted among white crepe myrtles.

Jolie glanced at the placid scene. She didn't feel like talking, but she dreaded her own company and didn't want to leave.

After a while, Martin stopped striding across the floor and took a seat on one of the smooth, flat stones that topped the terrace's low wall. He crossed his arms and looked at her, but it was at least a minute before he spoke. "I'm in the mood for a little trip. It's someplace I've wanted to see since I first heard Violet talk about it on that video of yours. I think you need to go along. We could leave soon."

"I've got this video for the museum I'm working on. Remember?"

"I remember. So when's your next meeting?"

"Friday."

"Today's only Monday. We could leave tomorrow, stay

two nights at Russell's in La Grange, and go on our little adventure the day after we arrive."

Jolie looked up at him. It now registered that he'd said something about Violet's video. "What are you talking about?"

He leaned forward. "Twining Roses. Wasn't that the name of the plantation where Violet met Grant? I think we should see if it's still there."

Twenty-Nine

Russell hugged Jolie and Martin at the green picket gate leading to Havenwood. "Need another dose of the past? Please be my guests."

Indeed, as Jolie stood in the dark, serene foyer, not a day seemed to have passed since their last visit. In the interim, could Rebecca really have died with a needle in her arm?

Russell led them up the stairs, carrying their bags.

"Servants still on strike?" Martin asked.

"They're making impossible demands."

***

After setting the faucets on the massive clawfooted tub to full force, Jolie lay back on the canopied four-poster and nibbled on two oatmeal cookies from a crystal plate on the nightstand. She could make out Martin's and Russell's chatter and laughter downstairs. Occasionally she caught the words. Martin was telling the story she'd heard on the way over about a French lop-ear rabbit named Warren, an eighth birthday gift, who would sneak up behind his mother's guests and gnaw on their heels. It relaxed her to hear their pleasure in each other's company.

The tub's proportions were so deep and long she could stretch out fully, let the water seep up to her chin and still have a foot left at the other end. As she soaked, she thought about how easily this trip had worked out.

She had found a Kenworthy in Oxford in an online listing. He turned out to be a pleasant-toned young man and a relative of Ruth Anne's. In an inviting tone heavy with Mississippi's accent, he explained that, yes, the family still had Twining Roses, but Ruth Anne had passed away about fifteen years ago, and her daughter Martha—from his flattened tongue it sounded like "Mawthuh"—lived there now.

After Jolie explained vaguely her reason for wanting to visit Twining Roses, he offered more information. Mawthuh had lived there all her life, even after she married. Her husband "Edwad" had died a few years back. Her children lived in Oxford and were good to visit her often. She loved having "kuhp-ny," and he knew she would love to have them come by. "Let me give you Mawthuh's number," he said.

Indeed, when Jolie reached her, Martha Kenworthy Tilton vowed in a butter-thick voice she "would just love to have y'all come visit." She wanted to hear all about her mother's friend Violet and how she met her beau at Twining Roses. Suddenly, Twining Roses, a place with substance only in Violet's memory, existed in the present.

As Jolie lay now in the watery cocoon, she hoped Twining Roses wouldn't be the disappointment Grant Milburn had been. At least Mawthuh promised a friendly reception.

At Martin's urging, Jolie had retrieved the alexandrite necklace from its safe deposit box at the bank. "Violet's story is our hall pass to Twining Roses," he'd said. "You've got to take along the visual aids."

After bathing, she slipped the necklace around her neck. The large central gem and smaller ones on each side picked up the soft incandescence of the bedroom lamps. In this warm light, the crystals sparkled with a ruby hue. Jolie turned back and forth, watching the stones shimmer in the dressing table mirror. How could the addition of nothing more than a necklace make her feel utterly beautiful?

***

When Jolie approached, Martin and Russell had moved on from Warren the rabbit to favorite eating-places in New Orleans, a topic of perpetual conversation among many affluent Southerners. Each man had a glass of white wine in his hand and a smile on his face. Under the soft whirr of ceiling fans on the side porch, Jolie thought they looked like the picture of Southern idleness and privilege. She crossed in front of them, cleared her throat, and traced the necklace with a model's sweeping gesture.

"My word!" Russell's eyes widened.

"And it's so right with those shorts," Martin said.

Jolie curtsied.

Russell brought her a chilled glass of the Viognier they were drinking. She sat down in a wrought iron chair with thick cushions and looked over at Martin. "So how much have you told him about events of late?"

Martin ran a hand through his gray-flecked black hair. "Pretty much everything."

"Including?"

"Yes, including."

Good. She wanted on this trip to get as far away from Rebecca's death as she could.

***

Twining Roses's abrupt elegance took both Martin and Jolie by surprise. Since he'd turned the red Avanti convertible off the main highway that led into north Mississippi, they'd seen only small homes and modest farms. The farther they had traveled, the more ragtag the homes had become. Tiny, dilapidated shotgun houses dotted the last few miles, their poverty a legacy of slavery, sharecropping, and little education.

Now they came upon this sudden testament to Old South

grandeur. Martin hit the brakes.

"Wow," Jolie whispered as she stared ahead.

Slender towers of Lombardy poplars lined a long drive. At drive's end, magnolias in bloom sheltered a massive brick home painted white. Dual staircases of gray-green ironwork curved from a ground floor to either side of the main floor entrance some fifteen feet higher. The design was styled for a carriage to arrive. Along a third story ran a full balcony filagreed in the same grape-leaf pattern of ironwork.

"Just think," Martin said as he cut the engine, "this house was old when Violet came here as a girl."

Jolie tugged at his arm as they walked to the winding stairs. "Look over there." She pointed to cultivated rows of color along the left side of the house. "Mister Kenworthy's roses."

Martin stopped and surveyed the scene. "Indeed they are," he answered quietly. "After all this time, there they are just as she said."

Jolie lifted a heavy door knocker with a large K engraved on its gleaming brass. As she let it fall against the glossy black paint of the double front doors, its loud clang surprised her.

In a moment, both doors opened to a woman with a wide country-club smile.

Jolie mentally wrote Martha Kenworthy Tilton's story. Although a widow, life had been gentle to her blond looks. She looked no older than mid-forties, although Jolie calculated at least another ten years could accurately be added to that. Probably she had known no hard work beyond gardening. Had to lighten her hair now, but its tone was subtle, its style a face-softening chin length. Kept her figure trim, either from the roses or from golf, judging by the tanned arms and legs. A slender but sturdy woman with blue eyes behind blue-framed glasses. Jolie knew hers was a simplistic caricature, but nothing about the woman suggested anything to contradict her suppositions.

"Y'all must be just completely worn out from your drive," Martha said after introductions.

"Not at all," Martin said in a drawl nearly as deep as the Mississippian's. Jolie smiled to herself at the slowing of his speech. He'd be calling her "Mawthuh" any minute with the same dose of molasses Martha's relative had used when Jolie had called him to track her down.

Martin said, "We made the long drive from east Tennessee yesterday. We're staying at a bed and breakfast in La Grange."

"How lovely." She smiled at them both. Mawthuh, Jolie figured, had them pegged as lovers.

Their host escorted them through a chandeliered foyer into a long living room. Persian rugs lay here and there over heart-pine floors polished to a luster. She walked toward a sofa covered in an impressionistic wash of pale yellow, ivory, and cantaloupe. A crystal vase brimming with yellow and peach-colored roses sat facing it on a marble-topped table. Martha gestured toward the sofa. "Please sit down."

Martha excused herself and returned with tall glasses of tea on a silver platter. After serving, she sat between the wide wings of a Queen Anne chair and stretched out her honey-hued arms. "Now, please tell me again, if y'all don't mind too much, just how it is Jolie came to call me. And please don't leave out one iota. This is such a fun surprise." She smiled broadly, her pleasure in their "kuhp-ny" obvious.

Jolie repeated in greater detail the story she had sketched only briefly for Martha on the phone. No mention was made of Rebecca. When she finished, she reached into a woven cloth shoulder bag and pulled out a DVD. "I've got Violet's story right here, if you want to see it."

"That would be wonderful! Let's go into the back room where the TV is. I'll let you fuss with that DVD player," she said to Jolie. "I'm always having trouble with the thing.

Somehow I seem to be putting it into reverse when I want to go forward, or else I go way past what I'm trying to find and spend the longest time getting to the right place."

"Don't feel bad," Jolie said. "A lot of people feel that way."

"You must be very smart not to," Martha said with her all's-well-with-the-world smile.

Jolie recognized the meaningless flattery even as she warmed to it. She popped the DVD in the player.

"This is exciting," Martha said. She settled back into one of the wicker chairs and patted the soft curve of her blond hair.

As the video played, Jolie did what she had done with Grant, covertly studying her audience's face instead of watching the screen. When Violet told about the drowning, Martha let out a softly audible "Oh!"

When Violet's story ended, Martha continued to stare at the screen. "How sad," she said at last in a hoarse voice. "I believe you said she died recently?"

"That's right," Jolie said. "Soon after we did this." She stuffed the DVD back in her bag.

"What a lot she'd been keeping in."

Martha stood. "If you're interested, I could show you the ballroom Violet talked about."

"Please," Jolie and Martin said together.

"The murals are still there. But that part about the Yankee general..." Martha eased out a soft laugh. "Well, I can show y'all where the soldiers carved their names. But I never heard anything about the general horsewhipping them. And feeding them nothing but grass for three days! Oh, my. I certainly never heard that."

"So," Jolie said, "were there really all those servants back when Violet visited?"

"Oh, yes. I don't know about ten. Ten sounds a bit excessive that long after the war. But I do know Mother never lifted a hand to do anything." Martha laughed again. "Nobody has help like that anymore." She eased herself up from the wicker chair. "Why don't I show you that door first?"

The door was in the foyer beneath a sweeping staircase to the third floor. Martha turned a crystal knob and opened it. "There they are," she said.

Jolie touched the crude, half-inch grooves carved by knives that might well have pierced the hearts of Southern boys. Beside her, Martin whispered the names. "Luther Randall. Jeremiah Cooper. Matthew Heddington." They counted 30 names in all. Names of men long dead, even when Violet had stood at this spot reading them.

"Would y'all like to see the ballroom now?"

She led them through French doors at the far end of a dining room to an enormous room beyond. "As y'all can see, Violet's memories of this room were quite accurate."

On long walls above the floor's shining parquetry, endless adventures with foxhunters, grape-gathering peasants, and bucolic lovers played out.

Martin came close to study the panels. "These are in excellent condition," he said.

"I had a man from New Orleans come up and clean them."

"Violet said the original painter was from there too," he said.

"Yes, but I'm afraid that was a little off. The records of the house show he came from Boston."

"Close," he said and winked at Martha.

Jolie reached into her shoulder bag. "I'd like to show you something Violet gave me." She lifted the necklace gently from the satin case, held it out, and waited for the expected "Ooh!"

Martha's brow furrowed. She bent toward the piece. "I was afraid of this," she said in words so low they barely heard her. She held out her hand. "May I?"

"Sure," Jolie said uncertainly. "Violet left it to me. This is the necklace Grant gave her the night he proposed."

"I see," Martha said. "And is this the same necklace she had on during the last part of the story? I was sitting too far away to see it very clearly."

"It's the same one."

Their host leaned back from her scrutiny of the necklace and closed her eyes for a moment. Her hand still encircled the piece.

Jolie and Martin waited for her to speak. Instead, she walked toward the French doors and gestured for her guests to follow. "Please," she said.

She led them back to the living room, to an oil painting on a far wall. It was one of many portraits in the room, and neither Jolie nor Martin had done more than glance at it before.

A dark-haired woman in her early twenties, almost life-sized, beamed down at them from inside her gilt frame. Her blue eyes had the same wide spacing of Martha's. She sat on a chaise longue, her gown spread out, one arm perched lightly on the chaise's back. Around her long neck glittered a gold necklace. In its center lay a large alexandrite with four smaller stones on each side.

Jolie gasped.

Martha took a deep breath. "Did Violet or Grant ever mention how he came to have the necklace?"

"No," Jolie said. "Grant's family used to have money. But they'd lost it by the time he was born. He was pretty bitter about that. So, I doubt he could've afforded it, but I always figured it was a family heirloom."

"Indeed it was a family heirloom," Martha said, looking up at the portrait. "That's my grandmother, my father's mother. The necklace belonged to a very well off aunt of hers who had no children. It was given to my grandmother on her twenty-first birthday. The portrait was painted soon after that." Martha's face had grown pale. "Why don't we sit down."

"When I was a little girl," Martha said once they were seated, "Mother told me the story of how it was stolen. The theft happened, no doubt, the same year as that house party. Its disappearance wasn't noticed until my grandmother wanted to wear it for Christmas. That would've been several months later. One of the black maids was new at that time. A silver ladle had turned up missing soon after she came to work for us, so when the necklace was discovered missing, she was arrested." Martha grimaced. "She spent seven years in prison over it. She was the mother of two young boys."

Jolie, open-mouthed, looked at Martin. He had closed his eyes.

"The necklace was never found. Mother told me my grandmother mentioned it in her will, with a full description, in case it might turn up, because it was to go to Mother, then to me."

"Insurance?" Jolie asked.

Martha shook her head. "Insuring jewelry wasn't done as often then as it is now, so she never got a cent for it." She absentmindedly touched a tanned hand to the hollow of her neck and looked around. "I used to hope it was hidden in the house somewhere and would spend hours looking for it. Every nook and cranny in this big old place."

Martha carefully laid the string of jewels on a table and stroked them.

"I'd like to step outside a minute," Jolie said.

Dizziness swept over her as the nicotine seeped into her lungs. She sat on the sweeping dual staircase at the front of the house and looked at the settled beauty of Twining Roses. Violet, nineteen years younger than Jolie was now, had walked up these steps. Perhaps she'd even sat on them and looked out over the green expanse of cotton fields.

Jolie stood up slowly and walked toward the rose garden. Violet had been there, pointing out the roses she wanted Mr. Kenworthy to cut for dance decorations.

She opened a low gate and started out along one of the gravel paths between the rows. Old-fashioned roses with wide faces grew beside long-stemmed ones with tightly curled buds. She walked by every bush before making her way back up the curving stairs.

Martha and Martin stopped their quiet conversation when Jolie reappeared.

She came near them but remained standing. "The necklace, of course, belongs to you, Martha, to your family," Jolie said.

Martha let out an audible sigh of relief. "That's very kind."

"I think," Martin said gently, "Jolie would understand if you wanted to put it on."

"Yes," Jolie said. "Go ahead. You've finally found it."

Martha lifted the necklace. Martin walked over and fastened the ends of the gold filigree around her neck.

"I have to go look," Martha said. She rose and moved toward a mirror. As she stood in front of her image, tears began to spill down her cheeks and onto the shimmering stones. "You've made me so happy today," she said, turning to Jolie. She walked over and hugged her. "Thank you. Thank you."

"It's only right," Jolie said. She tried not to let her disappointment show.

Thirty

"I want to talk to you!"

Jolie's pounding on Grant Milburn's door summoned both the mousey housekeeper and her employer.

"What do you want?" Milburn growled. "Why are you back here at the crack of dawn?"

"To talk." Throughout the night, Jolie had awakened thinking about the visit she would pay him this morning.

"Do you have to bang on my door like a jackhammer?"

"Let me in."

As soon as the door opened enough to admit her, she stomped through the murky light of the hallway into the living room and sat on the grease-edged couch. The rotten fruit smell filled her nostrils, emanating from somewhere in the back of the house.

Milburn, still unshaven, shuffled toward his caverned chair and dropped into it.

She pointed a finger and stared at him. "You're a thief. A lying thief."

"Get out of—"

"I went to Twining Roses yesterday," Jolie said. "Ruth Anne Kenworthy's daughter told me all about the necklace you stole. I even saw it in a painting of her grandmother."

His gaze, fixed on the floor, did not waver. Was he even listening? "Do you know," she shouted, "a woman who worked for them went to prison for what you did? Did you know that? An innocent mother with young kids spent seven years of her life behind bars. For you, you bastard!"

He covered his face with thickly veined hands and mumbled something.

"What?" Jolie leaned toward him, her voice still sharp. "What did you say?"

He moved his hands away only slightly. "I said I never knew that. But that wasn't my doing."

"Like hell it wasn't."

"I was young. It was a long time ago."

"That's it? You're defending what you did and the misery your actions brought on, and it's all ok because you were *young*? You don't feel the least bit guilty?"

He shrugged, then he met Jolie's stare with a cold glare of his own that gave her chills.

Jolie wasn't sure what she wanted from Milburn, but what he'd given her wasn't enough. She surveyed the dingy room. Glanced at the mantel with its collection of pictures. She walked over to the photographs.

He had been, just as Violet said, striking with his black hair and those cornflower eyes. In one photo, he stood with a diploma and a face not fully formed. Another showed him as a small boy with a man, woman and young girl whose hair was as dark as his own. In a third, a teen-aged, wet-haired Grant in swimming trunks held up a medal poolside and grinned.

She turned away from the mantel. "When I made the video of you, you kind of glossed over the death of Violet's father. I want to hear more about that."

"None of your damn business."

"You owe it to me, after the necklace. You owe me the truth on this one."

"I don't owe you anything. He drowned."

"I know he drowned. I want to know why." She moved closer to him. The suspicion that had suddenly risen in her mind turned her voice hard. "Why couldn't you save him, a swimming champ like you?"

Milburn didn't answer.

"It occurs to me," she said, "as I'm sure it did to you long ago, that he was the only thing that stood in the way of your marrying Violet." Jolie decided to risk whatever reaction might come. "You could've saved him, couldn't you? But you didn't."

He flinched, but his look remained icy.

She moved closer and leaned down so she was only inches away. "You could have saved him," she said in a contemptuous whisper. "You let him die."

***

Grant Milburn turned his head as the obnoxious young woman stood back up. He looked at her smug face. As he did so, it began to meld into Gilman's angry features, Gilman howling for Grant to save him, howling he couldn't swim.

There had been no time to grab life preservers when, several hundred yards from shore, a stealth wind flipped their craft. The wind muffled Gilman's yelps, even though he struggled only a few feet away. The little boat was tossed farther from them with every movement of the raging waves. Lightning crackled overhead, each sharp snap coming right on the heels of the last. One bolt shot into the lake between Grant and the shore.

A gush of rain pelted Grant's face. The boat blurred. The shore vanished.

A wave threw Gilman at him. He flailed only inches away now. Gilman lurched forward and grabbed Grant's neck with a jerk that nearly took them both under. "Help," he wailed, choking, coughing up water. "Help me."

Grant looked at the despicable face with its fear-filled eyes. Even in terror, Gilman seemed to taunt him, to remind him of his poverty, of his outcast religion, of what he wanted badly and could not have. He heard again Gilman's declaration from that morning: "Impossible!"

It had taken only one push of his hand. Gilman didn't even resist, all struggle pounded out of him. One push against the terrified face and the pleas muted and died.

"Why are you looking at me like that?"

The question jolted him back to his living room.

"Get out of my house," Milburn barked.

Thirty-One

The evening air sharpened the fruity scent of a mimosa as Jolie and Martin strolled through his back lawn and woods. Thunder rumbled faintly, too far away to threaten.

Jolie plucked one of the pink blossoms from the low tree and brushed its feathery strands across her cheek before letting it fall to the ground. "I still can't get over how differently Grant and Violet viewed things."

"And of course," Martin said, "both of them were absolutely convinced of their own veracity."

Jolie smiled at him. "You're the only person I know who casually drops a word like veracity into a sentence."

"Thank you, I think."

"So which one told the truth?" she asked.

"You mean, underneath the distortions, self-deceptions, and tricks of memory?"

"Underneath all those."

"Beats me," Martin said.

"I don't know if it's life-long resentment or what that makes Milburn so unpleasant," she said. "He really is a bitter old man."

"I don't wonder," Martin said. "He might even have let Violet's father drown, and still he didn't get the girl. To top it off, she aborted their child—and he's Catholic."

"But he married and had a son after that. Why not let it go?"

"Grudges are funny things. I think some people look for reasons to hold them. Some people make every effort to be unhappy."

Jolie picked up a foot-long stick in their path and tossed it at the trunk of a pine. "Well, sometimes life does suck. I think Rebecca would have agreed with that."

"Dancing the old ennui boogie, are we?"

"Maybe."

"I know the steps."

"You do?"

"Any person with more than grits for brains does. Remember the Spanish proverb, the one about living well being the best revenge?" He stopped walking and looked closely at her. "There's a lot to be said for that."

"There's a lot to be said for the money to be able to say that."

"True. But it doesn't cost a cent to stay awake to your senses." He pointed to the nearby mimosa tree laden with deep pink puffs. "Each one of those blooms is a fragrant little miracle. If you don't believe me, just look." He walked over to a weathered wood bench, sat down, and patted the seat beside him.

Jolie ignored the invitation and remained standing.

"What really helps me when I'm down," he said, "is to think of my life as theater."

"Sound and fury signifying nothing? Yeah, that's a spirit booster for sure."

"It's not that bleak." Martin leaned back and gazed at the mimosa. "It's more like this: My life is something I'm acting out on this proscenium stage. There's an audience I can't see because of the lights. I rush around on this little stage, worrying about the silliest things, getting furious about trivialities. And it's all just a play, just so much theater. In the next hall, someone else is on a stage with a different script and, like me, they think it's the only script that exists." He lowered his head to look at her. "Seeing things this way gives me a bigger perspective. It helps."

295

She walked a few paces, halted and faced him. "But don't you think life is worth taking seriously?"

"Life is. My own day-to-day comic opera isn't."

***

Jolie trotted up the lane in the morning's still-damp air, proud her long walk had become a jog. Yes, her lungs hurt. Yes, she cursed Sir Walter Raleigh with what breath she had left. But, by damn, she had run, or at least jogged, and the exhaustion felt triumphant.

She made the turn into her drive, slowing to cool down. As soon as she did, from the corner of her eye, spots of color caught her attention. The sensation registered before the thought. Her sinews knew something was awry. She jerked her head toward the color. Over the bright blue of her sports car, words had been smeared on the side in a garish yellow. *Back off bitch.* Her stomach clenched as the blood rushed to it. She glanced around the empty yard and crept closer. The other side bore the same message. Across the hood and trunk, the spray painter had continued his odd symmetry: *Slut* ran across either end.

Only then did she notice the tires had been slashed, the windows broken. An unconcerned blue jay pecked at the ground nearby. Jolie slumped to the grass, put her head between her hands, and tried to think. Between a jumble of thoughts crept the eerie sensation that someone had been watching her, waiting for her to leave, waiting for this opportunity.

She hadn't riled anyone around here lately to her knowledge. She'd bet anything the warning to back off had to do with the *Watchworld* story. No doubt, the crew had been poking around, shooting interviews.

"Penelope, I need to know something," she said when she

296

reached the producer by phone. "Who have you and your crew been talking to in Memphis?"

"We just wrapped up most of our shooting there. Let me think. We got bites with people on the street and Mayor Farrell. We might pick up something more later. Why?"

"When you talked to Farrell, did he seem threatening?"

"Not in the least. He was very accommodating. Downright gushy."

"How about the vice mayor, a guy named Ed Dempsey. Did you talk with him?"

"We didn't interview him, but he sat in on the shoot with Farrell. He was 180-degrees from his charming boss. He definitely didn't want us there."

"Tell me what he said."

"Well, when the interview with Farrell ended, Dempsey followed us out the door. He said, 'So John Beck put you up to this, right?' I told him I had no idea who John Beck was. Dempsey said Beck worked for the local paper. Then he started on some rant about him. I kept telling Dempsey, we've never heard of a John Beck. He kept insisting we did. Finally Raphael, the videographer, spoke up and said, 'Look, we got this story from someone who doesn't even work in news anymore, doesn't even live in Memphis anymore.' I think Raphael was worried Dempsey was going to hassle this Beck fellow for no good reason. Memphis has a real piece of work for deputy mayor. You're not getting hassled now are you?"

Jolie didn't feel like explaining.

When the sheriff's deputy arrived, he confirmed what she'd already guessed: Probably no fingerprints, although he'd dust. "Spray paint is spray paint, lady, not much we can trace there. We'll check the shoe prints, if you really want us to, but they sure strike me as your average-size, everybody's-got-'em Nikes. Looks like you got yourself just another case of vandalism."

"Has anything like this happened to anyone else?"

"No," he said. Jolie thought he looked barely old enough to have a driver's license. He scratched his unlined face. "We see our share of smashed windows, though, slashed tires, that kind of thing."

"But not the writing?"

"Not the writing. But I wouldn't let it worry me, ma'am, if I were you. Just keep your doors locked, keep an eye out, and call us if you see anything suspicious." Five minutes and some paperwork later, he was gone.

Maybe Dempsey hadn't done this firsthand, maybe he'd hired somebody else to watch her house, to sneak up to it at the right time, but he'd planned it. Just as with his intangible threat to John Beck, however, nothing could be proven. She knew there would be no prints, nothing to track down. You didn't spend as many years as a cop as Ed Dempsey had and not know how to be careful. The local sheriff's department wouldn't want to spend that much time on an incident of vandalism anyway.

Try as she might to pretend she felt no fear, she knew from the shaking in her hands as she poured a cup of coffee, all was not calm. Dempsey meant to unnerve her, and he did. But he wouldn't sidetrack her.

She took a sip of coffee, pitched it in the kitchen sink, and made a cup of cocoa. Then she opened a bar of dark chocolate, intending to take only a couple of bites. Moments later, the wrapper lay empty on the counter.

Was John right to have abandoned the story? Was she stupid to pursue it? She was too far along to give up now, especially with *Watchworld* on it. She assured herself yet again, no one would seriously harm her. They couldn't get away with it, not with all the people she'd talked to about Daunton and Dempsey.

However, she vowed to tell no one in Memphis about her

car. It might scare Penelope off the story. Probably not, but why take that chance? She might want to make it part of the story. Anyone else Jolie told would pressure her to do just what Dempsey suggested. She would not give him the satisfaction.

***

At the body shop, she tried to ignore the curious looks of the guys who surveyed her car. "Guess I got too close to somebody in traffic," she said, trying to make a joke of it. She arranged for a rental car and figured she'd tell anyone who asked that her car was in the shop for brake work.

When the sheriff's department called a few days later, the deputy said what she expected: No prints, common shoe size, brand, and style, nothing noteworthy about the spray paint.

At moments during the day and night, she would tell herself she ought to call Penelope and try to convince her to kill the story. Those moments didn't last. Yes, of course, she felt uneasy every morning when she awoke. Would she find something else trashed? But morning after uneventful morning eased her concern, made her determined to see the story on the air. She brushed away her fears each time they arose, and they began to rise up less and less.

Jolie found herself itchy to tell Nick about the upcoming *Watchworld* segment, because she thought he'd want to see it. But seconds after picking up the phone, she put it down again.

She dumped herself on the sofa with its misplaced tropical scene, grabbed a pillow, and held it to her chest. A corner of her heart missed Nick, but it didn't occupy enough space for her to call, even to relay information. She had ended things because things needed to end.

She thumped the pillow.

How fast it can change with any lover, she thought, and

how final that change can be, despite intense months or years together. In no more than the flash of an angry remark, the turn of a back, perhaps only the downward movement of a head, it is over.

Hands whose texture, shape, and color are so familiar she could pick them out from thousands of others. Suddenly no longer there. The particular quirks of a walk. Gone away. The unique and quickening scent. Elsewhere. Usually gone forever.

But no one, no matter who instigated the breakup, left a relationship unchanged. The change might be as minute and permanent as the way Sam Watson had taught her to parallel park. Or it might be as life-altering as the way her heart had opened for Rich and then knitted shut.

She went upstairs and opened the lid on a cedar chest at the foot of her bed. Under a stack of folders and papers, she saw the green silk cover of the wedding album. As she slid it out of the chest, her fingers remembered the nubby weave.

She had married Rich Peretti when she was twenty-two, not long out of journalism school. Her first job was with Battle Creek's single television station, a tight-fisted operation that counted on new talent from Michigan State's journalism school, let loose in a field with far more graduates than jobs.

Rich was the most popular anchor anyone in town could remember, especially among the all-important female demographic. They swooned over his deep, confidential voice, his thick, dark hair. Even from their living room couches, they could see the long lashes, the dimpled slits in his cheeks when he smiled.

Rich Peretti gloated on the attention. But his 26-year-old ambition chafed at being in the 95th market. When cooing women would ask why he wasn't working for a bigger station, someplace like Chicago or New York, he had no face-saving response.

He already had become the hometown idol when Jolie came to work a year after he did. The newsroom might be small by any standard, but it still sported the flirtatious repartee of every other newsroom in the country filled with young adults, and Rich Peretti was a master of the art. He also was the only guy with enough drive to interest Jolie.

Soon after their first date, when they talked until dawn, a videotape appeared on her doorstep. On it was a plea from him, shot in extreme close-up, asking her out again. He spoke of famous lovers who shared a passion for work: Robert and Elizabeth Barrett Browning; Georgia O'Keeffe and Alfred Stieglitz; Clark Kent and Lois Lane; Fabian and Annette Funicello. She answered him by leaving a beach ball on his desk and a note: "Wanna play?"

They talked shop and made intense love until late every night after work.

Jolie's past had included maybe a dozen lovers and a few very serious infatuations, but nothing beyond that. She first knew the depth of her feelings for Rich after their initial lovemaking. He held her face in his hands. He probed her eyes as if looking for an opening into which he might plunge. She softened her gaze, and it appeared.

"Finally," she whispered to him as he kissed first one eye, then another. "I thought you'd never show up."

One spring night on a full-moon impulse, Rich proposed, and she accepted. They laughed at her earlier vow not to wed before she'd hit a top 30 market. "I hadn't figured on you," she told him.

"We'll get there together," he said.

They became the darlings of Battle Creek, the glamorous young stars whose names appeared frequently in the small city's society column. They were sought-after party guests, favorite hosts for charity events. They knew everything in their lives had led them to each other and to this starting point.

Yes, they argued with each other, but what passionate, strong-minded couple doesn't, they reasoned? They never bored each other, and that mattered more. Each loved the other's quick mind and sassy attitude. Each adored the other's body.

Fourteen months after their wedding day, Rich received an offer from one of the network affiliates in Milwaukee. How could he say no? This was what they'd planned, this move up. Not only was it a considerably bigger market, it was more than two times his current salary. Instead of having to do both the noon and early evening news, he would anchor only the evening and one investigative report a week. A terrific gig. On top of it all, the offer came from the number one station in the market.

They decided he would return to Battle Creek or she'd visit Milwaukee every weekend until she could land a job there. Surely it wouldn't take long once she began looking. They decided against her leaving with him without a job. Her prospects would be much stronger if she stayed employed in TV news.

They began their strategy with confidence. But the demands of a small station meant she had to pull weekend reporting duty when someone was sick or on vacation, so they had less time together than expected. The market in Milwaukee, like everywhere else, was saturated with broadcasting degrees. She got encouragement and compliments from prospective news directors but no offers. Looking for work there in another field was unthinkable. She might never get back into television news if she left. Besides, there was no other work she wanted to do.

Her life was in a stall compared to his. She rode in her station's junker news cruisers while he bopped around on a helicopter. She felt lucky to get a petty theft at city hall while he reported on huge drug busts and police coverups.

She became derisive when Rich would tell her what he was working on and where he'd been invited. Little things about him began to rile her. She decided he was becoming conceited. She decided he'd been that way all along.

The ugliest argument came one Sunday afternoon just before he was to return to Milwaukee. As she paced the bedroom, she ragged him about buying a new car. "You didn't bother to consult me first," she screamed. "You act like a single man!"

When he answered from his seat on the bed, his voice was an incision. "If you only knew how married I've been."

"What's that supposed to mean? That you're turning down panting females to stay true to your wife?" She walked over to a window. A foot of snow had fallen since his arrival last night. Because of the weather, he had decided that morning to leave earlier than planned. Her outburst had interrupted his packing.

"Something like that, yeah." He leaned both hands back on the bed. "But you don't seem to appreciate it. All you can do anymore when I see you or talk to you on the phone is bitch. Bitch about how boring your life is here. Bitch about how I'm getting to do what I've worked hard at. Bitch about being stuck in Battle Creek." He fell back against the couch. "Honestly, Jolie, it sometimes seems like you don't want me to be successful. Like you wish I'd spent my life with you in a two-bit TV market."

"That's not fair, you bastard. It's not like I'm not trying to find something in Milwaukee."

"You're right." He hung his head. "I'm sorry. Something's bound to open up sooner or later."

"But in the meantime…"

"In the meantime, Jolie girl, I'm so tired of arguing, so utterly tired of it. And I'm tired of this lousy arrangement we have. It's not good for either one of us."

He patted the bed for her to join him. She sat down rigidly, and he stroked her hair. "If only we'd been able to make this move together."

"This is the very reason I used to swear I'd never marry until I was further along," she told him. "Top 30 market at least."

He laughed and kissed her. "My sweet, smart, ambitious wife."

She looked over at him. "How do you figure sweet?"

"Okay, smart and ambitious. And beautiful."

But that wasn't the end of the arguments. For several months more they struggled through similar exchanges. Each one left them more exhausted and estranged.

One Saturday night they sat by candlelight at Rich's favorite restaurant in Milwaukee, a place where the owner always brought over a complimentary bottle of reserve Chianti. "For my famous friend," he'd say and instruct the waiter standing nearby to treat them well.

Halfway through the meal on this particular night, Jolie pushed back her barely touched calzone. She was worn out from the drive in a pounding rain and too tired to eat. "All the way over here," she said, "I thought about us. You know how you said all I do anymore is bitch?"

He put down his fork, sighed, and fixed his gaze on a far wall.

"Well, you're right," she said. "I've been listening to myself lately. I hate what I'm hearing." She leaned forward as he looked at her, baffled. "The reason I'm so bitchy is because I'm still in Battle Creek...so appropriately named for us maybe...and you've gone on, and I'm not with you. I'm blaming you for having what I don't and for being where I'm not."

His brown eyes filled with sympathy. "You never were one

to let yourself off the hook, were you, Jolie girl?"

"No. And I'm not going to now."

"I know it's been hard for you," he said softly. "God, I try to think what it would be like if we were to swap places. I'd be miserable."

She winced. "Thanks for your pity."

"It's not…" But he stopped.

She crossed her arms on the table. "The fact is, I'm going to be miserable until I get my ass into a bigger market. And," she said, her voice hoarse, "if it's not where you are, then it has to be somewhere." She forced a brave smile. "I don't suppose you've heard of any job offers in Milwaukee lately?"

He shook his head slightly and reached over to lay a hand on her arm. She looked down at the tapered shape of his hand, at the smoothness of its skin. When, after a long silence, she looked back at him, his eyes were watering.

He spoke in a near whisper. "This hasn't come easily, has it, Jolie girl?"

She shook her head slowly as tears began to drop on her lap. "It's the hardest thing I've ever had to decide."

"I guess we were naive to think we could so easily hop from one market to the next together," he said.

"Naive. Dumb."

"In love."

They left the restaurant and walked in the relentless rain to his new car. He wrapped an arm around her, and she huddled against him under his umbrella.

Once in the car, he leaned over and hugged her. "You know, don't you, that no matter what happens to us, I'll always love you?"

She wiped away tears that had begun again. "At least there's that."

They saw each other only a couple of times more, once in

Battle Creek, once in Milwaukee. Rich waited for her to be the first to mention divorce, but both knew one already had occurred.

She began looking for prospects around the country. After three months of mailing resume videos, contacting former professors, and pumping colleagues in the industry for leads, a call came from Albuquerque. The station flew her out for an interview, and she accepted their terms on the spot. At the airport, she called Rich. She used the word divorce.

After two years in Albuquerque, she landed the job at WTNW in Memphis. The last she had heard, Rich was in Houston.

It had been five or six years since his postcard saying he was going there as anchor for the number two station. She'd sent him a congratulatory postcard in return. A postal clerk reading their messages on the sly wouldn't have guessed they'd known the exact and singular taste of each other's skin.

***

Jolie laid the silk-covered album of wedding photos, unopened, back in the cedar chest. She knew his home number would be unlisted, but the newsroom number was easy to track down on the computer. When she had a fresh cigarette and a tumbler of Glenlivet at hand, she called.

"Hang on," a hurried man said when she asked for Rich Peretti. She took an anxious drag and waited.

"Peretti."

On hearing the familiar, deep tone, a tingle of energy raced just underskin. The soles of her feet grew cold. She'd forgotten how his voice oozed confidence and sex.

No way did she want to risk being unrecognized. "Rich, it's Jolie."

She heard an intake of breath from his end. "Jolie?"

"None other. How are you?"

"I'm fine. Great. How are you? And where are you? Are you in town?"

"No, no. I'm back in my hometown, in fact. Singleton. You remember?"

"Of course I do. Visiting your folks?"

"You got a minute?"

"Sure. I've got to go into a meeting in about five, maybe ten, but until then I'm yours. What's on your mind?"

"I just got curious. I mean, you might have been dead for all I knew."

"I'm happy to report I'm not. What's going on with you?"

She gave him a condensed version of her firing and her life since, trying to sound as upbeat as possible. She talked about the story coming at the end of the month on *Watchworld*. She mentioned shoots for website videos. She skipped the kiddie birthdays. Jolie knew he was going to feel sorry for her but dammit if she'd ask him to. "So things are fine. It's a good chance to step back. Reassess. You know." She let out a long breath. "So what's new with you?"

"Things are pretty good here at the station. I got an offer to go to San Diego, but the station countered with more money than San Diego was willing to shell out. And since my wife's family—" He paused. "Did you know I was married?"

"No," she said, the word sticking in her throat.

"God, it *has* been a while. Claire and I married four years ago. I'm a father now, Jolie, can you believe it? One almost three now and another one on the way."

A wife wasn't too surprising, but children? They fixed him away from her too finally.

"It's great to hear from you," he said when there was no response. "So have you remarried?"

"No." She laughed, a high-pitched sound too like a nervous titter. It made her cringe. "No," she repeated, lowering her voice. "In fact, I'm just now, at least I think I am, looking at the tail end of a relationship that went on for about two and a half years."

"Sorry to hear that. Or maybe congratulations are in order."

"Neither really. There just wasn't enough there, I guess, to sustain us after I moved back to Singleton."

Until this moment, she hadn't thought about the similarities of the relationships. Or rather, of how they ended.

"So how's your family?" Rich asked. "Your parents doing all right?"

"Sure. My dad's retired and seems to be handling it okay. Mom's still a maven of Singleton society." She wasn't sure how much more of this she could stand. "Listen, Rich, can I ask you something?"

"Sure. What?"

"Do you remember us?"

The polished voice grew soothing, private. "Of course I do, Jolie girl. I remember a lot about us."

"I'm glad to hear that. Really I am."

"Why do you ask?" The voice was still gentle.

"It's not easy to explain. I mentioned this *Watchworld* thing and how I happened to get involved in the story. I won't go into any more detail than I have, but it's made me wonder about, well, about people's memories. I mean about exactly what people remember."

"You always were one to scrutinize. Comes with being so smart, I guess."

"Aw, cut the patronizing," she said, but she was smiling. "Here's the thing: When you remember us, what do you remember? What images? What times together? What exactly?"

"Whew. Let me think." He laughed. "One thing I think of is

308

how you showed up at my door one evening, this was very early in our relationship, and your hair was soaking wet. You'd locked yourself out of your apartment and couldn't find the landlord. You had on this red hood of a thing, a cape, something like that. And it made me think of Little Red Riding Hood. A very soggy Little Red Riding Hood."

"Jeez, I barely remember that. And I didn't remember at all what I was wearing." She paused for breath. "Listen, Rich, do you remember the first time we made love?"

"Yes," he said in a whisper. "Yes, I do."

"Remember the videotape you made for me and left on my doorstep after our first date?"

"That tape about all the famous couples! I'd forgotten that. God, I worked and worked to get it right. I couldn't ask anybody at the station to help me. I'd never have lived down their ribbing. And I kept messing up the focus, because I couldn't look through the viewfinder and shoot myself at the same time, and there was no autofocus on that sucker. It took forever to get it right."

"I didn't know that."

"Of course not. I was too cool to let you know."

"I see." She was breathing regularly again. She glanced at her watch, eager to be the one to end the conversation. "Look, Rich, I know you have to go in just a minute, but there's one more thing I want to ask."

"Shoot."

"Why…well, why do you think we fell apart?"

"I've thought about that, Jolie. Of course, I have. Seems to me, we were too ambitious for our own good. Maybe if only one of us, either one of us, hadn't been so itchy to—"

"No, I think you're wrong."

"I'm wrong?"

"We weren't too ambitious." Her voice became insistent.

"You're wrong there."

"Jolie, Jolie. Still playing offense for defense. Even when you don't need to. Okay, so why do you think we parted ways?"

"We were too young, that's all. I mean, if we'd met a few years later, if we'd both been settled in the same town, then maybe…"

"But that's the crux of it, don't you see? Because of our ambition, we never could be settled in the same town. I was ready to jump for San Diego only this past April if management hadn't come up with the bucks. My wife's quit work until the kids are older, so it wouldn't have been a big deal except that we are pretty comfy here in Houston."

"Sometimes I can't believe I never made it into a bigger market. Memphis just became so comfortable, and I knew I had it good with my old news director."

"You're top notch, Jolie. One of the best I ever worked with."

"I better let you get to that meeting."

"Yeah, I'd better go. But it's been terrific talking to you. Really it has. I'm so glad you called."

She listened to the warm tone of his words. It might well be the last time she'd ever hear that voice, the voice that once had said *I do* again and again until the congregation had begun laughing.

From now on, he was beyond her knowing. "It's been good to talk to you too, Rich."

She took a fresh cigarette and her drink to the porch and propped her feet on the railing. Damned if she'd give in to this sudden urge to cry. With a thunk, she dropped her feet to the floor and stubbed out the newly lit cigarette. She headed for the gravel drive, her arms pumping, her pace furious. She had no destination, but any place was better than here.

***

The woman gave the man a rueful smile as she handed him an envelope full of bills. "Half now," she said in her twangy voice, "and half after. As soon as I hear for sure Ed Dempsey's a goner, you can pick up the rest at the cemetery where we said."

"You gonna come to Reno after that?" He lowered his head and fixed his eyes on the well-shaped flesh underneath her red stretch lace shirt. "You gonna meet me there?" He put his hand on her breast and tilted his head up toward her.

"Sure I am, honey pie." What the hell, maybe she would. She looked at the man's doe-like eyes. She probably could have gotten him to knock off the bastard for nothing more than a free lay. Maybe Jerome too while he was at it. But this way was safer. This way he was in deeper.

She figured Daunton ought to get the same treatment as Dempsey. Beating up Monique wasn't the first time Jerome had hit one of the girls, but it was the worst. Still, she feared him enough to leave him alone.

The piss-poor excuse for a deputy mayor was something else altogether. She knew for a fact he'd caused Monique's death. The wired-up little bitch who'd been Monique's source claimed she had no idea the dose was lethal. She was lying sure as shit, but it was Dempsey who put her up to what she did. A couple of slaps had been all it had taken to weasel that out of her.

The one thing she regretted was that she wouldn't be able to brag to Jerome. He'd hated Dempsey from the get-go, hated the way he acted like lord and master over the girls. She knew Jerome hated him especially for taking out Monique, his property.

As for paying to kill Dempsey, she couldn't figure a better way to use the money Monique had left behind in a hiding place known only to the two of them. This dolt standing in front of her had agreed to get rid of Dempsey for five thou.

"I need me a kiss for good luck," he said. He leaned his 300-pound-frame toward her.

She shut her eyes and met his mouth briefly, then pushed him away. "You do me right and there'll be lots and lots more sweet stuff where that came from." She gripped his shoulders and looked hard at him. "But you go ratting on me, bragging to your sorry-ass friends, and I'll tell the cops where to find you. Tell them what you been up to since you been on parole. Remember, if I go down, you go down, and there won't be no picket fence for us. Nothing but concertina wire, and that ain't my kinda home."

"Mine either, sugar," he said.

He might be a convict on parole for knifing a man in a robbery, she thought, but in spite of that, for whatever reason he wasn't nearly as hardened to life as Daunton or Dempsey. Or herself. He was perfect, a john who thought she was the Virgin Mary no matter how many times they fucked, a fool who would do anything for her, including what she was asking. Why did only the dumb, fat ones fall for her? Of course, the pack of bills she had handed him, with the promise of more to come, had supplied whatever incentive lust might not have totally covered.

She held his round face in both hands. "Now remember what we said. I don't want no fuck-ups on this, you hear me?"

He nodded from the confines of her grasp.

"You know when I'm gonna call, right? And you know what to do as soon as you see his car leave?"

He pulled away from her hands. "I remember, sugar. I ain't stupid."

***

Two days after the call to Rich, Jolie learned from

Penelope Chisholm that *Watchworld's* executive producer had bumped up the story. It would air in five days.

Thirty-Two

Ed Dempsey stuck a tall plastic cup under the ice dispenser on his refrigerator, then added whiskey and 7-Up in equal measure. He took a long swig and scanned the TV listings for *Watchworld*.

Ed knew his boss would be watching, probably with some babe in his lap so he could prove what a big shot he was, getting interviewed on national TV. Dempsey wished those jerks had interviewed him too. He would have given them a soundbite they could stick up their New York asses. And that Marston bitch's ass too. He chuckled at what must've been the look on her face when she saw her little blue convertible. He'd taken care of it himself, not trusting some kid to even spell the words right. It had been a blast, made him feel like a sixteen-year-old again.

The way he figured it, he was only doing his job. Daunton helped him out. He should help Daunton out. He figured he owed the sleaze more than a string of jokes for the fun Daunton provided on demand. Dempsey had decided to get rid of that troublesome slut Monique, and he figured Jerome ought to be appreciative about that.

Maybe he should take it further with the Marston bitch. Maybe she needed a little more of his attention. That was something to think about, something interesting to think about. First, let's see how much she'd screwed them with this TV thing.

Ed settled back into his recliner, picked up the remote control on the table beside it, and turned on the set. As far as he could tell, this *Watchworld* thing wasn't going to touch him, but you never knew.

Just as the opening logo came on, the phone rang. Dempsey answered, grunted a few replies and slammed down the receiver.

All he needed tonight was some whiny whore at the Delray motel down on Lamar and couldn't he come get her 'cause she was all beat up and afraid to call a taxi? She couldn't get in touch with Jerome so would he please come? Said she was new on the job, just in from Kentucky. Dempsey thought the voice sounded a little like one of the old-timer girls, but who could tell? All those hillbilly bitches from the mountains sounded alike.

He didn't want to go get her, and he'd make sure she knew it. But he owed Jerome—didn't everybody?—so he set things up to record the show. Before leaving, he refilled the whiskey and 7.

***

"Me, too." Peyton Manning Marston tried to hoist his two-year-old bulk up on Jolie's lap. The space already had been captured by the imperial Lee Ann.

Jolie's niece and nephew formed part of the crowd waiting in her parents' den for *Watchworld*. Her brother Jeff and Bonnie Lynn, the kids' parents, had driven up from Chattanooga. Matty and Martin had come over. Charlotte brought in platters of raw vegetables, honey-mustard dip and miniature pizzas she'd made that afternoon. As far as Jolie could tell, her mother thought of this as just another chance to entertain.

"Okay, Peyton Manning." Jolie gave his blond curls a pat and pulled Lee Ann back against her. "Climb on, fellow." His parents insisted he be called not Peyton but Peyton Manning in the Southern tradition of two first names. When they weren't around, Jolie called him Peyt, and she sensed it was a relief to him.

He tried without luck to throw a leg over her, as Lee Ann had done. Finally, he gave up and jumped on her lap in front of his sister.

"No, Aunt Jolie," Lee Ann said. She turned her head of light red hair, so like her aunt's own at that age, and displayed a pout. "Just me. I was here first." With that, she pushed Peyton Manning, knocking him to the floor. He began wailing.

Bonnie Lynn, who still looked like the perky ex-UT cheerleader she'd been, never stopped her chatter. Jeff didn't seem to know he'd fathered.

"Lee Ann," she said, "because you pushed your brother…" she lifted the slender child from her lap "…you can't sit here any longer."

Lee Ann's lower lip came out farther and she lowered her head. It was an act, and Jolie knew it. She also knew it probably worked every time on Jeff who would think it cute and feminine. It was pretty cute, but Jolie loved her niece too much to let her get away with it.

"If you push your brother, sweetheart, you have to expect consequences." She reached down and encircled both children in her arms, drawing their attention by whispering. "Look, in a few minutes a big story is going to come on television. It's going to be on all over the country. And it's a story Aunt Jolie got on TV. So you can see why it's very important to me, right?" As wide eyes filled with awe, two little heads bobbed up and down.

***

The Delray was farther out Lamar than Dempsey had expected. Finally, he spotted the sign announcing the motel. Half the lights forming a rectangle around its name were out.

The red vacancy sign below it flickered erratically.

Dempsey pulled the white Lincoln into the potholed lot. A string of eight flat-roofed rooms faced the road. Boards covered two windows. At one end of the units, he saw a glass-fronted area with *Office* on the door. In its dim light, he couldn't see anyone inside.

What kind of sleazy shit was this? He thought Daunton's girls never worked out of dives. Jerome ought to run things classy, no exceptions.

As he put the car in park, a loud pop sounded. Dempsey looked around at the darkness on either side of the motel but couldn't see anything suspicious. He didn't like anything about this rescue operation. The slut would pay for this. And next time, Daunton was on his own when one of his girlies got in trouble.

A second pop sounded. Something jerked Dempsey's body up and threw it back against the seat. Another pop. His head smacked into the windshield, and blood began pouring out of him.

The shots stopped after that.

This was not a part of town where citizens reported anything to the police. It was well past dawn before Ed Dempsey's body was spotted in his car by the motel's daytime manager.

***

At five to nine, just before *Watchworld* was to come on, the clamor of conversations hit its highest pitch yet. Jolie walked in front of the television and turned down the sound. "Hey, everybody!" She waved her arms and a few murmurs died down. "Quiet, okay?"

The room grew silent except for Peyton Manning's

babbling of a Burger King jingle that had aired moments ago. "Sorry to interrupt," she said, "but it's almost nine. Could y'all please not talk while this is on?" She never used y'all in Memphis, but in Singleton it sometimes came out without thinking.

"Are you going to record it?" her father asked.

"Yes, but I want to hear everything the first time around. I don't care if you talk through the other stories, just not the one I care about. Okay?" She turned the audio back up, then lowered it again. "One more thing. No talking during the tease at the top of the show either."

"What does she expect?" she overheard Jeff say to her father and Martin. "Does she think we're going to give a Rebel yell through the whole thing? Give me a break."

She shot him a dirty look. Martin saw it and winked at her when he had her eye.

As the opening theme sounded to a dead silent room, Jolie wondered if she might have been too adamant. But better that, than try to shush them during the story.

Tonight, the announcer boomed, *a report on old secrets kept by the wealthy and powerful in a Southern city.* During the voice-over, pictures flashed of Memphis's skyline above the Mississippi River, of city hall, Ellis Standifer, and Rebecca. The shot of Rebecca was a freeze frame from Martin's video. *And—* shots of chickens jammed together in cramped wire cages stacked twenty high—*an investigative report on the horrors of factory farming and how it can lead to food poisoning from the poultry on your table. Plus—*flawless celebrity faces in close-up—*a conversation with Angelina Jolie and Brad Pitt about the movie they're making together in Borneo and what they discovered about the culture while filming there.* Angelina Jolie pushed back a strand of long blond hair from her forehead and said, *It's unconscionable. The forests are disappearing...to* *make chopsticks.* A loud driving drumbeat underscored her comments.

Jolie rose from her chair and sat cross-legged on the floor three feet from the screen. She leaned forward, her chin in her hands. It was a good sign they'd teased the Memphis story first. To earn a lead, it had to zing.

A glitzy logo scattered into a million tiny dots to reveal the set and its two anchors, a sparkling blond woman and a chisel-faced man. *Good evening, I'm Nancy Rundorff.* She turned stiff-necked to her partner and smile.

And I'm John Waggoner. Our first story tonight is one of long-held secrets, illegitimacy, and an unsolved murder among the powerful and elite in Memphis, Tennessee. Ross Witkowski has the story.

Ellis Standifer appeared, smiling and triumphant at a campaign victory party. Jolie figured the video had come from the network affiliate in town. *Watchworld,* an accentless male voice said, *has learned this man...the highly respected former mayor of Memphis...led a carefully concealed life before his murder, a murder that tonight is still unsolved. We discovered this woman* (another freeze frame from footage Martin had shot) *was his illegitimate daughter by a black woman. But the scandal doesn't end there. This beautiful young woman worked as a high-class call girl. And another shocker: She's dead now too. A heroin overdose just weeks ago.* The program cut to the reporter, standing in front of city hall who spoke for 20 seconds about Standifer's accomplishments and his secret daughter's line of work.

Next came an interview with homicide's Plonski, sounding put out, about Ellis's unsolved murder. After that, an interview with the pathologist who autopsied his body, followed by slo-mo'ed frames of Rebecca, usually referred to as Monique, from Martin's footage. A couple of opportunistic soundbites from current mayor Howard Farrell. More shots of Rebecca. On-the-street interviews with Memphians who, yes indeed, were just downright flabbergasted to learn that nice Standifer fellow everybody admired had an illegitimate black hooker junkie daughter. The reporter came on-camera to say Monique possibly was part of a secretive call-girl ring that served Memphis's carriage trade. Some of the affluent clients of this stunningly beautiful woman might even have been chums with her dad. *"A tragic life ending in an equally tragic death. Was that death an accident, or did this gorgeous young woman intend it? We may never know. This is Ross Witkowski reporting."*

Suicide? Jolie's mouth dropped open. Where had they come up with that? And when were they going to mention Jerome Daunton, maybe even Ed Dempsey?

Suddenly, the theme music started up again and the scene returned to the anchor desk. Chisel-face spoke. *Thanks, Ross. Up next, are factory-farmed chickens giving us salmonella poisoning?* Seconds later, a shampoo ad flashed on the screen.

Jolie shut off the power on the TV and banged her fist on top of the set. "Dammit! Dammit all!"

"Jolie, please," Charlotte said, "the children."

"Dammit to hell!"

Matty spoke, her voice soft. "What is it's got you so upset, Jolie?"

"They blew it, Matty! They absolutely blew it." She began pacing the room, slamming her fist into her palm. "It makes me sick. They went for the easy story. The trashy angle. Did no digging at all. And this suggestion that she killed herself? That's ridiculous."

"What were they supposed to uncover?" Matty asked.

"That she was definitely…not *possibly* but definitely…part of a prostitution ring, and that it's run by one Jerome Daunton who also runs a respectable answering service. The deputy mayor, Ed Dempsey, has a vested interest in keeping it in operation. And I think the overdose was murder, even if the cops don't think so."

Jolie looked to Martin.

"I agree," he said. "It stinks."

***

As soon as Jolie screeched into her drive and ran inside, she pulled out her phone and called Penelope's number. She left a message on her voice mail saying she'd call again in the morning.

When she tried at nine a.m., Penelope answered. "Why didn't you go into the prostitution ring?" Jolie said, her voice curt.

"Hi, Jolie. I wanted to, believe me. But I told you, they pushed up my airdate, and I had to go with what I had."

"Which was sleaze."

"The whole story is sleaze. So your point would be?"

"The point is..." Jolie paused for breath "...that you shouldn't have even bothered to go with what you had. You should've insisted on waiting until you had the full story. And this suggestion of suicide...where did that come from?"

"My editor stuck that in. Look, I know you are disappointed. So am I. But the pressure was on to meet the airdate. I would've needed another couple of weeks, at the very least, to blow open a well-connected prostitution ring, if indeed one exists. It might even have taken months. Our lawyers would never let us go with something like that unless we had an absolutely locked-down case. We didn't. At least I mentioned the possibility, but that was as far as I could go."

"Couldn't you have fought to push back the date until you

321

could do the story right?"

Penelope let out a tired sigh. "I would have, Jolie, if I'd been certain we could've come up with something that would pass muster with legal. I would love to have scored on the full extent of that story. But I just didn't see it happening. Not with the constraints of time and staff I have to work under.

"No reason you'd know this," Penelope added, "but we've had a drop the last three ratings books, which means the money's not flowing like it used to. We cut a couple of producers, so I have a shorter lead time for stories and more stories to turn around. The upshot is, I skim. I don't like it. It's not the way I want to do things. But there it is. I take my Maalox and go on."

"Investing in the economy size, are you?"

"Yeah, but I have been ever since I was a news producer twelve years ago back in Des Moines. The Maalox formula's part of my genetic code now."

Jolie smiled in spite of her anger. It had been too long since she'd had a conversation with another smart-mouthed newswoman.

"Listen, Jolie, I gotta run in a few, but you really did do a terrific job feeding me info for this. With our budget cuts, we're using freelancers more, so if you come across anything else, I hope you'll give me a call."

Jolie grunted.

"I mean it," Penelope said. "You're good. Maybe we could use you."

"Maybe."

"You'll just have to take my word for it that I would've liked to have done a lot more with this story, that I intended to. Before I go, I've got a question for you: Why did you leave news anyway?"

"Blew my mouth off on-air about how a story was nothing

but drivel. I died on a live feed."

Penelope laughed. "I knew I liked you. If we need a field producer down your way, okay if I give you a call?"

"Remember, I'm banned in Memphis."

"So what?" she said, still laughing. "You wouldn't be on camera live. We'd retain full censorship rights over you. Wouldn't let you call a spade a spade on *Watchworld*, no siree."

***

Too many changes. Too many decisions.

When Jolie awoke well before dawn, Penelope's offer ran through her mind. Although there was a good chance nothing would come of it, what if something did? Would she say yes?

Her identity had disappeared with her job. She was now without anything to show for her day on far too many days. At least she was earning enough with her video work, especially creating web videos, to pay her very modest expenses—well, modest except for cigarettes, and there were fewer of those now.

Jolie tried to return to sleep but gave up after half an hour.

Wearing only the tee shirt she had slept in, she went downstairs and turned on television. CNN carried a report of a drought in Texas. Next came news of an Israeli-Palestinian clash, a boy's dramatic rescue from a bridge railing, an oil spill off the Washington coast. And more. Always more. The images flashed by.

Jolie thought of the rush of stories hurled at audiences. Their relentless dramas lay beyond the viewers' control. Nonetheless, the onslaught, by design, played on their emotions. No wonder people felt powerless.

And there was so much news. Somewhere she'd read a typical weekday issue of *The New York Times*—not even the weekend had more information in it than the average person in the Middle Ages came across in a lifetime.

Jolie clicked through the channels. Local news, business news, sports news. She had watched the news machine's appetite grow ever more voracious. It gulped down stories, billed them as crucial, and forgot about them a week later.

Hell, Lizzie Borden, the legendary ax-wielding woman past generations saw as the epitome of cruelty (despite an acquittal) wouldn't lead two days in a row now. Just another whacked-up father and stepmother. Only if Lizzie had been beautiful would the story have run longer.

She walked away from the chatting match on TV and padded in bare feet to the kitchen to grind beans for coffee. While waiting for the water to boil, she went to the back porch and leaned against the rail.

There was a lot to be said for being here, for being on a peaceful back porch in early morning. She wondered if she could deal with the clamor of a newsroom again even if the situation should present itself. It would require an adjustment, no doubt.

While she felt no deep connection to Singleton, lately the town had begun showing itself to her in new ways. She'd begun to notice the good-heartedness of most of its citizens. She'd begun to see people as more than just her parents' friends—as men and women with their own struggles and hopes, every bit as vivid as her own. So what if most of them would never watch a Fellini film or stand before a Picasso? Most of the people of any given city, no matter the size, wouldn't either. And hadn't Martin proved to be as urbane and interesting as almost anyone she'd ever met? Still, her time here felt like only a stopover. Would it someday no longer feel that way? Would she be here that long?

The early jubilation of birds filled the moist air. On this

morning, she envied them. Their lives could be brutal, she knew, but they had moments of untethered flight, and they never questioned what to do next. Get food, build a nest, sing, protect their young. Get food, build a nest, sing…

***

Jolie sat on the porch later that morning leafing through a back issue of *The Atlantic* magazine. From a corner of her perception, she became aware of the now-familiar rumble of an Avanti. As she heard Martin shift for the turn into her drive, she tossed aside the magazine and hurried to the front door. A visit from an erudite grease monkey could be just the thing right now.

Martin had come in a black convertible, one from the '80s. The top was down, ready for the day's heat. He slid out of the car, looking decidedly ungreasy in a seersucker shirt and khaki shorts that showed off the tanned muscles of his legs. "Are you packed?" he said.

She walked toward him, stepping gingerly in her bare feet over the gravel drive. "Packed? What for?"

"A nice long drive. Let's say, to La Grange. Russell called last night and invited us."

"Invited you or invited us?"

He smiled, shrugged. "Can you think of anything better to do on a beautiful morning?"

"Well, no. But for how long?"

"Just overnight. I need to be back tomorrow evening."

"You know, Martin, you don't have to take me along every time you want to visit Russell."

"I know, but you're good for my reputation in this gossipy Bible Belt town." He walked around and opened the passenger side door. "Besides, you're the most interesting company around here. Now go get packed."

***

As Martin watched Jolie toss clothes into a suitcase, he said, "I think Dick Hargrove may be exempt as a suspect."

"Mary Ellen's husband? Why?"

"Her cousin Louis, the one you met, said she told him...Louis...not long ago she was getting bored with Ellis. She'd already started doing the dirty with some fifty-dollar-cigar Cuban from Miami who'd commissioned her to paint his portrait."

"She certainly didn't look like the grieving lover when we saw her at Louis's," Jolie said. "So you think the jealous husband motive is out? At least as far as Ellis goes anyway?"

"Louis said, even if Dick didn't know she'd switched lovers, he's been making it with some nineteen-year-old. Doubtful he'd go kill his wife's lover just to cover up for his own whoopee."

She tucked a hairbrush and cosmetics into the suitcase. "Paragons of respectability, aren't they?"

"It's the humidity," Martin said. *"What men call gallantry, and gods adultery, is much more common where the climate's sultry."*

"Who's that?"

"One who should know. Byron."

"We seem to have skipped that in English lit."

Thirty-Three

"My last guests told me that with enough of a marketing effort here in La Grange, we could pull in manufacturers *and* McDonald's." Russell cut his eyes from Martin to Jolie. "Carpetbaggers."

The trio sat around an oval table in Havenwood's dining room. Martin & Jolie had arrived the day before. In front of them now lay the remains of blueberry crepes and honeydew melon.

Russell poured more chicory coffee and left the room. When he returned, he carried a recent edition of *The Commercial Appeal*. He dropped the newspaper by Jolie's plate. "Big news in your old town." He unfolded the paper and pointed to the bold headline: *Deputy Mayor Murdered.* "Holding high office in Memphis doesn't seem to bode well for longevity."

Jolie grabbed the paper with its lead story about Dempsey's killing in the motel lot. This was one killing she was glad had happened, but she was shocked nonetheless. Interesting that another reporter, not John Beck, had written the story. She read the article slowly, absorbing every detail. When she finished, she passed the paper to Martin. "There is justice in this world at least some of the time."

***

La Grange's cemetery lay only a short walk from Havenwood. It seemed an appropriate setting to get away by herself to absorb the news. As she headed toward the graveyard, a sense of relief engulfed her. She realized she had been more fearful of Dempsey and what he might do next than she had ever allowed herself to admit.

The ends of a wide cul-de-sac formed the entrance. Beyond it lay acres of worn stones under sturdy oaks and magnolias. La Grange's population of dead looked to outnumber the living.

She meandered through purple blooms of vinca and skirted the occasional patch of poison ivy. Several lichen-covered tombstones carried the insignia of the Confederacy. Beneath them lay veterans who'd survived that hellish war and managed somehow to get back home.

Other stones showed clusters of family members, some young, dying in 1878. Yellow fever.

She leaned against the magnolia. Death seemed to fill the past and present.

What about Rebecca? Was her lovely, needle-scarred body now lying beside her mother's grave? In whatever cemetery it lay, she hoped Dempsey was nowhere near.

The newspaper story had mentioned that the homicide department at this point suspected no connection with the murder of Ellis Standifer. The weapons and locales bore no similarities. The investigation of Standifer's death, the report noted, remained stalled. Rebecca's name appeared nowhere in the article.

Jolie walked slowly out of the graveyard. She headed back toward the main intersection and what Russell had described as the heart of the town, Cogbill's store.

Inside Cogbill's, oak baskets, willow wreaths and a few antique chairs hung from a high, beaded ceiling. Old license plates covered a back wall. Oiled planks creaked beneath her feet as she scanned everything from 1926 music scores to squash rackets.

When she re-entered the bright morning, she carried a jar of Vidalia onion relish for her mother and two bars of lavender soap for Matty and herself. She sniffed the old-fashioned fragrance.

Under a light breeze, poufy cumulus clouds dotted the sky. In the yards she wandered by, owners tidied beds of geraniums and petunias before the July heat took hold for the day and called a halt to their labor. A stout man pulled weeds from the base of a thick oak.

He looked up, stretched and said, "Morning. How are you?"

Jolie said hello and walked on. The only sounds after that came from her feet on the cracked sidewalk and a mockingbird's melodious, ever-changing song.

The town's constant surprise was this: It lay only fifty miles east of the rush of Memphis. Yet *La Belle Village* somehow existed apart from the passage of time. Murder seemed unimaginable here.

So did loud traffic noise. A loud screech broke her reverie. A block away, a pickup truck, its chassis elevated a foot above its wheels, careened around the corner, its tires screaming. A teenage boy bounced behind the wheel. As he passed, bass notes thudded through her body. All was not serene here all the time.

She walked toward a small park just up the road from Cogbill's. Maybe there she could reclaim the quiet.

Near the entrance, an older woman perched on a bench, the grass beneath it worn away by generations of feet. Jolie looked at the woman's thin, straight back, at her gray-streaked bun, and timid face. Grant Milburn's housekeeper. She considered walking on but decided to speak.

"Hi, remember me?"

The woman looked up without interest. "Yes'm."

"You doing okay this morning?" Jolie heard herself phrase the pleasantry in a way she hadn't since small-town childhood.

"Yes'm." After a long pause, she said, "Yourself?"

"I'm fine, thank you." Jolie sat on the other end of the bench and leaned against its wood back. "Are you having a good summer?"

The woman's eyes followed a squirrel scurrying across the ground. "I reckon."

Conversations between her and Milburn must be a riot. "How's Mr. Milburn? Is he doing okay?"

The woman grunted. "Hardest person to live with I ever come across. Folks don't know how tough I have it sometimes." The woman shook her head and stared straight ahead. "My sister what works at cleaning offices thinks I got a easy job. I keep telling her he's no angel, but she don't want to hear it. She just wants to go on and on about how she's got things bad, about how she works her fingers to the bone. Now, I know she works hard. But my job ain't no bed of roses."

"I'm sure it isn't." Jolie squirmed on the bench.

"Take this morning, if you want a for instance. He complained about the coffee, he complained about the eggs. Said they were too runny when they were just the way I fix them ever morning of the world. Then he went to carrying on over how I wasn't rubbing his foot right when I put some liniment on it. Wasn't like I was doing it for my own sake, now was it? No, indeedy. I saw him hobbling and stiff-footed, that's why. But does he ever say one nice word for anything I do?"

The woman looked sourly at Jolie. "So I just decided to get me some air."

She shouldn't be surprised the mousey woman had opened up. Hadn't it happened enough times with people she'd come across in news? Whiners longed for an ear. At least she could find out more about Milburn. "I'm sure he can be awfully difficult to deal with."

"You got no idea. Always grumpy about something. And

he don't tell me nothing. Even when he does, it's not always the God's honest truth."

"What do you mean?"

"Sent me to my sister's once, saying he was going fishing. But next day when I come back, I noticed the cobwebs was still all over his fishing pole. I don't dust in the garage."

Nor much of anywhere else. "Maybe he used somebody else's rod."

The woman squeezed her lips into a tight line. "No'm. I asked him. I said, 'You take your old pole what sits in the garage?' And he said 'Yes.' Now, that was just a barefaced lie, sure as I'm here."

"He's not a very happy man, is he?"

"He sure ain't. Do you know, I don't think I ever saw him crack a smile."

Jolie couldn't imagine either one of them doing so. "Well, he has a broken heart. That's my rather romantic theory anyway."

The woman turned toward Jolie, for the first time showing an interest in her. "Now, what makes you say that?"

"Didn't you hear what he told me the day I made a video of him?" Jolie assumed she had been eavesdropping from behind the door.

"No'm. I used that as my chance to get some work done back behind the house."

Jolie briefly repeated the story of his failed affair with Violet, omitting the abortion. "So I think he never got over her."

The housekeeper frowned at the ground. "Now, you said her last name was Standifer?"

"Yes, although her maiden name was Gilman."

"She any kin to that mayor over in Memphis got hisself kilt?"

"That was her son."

The woman ran a pointed tongue over her lips. "Mr. Milburn sure did hate that man."

"He hated him?"

"Lord, yes. Whenever he come on the news, Mr. Milburn would rant and rave about how he had no business being mayor."

"Did he ever say why he felt that way?"

"No. But now that I think about it, maybe it was nothing but jealousy because of his own son."

"What about his son?"

"Lucas William? Luke they called him. A no-count boy if ever there was one."

"How so?"

"Any way you can think of. That boy was into trouble from the day he was put on this earth. From what I've heard tell, he was the cause of his mama's death what with all the sorrow he brung her. Drinking, gambling, in and out of jail. I heard talk of drugs, and I don't doubt it. Course his daddy was hard on him from the time he was just little, whupped him plenty. Mr. Milburn told me he did that."

Jolie hated to think of Grant Milburn as a father. No surprise his son turned out bad. "Where is he now?"

"Ten feet under. And burning in the Devil's own dwelling, if you ask me. Kilt himself in a car wreck about six years back. Heard tell he was drunk as a skunk. Wrapped a car around a tree and broke his neck. Stolen car, they say."

"So Milburn resented Ellis Standifer?"

"Lord, yes. He got the angriest I ever seen him once when that mayor come on the news with his mother. It was some kind of award, and they showed him and his mother both on this stage."

Jolie caught her breath. "Was this back in February?"

"I don't rightly know."

"This was the Curtis Foundation Award, right?" The last story she'd covered with Ellis.

"I don't recollect the name of it, only that Mr. Milburn was in a bad mood all that night and the next day too."

Jolie grabbed the bony arm. "When was that fishing trip? I mean the one when he didn't really go fishing?"

The woman pulled her arm back. "I don't recollect that either."

Jolie's voice grew insistent. "Was it also in February?"

"It might have been." The woman scooted a couple of inches away.

"This is important. See if you can remember."

The housekeeper looked at Jolie and bit her bottom lip. Jolie saw fear in her milky brown eyes and softened her voice. "Sorry, I didn't mean to frighten you. Take your time but do try to remember. Please. Was it February?"

The woman looked away, her eyes tracking a passing car. She shook her head slowly, as if moving it were an effort. "No, it was after."

Jolie's face fell. "You sure?"

"It had to be, 'cause I was finishing up a quilt for my sister's great-grandbaby when he took that trip. A pink and yellow and blue quilt. I don't like to quilt much anymore, it's hard on my eyes, but my sister she kept asking me to make her great-grandbaby one. That baby was born the end of March, so that was when I got it ready by."

"I see." Jolie was tired of the old woman's conversation. She rose, brushing twigs and dirt from the back of her shorts. "I better get going."

The woman watched Jolie get up.

"Goodbye," Jolie said. She began walking off.

Jolie was on the sidewalk when the woman said, "No, it wasn't."

Jolie turned. "Wasn't what?" Jolie said, walking back.

"Wasn't after. When I was finishing up that quilt. I was thinking I give her great-grandbaby that quilt when she was born, that I was getting it ready for then. But I give it to her before that. My sister wanted it to show at a shower for her granddaughter, and that was…Lordy, let me think…that probably was February, because it was several weeks before the baby was born. She asked me did I want to come, but I said no, I—"

"So Milburn saw the news about Ellis Standifer and his mother not long before he went some place on a trip? You're sure?"

The woman looked up at Jolie and nodded her head. "Not a doubt in my mind. What had me confused was the baby shower. I was thinking about the baby's birthin', and that wasn't until March. But now I recollect the shower was the very same time Mr. Milburn was gone. I'm not rightly sure of the date, but it was pretty early on in February. I know that because—"

"I've got to go."

***

She ran the three blocks to Milburn's house and beat on the door, once again doing so to confront him. When he didn't answer, she pounded harder. "Mr. Milburn," she yelled. "It's Jolie Marston. Let me in!"

After several more rounds of hammering with her fist, she saw a curtain part and close again. The door opened a crack.

"What do you want now?"

She shoved the door open and pushed past him into the dark, musty hall. She clamped a hand around his elbow and steered him into the cloistered living room and toward his worn chair. "Sit down. I want to talk."

"What the hell do you want to talk about this time?"

"I want to know why you hated Ellis Standifer. Was it because your own son was worthless? Were you jealous of the child Violet had by another man after she refused to have your child?"

He started to rise, but she reached out a hand to still him.

"Listen, lady," he said in a nasty tone, "I don't know who you've been talking to, but you've got some looney ideas."

Jolie fixed her gaze on his hard eyes, the eyes Violet had adored. "Why did you hate Ellis?"

"Who says I did?" he growled.

"Your housekeeper."

"She's full of it. When were you talking to her?"

"Just now in the park. She said you hated him, hated to see him on the news and especially hated seeing him that time he won an award and had his mother with him."

He folded his arms across his chest and pressed against the back of the chair. "She ought to keep her trap shut."

"He was everything your son wasn't."

"My son was a fool, and because of it, he's now a dead fool. Don't ask me anything about my son. I don't want to talk about him." He rose abruptly. "I don't want to talk to you period."

"Are you afraid of what I might ask?"

"Afraid of you?"

"Of what I might ask."

She stood and walked to the mantel. From it, she took the photo of Milburn with his medal. "Ah yes, the champion swimmer."

"I'm not going to talk about this again." He sat in his chair and waved her away.

Jolie thought he looked exhausted, even older than he was. He didn't sound weak, but he looked it.

***

Grant Milburn looked at the annoying woman who once more stood over him. He looked at her self-righteous little mouth, the hands on her hips.

Thanks to her snooping, he hadn't had a good night's sleep in ages. His mind kept running back to the past. It did him no good, but he couldn't seem to stop. It left him worn out all the time. Not sorry for anything, just tired of it all. He realized now, she would never give up. She would keep at it until she found out everything. He'd had enough. Enough. Enough.

He pulled himself up on the arms of his chair. "I have to go to the john."

Jolie smirked. "Are you coming back to talk to me or is this your way of getting out the back door?"

He shoved her away. "I have an old man's prostate." He shuffled down the hall. He opened a door and moments later slammed it shut. He opened another door, shut it.

He stood for several long minutes before the bathroom mirror. He was tired of everything including his own face. It was all going to be downhill from here anyway. He thought again about what he'd considered several times these last few pointless years, but this time he didn't need more convincing.

He lowered the lid on the toilet and braced himself as he sat. With his right hand, he encircled the rifle and held a shaking finger to its trigger. His left hand gripped the barrel and aimed it toward his mouth. He tilted his head back, closed his cornflower blue eyes, and clenched the trigger.

***

When Jolie heard the sharp slap, she didn't know whether to go toward it or run away. She reasoned the shot wasn't aimed at her. It came from the back of the house. Had Milburn or whoever been trying to hit her, he would have been nearer and the sound wouldn't have been muffled as if coming from behind a door.

Maybe it wasn't a shot. Maybe it was an unexpected clap of thunder. She knew that was a crazy thought, still she glanced out a streaked window. The sun shone blithely on.

A hallway ran behind the living room. Three doors led off the hall. Two were shut. She looked in the open room, a small space with a high, narrow bed. The housekeeper's? When she reached the first closed door, she called out. "Milburn?" She flung it open to find an empty, dark room with a sagging mattress. She walked out into the hallway and stood before the other closed door. After taking a deep breath, she gripped the dented metal knob and turned it.

She saw his eyes first. They'd frozen wide with a mixture of surprise and terror. The heavy head slumped against the back of the toilet. As she took a step into the cramped bathroom, a rifle clattered to the linoleum. She jumped back and grabbed the door frame for support.

After the dizziness passed, she stepped forward, but stopped abruptly. Blood and fragments of brain and bone had splattered against the walls, on the mirror, and on the squares of the green linoleum floor.

She ran from the room and made it to the kitchen sink as hot vomit rumbled into her throat. After washing out her mouth, she splashed cold water on her face, the top of her head, and the back of her neck. She kept telling herself she'd seen dead people plenty of times in her work. Yes, but she'd always known ahead of time what she'd find.

When she felt steady enough to walk, she returned to the bathroom and picked up the rifle gingerly with a towel to leave no fingerprints. She had to find out.

Winchester. Etched on the black barrel in letters and numbers so small she had to catch the light to see them: *Model 70. 30-06.* The rifle that had killed Ellis.

She put it on the floor, fled the room, and fumbled for her phone.

After she summoned an ambulance, she called Memphis homicide.

"Plonski." His voice sounded as harried as always.

"It's Jolie Marston. I have Ellis Standifer's murderer for you."

After talking to Plonski and summoning Martin, she poured a glass of water, and went out to sit on the front porch steps and wait.

Thirty-Four

Yet another violent death. She had to stop to count how many since Ellis's.

After having given a written statement to the La Grange police, Jolie had asked Martin if they could start back for Singleton. Now that she was back home, she barely remembered the drive.

She wandered through her cottage as the long twilight of July lit the rooms. In the hour since she had been home, she'd cleaned the refrigerator shelves and swept the back porch. Next she planned to clear out the downstairs hall closet. Doing anything that required sitting still was not an option.

As she opened the closet door, the cardboard box pushed to a back corner caught her eye. Except for a quick rummage through it some time back to find Ellis's photo—on her hunch Rebecca might be his daughter—she hadn't wanted to deal with what lay inside.

Now she dragged out the newsroom mementos. Beneath the Slinky, beneath the tacky Elvis prayer candle, rested the keepsakes of fourteen years. A complimentary profile of her in the Albuquerque newspaper during her stint there. A Colin Fisher column heralding her awards in news. A note from the governor thanking her for the most substantial, and most challenging, interview he'd ever had. One by one, she reviewed the thick stack.

How easily, how safely news had allowed her to exercise her crusading spirit. She had salved her conscience, found her redemption by reporting injustices. In tidy minute-and-a-half reports, she'd brought to light nursing home abuses, foster care inequities, animal cruelty. But it was crusading at one remove.

339

She had never narrowed the emotional distance between herself and the cause she'd covered. That would have been unprofessional. That would have been messy.

As she bent over the box, she thought about the countless deaths she had reported over the years: tragic deaths, deaths of children, deaths of entire families. But it was as if she had been an automaton, focused only on getting the story. She had felt righteous about baring the ugly lie of news, but had she been any better herself? She had berated news for its ruthless pursuit of ratings, but had she been any less callous in her pursuit of the story that might well have cost Rebecca her life? And for what?

At the bottom of the pile lay a book of poems by Leonard Cohen. The inscription read: *To my lovely. Always, Rich.* Jolie turned to an old favorite, "What I'm Doing Here," forgotten now for years, and began reading:

I do not know if the world has lied
I have lied
I do not know if the world has conspired against love
I have conspired against love…

"Mea culpa, Leonard," she muttered, closing the book without reading the poem further. "Youa culpa, mea culpa, wea culpa." She put the book and all the memorabilia back in, closed the lid, and carried the box to the attic.

***

"But how was it you were so sure?" Martin asked as he sat beside Jolie in his living room. Agnes sat across from them on the other Victorian sofa, stroking Eva. The dark calico had shown up at the Everett's door a few days ago and now purred on Agnes's eighty-three-year-old lap.

Jolie leaned against padded velvet, into the soothing comfort of Martin's '63 port. "I remembered," she said, "that

Ellis had been killed with a rifle. That stuck in my mind, because most shootings in Memphis are with handguns. A rifle seemed so quaint. Or vigilante. Odd, at any rate. And I remembered it was a Winchester 30-06."

The cat jumped from Agnes's lap. Jolie reached down to invite it over, but it stretched, yawned, and left the room.

"Picky little stray," Martin said.

"As long as it picks me," Agnes said, "I don't mind. Now, do go on, Jolie."

"Well, forensics matched the bullet from Milburn's shooting with the one that went through Ellis and lodged in his wall. The lands and grooves cut inside the rifle's barrel—that's what gives a fired bullet its spin—were a match. It's like our fingerprints. No two rifle barrels are exactly the same. That's because of little differences during manufacturing, and normal wear from shooting…that kind of thing."

"I'm just thankful," Martin said, "that Violet never knew Grant killed her son and might well have murdered her father too."

"I feel sure she never suspected her beloved Grant of either," Jolie said.

Agnes leaned forward. "Weren't you absolutely terrified when you went to his house? I'm so glad your dear mother and daddy didn't know what you were up to."

"I guess my itchiness to find out what was going on kept me too fixated to be scared."

Agnes made Jolie repeat parts of the story, then stood to leave. "Time for my beauty rest," she said. "I don't want to look a day over seventy tomorrow." She winked at Jolie. "I have an appointment with that good-looking young dentist who's new in town."

Jolie and Martin said goodnight to Agnes. Jolie scooted lower on the sofa, and momentarily closed her eyes. "Those videos. I look at those two stories and wish I knew what really happened." She inhaled the port's raisin bouquet. "I'm beginning to think there's no such thing as truth. Not when it comes to the past. Just different versions of it. Those stories of Violet's and Milburn's made me call up my ex-husband."

"Uh oh."

"It was as if we'd been in different marriages. We cling to different memories, even different reasons for why we divorced. And yet, neither one of us is knowingly fabricating anything. In a conversation with Nick, I came up against the same thing, and we're talking about pretty recent times when it comes to him."

She shook her head. "What finally struck me was this: When I look back on my 36 years, it seems like nothing more than some arbitrary collection of memories. I could easily have chosen different memories, and if I had, I would think of myself as having led a different life. Same situations. Same events. But it would be a different life. And whatever collection of memories I hold to is both a lie and the truth."

Martin patted her shoulder. "Good thought fodder. If I ever take up thinking again, I'll try to remember what you said."

"Don't bother. The whole experience, especially the phone call to Rich, my ex, was discouraging as hell."

"Sorry about that. I think you've convinced me to let my sleeping dogs…lie."

"While you pun on."

He lifted his glass to her. "So what's next? Any business lined up?"

"A couple of environmental videos for the city's public works department that sound interesting. And," she said, stretching out her legs, "I do have an idea, something I've been toying with since this morning."

"Tell me."

"It would take your untold wealth and my vast experience,

but it would be great fun."

"As I clutch my wallet, please do explain."

"I'd like to do a video on La Grange. It's a little treasure. I'd like to do a scenic tour of its old homes, the cemetery, Cogbill's, and the other places in town. Get Russell to tell a few of his stories."

"I love it."

"Do you? It shouldn't cost much, not with me donating time and equipment."

"And what do you propose we do with our little movie?"

"Donate it to the town. Let them sell it to folks who come through, put it online, or market it any way they like. It might bring in a little income to help fix up one or two of the old homes that need repair. Or they could just use the cash to throw a party in the cemetery."

Martin grinned. "Count old Moneybags in."

***

When Jolie returned home from Martin's, she realized she had forgotten to check the mailbox. In it, along with a bill and two credit card offers, lay a large envelope from Colin Fisher of the *The Commercial Appeal*.

As soon as she got in the door, she flipped on a light and ripped open the envelope. From it, she pulled a column of Colin's.

FIRED REPORTER STILL MAKING NEWS

Jolie Marston, formerly of WTNW, proved she still has a nose for news. It was Marston, fired back in February, who solved the murder of former mayor Ellis Standifer. (See story on A-1.)

*Her still-potent proboscis led her to the late
Grant Milburn, of La Grange. Undaunted, she
confronted the elderly man who had once been
the lover of Standifer's late mother. Before
Marston could call police, Milburn slipped away
and killed himself. Homicide chief Jim Plonski
admits his department had been stalled on the
case. So what does her old boss think, the one
who fired her? "She stayed with the story," said
WTNW News Director Brad Delano. "I'll give
her that." WTNW General Manager Jim
Trousdale was unavailable for comment.*

Jolie noticed a note tucked into the envelope. With shaking hands, she read it: *My sources tell me Brad was furious you broke the case. Good for you! Colin.*

Jolie held the column and note to her chest and shut her eyes against the tears.

Later that night, just before turning out the light, she thought about the video project on La Grange. It was the first time she had felt excitement about the future in a long time.

Her life seemed to have split into two parts, before and after news. Who knew what might be ahead? She was still young. "Ahead" could be a very long time.

Jolie lifted the burgundy bag of Runes from the bedside table and reached one by one for three of the smooth stones inside. She laid them face down in a row, wondering what she would find when she turned them over.

The End

Acknowledgments:

I am grateful to friends and family, including my husband Bill, for encouragement and support and to patient readers of early drafts. Ken Lewis at Krill Press has been an adept, helpful, and dedicated publisher, and I appreciate all he has done to bring this tale to you. Catharine Gallagher graciously lent technical and artistic expertise in cruciual ways and as creator of my author's website: www.sarahscottbooks.com. The Puget Sound Avanti Owners Association turned my research on the Avanti, that ever-futuristic car, into a fun outing. Most of all, my thanks go to Carolyn J. Rose, author of *A Place of Forgetting*, *An Uncertain Refuge*, *Hemlock Lake*, *Through a Yellow Wood*, and *No Substitute For Murder*. Without her generous mentoring, editing assistance, and inspiration, you wouldn't be reading this book. Every novice author should have a Carolyn, preferably one as witty and huge-hearted as mine.

About the author

During Sarah Scott's television career she was a news producer at WHBQ (then the ABC-affiliate in Memphis) and at CNN headquarters in Atlanta. She was the executive producer of *PM Magazine* in Memphis. She later headed the television department for the WA State House of Representatives. Sarah has written for magazines (*Billboard, American Cinematographer*) and newspapers (*Memphis Business Journal, The Olympian, USA Today*). Her essays have appeared in *The Seattle Times* and on KPLU (NPR) radio in Seattle. In Memphis, she served on the Board of Directors of the National Blues Foundation and scripted two W.C. Handy Awards shows hosted by B.B. King. A native of Athens in east Tennessee, Sarah now is proprietor of the eco-lodging Cedar Loft Cabin at Mt. Rainier in Washington. She lives an off-the-grid life with her husband Bill Compher, a renowned treehouse builder. She is writing the Jolie Marston sequel to *Lies at Six*. Visit her website at: www.sarahscottbooks.com.

CPSIA information can be obtained at www.ICGtesting.com
Printed in the USA
BVOW070405081012

302355BV00001B/8/P